HIMSELF

A CIVIL WAR VETERAN'S STRUGGLES
WITH REBELS, BRITS, AND DEVILS

WILLIAM J. DONOHUE

Published by Buffalo Heritage Press

BUFFALO
HERITAGE
UNLIMITED

Buffalo Heritage Press
266 Elmwood Avenue, Ste. 407
Buffalo, New York 14222
716-903-7155
info@BuffaloHeritage.com
www.BuffaloHeritage.com

ISBN 978-1-942483-09-0 (softcover)
ISBN 978-1-942483-10-6 (hardcover)
ISBN 978-1-942483-11-3 (ebook)

Cover art and book design by Goulah Design Group

Printed in the United States of America

10 9 8 7 6 5 4 3 2 1

❧ ACKNOWLEDGMENTS ❧

Family and friends helped me to write this book: Sue Donohue, wife and reader; Gene Donohue, cousin, consultant, resource, and founding 155th Regiment re-enactor; Jack Brew, cousin and lifeline to the main character; the late Mary Suchan, John's great-granddaughter; Elaine Kelly Pease, great-granddaughter of Captain Tim Kelly of the 164th Regiment; Patty McClain, proofreader and literary critic; Pat Wille, formatter and technical adviser; Jeanne Bowman, reader and literary critic; Bob Yott, Bath Soldiers and Sailors Home historian; Kathy Shaw, literary critic; Buffalo Irish Genealogical Society members; librarians at both the Buffalo and Erie County Central Library and the Clarence Library; Ben Maryniak, late Civil War historian; First Ward historians Barbara Sullivan and Tim Bohen; Ed and Sue Curtis, Salisbury Confederate Prison Association founders ; Michael Gent, reader and literary adviser; Judy Tamburlin, clerical help and reader; Tim Trabold, computer consultant and manuscript rescuer; Dr. Edmund Egan, medical adviser; and the volunteer staff at the Waterfront Memories Museum.

Lastly, let me mention in a most special way my editor, Carl Thiel.

❧ CONTENTS ❧

SECTION IV Descent into the Abyss

SECTION V Redemption

❦ PREFACE ❦

This story is historical fiction. It reconstructs the lives of Patrick and John Donohue, my great grandfather and great-uncle respectively, using historical information and family memory. What they said and what they did precisely I invented to bring these people and their issues to life.

Patrick returned home from America's worst war with only a shadow of his manhood intact. John had great difficulty tolerating heavy manual labor throughout a sixty-six hour workweek. The historical Patrick lived in twenty or more residences, a sign of his personal and financial instability, in some measure due to his alcoholism. He died in the Bath Soldiers Home, a residence for indigent war veterans. The Patrick of the book becomes a mature and contributing member of society. He is a composite of generations of struggling Donohue men and my hopes for myself.

The main female characters, Maire, Annabelle, Mary, and Millicent, are largely or entirely fictional. They are my way of saying their women are the major exogenous reason Donohue men have grown to greater selfhood.

CHAPTER I

Gram to the Rescue

In the winter of 1850, Maire received Margaret's letter expecting news of her grandsons—the children of her only child, Catherine—and progress she hoped they would be making by now. She had a neighbor read it to her, for she read neither Irish Gaelic, her native tongue, nor English. The neighbor read key sentences twice to make sure Maire understood what they meant. At the end of the second paragraph describing the boys' behavior, Maire cried out in anguish, "Read no more. I know what I must do."

Maire Elizabeth Joy had emigrated from Mallow, County Cork, Ireland, to the tiny community of Niagara in Southern Ontario in 1842 with Catherine and Catherine's husband, Patrick Donohue. They lived for two years in Canada before moving south and east to Rochester, New York. Maire moved on to Buffalo. She maintained her ties with her Rochester relatives, including Conal, Patrick's brother, and his wife, Margaret, who together had first finessed the whole move from Ireland and Canada.

Maire had been widowed after Catherine's birth and supported herself and her infant by sewing and doing fine needlework for wealthy Anglo-Irish women. She had every confidence she could do the same in America. She had also been a public figure in Mallow, where she functioned as a spree or festival organizer, a *seanachai* or public storyteller, and a healer. She pictured herself doing the same in any Irish community anywhere in the world.

She soon found a market for her old trade in Buffalo. Maire visited Rochester once a year when Patrick or Conal sent her the fare, as they usually did. Over the years in Ireland, and now in America, she became a legendary figure in their eyes. Above all, she was a delight to be with. Catherine and Patrick welcomed her charismatic presence whenever they could persuade her to come. Patrick often commented to his wife after Maire's visit, "She leaves a gift of peace and joy. We must treasure it. We'll never know the like."

Two weeks after receiving the letter, Maire appeared at Conal and Margaret's door. At fifty-eight, "Mother Joy," as she was known within the family, was still vigorous. Barely five-foot two, with broad shoulders, muscular arms, and thick waist, she wore her heavy, long grey hair in a bun.

Her bright blue eyes and broad smile conveyed to the anxious Margaret, "Don't worry. I can handle my grandsons." Laughing loudly and punctuating her remarks with stories from Buffalo and Ireland, she spent the evening chitchatting with Conal and Margaret about the boys, while Margaret threw their few clothes into a flour sack.

Margaret and Conal had gladly taken in the boys, John and Patrick, Jr., ages six and five, as they had promised their mother a few days before her death. Catherine, age twenty-eight, and Patrick Sr., age twenty-nine, had both fallen victim to the cholera epidemic that swept Rochester in 1849.

Conal and Margaret, both thirty-five and childless, were strongly committed to making a home for the boys and raising them as their own sons. Conal moved bunk beds from his brother's home a few blocks away and stacked them one above the other in the nine-by-ten-foot bedroom meant for the children who had never come.

Maire was very proud of the way her relatives had helped with the move from Ireland. Conal had come first, married Margaret a year later, and urged Patrick to follow. In 1844, Conal and Margaret had settled Patrick and Catherine in a small but comfortable cottage nearby, just north of downtown in the Genesee River waterfalls area of Rochester known as Little Dublin.

In Buffalo, Maire lived with her brother, Jack, a widower. He had asked for her help raising his daughter, Johanna, who had turned seven in 1845. The whole family appealed to Maire whenever they felt a pressing need that she could best fulfill. Having lived the first two years of her marriage in her mother's home, Maire was also keenly aware that living in the same house with a married daughter often bred conflict.

Conal found Patrick work as a cooper in the same flour mill where he himself was employed for three years. A year later, Conal helped Patrick build a cooperage business in small villages throughout the area. Weekends the four—Conal and Margaret, Patrick and Catherine—socialized together in pubs and at church events. They became best friends.

The year 1849 was a trial for Maire, who joined Conal and Margaret in nursing first Patrick, then Catherine. In one year, these strong, young individuals, one after the other, descended into helplessness and, finally, painful and miserable deaths. Throughout the ordeals, Conal, Margaret, and Maire could do little but wipe brows and butts and pray. The fact that Maire stood by them through it all like a rock, most notably through the death of her daughter, and did so with equanimity, wisdom, and a deep spirituality bordering on the mystical, only endeared her more to her Rochester family and built her legend to the point of canonized sainthood. In their eyes no pope could have raised her any higher. The way she handled her only daughter's death was a model of parent-child relationship. They could see she grieved Catherine's death deeply but remained strong for the sake of those around her.

Conal found Patrick's illness especially difficult, Patrick being a giant of a man at six feet two inches, with the arm span and strength to carry two loaded barrels from the mill floor down three flights of stairs to a waiting wagon. Conal, who was only five feet eight inches and of modest frame, regaled family and friends on Saturdays in Little Dublin pubs with stories of Patrick's progress in building his cooperage business and his feats of strength at the mill. Patrick, in turn, soaked up his brother's loyalty and cherished him for his goodness.

After supporting Catherine throughout Patrick's illness and death, her demise caught Margaret and Maire by surprise, despite the fact that hundreds were dying of the plague throughout Little Dublin, which was crowded, swampy, and overflowing with human and animal sewage. Those who nursed others often succumbed themselves to the terrible plague.

When it came time to bring John and Patrick Jr. into their home, Conal and Margaret were emotionally spent and unable to cope with the anger and turmoil that possessed the two boys.

In January 1850, Margaret, in desperation and with some guilt, wrote Maire sixty miles away in Buffalo. "Things are not working out. John and Pat simply will not obey or listen to anything we ask them to do. Nearly every day they run away and float through downtown Rochester begging."

After helping Margaret pack the boys' clothes, Maire sat in a favorite rocking chair before a blazing fireplace, her two grandsons seated on a rug and leaning into her knees. The boys cringed as Conal and Margaret told of their misdeeds and hung on their grandmother's every word. Maire's replies in the form of short stories appeared to be connected to what the adults in the room were saying, but actually, she tailored them to what she knew the boys would enjoy. Margaret and Conal smiled knowingly at her ploy.

When Margaret announced it was time for bed, the children begged to stay up. "Could Gram tell us just one story of Half Night O'Toole?" asked John.

"We'll have plenty of time tomorrow," she told her young audience.

After the children went to bed, Conal and Margaret told Maire a tale of the boys' antics far more graphic than those recounted earlier.

"The boys lived three days aboard a steamship in Rochester harbor with Russian sailors," Conal said. "Don't ye know, Mother Joy, we had police, pastor, and friends searching the city in vain. When Father Edwards was after finding them, he told the boys he was going to take them to his orphanage for bad boys."

"We were ready to let the Father have the two of them," added Margaret.

With each new saga they told, Maire's eyes widened and she exclaimed, "O, Glory be to God." She was convinced now that she had made the right decision. Difficult as times were for her, she knew she was the only one who could handle her grandsons. She had no idea how she would support the boys on the few dollars she was earning with her sewing, but she believed that God never gave a cross without also giving the grace to bear it.

The next morning, Friday, February 1, 1850, dawned clear and cold. A light covering of snow off Lake Ontario crunched beneath their feet as Maire and the boys hugged Margaret and mounted Conal's open carriage to begin the daylong trip to Buffalo. On board were the flour sack with the boys' clothes, Maire's small cloth bag of garments and personal items, and a basket of food that Margaret had prepared. Maire and the boys waved to Margaret as Conal clucked at his horse to move out.

Once underway, the boys clung to their grandmother. Roads rutted from a recent thaw and freeze threw the car from side to side. They hardly noticed how cleverly their uncle wove past wagons bringing grain to feed stores and beer to saloons, nor the smell of horse urine, especially acrid on a cold morning, nor the hogs boldly roaming the streets rooting for garbage.

After a ten-minute trip into downtown Rochester, Maire urged John and Pat to apologize to their uncle for the way they had been acting and to give him a big hug and kiss. They obeyed, then the three boarded a Tonawanda Railway train for Batavia, thirty miles west.

The trip to Batavia was the boys' first train ride and they took it with a mix of fear, excitement, and curiosity. After a spate of exclamations and questions, they settled down and began to open up to their grandmother, whom they trusted and loved almost as much as they had their dad and mom.

"And it was all so sudden," John said. "One moment Mom and Dad were home with us. The next they were gone. There's a hole in my heart and somethin' big is missin' inside a me." He lapsed into silence.

Maire leaned forward and patted the boy's knee. "I miss your parents almost as much as you do. I remember the terrible times in Rochester, what with hearses crawlin' over the streets every day by the dozens. I only saw the likes in Ireland, boys."

Pat spoke up. "Gram, before you came we were mad and acting crazy. We fought with our friends over anything and ran away when our aunt and uncle went to bed."

Maire gave the boys all the time they needed to express their feelings. She was no stranger to loss of parents. Hers had died when she was a young girl and she was raised in the home of an older brother, who treated her and his children as his personal servants. Maire left the house after years of mistreatment and abuse, swearing she would give only kindness and compassion to her own children.

No one else was with them at their end of the railcar, so the boys became quite comfortable with their grandmother. They took turns sitting in her lap and telling her all about what happened after she left Rochester. She hugged them and grunted, "I hear ye, I hear ye," again and again. Not a word of disapproval did she speak. When they fell silent, if she thought they still had more to say, she asked a question or two that got them talking once again.

When she figured they had said all they needed, she asked if they would like to hear a bit about Half Night O'Toole. "Or are ye too tired, now?" The boys seated on the opposite bench quickly straightened and nodded eagerly at the prospect of the story. "Well then," she said by way of beginning, "here's how it happened that one night, when Half Night was walkin' home . . ." Maire's eyes lit up and her cheeks burned a bright red as the spirit of the Celtic muse possessed her. From that moment, her audience of two was enthralled with her and her story. Nothing else mattered, not the scenery outside the window, not the steady rattle of the cars on the tracks, only the spellbinding adventures of their favorite Mallow character. She told numerous episodes of outrageous coincidence and bold bravado that followed no clear direction but always featured a remarkable conclusion. When she finished one story, they urged her: "Tell another one, Gram."

"Is it true no one knew O'Toole's real first name?" asked John, who knew the stories of the bold rogue by heart.

"Indeed, 'tis no lie, John. No one but his mother, and she was long dead when first the world heard of him. The whole of Mallow, old to young, knew him as 'Half Night' and nothin' else. Half Night preyed on constables, government agents, and English landlords. Hands came out of the dark and choked them, stole their meat, vegetables, and tools, which then appeared on the stoop of some poor family."

"The story I like best about Half Night is 'The Banshee of Braker Bridge,'" Pat enthused. "Tell it again, Gram."

So Maire began the tale with new details of daring thefts and unfortunate but humorous accidents that befell police and English authorities. "It was they as well as the neighbors who created the name and the Half Night legend that spread through County Cork." The train car resounded with peals of the boys' high-pitched laughter. "I never heard it quite like that before," John exclaimed, as he flailed his arms in the air and shook his head. "Are you sure you didn't just make it up, Gram?"

Maire reached across the aisle and slapped John gently on the shoulder, smiling broadly, her head moving side to side, her bosom and belly rising up and down.

"Of course not, John, sure am I insulted you'd think the like. My memory is so loaded with Half Night, new stories could I tell you every time I told you an old one." She laughed and laughed as she was reminded of similar reactions over past decades in the old country.

For two hours, the trio crossed the barren, snow-swept landscape between Rochester and Batavia, in a world of their own, oblivious to other passengers. When not absorbed in one of Maire's stories, they were distracted by deer, geese, and rabbits wandering near the tracks. They squinted curiously at the sight of Seneca Nation villages, one with a longhouse. Maire commented occasionally about houses and people and animals, whatever passed by. The boy's questions were satisfied by her brief explanations. The last half-hour of the ride, lulled by the clickety clack of the train, all three fell into a deep sleep from which, as they neared Batavia, the conductor awakened them.

After a brief delay and munching on the sandwiches Margaret had packed, they boarded a train for Attica, twelve miles and two stops southwest of Batavia. Maire sat for a while in silence thinking about her financial situation, made worse by adding two hungry boys to her charge. She looked up as though open to the presence of God and His mercy and generosity.

Pat fidgeted, then got up and wandered through the car, examining people, furniture, and shiny brass surfaces the likes of which he had never seen before. He stopped to watch a group of men play cards. A thick cloud of smoke from foul-smelling cigars hung about them as they called their bets in gruff voices.

Not understanding the game, he passed on, swaying from side to side with the motion of the railcar.

He dallied alongside four women travelers. A heavyset, dark-haired woman turned to her companions. "This boy is so cute. What's your name, son?"

"Pat. And I'm going to Buffalo. Are you, too?"

"Indeed we are, Pat."

The woman nodded at her companions and then at Pat, taken by his innocent poise and handsome face. Pat had finely carved features, accentuated by his light olive skin, round deep-blue eyes, and a head of wavy light-brown hair. His diminutive frame made him seem vulnerable and only added to his appeal.

The women smiled at him while they answered his questions in simple sentences he could understand. The dark-haired woman moved over and beckoned Pat to sit beside her, which he did with no hesitation. He put his hand up to her jade brooch and felt it. She laughed, thinking he probably had never seen one before. He answered the women's questions about his life in Rochester and told them about the death of his parents and about his grandmother from Buffalo.

Pat at first noticed nothing that the women were wearing. As their conversation went on, things popped out at him that had not been worn by his mother or other women he knew, especially their fur capes and big jade brooches. He had never met women dressed so well. He asked them if they made their own clothes, and where did the fur and brooches come from. He asked them about their homes. Were they cottages like his? Did they take lots of trips on trains?

One woman, thinking this poor little Irish boy probably never had enough to eat, remarked how thin he was. Her companions brought out bulky wicker baskets, full of aromatic food and drink: homemade bread, sweet rolls, jellies, butter, dried fruits, and sarsaparilla-flavored mineral water. Pat liked their company, the way they smelled, eating their food, and being the center of attention.

John stayed with Maire. He had considered roaming with his brother, but was more interested in having his grandmother all to himself, listening to her stories, and questioning her about his parents and grandparents and their life in Mallow and Canada.

Periodically, Maire stood in the center aisle and looked the length of the car to see what Pat was doing. A half hour after beginning his walk, he returned to their seat. Maire asked what he had done and seen. She leaned forward and wiped some jelly off his cheek. Pat said little. She asked again more insistently. He went into more detail about the card players and the women he talked to. She nodded approvingly that he had been so well received by adults. She was well aware that wealthy Americans often looked on her kind with disdain.

At Attica, they transferred to yet a third train. After fifteen hours in stations and trains, they arrived late in the evening at the newly built Exchange Street Station at Old Crow—as the natives called Exchange Street—and Michigan Street in Buffalo.

The four women saw Pat in the station, introduced themselves to Maire, and complimented her on her bright and personable grandson. Maire smiled and thanked them politely before they ran off to hail a hack. Her estimation of the upper class rose significantly.

Life along Michigan Street was picking up as Maire and the boys walked south. The night air was bitter. A cold wind off Lake Erie cut through their clothes and hastened their step. Maire took the boys firmly by the hand. She navigated their way across a narrow bridge over the Hamburgh Canal and through a crowd of shippers and sailors clustered around saloons and inns, drunks staggering out of side alleys, and brightly painted, gaudily dressed women on the prowl for customers.

Small gangs of young men and boys caroused on street corners as the travelers turned onto Elk Street. Maire crossed to the opposite side of the street. She avoided dark spaces and walked under gas lamps wherever possible. She was used to downtown and the First Ward with its saloons, two or three in every block, and drunken men weaving into her path. Twice, boozers begged Maire for change. She put them off with a courteous word: "Ah, love, I have to buy bread for the children."

A quarter hour's walk took them down cobblestone and then gravel and mud streets, over rail tracks, along the Buffalo Creek, past factories and cottages. The way was lit only at corners by gas lamps. At this late hour, houses and businesses were dark, their inhabitants long since retired for the evening. Maire relaxed as they turned onto Louisiana Street, whose residents she knew house by house. She often stopped to chat with them on her way home from church or delivering her goods to wealthy women on the West Side. Still, she sighed when they arrived at the four-room cottage on Louisiana that she rented with her brother, Jack, and his daughter, Johanna.

Forty-nine-year-old Jack met them at the door with a broad smile, took their luggage, set it in the dining room, and welcomed the boys to his home. Johanna—Jo for short—now eleven, stood leaning against a wall in the living room and greeted them without enthusiasm, her face clenched in a frown. Jack led the group to the kitchen, where they sat around a small table. He asked them about the trip and slowly got the boys to talk to him. He asked his sister how Conal and Margaret were doing. He was fully aware that the boys had been acting badly since their parents died. Questions about their behavior, however, could wait. Within fifteen minutes, he saw that the boys were tired and suggested there would be time enough to talk in the days to come.

Jack was a quiet, gentle man, nine years younger than his sister. Since moving from Ireland, he had worked for two decades on the waterfront, the last ten years in the massive grain elevators that dotted the Niagara River and Buffalo Creek. The harsh work was beginning to show on him. His face was furrowed and weather-worn, his short, thick frame beginning to stoop.

Their cottage was small like most of the houses in the Ward. The children slept in one ten by ten foot bedroom. The once green wallpaper was fading into brownish yellow. One window provided light and leaked cold air. Jo, as the oldest, secured the stand-alone bunk nearest the door. In anticipation of the boys' arrival, Jack had borrowed a double bunk bed from friends before Maire had left for Rochester. Pat was given the bottom bunk, John the top.

Jo had complained about having to share her bedroom with the boys, which her father dismissed with a wave of his hand, saying, "It can't be helped. You'll just have to get used to it." Jack occupied the largest bedroom. Maire slept in a smaller bedroom by herself. In all, the living arrangement was not as bad as many in the Ward, where the average home had two adults and eight children.

Their first Monday in Buffalo, February 4, 1850, Maire woke the boys before seven, fed them a hearty breakfast of fried bread and eggs that she had gathered from her chickens in a rear coop, and led them out to enroll in school. A cold wind and steady snow met them at the door. She pointed to the excavation of the Ohio Basin just across the street. "One day, there'll be boats moving around the basin. You boys'll be able to do errands for the sailors on those ships and help your granny out, but for now, it's off to school. This afternoon will we tend the chickens together."

She took the boys by the hand and marched them north down Louisiana to Elk and School 4, built in 1835. It was the first elementary school in the Ward. Residents called this wooden, one-story building the Little Red Schoolhouse. Maire knew the boys would have to go to work by the time they finished the sixth grade, but she did not want them to bear the ignominy she bore as an illiterate. When she was a child in rural Cork, there were only hedge schools.

She led the boys in to see Mr. Smith, the principal, short and middle-aged, with a mustache spread across his upper lip. He had robust shoulders and a voice that rocked the windows when he was angry. Parents knew him for strict discipline and using a thick ruler to back it up, but they also judged him to be fair and having the best interest of students. Thus, he gained the support of parents and guardians. He knew how to communicate with them. He was very supportive of and occasionally provided guidance to his six teachers, all females of various ages. They respected and liked him. The only noises Maire heard that day were teachers speaking in the six classrooms of the school and students answering in unison.

While waiting for Mr. Smith to finish with another family, Pat pleaded, "Gram, we already know how to read and do numbers from Rochester. Why can't we stay home with you?" Pat was exaggerating wildly. John had learned to read only the most simple sentences in first grade in Rochester. Pat had not been to school yet and read only the words he had picked up watching his mother practice his brother reading.

"Who do you think you're foolin', Padraig, me boy? You'd be after runnin' like wild rabbits around the Ward. Well, your runnin' days are over, at least till the summer. So you think you know readin' and arithmetic, do ye? We'll see. Don't forget. I'll be talkin' with Mr. Smith about every day." Maire was beginning to understand her youngest grandson was given to stretching the truth.

Maire heard from his teacher, Miss Eckert, two months later that Pat tended to be a practical joker and clown. He got a big kick out of playing tricks on his classmates. He tied a black string to the lower hinge of the classroom door and tripped Thomas O'Leary as he left for the outhouse, which stood a few yards from the back door of the building. Everyone laughed except Miss Eckert, who shouted at O'Leary to pick up his feet. At that, the kids laughed louder. Pat tried the stunt again the next day. This time, Miss Eckert was watching, caught him red-handed, and gave him a whipping with a willow switch she kept ever at hand.

Undaunted by his occasional punishment, Pat delighted in finding ways to amuse his fellow students. The unfortunate "Fatty" O'Leary—a nickname the boy had earned his first day in school—was short, overweight, and a dependable object of jokes, practical or otherwise. His clothes were either too big or too small, hand-me-downs from his older brothers, and certainly too few. They harbored a bouquet of body odors that his smell-hardened classmates mocked with fingers to nose. Pat played tricks on O'Leary, like stealing his hat or rubbing machine grease from Uncle Jack's shed on his jacket.

Pat was regularly in the principal's office for a ruler across the knuckles, which Maire supported with another whipping when she learned about it, usually the same week. She was embarrassed about her grandson's behavior in front of such an important person as the School 4 principal as well as his teacher. It was a sign of her lack of discipline at home, she felt. She mustered up as much anger as she could and gave Pat a sound spanking. Her whippings, though, could not escape her innate tenderness and sensitivity to Pat's loss of parents. Pat developed a healthy fear of the principal and his teacher, but not of his grandmother.

When Miss Eckert readied Pat for a well-earned switching, she often remarked, "Why can't you be more like your brother?"

John, indeed, was well behaved, a model student. He enjoyed math and made progress in reading and writing. Miss Eckert referred to John as her "prize pupil." He did little tasks for Miss Eckert, like cleaning the blackboard and buying chalk from Hershey's General Store on Elk Street and Chicago. He made good friends among schoolmates and played with them after school and on weekends.

Within a year, Maire trusted him to pick up material from Miller Levy, a cloth merchant on Elk Street. Levy allowed her to pay on credit as she converted the cotton and linen cloth to chasubles, stoles, maniples, albs, and surplices for area churches. John tarried at the shop while waiting for his grandmother's order to be filled and watched tailors cutting cloth and winding it into long rolls. He listened as customers talked with Mr. Levy about their orders and Levy gave directions to his two workers. After a month, John was trusted to do the complete transaction: order, pick-up, and payment.

Both John and Pat came to know many boys in the Ward, as it was a very tight-knit community. Patrick Murray Dolan or PM for short was the same age as Pat and about the same size, but with dark hair, dark eyes, and fair complexion. He was an only child and lived on Kentucky Street, two blocks from where the Joys lived on Louisiana. Walking home with the Donohues after school the first week, he trumpeted to his new friends, "The Ward has everything: railroads, factories, a river, canals!" He waved his hand, pointing them out. "We'll go exploring as soon as your gramma and my ma let us out to play. Let's go down to the harbor and watch the boats. We can even ride on trains, but you can't say a word to your gramma." Pat was excited at the prospect of exploring the Ward's many mysteries. He had little interest in school and books and blackboards. He yearned for a change of pace. John was a bit cautious, but he would go along to see that his brother avoided trouble.

On a July day, when school was out, the boys walked south on Louisiana, crossed over the Ohio Street Bridge, turned west on Ganson Street, and walked along the Buffalo Creek. The day was bright and sunny and everywhere they went they were greeted by new attractions. They crossed over rail tracks toward a grain elevator that dominated the landscape. Track crisscrossed the area along the south side of the creek. Engines released and connected cars. Cars rammed into other cars. Booming noises echoed off the grain elevator walls. With each boom, the boys ducked and covered their ears. The sweet smell of grain hung in the air.

Pat pointed at a lake freighter tied up at a dock alongside the elevator. "I wonder what's in that boat?" he said.

The other boys hesitated to go closer. He moved on ahead a few paces, studied the scene for a minute, returned, and whispered, "Let's get behind those barrels so we can see better."

The three boys ran behind a stack of wooden barrels and climbed up on the first row. For the next half hour, they watched a crew lift barrels of grain from the hold of a schooner, the *Jenny Lind*. The boys ducked when a sailor climbed the mid-mast to untangle lines high above the deck. When they realized he was far too occupied to pay attention to them, they relaxed, stood, and gazed about.

Men were loading barrels into open, hand-propelled cars that whined as they ran across rails into a large brick building, the grain house. Soon an empty car appeared on a track on the other side of the grain house. Two men pushed it back to the dock.

"What are they doing?" asked Pat. "What's that stuff they're moving?"

PM replied, "I don't know. My dad'ud know."

Just when they were about to leave, when none of the workers was looking, Pat jumped down, ran forward, and swiped a dust-covered soft hat from an untended handcar. The boys applauded his daring and laughed out of control at the oversized hat, cocked slightly to the left side of his head.

That evening, PM approached his father, who was reading the Buffalo *Daily Courier* newspaper. Mr. Dolan worked at the Dart Elevator, recently built at the mouth of the Buffalo Creek. He explained the grain milling process to his son. "Farmers plant wheat in Ohio or Indiana in the fall of the year and harvest it in the spring. It's packed in barrels or sacks and shipped by boat to Buffalo. Then it's unloaded, as you saw, at the various grain elevators on the waterfront. Some of the grain is stored until it's shipped on rail cars to flour mills as far away as New York and Philadelphia.

"By the way, Pat, what you saw is the old-fashioned way of emptying a boat by hand. At our new elevator, steam-driven machines do it. Before that, Irishmen's backs were the cheapest machinery," he added wryly. "Some Sunday I'll bring you boys to see the inside of the elevator."

Mr. Dolan lifted the newspaper from his lap.

"Now, can I read the paper, son?"

"Thanks, Dad," said PM and ran out to tell his pals, John and Pat.

"That was grain, maybe wheat, in those barrels we saw. My dad said he'd take us to his mill one of these Sundays. He knows a lot about wheat and where it comes from and stuff."

In the middle of the night, John awoke to the sound of his brother sobbing softly. "Pat, are you okay?" John got out of his bunk below Pat's, climbed up the ladder, and crawled in next to his brother.

"What's wrong?" he said and put his arm around his shoulder. Pat stopped sobbing and mumbled, "I miss Ma and Da. It hurts even to think about them."

"Me too, Pat, every day."

He continued to hold his brother and rub his back until he fell asleep. John swore to himself he would always be there to protect him. Jo said nothing, but her loud sighs made it clear she was annoyed at being awakened.

CHAPTER 2

Hard Times

Two years after bringing the boys to Buffalo, Maire was concerned about keeping them fed. She believed strongly in God, but was a very practical woman. For months, she had struggled to provide for the three of them. One night in mid-summer after Jack had left the supper table, Pat asked for more to eat. Jo stopped clearing the table and looked at Maire washing dishes at the sink, wondering what her response would be. Maire regarded the boy with a pained expression. "I'm sorry, love," she said, shaking her head. "There isn't any left."

"Why didn't you make more?" asked the boy.

Maire choked and answered that she couldn't. There was no more.

"But I'm still hungry," Pat complained.

Maire looked over at his brother. "And you, John? Are you still hungry, too?"

John slowly nodded. Grimacing, their grandmother shook her head again and turned to resume stacking dishes in the sink. She reminded Jo to bring her the rest of the supper dishes and utensils.

Maire went to bed that night, but did not sleep, sick at heart that the boys had to go without food. She had done all she could, worked her fingers to the bone, but it wasn't enough. Maybe God was trying to tell her something. After lying awake for hours, she saw what Divine Providence had already given her. At four in the morning, she fell into a sound sleep. That evening after supper, she said nothing to the boys, only that she was going over to see her cousin, Theresa.

Theresa Haggerty had migrated from County Cork at age fifteen and spent four years in London, where she became quite literate serving as a nanny to a wealthy family. She accompanied the eldest son and his young family across the ocean to Vermont, but left them within a year when he approached her sexually after his wife became pregnant for the third time in three years.

Theresa had relatives in Buffalo and moved there in 1830 at age twenty. Two years later, she accepted the proposal of Colin Haggerty, who had settled in the First Ward after completion of the Erie Canal. While not abusive as some husbands were, when he wasn't working, Haggerty drank heavily. Unlike many women in the Ward, Theresa did not accept his behavior passively. Their home became a house of coldness, tension, and hostility over the next few years.

Theresa was a few inches taller than Maire, with dark hair, a thin frame, smiling face, and piercing green eyes that looked intensely interested in everyone she addressed.

She was now forty-two and had lived alone for eight years, ever since losing her husband in 1844 after eleven years of marriage. Coming home from a late evening of drinking, Theresa's man had staggered into the Buffalo Creek at the foot of Alabama Street and drowned.

Theresa was pleasant to one and all and her neighbors looked out for her and guarded her home. She worked in the law office of Nathan K. Hall, including the two years he spent in Washington as Postmaster General, and then upon his return when he was appointed federal judge. She had grown close to the judge and one of his partners, the future president, Millard Fillmore, when she nursed both men's wives during prolonged illnesses. Hall had incorporated her into his home. His son and four daughters called her "Aunt Theresa." In 1844, ten years after he had formed a partnership with Fillmore, he started her in his practice as an assistant clerk. Her neighbors learned they could take counsel with her whenever they had dealings with government.

In her personal life, she protected her privacy and independence and never took in boarders. She didn't need them to get by and she did not want them.

Theresa considered herself lucky and did not remarry. She had a tidy bank account that served as her rainy-day fund from a small insurance policy Hall had taken out on Colin through his church. She enjoyed warm relationships within the Hall family and was happy with the work she was doing in his law office. She had a diverse social life through work and St. Bridget's Parish, where she helped tend the altar linens. Still, she rued the fact that she had never had children.

When her grandsons got home from school a week later, Maire called them into the kitchen and sat them down at the table. She had put off what she was about to tell them as long as she could. A little troubled by feelings of guilt, she fumbled for the right words to say what she had decided. John and Pat knew from experience that a somber expression meant she was about to talk about something serious.

Seating herself opposite them, she regarded them both with a tender gaze. She laced the fingers of both hands together on the tablecloth. Drawing in a deep breath, she began. "Boys, I have something to say. Listen now, carefully.

"There's little money in me apron to feed the two of you. Remember, your Uncle Jack contributes enough to feed only Jo and himself. And winters he can't do that because he's out of work. You know I shop and cook for all of us and we all eat together, but 'tis I who really feeds us three. I pay our fair share toward the rent and upkeep of all of us. I wouldn't have it any other way. I've never been a burden on Jack since I came to live with 'im. Even then with Jack and me both workin', it's not enough to feed us proper."

John stared at his grandmother as she spoke; his brow lowered as he tried to absorb what she was saying, but he just wasn't getting it. Pat refused to look at her, choosing instead to look down at his feet. He didn't understand where she was going either, but he didn't like it.

"Just last night," Maire continued, "the two of you said again you were still hungry. By the way, so were the rest of us." She straightened in her chair. "Somethin' had to be done." She paused still looking for the right words. "I talked with your Aunt Theresa. She says she could keep one of you. It should be you, John, said I, because you're a year older and the break will come easier to you. I love you like my own soul, but love won't fill your plate. Do you grasp it, boy?"

John did not want to understand. He would miss neither his cousin nor his uncle, who stayed pretty much to himself, but he could not imagine life away from his grandmother and his brother. He turned away as tears flooded his eyes. Pat looked on silently, mouth open at the sudden news and at his brother, crying out of control.

Maire rose. She was feeling all the hurt in John's heart and placed her hand on his shoulder. John pulled back slightly but then leaned in to her touch. Her voice quivered. "Now, John, don't cry. Aunt Theresa, you know, lives only two streets away on Mackinaw. An extra bedroom has she you'll have all to yourself, lad. She refuses to take in boarders because she doesn't need the money." She was pleading now and the hurt of the situation was choking her voice. "That tells you a lot. Pat will call on the way to school every mornin' and you two can stroll home together and play every afternoon. So it won't be so bad."

Her voice quivered. "Of course, I expect you to visit me every day to see if I have an errand for you: tend the chickens, pick up material from Mr. Levy, deliver a vestment. You know what I mean."

John blurted out through his crying, "I don't care! I want to stay here with you, Gram."

She raised her tone and in a loud, trembling voice said, "John, listen, lad." She was beginning to shout, angry not at John but at their plight. "The food on the table tonight tells it all. There wasn't enough. The two of you are growing boys, eating like hungry young pups. And that's the way it should be, John."

She gained control once again and steadied her voice. "Aunt Theresa has a good job at President Fillmore's law firm downtown." She forced a smile and said, "No doubt, you'll come to know some of her important friends. She'll be able to take you places you'd only see from the outside with the likes of your granny. Excitin' 'twill be, son." She thought to herself, *This is all wrong. Mother of God help us!*

Maire hesitated for a few seconds, steeling herself for any further response from either boy, but except for sniffling, John made no sound. Pat sat stiffly, a frightened expression on his face, and said nothing.

Maire forced a smile and found additional words. "I hope there'll be food enough so we can all eat dinner here every Sunday. Theresa has always wanted a son of her own. She'll be after treating you like the son the Lord never gave her." That was true, she thought to herself. In a month or two John would see it was all for the best.

The weight of her words now hit John fully. He felt abandoned once again, just as he had when his parents died. He was losing his grandmother, who meant more to him than anyone else in the whole world. He was sick to his stomach. He hardly knew Aunt Theresa. No matter how nice she would be to him, she was not his gram. He was terrified at the thought of separation from her. After slowing his crying and wiping his nose with his hand, he suddenly broke out again, crying even louder. He stammered and shouted, "But I don't want to go to Aunt Theresa's." He repeated again and again, "I don't want to go . . . I don't want to go . . . I don't want to go."

Gram said nothing—in truth, she had run out of words to say—and only held him tightly. When he stopped crying after several minutes, she said, "John, take my hand and let's go over and see where you'll be livin'. Pat, come with us. Aunt Theresa is a grand lady and you'll be needin' to get to know her better, too."

Maire and her grandsons walked two blocks to Aunt Theresa's flat. The walk helped calm their feelings, but there was still a whale of hurt, anger, and fear in all three hearts.

Theresa greeted them warmly, exclaiming how nice it was of them to visit her. She looked up questioningly at Maire, who nodded toward John. Clapping her hands, Theresa asked if the boys would like cookies and milk. Neither boy smiled at the offer and only grunted when they were served. Theresa and Maire let their impoliteness pass. They knew how difficult this was for them.

The two women talked about the unusually pleasant weather, Maire's new order for a surplice from St. Louis Church, and the law case Theresa was writing up. Maire raised her voice and pointed out to Theresa that John had gotten the cloth and delivered the surplice all by himself, but she could see that John was not buying her effort to build him up.

After an appropriate amount of time for the visit, Maire stood up and announced matter-of-factly that it was best they be going. She did not want to impose on Theresa any more than they already had. Theresa frowned and waved away her cousin's statement, but stood up. This visit was at an end. Theresa asked John to visit her every day after school, as soon as she got home from work.

John did as Theresa asked. He visited her three times that week. His first visit was awkward and Theresa was hard-pressed to get him talking, but by the third visit, John chattered on about his school day without much prompting from his aunt. Bonding was beginning to take place.

That first day, Theresa sent John home with a half loaf of bread. She would have sent a whole loaf but did not want to offend her cousin's pride. She excused the gift by asking John to tell his gram she was afraid it would go stale before she could eat it all. "Better you have it than it go to waste." After the second visit, John brought home a small packet of stew meat.

Eight-year-old Patrick, enjoying the taste of meat for the first time in a week, declared that if Theresa was giving them food then there was no reason for John to leave. Maire shook her head. "No, my love, I'm sorry, it doesn't work that way. If John lives here, he's mine to feed. I must talk to your aunt about the food she keeps giving us."

A week later in mid-August, Maire walked to Theresa's with the boys once again, John pulling a wagon borrowed from PM, loaded with clothes and a few personal items.

As Pat returned home with Gram but without John, hurt swelled in the pit of his stomach, in spite of all Gram was trying to say. He was sad beyond words and blind angry with Gram.

"Gram, we're a family and John should be here with us."

"Pat, a family we'll always be. A few streets can't take that away. You'll see."

He left the house that afternoon and walked aimlessly through the Ward, until he encountered a gang of six boys from school. He played Mr. Fox and jacks with them till well after dark and momentarily forgot his hurt and anger. The gang called themselves the "Rounders," a name given them by an old Irishman from the Flats when rebuking them for their rowdy behavior. Each section of the Ward had its own name. Among First Warders, they didn't come from the Ward; they came from Hakertown, Rogues Hollow, Uniontown, or the Flats. The poorest came from the Beach, a shantytown of several hundred shacks on the lake.

Their leader was a boy Pat knew only by his nickname, Bugsy. He liked Pat for his brash ways and willingness to plunge into whatever adventures he suggested.

After playing with the Rounders for a few days, Pat joined them roaming the farmers' market on Elk Street. He got John to come along. The boys dashed into this jungle of colorful vegetables and small animals, enclosed by walls of horse-drawn wagons on each side. Subtle plant smells and pungent, fresh horse manure flooded their noses. They peered at baskets of apples, pears, peaches and plums, squash, turnips, carrots and corn, animals hanging limp by their feet or squawking in their pens, clothes, pots and pans, and myriad other household items. Over the voices of their neighbors, the sounds of neighing horses and chickens clucking wildly as their heads were twisted, farmers shouted: "Fresh corn, beans, carrots, and potatoes . . . golden juicy peaches from the shores of Lake Ontario . . . rabbits, ducks, chickens slaughtered this morning."

The gang ran in and out of the stalls. One distracted a farmer by knocking over a basket of tomatoes. The rest grabbed produce from the other side of the stall. Then they all ran.

After a half hour of these antics, Pat grew bolder. He climbed up on the back of a wagon and began tossing pears from a bushel basket to his pals. Cursing profusely, the farmer lunged at Pat and almost caught him, but the boy evaded him, laughing like a fool.

As Pat moved out front of the gang with his devil-take-the-hindmost deeds, Bugsy grew resentful. He was big for his age and traded on his size to become leader of the gang. When they had run a distance from the market, Bugsy pushed Pat to the ground. "Get lost, ye termite, or I'll bust in yer face."

Pat's face was red with embarrassment and anger. John pulled on his sleeve and the two walked off. Seeing a paving brick by the side of the road, Pat picked it up and turned back toward the gang. John said, "Pat, let's go home. We don't want any more trouble today." John was afraid that the gang would beat his brother to a pulp and him as well. Pat ran back toward Bugsy who was walking in the opposite direction and walloped him over the skull.

Bugsy fell to the ground screaming in pain and holding his head. Before Pat could hit him again, John and the other boys rushed him, wrestled the brick away, and held him to the ground. Bugsy lay flat out on the ground, rubbing his head and moaning. He had only one true friend among the boys, and that friend stood off to the side. The rest of the boys resented the way

Bugsy bullied them and did nothing except break up the fight. Pat was furious with his brother and the other boys. He struggled to break their grips, but could not. Finally, he gave in, relaxed, got up, and walked away.

The next day, John had a long talk with his brother. Pat understood it was futile to fight with Bugsy and his gang. He knew John was right. Gram would be deeply disappointed in him if he got into trouble with the boys' parents or, worse, with the police.

From that point on, a truce reigned between Pat and Bugsy. Both acted as leaders, but were careful to defer to one another when decisions were being made.

John dropped out of the gang, uneasy with their rowdiness and thieving, but said nothing to his grandmother or aunt about his brother or the gang.

The next night, Pat came home with a rabbit. John had been visiting with his grandmother and was just leaving. Pat cut open the rabbit and yanked out its organs. On a hook on the chicken coop in the back yard, he hung it up to bleed. "We'll eat this bunny tonight, if we figure out how to skin it. But we'll need a couple of potatoes and carrots," he said. John skinned the rabbit. Pat went back to the market and begged vegetables from a sympathetic farmer who was just pulling a tarp over his wagon. As he walked home, he thought to himself, *I can tell tales and beg with the best.* He was very proud of himself.

"I suppose this rabbit shed its skin and hopped up to you on Elk Street, and the vegetables on his back, so as we'd have a full meal," chided Maire.

"No, Gram," maintained Pat wearing an expression of angelic innocence. "A farmer was closing his stall and wanted to get rid of 'em. We happened to be standing there. He asked us if we had anyone to cook them up. John said you, Gram, often cooked for a whole village in Ireland." Maire laughed. What he alluded to without knowing it was a custom called a "spree." She knew the boys had only the faintest idea of what a spree was.

Since there was nothing but two onions and some flour in the pantry, she didn't press the issue. At least John would have a farewell meal worthy of the name. Gram sent John over to fetch Aunt Theresa. The meal, with the six of them eating all they wanted, eased the transition a bit. Pat put his angel act in his memory bank for future use.

Over time, the boys got used to parting ways at the end of the evening, but that first departure brought on clenched faces and tears.

In June of 1852, at age fourteen, Jo left school after the eighth grade and went to work as a clerk at Sherman's Dry Goods Store at Main and Swan Streets and added a few helpful dollars to the household. Something clicked with Maire when Jo started working that Pat should not be sharing the same bedroom with her. She began to look at Jo differently and noticed the changes that had come over her body. Not one to dally over decisions, she talked to her brother and the same evening switched bedrooms with Pat. She now slept with Jo.

Over the years, Maire Joy became the delight of many of the Buffalo Irish clergy, telling at parish socials the same stories that had made her so popular in Mallow. She befriended Bishop John Timon at St. Patrick's Church at Ellicott and Broadway in 1847 and continued their friendship at St. Joseph Cathedral, which the bishop dedicated in 1855.

The bishop—once Prefect Apostolic of the Republic of Texas—was stocky, short, only five feet, with a large head of wavy white hair and a broad, severe face set off by big round, piercing dark eyes. He had a preaching voice that rocked the ushers standing in the back of church.

In late 1855, before leaving for Europe, the bishop was looking for an event that would build on Irish culture. He had participated in a spree on his last trip to Ireland and imagined a similar event that would raise money to cope with the social evils of the community and, above all, raise Irish pride and self-respect. He believed that a spree was no substitute for proper institutions to care for his poverty-stricken flock, but he also wisely noted to Father Martin Corbett, whom he had placed in charge of the St. Vincent de Paul Society on Fulton Street and one of the few priests he trusted, that nothing could substitute for self-respect. That surpassed anything money could buy or build.

He knew Maire had organized sprees in Mallow, so she would be the right person to consult about putting on an Irish festival in Buffalo. Maire attended mass almost daily. One morning he approached her after mass. "Maire, my heart is sick with the evils besetting our community. Our people have lost their soul and their way. Back in the old country, the spree was the way to spring the people out of their grief and sadness. Do you think we could do it here?"

"Sure I don't know why not, Your Excellency! Are all the *seanachaithe* dead and gone? Don't we have the best entertainers in America? We could bring in pipers, singers, dancers, and *seanachaithe* from New York and Chicago. And we could start it with a parade along the Canal to the cathedral."

"Maire, I love the way you think. I'll have Father Corbett start talking to you about this grand event. Will you help us?"

"You needn't ask. T'would be the pleasure of me life to do it, Your Excellency."

On a Saturday in early 1856, Pat wheeled home in PM's wagon one of the biggest watermelons Maire had ever seen. "Now where did you get that, son? I know they don't grow in the fields off Catherine Street!"

"Gram, they leave some of them in box cars coming up from the South. See, this one's got a slash in its side. So the fancy ladies don't want it and the men in the market can't sell it."

Maire had her doubts, but she knew when Theresa and John came over for dinner on Sunday she would have something special to serve them. She was also tired from sewing and delivering a chemise on the West Side. Today she just didn't have the persistence it took to question Pat and to wade through his half-truths.

Chapter 3

Life in the Ward

After returning from Europe in March of 1856, Bishop Timon approached Maire once again about organizing the Irish festival. Father Corbett had talked with Maire about her ideas while the bishop was away.

The priest appeared at her house in the bishop's brougham to bring her to the cathedral church hall. He was as tall as Bishop Timon was short, a humorous pair when standing side by side. To add to the contrast, Father Corbett had a finely chiseled face, round smiling eyes, and a head of thick dark, unruly hair.

Maire motioned Pat into the coach and wrapped him in a heavy wool blanket. She was honored to be riding in the bishop's carriage, but had not expected the austere state of it. The brougham was almost as bare as an open wagon, except for its black, varnished wood coach. It had unpadded wood benches, open windows, and one riding lamp. The bishop's coat of arms painted modestly on both doors was its only distinguishing feature.

Buffalo was in the midst of one of its coldest winters in years. Nonetheless, Maire sat on the outside with the priest, who drove. She enjoyed conversing with Father Corbett. The ride across streets she often walked was an added luxury. Pat was thrilled just to be riding in the bishop's carriage. He peered out the windows at streets he seldom saw after dark.

The streets were quiet. A few workers were making their way home on foot from workplaces clustered on the Niagara River, downtown, and in the

Buffalo harbor. Many men who knew the bishop's carriage by sight tipped their hats and shouted a word of greeting to him. Father Corbett acknowledged their greetings with a hearty "God bless you and your families," imitating the bishop's usual greeting. Maire smiled at the priest's puckish sense of humor.

Maire and Father Corbett chatted about the weather and the bishop's remarkable accomplishments. She asked him about his work aiding the poor through the St. Vincent de Paul Society. She thought, as he described it, *I could have used it many times meself, but there were those who needed it more.* Father Corbett's descriptions of Irish degradation filled the rest of their short voyage across the Ward and downtown to the cathedral on Franklin Street.

They were early for the meeting, and with time to burn he stopped the carriage to gaze at the cathedral looming majestically above them. "Maire, the cathedral is the crown jewel of the bishop's labors. After mass tomorrow, 100 yards or so into your walk home, take a minute to look back on it." He went on pointing out its features: its magnificent spire, its arched front gate, its stately buttresses, and St. Joseph holding the Child, the two standing guard over Buffalo's Catholics. "Remember, the bishop has not been here a decade and he's already positioned Buffalo's Roman Catholics proudly alongside not only the elite of our city, but of Christendom everywhere."

The bishop had gathered a hundred prominent Irish Americans, many of whom served on the cathedral building committee, to organize the first Buffalo Irish Festival. Members of the audience were whispering to one another. They were eager for the bishop to begin, not because they wanted the meeting over and done with, but because they enjoyed listening to this unusually bright, independent, and forceful man.

Everyone remained bundled up, the women with their hands up to their wrists in rabbit-furred mufflers. A large oil-fed boiler served both the church and its downstairs hall, but barely took the chill off.

The bishop wanted to hold the festival on the feast of St. Patrick, Monday, March 17, 1856, but he resigned himself that it was not to be. He hoped instead for a summer festival. Everything takes time, money, and skills, all in short supply. He thought to himself: *God, give me patience with my priests and people, most of all with myself. I'm not Jesus that can just wish things into being.*

He moved to center stage at exactly 7:00 and stood before the assembly. Flashing through his thoughts were his rides through Irish neighborhoods, stopping to visit families he knew—and he knew many—and to talk to men on the streets. Irish males were acting out in embarrassing ways, drinking and carousing, fighting and getting into trouble with the police, and filling the dockets of the city's courts. He knew they were intensely disliked by the Anglo-American population for their behavior. He had read the signs all over town saying, "Irish need not apply." The natives expected him to rein in his fellow Irish and teach them how to act.

There were Irish women at the doors of every social institution and church, bedraggled, hungry children in hand, begging for handouts. Catholics were not assimilating into the American masses as he hoped. They were losing the pride and culture they had fought so hard to nourish during hundreds of years of British domination. All sorts of anti-Catholic, anti-Irish societies were forming in Buffalo and throughout the country. In large measure, the same social dynamics were not found among German Catholics. German Catholics disliked him for the way he favored the Irish population. The truth was, the Irish needed his leadership and correction far more.

He had already established several new parishes, St. Joseph's College, St. Joseph's Boys' Orphanage, and Sisters of Charity Hospital. He intended to do much more as soon as he raised the money. He proposed to move thousands of Irish into rural communities to own land and farms once again, as they had in Ireland. The Protestant newspapers derisively called the plan "Timon's Colonization Program." *But never mind, it could work. Living in the slums of the cities brings nothing but squalor to people who have no history in them.*

He decided not to speak about the negative circumstances of the Irish population, believing them clearly visible to his audience every day. He would focus on his festival agenda.

"Ladies and gentlemen," he began in a voice loud and strong, amid the dying whispers and coughs. "Thank you for coming out on one of Buffalo's more inclement evenings.

"The interests of the diocese compel me to undertake more voyages seeking assistance from wealthy Catholics. On my last travels through Europe, my first stop was in Rome and the Vatican to ask for the Holy Father's blessing on our endeavors here in Buffalo and, to be sure, to ask for a significant donation. Pius IX was most generous. I used his good example to secure even bigger donations from rich Catholics throughout Europe and Mexico and will soon approach similar individuals in this country.

"Before I leave, I want you all to work with me to organize a grand event whose purposes will be twofold." The bishop lifted his outspread hands. "First, we must show our Protestant friends and neighbors and the people I will be begging from our willingness to help ourselves. We will raise from our own what funds we can.

"Secondly, this event will have another, more fundamental purpose. Our Irish brethren suffer not only from a lack of wealth, but far worse than that, from a lack of pride in themselves and their own heritage. In the face of the most dehumanizing and degrading persecutions ever perpetrated on any people in Europe, the Irish have always celebrated their faith and their culture like no other people on the continent.

"Many of you attended sprees in Ireland, so you know what I propose to do in our own uniquely American way here in Buffalo. I have asked Mrs. Maire Joy to speak briefly about the sprees she organized in Mallow, County Cork, and to suggest a few ideas to get us started. We want to inspire our people to rise above their sad conditions through faith in God, a disciplined family life, sobriety, and hard work.

"We beg your kind prayers, dearly beloved in Christ, that the Mother of Our Savior be our keeper throughout our journeys and make our festival a grand success."

Bishop Timon turned toward Maire and nodded. She stood up and bowed her head for a moment to utter a silent prayer and to gather her thoughts. She was nervous standing before such important people, but focused on giving a performance that would capture her audience. The crowd began whispering again. She raised her head slightly and waited for them to focus on her. Then she looked over them and gestured to a group of bagpipers who had gathered unnoticed in the rear of the hall. With a loud wail that pierced the stillness and sent shudders through every person there, the six musicians blew an ancient Celtic ballad, "The Winds of Galway." A dozen smiling girls in ankle-length, green cotton costumes trimmed with white lace step-danced onto the stage.

The moment they stopped, with gas lights turned low and in darkness broken only by large candles burning in the four corners of the hall and alongside her, Maire told a shortened version of Fionn mac Cumhaill, Finn McCool in English.

"You have all heard that Fionn mac Cumhaill received his father's magic spear and became the leader of the Fianna, who for centuries protected the high kings at Tara. Well, it seems that on our Bishop's last visit to Ireland, he ran across a giant of a lad high in the Boggeragh Mountains, nearly seven foot tall with arms that, when swung in a circle, could create a windstorm. He was said to be runnin' at the fore of a band of red-haired brothers and scarin' the bejesus out of any fool Brit who dared wander into the high heather."

She held up a large piece of print paper on which she had drawn, quite adeptly, the giant carrying a huge club and followed by a dozen smaller men.

"Well, the bishop ran the boys through one of the famous retreats he gives his priests. He recruited the leader and five of his best to join him in Buffalo. The lads found a skiff on the shore of the westernmost Aran Island, rowed their way to Canada, and were in Buffalo two weeks before him. There they perched atop the tallest elevator in the harbor, roamed the city by night invadin' Know Nothing meetings, demandin' they make their shops more safe and double workingmen's wages. You know, tonight the Fianna are buggerin' the St. Louis trustees, leadin' em through downtown to the cathedral to confess their sins of pride." The audience laughed loudly. They were all aware of the feud between the bishop and the St. Louis Church trustees that had continued on and off since he arrived in 1847.

Bishop Timon stood and shouted, "Wouldn't I love to see that procession. Hurry on, Maire, I have to get upstairs," and everyone laughed.

Maire paused to let the laughing die down and then continued. "Spread the word to your friends in the Ward, ladies and gentlemen. These heirs of Fionn and the Fianna have the Ohio Street saloons and the Beach in sight and they'll be drivin' the whole pack of them, Celtic, German, and Know Nothin's all, back to a barren Aran Isle on a slow barge in January."

Someone muttered loud enough for everyone to hear him, "Sure, I'll stay sober that night, love. That boat's not for me." Again the crowd laughed. They were very much into Maire's story. Then she went on.

"Before they do, they'll be holdin' their games at our spree on the Canal. Can you imagine the beer bellies with thorn in foot tryin' to pluck it out while runnin' and bendin' beneath a knee-high stick, or jumpin' their own height? Sure they'll all be glad to take to the barge." Now she had the crowd laughing at the thought of watching Know Nothings, St. Louis trustees, and Irish scoundrels put through Fianna trials, and then crowded together on the same barge crossing the Atlantic. She bowed and moved off.

Before she could sit down, the assemblage exploded in applause. She beamed ear to ear. Her aim was to get the group thinking "spree" and in the right mood. She knew she had succeeded.

Bishop Timon sprang to his feet and with Father Corbett called for and captured ideas and commitments shouted out by the crowd for over an hour on large paper tablets pinned on wooden stands.

When the discussion was done, he asked them to bow their heads. He prayed a short but fervent prayer to his heavenly Father, blessed them and their families, and dismissed them in peace. The festival was on its way.

Pat rode home, awestruck by the bishop and his grandmother even more so. Why, she was every bit as great as he was!

John had finished his last year in school, the sixth grade, in 1855. Theresa talked to him about remaining in school through the eighth grade and then going on to high school. She told him that education would open up opportunities that only people like the Halls and their kind enjoyed.

John, however, decided work, not school, was for him. He was looking forward to the day when he could live on his own and help his grandmother.

Besides, he could see no further use for book learning. Theresa fought back her disappointment and said nothing more. She knew talking education was a losing battle with most of the children of the Ward whose families were struggling to put food on the table each day. John was influenced by these children. Still, she had hoped for more from him. He had such promise, and going to work shining shoes or running errands for sailors following the other boys in the Ward was such a waste of his talents.

Of his ten classmates, only two went on two years later to Central School on Court and Franklin Streets, the city's only high school.

Pat's thoughts for the past year had focused exclusively on work. He hardly paid attention in school. All he thought about was getting through the daily boredom of his classes. He too lacked the slightest insight that further education could advance him beyond the fate of a day laborer. The very survival of his family depended on his finding a job as soon as he was legally allowed. Gram and Uncle Jack were as close to starving as a winter lasting into April or a deferred vestment order could bring them. They talked up work to Pat as soon as he reached the fifth grade. Pat turned twelve on Tuesday, March 25, 1856 and quit school as soon as he finished the sixth grade.

The Ward afforded opportunities for children and adults to find employment from the time they were ten. Even while still in school, Pat and John earned money shining sailors' shoes outside the many saloons on Ohio Street. The other shoeshine boys avoided the places where Pat set up his and his brother's stations, not only for fear of tangling with Pat, but with his gang as well.

The Buffalo harbor was full of ships and barges from Great Lakes states, Canada, Europe, and the East Coast. The Canadian government had constructed the second edition of the Welland Canal. Because of it, ships from all over the world now had access to Buffalo and its mercantile and marine facilities. English, Scottish, French Canadian, Irish, German, and Scandinavian sailors walked across the Ward from the docks to hotels, clubs, and restaurants downtown. Buffalo's downtown stretched from the Erie Canal at the foot of Main Street a dozen blocks north to Chippewa Street.

John and Pat found street corners with abundant foot traffic and explored how best to attract and keep customers. John smiled and talked in pleasantries. Pat engaged in more personal and direct talk that sometimes got him a dime and twice a cuff on the mouth. The last occasion, an English sailor wanted to give him a shilling. Not recognizing the large foreign coin with a woman's face on it and fearing he was about to be duped, Pat asked, "Who's this supposed to be?"

"Why, the most revered woman in the world, me boy," said the gob.

Pat scratched his head. "Wotja mean, Mary, Mother of God?"

"No, ye scamp, that's the Queen of England," and he swatted Pat lightly across the mouth.

Within a few weeks, John saw how men earned money outside the law. He made up his mind to shun such behavior. Pat saw the same thing and was drawn to the thrill of it.

Evenings, Pat led his gang to railroad cars awaiting switch engines to continue their journeys across the East and Midwest. The cars stood idle by the dozens in rail yards in the middle of the Ward and in the Valley, the next neighborhood east. Pat pointed out opportunities to his boys and plotted the best strategy so they wouldn't get caught. After he sliced freight car seals with iron clippers borrowed from Uncle Jack's backyard shed, four gang members pushed and pulled open the heavy doors. Many nights, they opened dozens of cars before they discovered valuable, portable cargo.

The boys loaded up as much as they could carry and moved quickly through the darkness across junk-filled yards, vegetable gardens, and grain fields—for there were still a few small farms in the area—to an unused shed on Alabama Street. The shed filled up with lumber, hardware, and other items Pat sold to a barkeep who asked no questions.

Pat proudly added his share of the take to his shoeshine earnings and handed it to Gram. At her quizzical expression at such large amounts, he exclaimed boldly to her face, "We're getting good at making the shoes shine like stars, so the tips are better." Gram was pleased and put any questions she had out of mind. The money Pat gave her would allow them to eat meat three or four times a week.

After a few months of this illicit behavior, a neighbor became suspicious and alerted the Buffalo police, who in turn notified railroad cops. The end for Pat and his gang came suddenly. They were beaten with nightsticks and taken downtown to Precinct #1 on Terrace and Evans Streets, which served as police headquarters and contained the city jail. Pat sat in a cell, aching, head full of lumps, with five other boys, glumly anxious about what would happen to them next.

That night Gram and Uncle Jack were awakened by a loud, persistent knocking on their door, as were the other parents, all of whom lived in the Ward. Uncle Jack opened the door to a police officer, a smallish, somewhat embarrassed rookie. Maire spoke first. "Is it about my Pat?" she asked, fearful of the reply. She had gone to bed worried because Pat had once again not returned home from playing outside before she retired. The officer apologized for waking them and told them Pat was in jail downtown for larceny, burglary, and selling stolen property. Parents were to appear at a hearing at 10:00 a.m. at Buffalo City Court on Clinton and Washington Streets.

Gram did not go back to bed that night. "Jack, I wonder if some mistake's been made. Sure our Pat would never do such things." They talked about Pat's habits over the past months and concluded she had given him too much freedom to hang out with his friends. "He could have been led astray by some of the older boys," Jack offered. Finally, Maire concluded, "Jack, I'm beginnin' to think the boy might have been into more mischief than I saw. Maybe I'm gettin' too old to raise a young scamp in the Ward."

She talked with her brother further about how this could have happened, "Sure and it was my fault, Jack. I was only too glad to see him bring home the extra coins. I shut me eyes to what he was doin'." She decided the only person who could help her was the bishop.

Maire approached Bishop Timon after the 7:30 morning mass at the cathedral. He listened to her confused statements and pieced together the gist of the story. He liked the fact that she blamed herself for not keeping a firmer rein on her grandson. *The truth is the boy needs a father*, he thought. The bishop agreed to appear at the arraignment at mid-morning.

There he listened to what the police and a few adults from the Ward had to say about what had been going on for months. When the judge was about to make his disposition of the case, the bishop rose and asked to approach the bench. The judge acquiesced. Bishop Timon spoke so that all could plainly hear him. "Your honor, these boys have done a grave injustice to our community, but I would like to salvage them from a life of crime that would be a burden on their families as well as on the city and its citizens."

Judge Wente believed the bishop to be a man of integrity and action, who was not about to whitewash what the boys had done just because they were Irish and Catholic. To the contrary, he felt Bishop Timon would use his influence with the parents to correct the boys' behavior and make good on what the boys had stolen from the railroads and stores. He listened to the bishop's deferential request, already knowing what he would do if the bishop asked that the boys be placed in his custody. He did so readily, grateful to have the bishop's intervention. There were so many delinquents and so few resources.

That afternoon, the bishop held an arraignment of his own in the cathedral church hall, attended by all seven boys and their parents. The boys were downcast and not a little sore. Their fathers, or uncles if fathers were absent, had whipped each of them while the bishop tactfully waited outside. He would have liked to have done the same. Two First Ward beat-policemen were present at the request of the judge and the bishop. They, too, waited outside until the boys' cries abated.

The bishop, with the two officers beside him, interviewed each boy singly and then brought parents and children together. "Your sons have acted like common criminals, breaking into rail cars, warehouses, and stores. They kept the stolen property right there near you in an abandoned shed on Alabama Street and sold it to a saloonkeeper on Ohio Street, who peddled it from his own bar and in other saloons nearby. He used young men from the Beach to sell it to sailors and travelers coming off boats, trains, and barges."

One of the parents pleaded, "But Bishop, we knew nothing about it. We thought the boys were doing what all boys do at their age." A few other parents grunted their agreement.

Bishop Timon waited to speak until he had better control of his temper. He surveyed the group before him, quite representative of his flock. He knew well their hardships and felt sympathy for each. Still he shook his head, arranging his spectacles on his nose.

"I understand your plight, living hand to mouth through the good weather when the men are working and then half starving when the lake freezes, but let's be honest with one another. This behavior has been going on several nights a week for months. Numerous robberies occurred right in the Elk Street Market, to such an extent that farmers moved their produce to markets in other parts of the city." The bishop tugged at his cassock sleeves before going on. "You had to know your sons were up to no good. Oh, sure, boys will be boys and get into a certain amount of mischief, but their actions were not just practical jokes. They committed felonies that could land them in jail for years.

"The boys had two motives, I say. One was the thrill of it. The other was money and you were complicit in the latter. You can't tell me your sons began to hand in more money than you'd ever seen from them and that you thought it came from fruit picking, ferrying men across the creek, shoe shining, or running sailors' errands, now did you?"

He looked out over the crowd to see if there were signs they agreed with his logic. Indeed, he caught several reluctant nods. He waited a moment and then went on. "I know some of you are hungry day after day, but winking at your sons' criminal behavior is wrong, not just before a city court judge, but before God. How were these boys able to stay out till late at night without you disciplining them?"

Again, he paused. The parents looked down or away. They knew he spoke the truth. "If your boys continue on like the last year, they will all be confined, most likely outside the area, for most of their lives. You parents will be forced by the court to make good for what they've stolen and for the damage they did. Do you understand what you must do?"

A chorus of voices responded, "We do, Your Excellency," and promised him it would never happen again.

In a much lower voice indicating he was about done, he said, "I can only go before the court once on your behalf. The judge is no fool. Recognize the mercy he has shown and the confidence he has in me that I would work with you. Your sons must see the seriousness of their deeds and go through a complete change of heart. I will stand by you this once and once only.

"Father Corbett will approach railroads and stores harmed by your boys and acquaint them with the full details of what has transpired. I want a few of you parents to accompany Father Corbett at each stop. You will have to beg the offended parties to forgive your sons and assure them it will not happen again. I will get a full report on all that is said and can only hope the parties will be merciful. I know you parents are not able to make full restitution or come close to it."

Lastly, with forefinger raised in reprimand, he chided the parents for allowing their sons to appear before a Protestant judge. "What must he think of us Irish?" he asked. "What else but thieves and delinquents from broken families . . . boys abandoned by their fathers and living on the streets, preying on the law-abiding citizens of the city!"

The bishop kept Pat, Maire, and Jack after the others had gone home. Bluntly, he told them, "Pat was the leader of the gang, and I hold him more responsible than the rest for all the evil the gang has done." He grabbed Pat by the arm with such pressure that the boy squirmed and tears came to his eyes. Pat feared he would never let go. Bishop Timon then asked him probing questions with all the skill and force of a New York district attorney. Pat's answers came quickly. He admitted he was the brains behind every break-in, the terms of sale to the saloonkeeper, and the division of money each boy received. Gram and Jack twisted in anguish and disbelief as they listened.

Finally, Pat began to sob and with head in hands said several times, "I'm sorry Gram, Uncle Jack. I promise I won't do it again."

The bishop took Maire aside and told her, "You must get control of your grandson or lose him. He will not see his fifteenth birthday a free person, perhaps not alive, the way he's going."

Then he asked Jack to step out with him for a moment. "I see Maire takes a hand with raising Jo. It's because you saw a woman's presence was needed to raise a young girl. Pat needs a man the same way Jo needed a woman. I'm asking you to talk with Maire. Tell her what I suggested, and take a stronger role with that boy. He needs a father." He hesitated for a moment. "Jack, that seems to be what God has in mind for you."

32

Jack was reluctant, but he knew that the bishop was right. He would have to step up and take the place of Pat's father or the boy would likely go the way of so many boys in the Ward.

That night, Jack slapped his leathery right hand across his nephew's backside, a whipping that Pat would recall with a pained expression for the rest of his life. Maire watched and then clenched her grandson's neck until his face turned crimson red. "I'll be after tellin' ye, son, I will send you back to Father Edwards and have him keep ye in his home for wayward boys for the next five years. If ye can't make up your mind to go straight and narrow, we'll be on the train tomorrow, first light."

Pat wanted nothing to do with an orphanage in Rochester. Losing his gram was his greatest fear. He put his head in her lap and said, "Gram, I love you more than anything. I won't ever do it again. I promise. I truly promise, Gram."

Later that night, Jack and Maire discussed what they must do and agreed they would act more like parents to one another's children. No more Jo belongs to Jack, Pat belongs to Maire.

Pat met with his gang one last time and told them his days as their leader were done for good. From now on, he would stick with his brother, work the shoeshine business, and play baseball. Pat and John had watched older boys carve a baseball diamond out of a field on Ohio Street and had become very interested in playing themselves.

On Saturdays, Pat packed up his shoeshine kit and followed his brother downtown, where they watched a mix of immigrants and Americans heading west: families, businessmen, sailors, vagrants, thieves, and women of the street, disembarking from trains and barges at the western end of the Erie Canal near the foot of Main Street. Buffalo was the transfer point for anyone wanting to secure free land, build rail lines, or mine for gold in the West. The boys catered to sailors, gamblers, and businessmen who frequented the hotels, taverns, brothels, and dives north of the canal.

CHAPTER 4

Sex Education and Shoveling Coal

John and Pat enjoyed talking to the women who dallied outside in good weather when business was slack. Dressed in long, flowing, loudly colored dresses that exposed large expanses of bosom, they spoke of the seamy side of Buffalo nightlife, the likes of which the boys had never heard . . . and these women were funny. Their language sparkled with crude phrases and outrageous stories about big-time businessmen, politicians, entertainers, and even clergymen, a few of whom the boys had heard of.

One, Kitty Hennigan from Limerick, worked in the Duncan Hotel on Canal Street. She was tall and in her late thirties, with long, dark hair; a rouge-reddened, prematurely wrinkled face; and narrow blue eyes that held the boys fast. The tight bodice of her long, pleated dress accentuated her ample bosom. She had moved from New York to ply her business because she thought Buffalo offered more opportunity. It was just opening up and there was less competition.

Kitty found it amusing to trade stories with the boys about the men they met downtown. "Ah, that rich contractor, Timmons, is a queer bastard," she said to them. "He comes by of an evening and hails one of the girls, me if I'm standin' out here, to his fancy carriage. He takes us for a ride and has us rub his crotch, raise our Mother Hubbards, so we bare our bottoms, and sit on his cock.

"Strange business, it is, boys. Last night, just as he left me off, I was stopped by a cop. Wearin' me straw hat was I, so he let me go. If I wasn't, I'd be in jail. Now figure that, boys, but that's life in Buffalo."

John and Pat did not understand what she meant. They knew that hundreds of men had crowded into the hotel hall on Independence Day evening to watch Kitty dance naked for two hours. They saw men take women upstairs in the Duncan Hotel and in the other hotels and bars along the strip, but they knew nothing about what was done once the doors were closed.

"Miss Kitty?" asked John. "Why do you spend so much time with these men?"

"Oh, they like to see me take off me clothes and look at me boobs and private parts."

"And they pay you for that?" asked Pat a little skeptically.

"Well, boys, you save up your money and one of these days, maybe on a birthday, I'll take you to my room and show you a thing or two."

"How much will it cost?" asked John, always the practical one.

Jo, Gram, and Aunt Theresa were extremely modest around them, and they were curious about the female body. They had been around mothers nursing their babies, mostly Irish women who took care to cover their breasts in the folds of their dresses. They had seen nude paintings of women in saloons and in sailors' private quarters, but they had never seen the naked, female body in the flesh.

"Well, if you can save fifty cents each, one of these afternoons I'll take you upstairs," replied Kitty.

It took the boys three months to save $.50 apiece, because they had to give Gram and Aunt Theresa most of what they earned running errands and shining shoes . . . but not quite all. They grew anxious to see Kitty undressed and pushed her several times to make good on her promise. On a very hot day in mid-August, Kitty took the two boys upstairs.

The madam was a fiftyish, heavyset woman who wore a faded red wig above a face that frightened the boys, so deep were the lines that crawled up her neck and wrinkled her cheeks. She stood at the top of the stairs, smiling wickedly and asked, "What have our young gentlemen in mind this afternoon?"

"This is John and this is Pat, my two best friends," Kitty said introducing the boys. The boys' "hello ma'ams" were barely audible. Kitty told them to pay the madam. John handed her a handkerchief of nickels, dimes, and pennies. The boys turned quickly and followed Kitty down a grey hallway, dimly lit by two gas lamps hung high on opposite walls. They entered another semi dark room with a large bed at the far end, covered by a red comforter and big pillows. A small bar stood off to the side with two bottles of Canadian whiskey. Near the entry were large, plush chairs around a small table with a lit candle in the middle.

Kitty closed the door and teased the boys with a gentle but provocative sway of her hips and bosom as she strutted to the bed. Facing the boys, she slapped her thighs and said "Well! Here's what ye came for!" Grabbing the hem of her red velvet dress, she raised the garment ever so slowly over her legs . . . thighs . . . waist, watching with pride and amusement the boys' eyes stop, and then slide upward. Their gaze followed her dress as it rose above her thighs and stopped at her wide waist to expose black pubic hair; ran quickly over her rippled stomach, and stopped again at the large brown nipples of her broad, heavy breasts. They never noticed she wore no undergarments. She then sat on the end of the bed, propping up her breasts in her hands, laid back, and opened her legs.

The boys stood fast, their eyes bulging.

"Come, boys, you needn't hold back," she said in a low voice. "I got customers awaitin'!"

John hesitated but Pat moved closer. With the kindest of smiles, she took his right hand and guided it over the hair between her legs. Then she did the same with John, who followed once his brother made the first move.

"Now stroke it gently, gently me lads," she said to the brothers. "You do damage to her and I'll starve." Both boys reacted the same way, trembling and pulling away slightly, but then did as commanded. Laughing in her rough voice, Kitty pulled them to her, and hugged and rubbed their faces deeply into her bosom.

She ushered the boys out shortly afterward. She did indeed have a customer waiting.

The boys walked toward home, stopping along the way, putting down their shoeshine kits to be able to talk more freely.

"Did you think Kitty would show all she did?" asked Pat.

"I had no idea, but I liked what I saw," replied John. "Her breasts were big and her brown nipples rubbin' on my face made me move all over."

"I could have had her rub them on me forever. My hands were tingling," said Pat. "Rubbing her muskrat was something wild. Did you see her start to pump up and down when she grabbed my hand and rubbed herself hard from between her legs to her button?"

"What was that big crack she had where we have our pissers?" asked John.

"I just don't know," said Pat. "But we can ask some of the older boys and find out."

"I didn't like the smells that came from down there," replied John. "Never smelled anything like it."

"Well, it was the best money we ever spent, John, wasn't it?"

"No doubt about that," answered John.

They coached one another to calm down and watch what they said as they were about to enter their grandmother's cottage.

Not long afterward, with only a few questions asked of older boys, John and Pat got the idea of what men and women did in bed together.

In 1857 at fourteen and thirteen, the brothers were quite small for their ages, less than five feet each. Their faces favored one another, with fine features and wavy brown hair, except that John's hair was dark and Pat's light. Pat was olive-skinned, dark enough that older boys kidded him that his mother must have been black. He was upset by their remarks, but said nothing because of their size. He began washing his face with brown soap to lighten it. In spite of their complexions, many adults took the two boys for twins.

That summer, they boarded ships moored at the docks along the Buffalo Creek and offered to run errands for the crew. "My Gram will wash your dirty clothes, sailor. Fifty cents is all she'll charge you and she'll do it in lye soap. Gram makes her own brown soap and it cleans really good," promised John.

There were plenty of other boys offering the same services. Pat moved to the gangplank of any ship he considered his territory and wielded a bat on the heads of the first boys in line if they didn't cede their places. Most backed off rather than get in a fight. If they fought and lost, they went to bed for days with bruises of the head, face, and groin. If they won, they still suffered a world of hurt and endured a fight that could resume the next day or sometimes for days thereafter. All the boys around his age in the Ward learned not to tangle with Pat.

The first time he beat up an older boy, he told John it made him feel tough, like a man.

Within an hour, the boys had sacks of clothes from a half-dozen sailors, which they brought home to Gram, and money to buy pipe tobacco and candy for the sailors. John wrote down their names, ships, and what they requested. They spent the day between home and stores and docks.

Often the sailors, with time to waste, showed the boys the crew's quarters and the mess room. They fed them large slices of bread, dripping with butter and jelly. If the captain had gone into town, they took them into the pilothouse and explained how the engine ran and the ship steered. They let them look across the lake at Fort Erie through binoculars that hung in the pilothouse.

On an August day, Pat took his clothes off down to his drawers and jumped from the railing of a lake freighter into the Buffalo Creek, performing swan dives and flips that no other boy would even attempt. He soon became the darling of ships' crews, who gave him free access to come aboard.

Many Saturday afternoons that same summer, Pat and John rode rail cars east to South Buffalo or west to the waterfront and back. Once, with a few coins in their pockets, they caught a freight train, got off in Ebenezer, and walked to a candy store run by a German family. Pat and John bought long sticks of saltwater taffy made before their eyes. Outside the store, they met children their age, blonde boys in leather pants and corn silk-pigtailed girls, who spoke only German. The language difference was somehow no barrier. The children took them to an orchard where they gorged on cherries, peaches, and plums. Both boys learned that children could be very different and yet get along well.

Toward evening, the boys jumped a freight back to Buffalo. On the way home, John said to Pat: "Those kids were like no other kids I ever met. I never felt a fight comin' on, not even the hint of it, the way I do around the boys in the Ward." He put a hand on his jaw and thought for a few seconds. "Must be something about their strange religion that makes them different," he said. "I never felt so calm; kinda lost in what we were doing."

"I didn't think much about it," answered Pat. "They were nice and I had a good time. Best fruit I ever ate."

The train pulled into a yard in East Buffalo and the boys jumped off. On the way home west of Fillmore Avenue, a gang of German boys chased them up Clinton Street, taunting and jeering. The chase ended within five blocks as the area became more heavily Irish.

Pat turned around and shouted back, "We'll even the score when we see you Krauts crossing the Ward to the lake. Your lead arses will be flying off the Louisiana Bridge."

He walked off slowly just to let them know that if they came after him he wouldn't be running. Later that summer, two older German boys from Smith Street suffered broken legs when they were pushed from the Louisiana overpass.

Once John and Pat grew to near adult height, they became temporary day laborers: grain handlers lifting fifty-pound grain sacks from the holds of boats, canal diggers excavating the Union Ship Canal, and cement carriers on the break walls that protected Buffalo's harbor. At the Ship Canal, they learned to drive a team of horses. Pat especially liked holding the reins and steering those large beasts.

At all these jobs, they earned \$1 for a twelve-hour workday, half the wage that men earned. Neither boy thought any further about school. They looked up to the older men who were stronger and made more money. They wanted to be like them.

Pat was envious of his brother the day John turned fifteen, February 2, 1858. As soon as the shipping season started he would join hundreds of men, shoveling coal out of rail cars and barges onto the dock at the North Pier. In mid-March, the ice on the canal, the lake, and the creek melted and the boys headed for the harbor. Both boys were anxious about spending the day apart, but neither one shared his feelings.

"Think of it, Pat. I'll be making fifteen cents an hour shoveling coal. There's work every day and they pay better than the scoopers . . . I'll walk with you downtown, if you're setting up there today."

"I'm going to the new hotel that just opened at the foot of Main Street, the Ferguson," announced Pat. "They say it's owned by one of the railroads."

The newest hotel was patronized by businessmen from all over the world. Miss Kitty had opened her own business on the third floor with a staff of three girls. Among her clients, Kitty claimed big railroad, shipping, and construction men. She liked Pat and he liked her, too. He was attracted to her and was trying to think of ways he could persuade her for a dollar or two to do more than show him her private parts.

She had encouraged him to stop by that morning, so that she could introduce him to the manager who might take him on as the hotel's shoeshine boy. The Ferguson had a stand at the entrance to the restaurant. If Pat secured that position, he'd be able to bring home \$5 a week easy and still have \$1 to play with. He was excited to make more money, help Gram live without financial worries, and have enough left over to frequent saloons and downtown shows.

As they walked, they talked first about Gram. "Pat, do you notice that Gram has to sit down halfway through cookin' Sunday dinner? And she's using a cane going to church."

Pat nodded thoughtfully. "That scares me, John. I can't imagine life without Gram."

"Maybe with our new jobs we can earn more money so Gram could rest more and even see a doctor," said John.

"I'm with you. I will get that shoeshine post in the new hotel. Bet on it, John. Gram's goin' to be with us for years . . . Seems you're much happier with Aunt Theresa these days."

"Aunt Theresa is a great lady and easy to live with. We talk a lot about Ireland and her trip across. She's had quite an experience as a nanny and a wife and now she's risen to a good job in President Fillmore's law firm." He looked off across the creek and then commented: "It's taken two years, but I've grown to like her a lot."

"You know, John, you've lived with two women who are the best subs for our ma you could have found."

"Yah, brother, I'm a lucky boy. God has blessed me. I know I'm sounding like a girl, but that's how I feel."

"Well, you should, and I feel the same way about Gram. Are we playing with the Junior Traveler's on the new ball field the boys carved out off Ohio Street?" asked Pat facetiously. He knew nothing thrilled his brother more than baseball.

"I'll be there with you, Pat. I think this year you'll be the pride of the Ward and we'll take the league."

"The bases are just four pieces of canvas someone stole from the Dart. The outfield and infield are like playing on a rock pile, but it's goin' to be more fun this season, John, playin' on our own field. And I think there will be more people out to watch us."

It was clear to John that Pat could hardly wait for baseball to begin. Baseball was his big outlet.

They were now approaching lower Main Street and the Ferguson. John would continue on a block north to the coal docks on Buffalo Creek.

"Pat, I'll come by your stand and we can walk home together," he promised his brother. "I have to see the newest hotel in Buffalo and say hello to Miss Kitty."

As he approached the river, John caught sight of a line of men and boys a hundred yards away. He picked up his stride, afraid he might arrive too late to be chosen. The morning was cold and the wind off the water had the men hunching shoulders, hands in pockets, and shuffling from one foot to the other. Once in line, John stood silently for a while and then asked a man he recognized from the Ward about the work.

"Mr. Slattery, do you think they'll hire all of us? There must be 200 men here."

Slattery stood straighter for having been asked his opinion and sniffed. "Rail cars, ships, and barges are arriving every day loaded with coal. The pier is empty now, but they'll pile coal up in small mountains the length and breadth of it. So they'll need every man they got shovels for."

"Oh, that's good. Are they hiring young fellows like me?"

"If you can shovel coal for twelve hours, they'd hire you if you were a midget. Lots of the men you see here won't make it through the first day."

"Why not?" asked John.

"They've lungs that won't take in enough air, or arms that were hit by booms and the like," replied Slattery. "They show up hoping to disappear in the crowd, but mind you, the bosses are keen-eyed bastards and they toss them out as soon as they see them doggin' it. If they last, it's because they got a friend somewhere upstairs, if you know what I mean, and I don't mean God the Father."

John didn't know, but he didn't want to appear ignorant.

"Have you a bandana to wear over your face, John?"

The boy nodded, pulling down the collar of his coat to show a red cloth around his neck. "I was told by my aunt to expect the sun to go dark by noon from the coal dust."

"You've got a wise aunt. You don't want that shit in your lungs."

Mr. Slattery rubbed his nose with his right knuckles and sniffed. "Let me give you another bit of advice, John. You'd be smart to go straight home after work and go to bed early."

As they talked, the line shuffled forward, eventually passing into a shed about the size of two horse stalls, where two men sat behind a table. John gave them his name and address, signed his name, and was given a wide, scooped shovel. He was told to join the group twenty yards away near the line of barges tied up at the dock.

A large man in brown coveralls stood up on the bow of the first barge. The wooden barge carried a hundred tons of coal, was ninety feet long, fifteen feet wide, and three and a half feet deep. In the bow was a pilothouse with a kitchen and sleeping-quarters for the pilot and captain. The stern held a small barn for two horses and quarters for their 'hoggee' or driver.

The man yelled out in a high voice in order to be heard above the wind. "Men, you're going to be divided into groups of five. The task is simple. You shovel out the coal onto the dock alongside each barge. It should take five men a day to shovel out a barge." He coughed and spit out a wad of phlegm. "When it's empty, the five of you skip to the first untended barge and shovel it out. We break at noon to eat and again at four. Normally we end the day at 7:00. It's now 7:30. We're a little late starting, so we'll work till 7:30 this evening. You'll get paid for eleven and a half hours. Tomorrow morning I want all of you ready to climb on board at 7:00 sharp. Is that clear?"

The men nodded and moved to separate barges in groups of five. John was in the second group. He climbed quickly up on the barge and looked to Mr. Slattery to see what to do. Slattery was leaning on his shovel, waiting for the last men to pass by to the next barges. Then he picked up his shovel and in a slow and easy motion began throwing coal on the dock. John picked up his and did the same, but with lunges into the coal and a faster pace. In a few minutes, his shoulders and arms ached. He understood what Slattery was doing. Two hours at this pace would finish him.

Fine black dust began to rise from the pile. John saw Mr. Slattery pull out his bandana and tie it around his face beneath his eyes, so he did too. Cold winds blew off Lake Erie, 200 yards away, and drilled into his body. The crunch of shovel on coal permitted no conversation.

Within an hour, John was tired and bored. He thought his arms would fall off. By 11:00 a.m., he could think of nothing else but breaking for lunch. When the noon whistle blew, he struggled down from the barge and walked to the shed, where he picked out the new tin lunch box his aunt had bought for him with "John Donohue" painted on it in bold black letters by his uncle.

Men sat alone or in groups to eat, depending on their moods. He heard one cry out at what was in his lunch, packed by a wife or sister. "Ach, liver sausage again! That woman is trying to kill me." The complainer chomped into it, nonetheless. John found space alongside Slattery in an empty barge out of the wind and devoured his lunch. The two said very little, content to close their eyes and rest.

After lunch and a fifteen-minute nap, the whistle blew and John returned to his crew, noting that one man was missing. Apparently, the work proved more than he could handle. They finished shoveling out the barge half an hour before quitting time, walked past mounds of coal, and started on the first unmanned barge as they had been instructed. Once the sun set, it grew increasingly difficult to see clearly within the barge or across the dock. Shortly after starting the second barge, the whistle blew to halt work for the day.

John felt too tired to join Pat and walked the half-mile straight from the harbor to Aunt Theresa's flat, took off his work clothes in the shed at the back of the house, washed the coal dust caked on his face, neck, and hands in a pail of cold water, and fell into a chair at the supper table. He answered his aunt's questions about his first day on the job without his usual enthusiasm and gratefully accepted the hot stew she set on the table before him, cradling the warm bowl in his chilled hands. Theresa let the boy eat his supper in silence. With stomach full and eyes drooping, John went to his bedroom. Within five minutes, Theresa heard loud snores. At six the next morning, she woke him up for work.

For the next month, John forced himself back to the coal dock. Each day was a new shape up, so John was with a different crew every morning. Within a week, he got smart and stood with men he knew were steady workers, in order to be chosen as one of their crew. They were older men, two Germans and two Irishmen. They grew to like John because he worked hard, was respectful, listened, and asked smart questions.

John became a regular among those who were still working from the first day on. Many men had left, but none from his crew. So many Irish, English, and Germans were flooding into the city there were plenty to take their places. Evenings after work, the route home was pure torture, tired muscles clamoring for rest, while being whipped by winds that gained speed over the full length of Lake Erie. Mornings he rolled out of bed headfirst.

Four weeks into the job, he hardened to the labor. In the months ahead, his body bulked up almost to that of a man's with bulging biceps and forearms. He would grow to five feet six inches and 140 pounds over the year shoveling coal. Most days his mind went numb. He stared off into downtown Buffalo and its rising buildings. He was determined to remain until he heard of something better. There was nothing through the end of the year and the end of the shipping season.

The second Sunday in April was the Junior Travelers' first game. The Junior Travelers, or just the Juniors, was the name given to the team Pat and John played for, a team for boys sixteen and under. Pat played center field because of his speed and ability to cover a large area of the outfield. He got on base the first at bat and stole second and third base with a flair that had the few bystanders cheering and shouting. Pat hit the ball hard between infielders the next two times up. Again, he stole second and third.

John also fielded well and got on base almost as often as Pat, but his skills went largely unnoticed. Still, he was satisfied with the way he played and cheered for his brother as vigorously as anyone there. Pat, absorbed in his own exploits and adulation from teammates and the crowd, talked with his brother only about himself.

After the game, John and Pat headed with other players for Kennedy's. By his second beer, Pat was trading stories with other players. His tale of Mick of Mackinaw Street, who couldn't read his own name and so was deported back to Canada, left them all guffawing. John left after an hour and two beers. Pat drank steadily until almost midnight.

Aunt Theresa asked John questions about the people he worked with, especially the bosses. She fed him information about men she met at work, mostly positive examples of character and business success. She went to most of his games and quietly complimented him on his play. She found ways to comment on youthful mistakes without criticizing and asked him questions that expanded his thinking.

CHAPTER 5

Pat Goes to Work

Pat turned fourteen on March 25, 1858. He was anxious to land a full-time job and contribute like a man to his household. His friend PM had turned fourteen a few months before him and his father had gotten PM a job as a laborer at the Dart Elevator. John was still working full time on the coal docks. Pat pressed Uncle Jack at the supper table about joining him at the Dart.

"Why don't ye stop by Jim Kennedy's? He's got the labor contract from Fingy with the shippers." Jack went on to explain how the system worked. Men and boys lined up at Kennedy's at 6:30 every morning for the shape-up. If Kennedy had orders from shippers, he sent crews of men to the mills and elevators where boats were loading or unloading. Kennedy took a percent off the top of wages and paid the men at the bar. To find work through his shape-ups and get paid, a grain shoveler or "scooper," as they were called, had to drink at his bar.

The next day, Pat went to see Jim Kennedy, the proprietor of Kennedy's Saloon and the sponsor of the Junior Travelers. Jim was a man of average height, stout, and muscular. He had a full head of dark brown hair and sported a handlebar mustache. A ragged scar curved down toward his ear just above his right eyebrow, the result of a fight with a stevedore whom, men at the bar said, he had cheated of half his pay. He wore an apron over a burgundy-colored vest rumored to conceal a revolver.

Pat ordered a beer at the bar and asked the bartender if he could talk to Mr. Kennedy, who quickly appeared from the back room. "It's great to see you. You playin' for the Juniors these days?"

"Indeed I am, center field and battin' lead-off. Will you be sponsorin' us again?"

"That I will. Would it be for a real job you're askin'? If it is, you've but to say the word."

"I am, sir. My gram is gettin' older and shouldn't be workin' like a young girl any more. I need to help out and support the two of us."

"Well, that's good thinkin'. Suppose ye come fifteen minutes early tomorrow into the bar and find me. That'll be a quarter after six or so. I'll see you make the count. Glad to have you, lad. I know ye won't disappoint me, now will ye?"

"Thanks. I'll be here early and work I will as hard as any man." Pat had a habit of adapting his speech to the manner of the person he was talking to.

Pat began work with three other fourteen-year-olds in a gang of twenty, unloading grain at the Dart Elevator at the mouth of the Buffalo Creek near the east end of Lake Erie. Uncle Jack had worked as a grain handler for seven years at the Dart, rigging the conveyer belt and buckets and repairing them when their lines broke down, which they often did.

The night before Pat started work, Jack counseled his nephew, "Whether we're liftin' sacks out of the hold or tendin' the buckets, we always wear a bandana, don't ye know. The dust is like breathin' in a sandstorm. It'll fill your lungs so you can't talk for coughin'. Tomorrow, we're unloadin' sacks by hand."

The next day, Jack walked with Pat to the Dart and lined up in front of him. Built of oak and weighing 225 tons, the *Evergreen City*, a triple-masted schooner, was 190 feet long and carried 550 tons of grain. It had a boxy hull, a blunt stern, and a pug-nosed bow. Standing at the dock, Pat said to Jack, "This looks like an overgrown canal barge."

Jack laughed. "Sure enough, Pat, but it can carry more grain than any ship on the lakes."

The ship at dock was loaded with sacks of grain and thus management could not employ Dart's famous conveyor system. The crew of grain shovelers descended into the first hold, Pat and Jack with them.

At fifty-eight, carrying one fifty-pound sack was no test of strength for Jack. Though not a large man, he had thick arms, stooped shoulders, and gnarled fingers from years of working the elevators. He put his hand on his nephew's shoulder. "Now let me tell ye. Make sure you grab each sack and hold it with both hands. You drop one, you'll kill the man beneath you. You lose your footin' and fall, your grandmother will be burying you in the mornin'. Above all, don't rush. Take your time." He lifted a sack with one hand and pulled it to his right hip, raised his right foot onto the first rung of the ladder, and called over his shoulder, "I'll catch ye at lunch."

For Pat, the first day lifting sacks up a twelve-foot ladder and depositing them on a handcart on the dock was pure torture. His arms began to shake after two hours. His shoulders and neck throbbed with pain. The bandana did little to stop dust from caking in his nostrils. He choked trying to breathe. March winds off Lake Erie lowered the temperature below forty degrees. He sweated while carrying sacks and then chilled in between.

At noon, he shook out his bandana, grabbed his lunch pail, sought out Jack and PM, and slumped against the leeward side of the pilothouse. He gobbled his lunch, said little, and fell asleep, only to be awakened with a start by the boss foreman's shrill whistle ten minutes later. The afternoon dragged on. Occasionally, Pat dropped off the line, went to a five-hole outhouse a few yards from the elevator, and rested for five minutes. He had seen other boys and a few older men do the same. Only fully-grown, young men, who had worked these jobs daily for years, were able to keep a steady unbroken pace. They covered for the rest of the gang, who were often relatives or friends.

Pat trudged home on sore legs that night with his uncle.

"How you doin'?" Jack asked, smiling at his nephew's discomfort.

"Uncle Jack, I thought lifting sacks would be little more than playing baseball. I'd run up and down the stairs like runnin' the bases."

"I know how 'tis," Jack sympathized, but dismissed the boy's comment with a wave of his hand. "Ah, you'll be used to it in a month. Just get plenty of rest tonight. The worst thing you can do is be out drinkin' like a sailor and then have to muscle those sacks the next day."

Pat thought to himself, *Don't worry about that, Uncle. I'll be lucky to make it home, and if I do, I hope I can get up tomorrow morning.*

Pat hung in bed an extra five minutes moaning when Gram called at 5:30 and struggled with all the character he had to make it through a day's work. Only his pride and the shame he would feel before Jack, John, PM, and the rest of the Ward kept him going. He learned from other workers to rest when the foreman walked off or to slow down if the foreman was not directly overseeing his work.

At the end of the week, Pat went to Kennedy's bar to be paid. When he received his first wages, he forgot all the job's miseries. He stared at the money in his hand—$12 in coin—and smiled proudly. He was finally a man earning his keep.

His uncle had warned him the night before to drink no more than two beers and stay only a half hour. Perhaps because he was a stranger at the bar or because he was eager to dump his coins in Gram's apron, after two beers, he went directly home.

He exaggerated his steps, widened his eyes, and opened his mouth in a huge grin as he approached Gram standing in the kitchen making supper. He counted the coins slowly as he lined them up on the table before her, ten whole dollars. The delighted look on his grandmother's wrinkled face made all the backbreaking labor worthwhile. She could not have been more pleased and more proud of her grandson.

Like his brother before him, Pat transformed into a working machine over the next six months. By Christmas of 1858, he had grown four inches and gained twenty-five pounds. He was now five feet four inches and weighed 130 pounds, with hardened muscle through his neck, shoulders, and arms.

Pat relished his newfound strength and size and challenged other young men to arm wrestling, ball throwing, races, whatever would show off his prowess. Wherever he went, he walked with the confidence of a man approaching the peak of his development.

Each week he gave Gram $10. After work, he joined coworkers at Kennedy's. The requirement to have a few beers in order to be paid was no hardship at all. He enjoyed Jim Kennedy and the gang that hung out there. Kennedy's became his second home in the Ward.

In response to the added income and her own aging—she was now sixty-seven—Maire cut down the number of church vestments she produced or repaired and let her customers know it would be months before she got around to their order. Most stayed with her. Her work was exceptional, as good as or superior to the big supply houses of New England and New York. Besides, they enjoyed doing business with her.

In the heat and the cold, she walked twenty blocks to mass at the cathedral most Sundays and frequently during the week. It kept her young, she said.

No one preached like the bishop. He was the real thing. His words wafted her up to the Almighty. Often she stayed in church afterward to relax in the company of God and his saints. A Catholic church had a special feel for her. Maybe it was the presence of the Blessed Sacrament, maybe the statues, candles, and stained glass. During mass, she prayed the rosary, the Crown of Mary as she called it, moving her fingers slowly over the ten beads of each of the five decades, as she mouthed the Hail Mary like a mantra. Often, she just sat in silence and let her mind drift to a single thought: God.

She was aware of the struggle her body was giving her and sensed her end would not be long in coming. She had little fear of death, but while life remained, she thought to herself, *I will enjoy every moment of it, every friend, everything I can be present at, and especially Bishop Timon and his new cathedral.*

At sixteen in 1860, Pat continued his sterling, if occasionally erratic, play for the Junior Travelers. John's play was ever steady. His teammates and the crowd of older First Warders who attended the games began to recognize John for his leadership and skill on the field.

On July 4, the Junior Travelers played a double header in their home field off Ohio Street against the Windpipes, who came from Town Line, a hamlet between Lancaster and Alden. Family members and a few friends stood behind both teams. Some spread out on blankets with baskets of food and drink. The Windpipes were both baseball team and marching band. They unloaded their wagons and marched around the field carrying flags announcing their secession from the Union, if the Republican Abraham Lincoln was elected. The Juniors were stunned at the sight and began laughing and hooting. The game took a half hour to begin.

The Windpipes went to bat first and scored five runs in the first inning. The buzz among the First Warders quickly changed to "These farm boys can play." The Windpipe pitcher was a tall, leathery lad who threw the ball so fast it made a whacking sound as it hit the catcher's mitt. "Oh boy," said one old First Warder to his young nephew, "this looks bad." In the Juniors' half of the inning, Pat was first up. He swung late on every pitch and struck out. The other batters went down in order and walked slowly, heads hanging, out to their positions. The crowd began to fear this game could be a total embarrassment. A few people drifted away, which made the Juniors feel worse.

The next inning, Pat did not sit with his teammates when they went up to bat. He stood off to the side and swung a bat in time with the pitcher's throws. In the third inning, Pat fouled off the first pitch, but then smashed the next one between the left and center fielders who were playing in, fooled by Pat's small size. The ball bounded past them into the uncut high weeds surrounding the baseball field. Pat rounded the bases and scored while the Windpipes' left fielder pawed through weeds in vain. Pat's feat gave a lift to his teammates. "This pitcher can be hit," they said to one another. "All he's got is a fast ball."

John batted next and hit the ball hard but right at the center fielder. In the fourth and fifth innings, the Juniors caught on to the Windpipe pitcher, scoring four runs in each inning.

In the sixth inning, Pat came up with a man on third, dragged a bunt toward the second baseman, and beat the throw to first base. He sped past the bag, ran over second, and on to third standing up, surprising the fielders and beating the throws. When the throw to third got away from the third baseman,

Pat kept on running and scored, tying the game at ten apiece. The small crowd went wild. In the seventh inning, he faked a bunt down third, drawing the third basemen toward home and then swung hard hitting the ball down the line past him.

Before the next pitch, with John batting, Pat yelled to his brother not to swing. Pat's quick strides ate up the seventy-five feet between bases. Again, he yelled to John not to swing and stole third. With two strikes on him, John laid down a perfect squeeze bunt and Pat crossed home plate standing up. He was three strides toward his grandmother sitting along first base before the throw came lamely to the catcher. Gram cried big tears of joy and pride.

In the field, Pat had played a very short center and plugged two base runners trying to advance to second base.

Jim Kennedy approached Pat after the game. "Pat, you're the pride of the Ward. Come, ride in my carriage and have a drink on me." Pat hesitated but his teammates urged him to take the ride and set up a few for them.

He climbed into Kennedy's covered trap and made the short trip to the Ohio Street saloon. An occasional fan walking home from the ballpark cheered Pat as he passed by.

Pat was the star but had the good sense to compliment his fellow players and even the other team. The opposing players got in their wagons and joined the Juniors at Kennedy's. At the bar, Pat joked with the Windpipes, telling them they should move to South Carolina. They weren't joking when they told him they already had plans to move. Two hours and three empty half-kegs later, the Windpipes left for home, Pat's new best friends.

After every game in the Ward, Pat presided over the bar from the same stool and told the opposing teams, usually Germans, stories about First Ward chaws. They told stories of a few of their own characters. *It was great to hang around these young men, throwing down a few with them*, he thought. He felt now he was a man among men.

After work on Saturdays, he crowded into E. H. Hales's barbershop on the corner of Seneca and Michigan with a bunch of old timers and listened to gossip, local news, and chaw-stories. There were no Irish barbers at the time, so First Warders chose two in or close to the downtown area as their favorites. Pat laughed until he cried at the stories. He was a happy soul and loved the life he had in the Ward.

On a September evening that year, 1860, Jo surprised her father and the rest of the family, quietly announcing at supper that she was going to marry a young man named Harry Crawford. She was now twenty-two and had been working at Sherman's Dry Goods Store for eight years. The young couple had met at Sherman's and dated on and off for the past two years.

Her usually reticent father looked at her and exploded: "What are ye sayin'? Are ye pregnant now, is that it?"

Jo shook her head. "No, I'm not."

"Well, why haven't we heard the lad's name before, or even that the two of ye have been seein' one another?"

"Dad, don't worry about it. Neither of us wants a big wedding. He's Protestant, but willing to marry me before a priest. It took us a while to get his parents to agree to it. We're going to talk to Father O'Connor about it next week. We've been saving our money and will pay for the reception. It won't be much. We're only inviting family and a few friends from Sherman's."

Jo was ready with answers to most of his questions before he asked them. Jack knew his daughter was levelheaded and had made up her mind. As Jo explained the details to him, Jack's expression softened, but he refused to give his blessing immediately. She was pretty, like her mother; of course, she would have suitors. His "little girl" was truly a woman and leaving.

Maire said nothing, but Jo read her smiling face as approval.

Within a month, Jo was married and moved to a small apartment on Ellicott Street.

Two years after Pat joined Kennedy's gang, grain handlers successfully pressured saloon bosses, Kennedy among them, to raise what they were charging the Great Lakes Association shippers. In the early spring, just as the shipping season began, shippers countered by bringing in colored men from Cleveland who worked for less and took their jobs.

Punch Leary, the oldest member of one of Kennedy's scooper gangs, talked to every man who entered the bar the next day. "Men, these niggers think they can steal our jobs and get away with it. We have families to feed and they'll not go hungry as long as we've two good arms to swing a club. Are ye with me?"

"We are that," agreed Timmy McLaughlin. "We'll give them a whipping that'll send them back to Ohio. They'll be lucky to get out of the Ward alive, the fekkin' bastards."

Tim came from a large family with five brothers, all well over six feet tall with broad shoulders. "Get yourselves a blackthorn or a length of pipe. They'll be comin' down Louisiana about eight tonight. Bring every man you can talk to. I hear there's two gangs of them, so they'll be at least fifty. Dress warm. We could be out in the weather for some time," he warned against the cold winds and lake effect snow lashing the south side of Buffalo.

John met his brother on Louisiana with fifty other men from the Ward who were drinking whiskey Kennedy had given them. Pat downed several belts and was shouting with the other men. He yelled to John to join the group, but John said he was angrier at the shippers than at the coloreds. "They get only the worst jobs most whites won't take. That pits them against Irish like us. They have to eat, too."

"You're crazy, John. We have to fight for our own. We can't let them take our jobs. Who cares about a bunch of niggers!" Four men crowded around John, poking him in the chest. "Either stand with us or get the hell out of here," Pat ordered his brother. John stood his ground and begged Pat to leave and cool off. Clenching his fist, Pat nosed into John's face and swore at him.

John saw that the crowd, including Pat, was out of control. He broke off, hurried to Maire's cottage, and told her what was happening. Maire sent him over to Father O'Connor at St. Bridget's. He was the only one she felt could have any influence with Pat and the others.

But it was too late for the priest to intervene. The coloreds were already walking north down Louisiana toward their rooming houses on what was called the "nigger block" on Water Street between Canal and Commercial Streets. Seventy First Ward men led by a few who held torches shouted "nigger scabs" and rushed into their midst from two sides, swinging pipes, bats, and heavy blackthorn canes. The coloreds were caught by surprise and unarmed. There were screams of white anger and black pain as blows smashed into heads and limbs.

Pat charged just behind the McLaughlins, swinging a blackthorn with both hands. "You fekkin' niggers!" he screamed. "Take our jobs and we'll give ye to the slave hunters in a pine box."

Several Negroes turned and ran back toward South Street. Pat caught up with one, slamming him in the head and shoulders. The man fell, bleeding and groaning. Pat kicked him viciously in the groin and side before moving on in search of another quarry.

Negroes defended themselves with uprooted stakes and paving bricks and got in good blows of their own. Men grunted and howled in anger and pain. The sound of windows shattering split the air. A few Negroes broke from their gang and ducked into alleys. Women and children lining the way on porches shouted encouragement to their men and chased the Negroes into their backyards, skirts aloft and pokers swinging.

Most Negroes hung together and were chased down Louisiana to Elk and then up Elk several hundred yards to Michigan Street, beaten savagely as they ran, worse if they fell.

51

At Michigan Street the fighting stopped as police and coloreds from the canal district and the East Side joined the melee, too late to save several Negroes from cracked heads, broken limbs, and internal injuries . . . but soon enough to lock Pat and several of the leaders of the Irish mob in a paddy wagon.

Pat slumped on the floor of a cell in the police holding center on Terrace and Evans Streets that night, along with Tim McLaughlin, three of his brothers, and half a dozen others. The city jail, even with three to a cell, would not accommodate more than ten. Another ten were booked and transferred to the county jail on Root Street on the lower West Side. Pat lay on the floor of his cell with nothing but a blanket wrapped around him. Like most First Warders, coloreds were his natural enemy. He believed they were more animal than human. Nothing made Pat madder than to see cartoons in the Buffalo Know Nothing newspaper depicting coloreds and Irish in the same beast-like manner. After an hour of animated talk with cellmates, he fell asleep and slept soundly, pleased that he had bashed in a few black heads and groins.

The next morning after mass, Maire tried once again to trade on her friendship with Bishop Timon. "Bishop, Pat's done it again; he was front 'n' center in that riot with the coloreds last night and the cops locked 'im up. From all I hear, he beat one man with a blackthorn and sent him to the hospital. The man may not live."

The bishop knew what Maire was asking. Looking the woman in the eye, he said, "Maire, I think it's time we let the courts do whatever they're going to do with Pat and pray to God the colored man doesn't die. Pat's anger will land him in prison for life or even get him hanged."

By the time she arrived home, she realized that the bishop was right, and was thinking about what was good for her grandson. She also understood that the bishop was embarrassed by the riotous behavior of Irish men, whether aimed at the shippers or coloreds.

After Pat spent a day and two nights thinking about what he had done, the bishop changed his mind and sent Father Corbett to bail him out. John joined him at the downtown jail. It was a Wednesday morning. On Tuesday just before lunch, John had talked to the foreman at the coal dock about missing work the next day. He inquired of the company manager on site, and was told before the end of the day that it was all right. They feared they would lose John, one of the better workers, if they refused his request.

Pat greeted the two with head high. He had met other young men in the jail who applauded his actions, making him even prouder of his part in beating up colored men. Happily for Pat, the men he beat recovered. Another, whose head was bashed in by other First Warders, did not.

Father Corbett led the two brothers to the street where Bishop Timon was waiting with his brougham. "My young gentleman," said the bishop to Pat with a grave face, "please get in. John can sit with Father Corbett on the driver's seat."

When their route took them north on Main Street rather than south, Pat, uncertain about what the bishop had in mind, asked where they were going. Only then did the bishop allow himself a half-smile. "We're going to church."

Father Corbett drove the carriage east down Batavia Street and turned north on Michigan, stopping to allow a funeral cortege to pass into the Michigan Street Baptist Church, a small, red brick building with an artistically designed facade. John observed that there must be 200 Negroes crowding into the church. He had never seen so many. They were garbed in various states of dress clothes, clean and neat, the best they had. He looked down at his own disheveled clothes and winced. He knew Pat looked even worse.

The bishop directed Father Corbett to rein the team to the side of the street. Father Corbett got down, opened the door to the wagon, and waved to Pat and the bishop to get out. The bishop walked a few paces to the front steps of the church. When all the people had entered, he followed them. He nodded in recognition to Rev. J. S. Martin, a tall, light-skinned Negro with bright, compassionate eyes standing at the head of the casket, who nodded back. The bishop led the way into a rear pew. Pat's nerves were on edge. It was a strange and threatening feeling to be white in a crowd of colored people.

Colored people were jammed into the sanctuary, pews, and aisles. Reverend Martin welcomed the congregation, spent several minutes giving his condolences to the family, and announced the opening hymn. The ceremony began with a powerful a cappella rendition of a Negro spiritual by the choir, as six tall colored men in dark suits positioned the casket alongside the front pew in the center aisle. The church had no organ. Pat began to sweat and look for a way out. He thought the hymn would never end. The strong voices surged against him like a stormy wave hitting the Lake Erie shore. Roiled emotions welled up in him. The muscles of his upper body tightened and he coughed trying to control himself. John was equally uncomfortable, as was Father Corbett. Not only was the singing very emotional, but they were the only whites in the church, except for three visiting ministers who sat in the sanctuary in their full ceremonial vestments.

As the choir and congregation sang the tenth and last verse, a tall man in a black suit opened the casket to reveal the body of a young Negro man. His widow in the front pew alongside the casket cried out at the sight of his face, threw herself over him, and stroked his stiff head and neck with her gloved hands. A man alongside her in the pew rose, held her by the shoulders, and consoled her. Her sobs and moans blended with the strums of the bass, filling every corner of the church. The bass strummed louder, the only instrument accompanying the choir.

The white men in the last pew could not take their eyes off her. At last, she grew weak and sagged into her friend's arms. The man guided her back into the pew. Her sobs slowed and grew quieter. Reverend Martin then pronounced in undulating tones the 23rd Psalm, "The Lord is my shepherd I shall not want." Congregants punctuated the reading with "Yes, Lord . . . Save us, Lord . . ."

He finished and sat down. A large woman rose and sang the same psalm in a contralto voice that ranged easily over the lows and highs of the melody and built tempo and intensity with each verse.

Then Reverend Martin looked straight at the congregation and recited from memory St. John's Gospel story of Jesus resurrecting his friend, Lazarus. At the end of each sentence, voices from the congregation shouted out short phrases of support and commitment.

The Reverend Martin put down the lectionary and stared long in silence at the casket as though desperate to grasp the evil behind this young man's death. "Son, we are a cursed race in a world that hates us. We are its slaves and servants, its diggers and its domestics. Our faces are pushed into the dirt and they murder us for our blackness." On and on he went, describing how the Negro race was the very imitation of Jesus, persecuted and tortured, and finally murdered. Repeatedly, he laced his address with the words, "And you, my beautiful son, you were murdered by the evil men of this world, but Jesus conquers them and you rest with Him for all eternity."

Throughout it all, the widow moaned. The other women vocalized their support. Men's voices, too, could be heard every time he paused, saluting what he said.

The number of bodies in the room raised the heat to an uncomfortable level. Women waved their fans. Men perspired in their dark coats until the room became musky. Pat grew faint and gripped his brother's arm.

When Reverend Martin finished after an hour, he called on seven other ministers, both Negro and white, including one from as far away as Batavia, whose strident voices and powerful images played with people's emotions like stones shaken inside a jar.

The last clergyman to speak was the bishop. The three whites in the last pew were accustomed to his booming voice and bold imagery, but he was carried to new heights by the occasion and the preachers who preceded him. He condemned the hate-filled actions of First Ward Irish and the inhuman greed of the Great Lakes Association owners, which pitted poor men of both races against one another.

After three full hours of preaching and singing, the ceremony ended. The congregation stood and slowly followed the casket out the front door. Pat was drained. He could barely stand up. He held on to his brother's arm to steady himself as he tried to walk out.

The bishop spoke quietly to Reverend Martin, who bent down to put his ear close to the bishop's mouth. He was grateful and let the bishop know it with the press of his arms around his shoulders.

The bishop, Pat, John, and Father Corbett climbed back into their carriage and drove south on Michigan Street to the Joy residence on Louisiana Street. Gram and Jack met them, questioning and exclaiming in frustration and relief.

Short as he was, the bishop's presence dominated the room. "Pat will tell you about his stay in the mayor's hotel downtown." Turning toward the erstwhile prisoner, he said, "I am sure they didn't feed you quite as well as your gram." Putting a hand on Pat's shoulder, he said, "Before I leave, I need to talk with you."

They stepped outside into the late afternoon sunlight. The bishop pointed to the creek and said, "Let's take a walk." Pat obeyed willingly.

The two men strolled slowly along the north bank of the Buffalo Creek as it wound through the Ward and the Valley, until recently a part of the Buffalo Creek Reservation. All the elevators were downstream. Where they walked, the creek was shallow and unnavigable. Currents of green water reflected sunshine and clouds.

The bishop commented on God's handiwork all around them, swinging his right arm in wide semi-circles. Eventually, he got to the point.

"Pat, I hope by now you understand how wrong is the hatred you and many of our kind bear toward people of color. How wrong it is for the Church of Rome, founded by Jesus Christ on the love of God for all human beings, to hold colored people as slaves this very day!

"What do you think has gotten you into so much trouble?" the bishop asked.

"I get angry quick . . . and then act without giving it much thought."

"That's real insight. Do you think you are easily influenced by your friends and others around you?"

"Maybe so, Bishop, but how do I escape them and learn to think for myself?"

"That is one of life's great questions for all of us. Maybe that is the ultimate meaning of prayer: moving off into another world where only goodness exists." The bishop realized he had killed the conversation with his one-line sermon. He walked a while, saying nothing and just letting other thoughts come to mind.

"I use to drink when I was young. Drank with my father and grandfather. Loved drinking with the family back in Ireland. But once I became a priest, I decided never to drink alcohol again. Do you think alcohol has anything to do with the difficulties you've gotten into of late?" Pat said nothing in reply.

"Why do you think Kennedy brought a few bottles of whiskey to you men before the colored men came down Louisiana Street?"

"I never thought about what alcohol does to me, but I guess I lose control of my temper easier once I've had a few drinks. No doubt, so do my friends. That's why Kennedy fed us whiskey . . . Come to think of it, he only took a sip or two before heading back to his saloon." Pat looked down at the ground.

"Maybe he made fools of us. We did his dirty work."

"Just one last suggestion, Pat. The church in her wisdom helps us with confession. I know it's not easy for us men to confess our sins. So the church makes it a commandment that we go to confession at least once a year. That is the bare minimum and misses the true value of confession. Beside the grace that comes with the sacrament, confession can help us change. It starts if we do it often enough, like once a month, by guiding us more deeply into our own character."

"I get what you're saying, Bishop. Time thinking about the bad things I did can help me bring greater control over some of my rough spots."

"That's the real value of confession, Pat," replied the bishop. Then he changed the subject to the beauty of a creek gurgling. Just before turning into the home on Louisiana, the bishop said, "Promise me you'll go to confession, receive Holy Communion, and spend time in prayer every day. And take the pledge. Father Corbett will administer it to you if you ask him."

"I will, Your Excellency, I promise. Thanks."

The bishop gained confidence that Pat was sincere and would make the changes that would propel him toward a safer future.

Then he pulled out the strongest argument he felt he could use on Pat. He put his hands on his shoulders, looked him straight in the eyes, and shook him gently. "If you don't deal with your anger, you'll spend most of your life in jail and crush your grandmother, who loves you more than anyone in the whole world."

Pat's voice grew raspy. "There's no one I love more than Gram and I never want to disgrace her and the Donohue name."

They headed into the house, where the bishop had Pat repeat his promises to Gram and Uncle Jack. John said nothing, but his face made it clear he was happy for his brother. The bishop pulled them all into a circle, blessed them, and took his leave.

The next day, John and Pat went to work for the bishop as janitors in his empire of Catholic institutions. The boys would soon turn seventeen and sixteen. Life for both had taken a turn for the better.

CHAPTER 6

Off to War

Neither Pat nor John paid much attention during the first half of 1860 as the older men at Bishop Timon's various institutions discussed the pending presidential election. Many of the men knew Bishop Timon well. In fact, they were all hired by him in one way or another. They listened to his sermons or discussions of his sermons. Those who could read loyally bought his newspaper, the *Sentinel*, and were heavily influenced by his point of view and that of his editor/publisher.

John and Pat were much more interested in women and baseball. They were influenced by the friends they played ball with, attended dances with at St. Bridget's, and accompanied to downtown dance halls. Occasionally, they squirreled away a quarter and attended musical shows featuring New York talent. Both boys liked to dance, which made them popular with girls. Pat and John knew girls they were attracted to, but they preferred to run with the crowd rather than with any one girl. Settling down and marrying was the last thing on their minds, even though several friends their own age had already done so.

Both joined Maire working with the bishop's Irish Festival committee. The festival, held the weekend of September 3, 1860, had taken much longer to organize than Bishop Timon had dreamed. Seanachaithe committed and then canceled because of delays caused by the festival committee itself. Games were slow coming together. City fathers balked at making the open space along the

Niagara River available. Only when it became apparent that Bishop Timon had taken charge and Father Corbett was making the behind-the-scenes arrangements did everything begin to come together in a timely manner.

Ten thousand Irish participated over two days from all over Western New York and southern Ontario. Mayor William Fargo opened the festival on Saturday on the grounds along the Niagara River. The festival culminated with a Sunday noon high mass concelebrated by three bishops, two of them from Canada.

A parade mobilized after mass in front of the cathedral and proceeded down the path along the Erie Canal to an open park-like area near Fort Porter on the Niagara River. It featured marching bands, Irish dancers, three groups of bagpipers, and over 1,000 well-behaved paraders led by a contingent of mounted police from the City of Buffalo. Marchers were dressed in a motley mix of green. The bishop himself walked at the center of the parade with only Father Corbett at his side. Both clerics dressed in black suits and black shirts open at the collar. The bishop had spread members of his committee throughout the parade, both among onlookers and marchers. The day was sunlit and warm, a perfect late summer day.

Everyone was in a jovial mood and enjoyed themselves. Heads were high. Backs were straight. The bishop's message of Irish pride hung subtly in the air. The two days featured step dancing, storytelling, games of chance, hurling, a rowing regatta on the river, and the main event: an imitation of the *fianna* trials consisting of foot races, hammer throwing, high and distance jumping, and other games of physical skill.

Perhaps the best received was a forty-five minute concert toward the end of the festival, featuring time-honored Irish instruments: harps, bagpipes, tin whistles, bones—the most ancient of Irish instruments—and bodhrans, Celtic drums that looked like and may have evolved from tambourines. The combination was loud and penetrating.

Fifteen minutes into the concert, three young boys began a spontaneous step dance before the stage. Soon the grass in front of the musicians filled with dancers of unequal ability but contagious enthusiasm. Bishop Timon and Father Corbett were among the first to join in. Musicians and dancers prodded one another into group and individual displays. It was the most serendipitous event of the program and the one most remembered afterward.

Bishop Timon closed the festival Sunday night, surrounded by 1,000 participants. He thanked them for the civil way they had conducted themselves, had especially kind things to say about those who had come from afar, reminded all Americans to vote in the coming elections, and closed the festivities with a brief prayer and blessing.

On the way home, Gram pointed out to Theresa and the boys how perfectly the festival had come off. "It was all because of the way the bishop organized it," she said. "There were police everywhere and he allowed no alcohol for sale. So if you were goin' to drink heavy, you had to bring it in your own wagon."

The *Sentinel* covered the festival in glorious detail and ignored some of the drunken revelry accompanying it in spite of the bishop's and the police department's best efforts. The other papers doted on the latter and gave scant notice to unique festival events and the generally family-friendly atmosphere. The business community breathed a sigh of relief that the festival was over and conducted in such an orderly manner.

Abraham Lincoln was elected president of the United States on Tuesday, November 6, 1860. The men in the Ward voted solidly for him. He had dodged the question of freeing the slaves and run on a save-the-Union platform that included opening up the West to homesteaders, keeping territories and new states free of slavery, and building a transcontinental railroad. First Warders saw this as good for them. An open, accessible West without slaves would drain off workers from the East, both immigrants and natives. It was sure to leave more jobs in Buffalo for them and maybe even raise wages.

South Carolina, having long threatened to secede if Lincoln was elected, voted for secession on December 20, 1860. Five other states in the Deep South followed in January. The threat of war caused many in the Ward to become more personally engaged in political and war-related conversations. War was in the wind.

At mass on Sundays, the congregation heard the bishop defend the new president's position against secession. He proclaimed that war was not only inevitable, but morally defensible. He quoted from the Epistle of James, Chapter 4, and from Matthew, Chapter 24, to support his position. The Union must be saved, he said, even if it meant going to war.

He took a more equivocal position on the abolition of slavery, but followed Pius IX, saying it was wrong to hold any one race in bondage. At work and in the pubs of the Ward, the older men agreed with the bishop that the Union had to be saved for the good of the Irish race, but most were for keeping coloreds exactly where they were. In fact, if they could ship the blacks, who were concentrated on Canal and Michigan Streets, to Liberia, as Lincoln once suggested, they claimed they'd gladly pay for the boats.

John told Pat as they finished work on Saturday, February 2, 1861, John's 18th birthday, that the likelihood of war and serving in Lincoln's army was weighing on his mind. He wanted to hear what Gram and Uncle Jack had to say about it the next day at dinner. Pat also heard talk of war from coworkers and fellow imbibers at Kennedy's. But his head was not in it. As much as he resented and disliked the long hours of work, the rest of his life was just great. There was nothing like being a young man in the Ward. He was happy at home. He adored Gram. He had his own stool at Kennedy's. He was recognized throughout the city for his baseball heroics. He had money, girls when he wanted them, male friends when he didn't . . . what else was there?

On Sunday, John asked, "Uncle Jack, what does it mean for the Union that so many Southern states have seceded?"

"Well, it means South Carolina and five other states are after being no longer a part of the United States. Several other slave states will likely follow. Mr. Lincoln will not stand by idle. Understand, John?"

He nodded in assent, but there was confusion in his mind. Unlike many of the young men at work, John was not keen on fighting. Life was only now becoming enjoyable. He had enormous pride in working for Bishop Timon. He had grown to love Aunt Theresa and had a great social life. He had no desire to leave Buffalo and go off to war.

"Do you think we will be forced to serve in the Union Army?"

"No, John, right now there are thousands of men wantin' to join. The papers say it could be all over in a couple of months. So you might think about waitin' to volunteer."

From that day on, John read the *Sentinel* whenever it was published and listened intently to Bishop Timon's sermons, as well as conversations at work and in the barbershop.

On April 15, 1861, the day after the fall of Fort Sumter, Lincoln issued a declaration of war and called for 75,000 volunteers. John decided to wait until Pat turned eighteen the following March and then to enlist with his brother. Pat could have enlisted at 17 with his grandmother's permission, but she told them both it was better they wait. Her thinking was a little maturity might blunt Pat's rash behavior and save him from being killed.

"I love Gram an' all," Pat told his brother, "but the minute I turn eighteen, I'm joining up. An' no one is gonna stop me!" Pat's attitude toward the war had changed 180 degrees.

John winced. "The papers are saying it would be over in six weeks. With any luck we may be able to escape the war altogether. I say we see how things break."

"I want to get out of this town and fight," said Pat. "Are ye comin' with me or are ye stayin' home with the women? You decide. I'm goin'."

John shook his head. He could see his brother was not going to be dissuaded by anything he could say.

Pat's young coworkers were looking forward to leaving work and doing something patriotic, traveling on steamboats, seeing other parts of the country, and fighting a war. A smoldering fire blazed in him, too.

Over the next year, John read about the armies of both nations—the United States and the Confederate States—fighting and dying with no decisive victories won by either side. It became clear to him after the First Battle of Bull Run, July 21, 1861, that Southern generals were much better at preparing and leading their troops than Northern generals. The fighting had turned into an honest-to-God war, a civil war, as the papers called it. And it seemed it would go on with no end in sight.

In June, Uncle Jack warned John and Pat, "The President and Congress are thinkin' about a draft. Maybe you should join one of them regiments being formed in Buffalo. The papers say if you're drafted you won't get any bonus money." Both boys had seen advertisements for sign-up bonuses of $500.

Pat quit his job with the diocese in a dispute with his supervisor. He resented taking orders from a man he considered a puffed-up fool who knew less than he did about maintaining buildings and grounds. Pat exploded when a job cleaning a classroom took twice as long and was made twice as difficult by the supervisor's stupidity. He walked off before he punched the man in the head.

When the bishop heard about it, he expressed his disappointment to Maire. He worried that Pat would join the saloon crowd after work. Maire agreed, but had no comment. She knew Pat had never left his mates at Kennedy's. He was there almost whenever he wasn't working. Still, he was a man now, working full time and giving her most of what he earned every week. What he did on his time, she believed, was none of her business.

On the day Pat quit, he hired on at the Union Iron Works on Catherine Street in the Ward as an unskilled laborer raking slag from the first of three blast furnaces to be built, called the Pioneer. The work was dirty, long—sixty-six hours a week—and exhausting. It paid $2 a day, one of the highest paid jobs for unskilled labor anywhere in Buffalo.

His first day on the job, the emergency wagon ran down Louisiana as Maire was chatting with Carrie Duggan, a neighbor. The women stopped talking in mid-sentence and gaped as the ambulance clanged past and turned left on South. They listened to it rumble on for a few blocks to what they knew was the Iron Works. "Oh, Carrie, that place'll be the death of Pat if it isn't him the wagon's loadin' on his first day."

Gram hurried to the corner of Tecumseh to trade news with other women who gathered wondering if it was their man the wagon bore away. When the men exited the gate about noon, they brought word it was young Joe

McNamara who was burned when something exploded into his chest from
Furnace Number Two.

When Pat came home shortly after 6:30, Gram hugged him like he was
a long-lost relative just arrived from Ireland. "Gram, what's with this crushin'
me bones? And now look at ye, you're filthy as one of the men from the Iron
Works." Then Pat turned serious for a moment as they talked about the Iron
Works and Joe McNamara.

Dinner was a roast of beef and creamed green beans. "Gram, what day is
this? Did I work through a Sunday, missin' mass? Sure, I must'a." He liked to
imitate his grandmother's speech. She laughed. She enjoyed being teased by her
grandson. Jack laughed as well and relished the surprise of Sunday dinner on
a weekday.

John, Pat, and PM began attending rallies of various prominent
Buffalonians who were forming regiments and recruiting volunteers.

On August 15, Colonel Michael Corcoran was released from Confederate
prison. Fighting with the New York 69th, he had been captured at the First
Battle of Bull Run thirteen months earlier. He remained in prison more than
a year refusing parole, because it required signing an oath never again to fight
against the Confederacy. Four days after release, he was at the War Department
in Washington where he was promoted to brigadier general and authorized to
raise a brigade of New York volunteers. Within a week, word was on the streets
of the Ward that Corcoran had asked Buffalo attorney John McMahon to form
a regiment of Buffalo Irish.

John met his brother at Kennedy's after work. "Are you interested, Pat? The
poster at Hacker's Grocery Store advertised a rally recruiting young men to
serve in a new Irish regiment. They're offering bonuses from the state and local
governments, including 160 acres."

"I'd turn my bonuses over to Gram," bragged Pat, "so she could slow down
a little and maybe do her sewing just for Bishop Timon. I like the idea of
getting 160 acres. Wouldn't it be fun to have a place in the country just to get
away from all the dirt and crime of this place?"

John, Pat, and PM, along with 500 men mostly from the Ward, attended
two raucous rallies held in a Main Street hotel theater. They drank free beer
and listened to John McMahon and Hugh Mooney exhort them in the name
of all the saints of Ireland to join up. Afterward, the three went to PM's house
and stood around the backyard, discussing what they had heard and seen.

"Every meeting so far," groused John, "is green with Irish bullshit, which
as we know is brown and smells like everyone else's. Look at what I picked up
at this last one." He showed Pat and PM a brochure whose cover read in large
capital letters:

TO ARMS! TO ARMS!
ONWARD THE GREEN BANNER REARING,
GO FLESH EVERY SWORD TO THE HILT.
ON OUR SIDE IS VIRTUE AND ERIN,
ON THEIRS IS THE SAXON AND GUILT."

"I'm not volunteering for the money or because of some Irish crap. I'm in as long as the president needs me. Are you with me, Pat, PM?"

"I am," said PM. "The Union has to be saved or we Irish go down with it." Pat nodded in agreement.

On their last night home before enlisting and being assigned, Maire invited John and Theresa for dinner. Afterward she asked the boys to help her doing dishes. Theresa joined them.

"Boys, I'm hearin' there's not a paper that doesn't list men from Buffalo dying in the war. Lots of them from disease, so your uncle tells me, more than are shot. Wash your hands before eatin'. And stick with Mr. Tipping. He'll get you through if anyone can. Don't forget. Say your prayers morning and night. It's the Good Lord who will protect you."

With that, she threw her arms around the two of them and hugged them till they felt glued together.

Pat laughed, "Hold on, Gram, we haven't even made it through Camp Porter. We're some time before seein' the first rebel and I promise you, I'll shoot the first one I see and send his buttons home to ye. You can sew them on the bishop's cassock."

They all laughed. Theresa asked them to stay as far out of harm's way as possible. "We want you home with us," she said. "I'll be sayin'a rosary a day until you come home safe."

John and Pat joined 500 men, mostly from the Ward, in the 3rd Regiment of the Corcoran Legion on August 27 and were stationed at Fort Porter near the Niagara River. They could walk home in less than an hour.

During the six weeks they trained, the regiment was housed in ten sixty-by-eighteen-foot barracks at the fort. Fort Porter covered five acres on which a square masonry redoubt had been constructed between 1841 and 1843, with crenelated walls surrounded by large earthworks and a moat. It was bounded by Porter and Busti Avenues and the Erie Canal. From the redoubt, one could look west to the juncture of Lake Erie and the Niagara River, a mile north of Buffalo's expanding downtown, one of the more scenic views in the area.

Training was overseen by captains and lieutenants at the company level, who barked orders to sergeants from new manuals they held before them.

The training consisted of marching with stick-rifles in hand in columns four abreast, turning left or right while maintaining orderly rows; quick marches at double time; physical exercises to build up strength and endurance; and once a week a ten-mile hike north to a firing range in the far reaches of Amherst. There the men broke down and practiced firing Enfield and Springfield rifles. Fatigue duty each day included policing grounds, cleaning latrines, serving and cleaning up after meals, and rebuilding parts of the fort's buildings and walls that had fallen into disrepair.

On October 10, the 3rd Regiment's commanding officer, Colonel John McMahon, staged a departure ceremony, long on speeches. Pat, John, and PM were eager to get going. No high rhetoric, no matter how brilliant, could have held their attention. As soon as the ceremony ended, the regiment scattered gathering about their families and close friends. Maire had only one extra rosary. She shoved a small black leather bag containing the rosary into Pat's jacket pocket. She thought he needed it more than John.

John and Pat charily hugged Gram, Theresa, and Jack again. They knew they had to leave them and they wanted no further leave-taking. A handful of city officials and interested citizens watched and talked among themselves before dispersing.

After what seemed like a day of agony standing around and then saying good-bye to families, the 3rd Regiment marched two miles from Fort Porter to the New York Central Exchange Street Station in a column four abreast. Four hundred, including John and Pat, crowded into ten cars, chartered by the state at the behest of General Corcoran. Amenities included only padded benches and two coal-burning stoves per car.

The Central ran a series of roads between Buffalo and Albany, not as yet organized into a single system. Altogether, it was a twenty-hour, uncomfortable, constantly interrupted trip. The land between Buffalo and Albany was flat and dreary until they reached the Mohawk Valley. The men of the regiment slept whenever smoother rail sections allowed. They disembarked at Rochester, Syracuse, and Utica to eat sandwiches and gulp down nickel beers in restaurants close to the depots.

At Albany, they embarked on a steamer that sailed down the Hudson River to Staten Island and Camp Scott, a farm commandeered by the state at the start of the war. Sibley tents spread across gently rolling hills with only sparse green trees and bushes to break up the monotonous sea of white. The camp was sectioned off by regiment and further divided into companies. Pat and John settled into one of the conical tents with four other men before being ordered to the parade grounds.

After a day installing gear in tents, being assigned officers, and doing light fatigue duty, training began in earnest the next day, October 13. There was some excitement at the end of drill that first afternoon, as the men were issued 1858 muzzle-loading .58 caliber Springfield rifles without ammunition. With ramrods, the rifles weighed nine pounds. They also received kepi caps, wool uniforms, flannel underwear, two pair of socks, and boots to replace the hodgepodge of clothing worn at Fort Porter. Next came a cartridge box to be strapped over the left shoulder and under the waist belt on the right hip, a bayonet and scabbard, a haversack for rations, a canteen, and a knapsack containing half a pup tent and a gum blanket.

A Union soldier fully equipped carried an extra forty-five to fifty pounds, putting him at a decided disadvantage with his Southern cousins, who bore no more than twenty pounds and were therefore faster and more agile afoot.

A company consisted of 100 men with five first sergeants, each assigned a squad of twenty men.

George Tipping was a sergeant in Company I, comprised of men from Buffalo, including John and Pat. Older at age thirty-five, a quick study, and from the Ward, he had earned the respect of the men in his squad at Fort Porter. He studied the manual thoroughly beforehand and drilled his squad into superior shape and military precision.

While at Fort Porter, Pat resented the rigorous drills imposed on their squad by Tipping, but at Camp Scott, he realized he was in better shape than most recruits thanks to Tipping. Above all, he noted to John, Tipping was fair in making work assignments and meting out military discipline.

Hugh Mooney was the company's second lieutenant. He managed a tavern and inn on Ohio Street in the Ward, and had a good sense of what it took to maintain an organization. Like Tipping, he spent most of his time among his men, many of whom he had grown up with. He was one of them and did every company drill with them.

Corcoran assigned a first lieutenant, James Worthington, to Company I. He was a New Yorker and held himself aloof from the company.

The captain of Company I, John Byrne, a native Buffalonian, did little but parade around in his dress blues.

None of the regiment's officers, commissioned or non-commissioned, had any formal military training, let alone battle experience.

New York State ordered General Corcoran, given the undersized units in his command, to reorganize his brigade into full-sized regiments and companies. Word of Corcoran's reorganization plan leaked out before he implemented it. Buffalo Companies I and K were to be joined with New York

City companies to form the 155th Regiment. Fights broke out between Buffalo and New York companies, who were just as unhappy with the reorganization.

Though smaller than many of the men, Pat surged about the camp with five of his pals from the Ward, looking for New Yorkers to attack. They did not have to go far, as units were grouped side by side. Pat surprised a burly sergeant from Brooklyn. Without a word, he suddenly leaned forward and plowed a shoulder into his stomach. The fight was on. A circle of soldiers from both cities formed around them and yelled encouragement to their native sons.

Shouts went up from New Yorkers: "Bash his fekkin head in, Sarge." "Kick his ass." "Crush 'im, Sarge." From Buffalo men: "Show 'em the ground, Pat." "Bloody the bastard." The New Yorker swung the butt end of his rifle at Pat's skull. Pat ducked and dove forward into the sergeant's mid-section. The man settled onto his backside, gasping for breath. "Now you got 'em, Patty boy," yelled PM, who was standing closest to the fight to make sure no New Yorker attacked Pat's unguarded back.

Pat was on the sergeant so fast that all the man could do was cover his face with his hands. Pat kicked him in the groin with his right foot. The sergeant doubled up, bringing his hands down. As if executing a mortally wounded enemy, Pat drew his right hand to his shoulder and smashed him in the left temple. The man slumped back, unconscious.

Once the sergeant crumbled to the ground, the conflict gained momentum and became a general brawl. Four companies of men were kicking, punching, and swinging guns, tree limbs, and shovels, whatever they could grab. Pat waved his cap, urging his fellow Buffalonians to fight on. He himself watched, laughing atop the fallen sergeant.

John was on campsite cleanup duty when the melee erupted. He ran over and pulled his brother off the sergeant just as an armed provost marshal battalion raced in to restore order. Many of the 155th spent the night in the brig. The one who had a hand starting it all spent the evening joking, playing cards, telling stories, and drinking beer.

The Legion remained in Camp Scott for four weeks under the shadow of reorganization. Officers kept the men separated by company and busy rebuilding barracks and wharves. They did very little military training.

Meanwhile, the man who would determine the fate of the Corcoran Brigade, also called the Corcoran Legion, was sitting in Norfolk, 400 miles south. Major General John Adams Dix, commanding officer of coastal Virginia, prevailed upon Henry W. Halleck, general-in-chief of the Federal armies, to send him additional troops to counter a possible attack by a much larger Confederate force. Halleck ordered several brigades, including the Corcoran Legion, to join Dix's small force of less than 10,000 men.

CHAPTER 7

Fortress Suffolk

In November 1862, the Legion set sail in twenty steamships of varying sizes and types carrying 100 to 200 men each. A Navy frigate accompanied the flotilla, lest it run into one of the Confederate privateers operating along the coast, generally south of the Mason-Dixon Line.

Within a week, the motley armada sailed into Newport News, Virginia, about a dozen miles from Fort Monroe. The next day, November 12, General Corcoran carried out his reorganization plan and formally mustered his soldiers into the service of the United States.

He reassigned his officers to fit the new structure of the Corcoran Irish Brigade. John McMahon's all-Buffalo 3rd regiment, depleted through desertion from an original 570 volunteers, counted 400 men who made the trip to Staten Island. For reasons known only to Corcoran, instead of keeping Buffalo men in a single regiment, he assigned two Buffalo companies to the 155th and three to the 164th. He made up the balance of the 155th with companies from New York City and Binghamton. The 3rd Regiment ceased to exist. Corcoran assigned New Yorker Colonel William McEvily to command the 155th and Colonel John McMahon the 164th.

Special Order No 14   *November 20, 1862*

Hereinafter the special regiments constituting the command known as Corcoran's Irish Legion will be designated in the brigade organization in the following order:
The 69th Regt NYSNG – Col Murphy – 1st Regt of brigade
The 170th Regt NYS Vols – Col McDermott – 2nd Regt of brigade
The 164th Regt NYS Vols – Col McMahon – 3rd Regt of brigade

69

The Albany Regt NYS Vols – Col Bryan – 4th Regt of brigade
The 155th Regt NYS Vols – Col Mc Evily – 5th Regt of brigade
  By Order of Brig Genl Corcoran

To avoid further rioting, Companies I and K were assigned to duty in and around the camp under First Lieutenant Worthington. They spent the next month working in Fort Monroe Hospital and doing clean up and maintenance on the fort. Once again, Pat was ready to break loose, but there was no place to go.

In a letter to his wife, Sergeant Tipping wrote on November 30:

Last night there was quite a fuss in the town. Two of our lads broke into a house and half-killed a man. Corcoran got wind of it and he came to me, wanting to know who they were. I knew them, but I was not going to tell him. He wondered why I did not shoot them down. The man that got beat was the boss carpenter for the General. He thought a great deal of him. Today, when we were at mess, one of them was caught. The Articles of War were read out for him. They think he will be shot. He is in confinement. He is one of the Buffalo boys. One thing is sure – he will be drummed out of the regiment with his head shaved and branded.

Tipping wrote on Christmas Day:

Well, Lizzie, I am glad to hear you got that small present I sent you.
The colonel gave all the boys – all the boys – a Christmas whiskey. They are all in the house now and half-drunk. There are 10 geese and 12 turkeys for every company in the Regt, so you see that we have quite a time of it.

On December 29, on orders from General Dix, General Corcoran set sail from Hampton Roads down the James River and up the Nansemond with 3,000 men. They would increase the Suffolk garrison to almost 13,000.

On January 2, 1863, as part of the fifteen-mile defense line around the Village of Suffolk, Company I was ordered to improve Fort Dix, one of seven forts composing Fortress Suffolk. The forts were the redoubts of Dix's defense line connected by trenches and fortified with moats.

Soon after encamping in Suffolk, Tipping warned his squad that, quiet as it seemed, they needed to be alert. Rebel scouts were coming out from Fort Huger, fifty miles north on the Blackwater River. Two members of the brigade, who had arrived a week before them, had been taken prisoner by a rebel scouting party. He repeated again: "Stay on sharp lookout on picket duty."

Pat hated building fortifications and told Tipping he'd rather be on picket duty any day. The days were wet and cold. Sibley tents were in short supply. There was no time to construct shacks, so the men spent miserable nights in pup tents. The ground was wet and cold. Only the lice were out crawling and looking for hair and warm clothes.

Once assigned picket duty, Pat found it just as boring as fatigue duty. Out of sight of Tipping, he sought out PM at his place of picket duty. Companies I and K generally served side by side. PM was less than 100 yards down line. On two occasions, they rambled through the countryside meeting local farmers. A few were Unionists and spent time conversing with them. Many loyalist farmers let them know they hated the very sight of them. These they passed by quickly. Pat didn't talk to former Negro slaves, who had escaped their owners and attached themselves to the Union Army. He found them shy and almost impossible to understand. PM was more comfortable with coloreds and enjoyed listening to their stories of slave life.

Back in camp Pat was able to buy whisky on credit—the 155th had not yet been paid—from the regimental sutler. Alcohol was a relief from boredom. It made him feel good.

While on picket duty, Pat got into the habit of reaching into his pocket and tolling the beads of his rosary.

One day, in spite of his brother's urging to remain at his post and alert, Pat went off over farm roads, pretending to himself that he was a regimental scout. Tipping was in the field inspecting his squad. When he found Pat absent, he sent him to the brig for three days and for punishment ordered him to clean latrines.

Pat despised this duty. After getting out of the brig, he remained faithfully on picket duty for the next week. Then he sauntered off, convinced he could avoid the brig by returning to his post in the late afternoon.

Tipping appeared at the picket line looking for Pat about mid-afternoon. "John, I'm goin' to teach your brother once and for all. We need a party to take two teams of horses and haul logs from a mill out the Edenton Road. I'm detailin' the two of you and four others to drag in a few hundred logs to where the engineers set their stakes. You supervise, but Pat is to hook up the logs and lead the team back to the fort. I'll be there to deal with the mill owner and assure him he'll be paid. Understood?"

Pat and John had managed teams of horses in day jobs they held in the Port of Buffalo. It just seemed to come naturally to both of them.

"We're with you, George," said John as he turned to search for his brother. He found Pat in their tent, suffering from a pounding headache after drinking a bad batch of corn liquor. With the rest of the squad, they headed down the Edenton Road in a parade of work gangs from Companies I and K.

Sergeant Tipping was there when Pat and John led two teams of horses into the mill yard. Piles of logs, eight feet long by ten to twelve inches wide, lay strewn about. Pat reached under his jacket for his flask and sneaked a long drag of whiskey. Within minutes, the gangs had two logs each chained behind the horses and started their way back to the earthworks.

Instead of leading the horses, Pat rode the logs while holding their reins. John walked 100 yards behind him. As Pat mastered the balance it took, he began to jump from log to log, yelling and attracting attention and drawing laughter from other soldiers as he passed. As they approached the defense line, Pat jumped from a log to the ground and bounced back on again. After a half dozen successful tries, the log turned beneath his feet. He lost his balance, causing the log to crash into the horses' hind legs. The horses bolted and Pat was thrown sprawling against a tree.

Men rushed forward. Pat screamed that his back was hurt. Others chased after the team. One horse was being dragged by the other, a bone protruding from its lower leg. As the weight became too much the horse stopped, stomped, and threw its head in a circle, neighing loudly. Men turned away, gasping. As shock took hold of the poor animal, it grew quiet, letting out an occasional snort. Tipping put his rifle to its head and pulled the trigger. The shot resounded throughout the camp. He then turned toward Pat and swore at him, his face aflame in anger. "You stupid, goddamn bastard!" Another Company I man yelled at Pat: "You should be shot, you ignorant son of bitch," and slapped Pat in the face. Other men shouted similar epithets. Reg O'Donnell, face brimming with anger, yelled, "Oh, leave Pat alone. He was just having some fun." One or two others muttered similar statements. Bill Keefe walked up to O'Donnell, pushed him to the ground and drew his knife, before Tipping rushed into their midst and screamed at all of them: "What the hell is the matter with you men? Now shut up and get back to work or you'll all spend the next three days cleaning latrines." The men quickly went back to work without further words.

Tipping ordered two men, "Stand Pat up." Pat groaned in agony. "Now join that gang fillin' gabions. We'll see how funny you can be when you're shoving them in place." For the next two hours, Pat hacked down saplings in a nearby swamp and dragged them in bundles to the earthworks, where three men wove them into baskets. When several were completed, Tipping, who had stood watching the whole time, ordered Pat to fill the baskets with mud and rock and wedge them against the logs to hold them in place.

As the men labored over the earthworks, they sweated and cursed profusely. A mix of snow and rain over the last week had turned the ground into four or five inches of clay mud. Pat moaned while filling the baskets. Every time he slacked off, Tipping prodded him in the back where it pained the most. "Well, wise guy, put your shoulder into that one," he said, and Pat moaned even louder as he pushed a gabion against a wall of logs.

Led by First Lieutenant Worthington, Company I spread out in picket outposts of six men each, 50 yards apart, 500 yards north of Fort Dix. It was Friday, February 22, 1863, a cold, moonless night. Ice formed on puddles between patches of snow. The men wore their wool issue uniforms, but after remaining motionless for half an hour, teeth chattered and bodies shook. Tipping stationed six men near a farm road at the edge of woods, arrayed in a semicircle, so that each man was no more than five yards from the next.

The sergeant instructed his men, "Every so often, call to the next man. Make sure he's awake. Rebel scoutin' parties come through all the time. Local militia pick off the lone soldier, so keep your guns loaded, pointed down if it begins to rain. If you hear somethin' strange, a branch or ice crack, call to me." Tipping positioned himself just off the road.

The men took up their positions. John was five yards from Pat on his right. Late that night, he walked quietly over to his brother. "Pat, I think I just heard movement out west of us, maybe a quarter mile." They listened carefully, but heard nothing and relaxed a bit.

A minute later, John was certain he heard the sound of rustling feet on frozen road in the distance, but he couldn't see a thing. Without a moon, the night was black as a crow. When three deer came traipsing past, John breathed a sigh of relief.

Seconds later, they heard the crackling of tired feet on ice. John asked the man farthest left to alert Tipping, who came quickly.

"George, let's move up a few feet. It may be deer, but I don't think so."

The two moved a few paces forward and stood silently for several seconds before the sound of feet breaking thin ice reached them.

"You're right," whispered Tipping. "They're comin' fast and there's more than a few. Warn the other squads on the right. Make sure their muskets are loaded and triggers fully cocked. I'm runnin' over to Sergeant Berrey's squad to post them up. When they get closer, ask them to identify themselves."

With that, Tipping ran across the road. When the rebel scouting party was some distance off, John, back in line, took a deep breath and yelled out, "Gentlemen, y'all identify yuhselves!"

The shuffling stopped. There was a pause and then a loud voice returned, "We all are the 71st Virginia Volunteers. Who are you?"

John did not hesitate. "We all are Suffolk militia."

With some hesitation, the tramping restarted. John, standing behind a tree, pointed his gun at what he thought was the lead soldier and fired. The rebel squad halted and fired in John's direction. The two sides exchanged shots and then ceased firing, hoping the enemy would fire again and give themselves away. An eerie blanket of suspense smothered the field.

John was not sure he heard anything move. He could see nothing. He knew the rebels could be crawling alongside the road and would soon rise and charge. He reloaded and fired a second shot to draw their fire and then lay behind the tree. Nothing. Two of John's squad fired. Still nothing in return.

A voice boomed toward them from perhaps fifty yards away. "Lay down your arms and yuh won't be killed. We got yuh two to one."

The Confederate officer hoped he was facing a squad of green soldiers who had never fired a shot in battle before. They might surrender without a fight.

John sensed it was a bluff. "Come and get us, reb." To his fellow soldiers, he muttered,

"Stay calm, boys. I'll fire first and then you fire ten seconds apart."

John heard a group of men get to their feet and start running toward them. The sound of running soldiers was a combination of feet hitting the ground and the jangle of gear on their backs. He fired. A volley of shots rang out from the other side of the road.

John yelled, "Fire! Fire!"

The rebels dropped to their knees or sprawled flat on the ground. They could see from the flashes that they were caught in a crossfire. The officer directed his men to run to the rear as fast as they could. The two Company I squads reloaded and got off two more rounds each before the sounds of running men faded in the dark.

Companies A and B from the 155th ran up to join Company I. The rebels disappeared in the night, but three wounded soldiers lay moaning alongside a crumpled sergeant, blood splattered all over his yellowish-brown jacket from a direct head wound. A half-dozen muskets lay strewn along the road. Blood in the snow indicated at least one other bullet had found its mark. Company I cheered. It was their first taste of battle. It was also their first sight of rebel soldiers, the dead sergeant graphically displaying why Union soldiers had nicknamed the Confederates "butternuts."

All had a story to write home about. Captain McNally joined the men to learn exactly what had happened, for he had a report on the engagement he needed to file the next day. When they returned to camp at dawn after picket duty, Sergeant Tipping called a few members of his squad together and asked them how John had conducted himself. The squad, to a man, praised John for his calm and quick thinking.

Pat stood quietly off to the side during the discussion, beaming with pride. Like the other men, he felt that John was a man's man and a soldier's soldier. Whatever his brother told him, he would follow without hesitation.

CHAPTER 8

The Siege of Suffolk

In the days that followed, the companies of the 155th divided their time between twice-daily drills, fatigue duty building earthworks out of logs and soil, and picket duty. Fatigue duty was dull, often exhausting work, exposed to rain and snow. Many drank as much whiskey as they could buy, which, contrary to their beliefs, did nothing to relieve the frostbite many suffered. Drunk and unhappy soldiers brawled.

Tipping kept Pat under control by sending him with his brother to scout the surrounding area. On his first day out, after walking in silence a half mile in advance of their line, Pat said to his brother, "I like this scouting duty. It beats fatigue and picket duty or even just lying around our shed. But what are we supposed to be doin'? I see you writin' notes on a map."

"Well, brother, scouting is always about the enemy, where he is and how he'd use roads, crossroads, railroads, hills, woods, swamps . . . that kind of thing . . . or how we'd use them. Now, look at this map and the notes I've written on it."

Pat studied the map for a few seconds, but the words John had written meant nothing to him.

John saw his blank stare and said, "Let's sit over there and maybe I can explain it to you."

The two rested against trees and drank from their canteens. Then John spread out the map on the ground.

"Our engineers prepared this map of the area north of the village of Suffolk. You see the different colored lines? The farm roads are green, the local roads red. Terrain features are marked and some labeled like this swamp over here. They use upside down Vs to show hills with the height of the hills marked just on top of the Vs. Why do you think they mark the height?"

"Because the highest hill could be the best point to see approachin' soldiers."

"Right you are, Pat. It could also be the best place to position artillery," said John.

For the next two hours, the brothers walked narrow farm roads. "Pat, you take a turn adding the roads we discover to the map and draw on the map other features that might help an army attack or defend itself from attack." Pat very dutifully followed his brother's instructions.

On their way back to camp, Pat thought about what he had learned, but then asked his brother, "Where did you learn so much about scouting? You had the same training I did, almost nothing."

"Oh, George decided I had some ability to scout, so he gave me a manual to read."

"Where did you keep it? I never saw it," said Pat. "

"I kept it under my bedroll in our tent. After I read it through, he took me out with an engineer and I listened to them as they studied their maps and made changes to them. The third time out, George told me I was ready to go alone and could pick someone to go with me. So I picked you."

"Well, I'm glad you did. Thanks."

"You catch on quickly, baby brother," and he gave Pat a light shove on his chest.

Pat smiled and tapped his brother back on his right shoulder.

Life at Suffolk was mired in a three-month period of rain, snow, and ennui. A few men returned home on furlough and never came back. Morale sank. The men had not been paid since leaving Staten Island. Even worse, word came through letters from home that the promised bonus money was nowhere to be seen. Two more men disappeared. One, according to a letter from Tipping's wife, had slipped back into Buffalo and was hiding in a shack on Times Beach.

Slogging around in snow, mud, and water led to painful sores and frostbite. John contracted pneumonia and was hospitalized for a week. At various times, half the regiment was off duty, sick in their shacks or in the hospital. Some were faking it. Many were not. Tuberculosis spread easily among them, since seven or eight men slept together in Sibley tents or in shacks. Two men died of it.

The most frequent complaint was boredom, which the men fought with cards around makeshift stoves in their quarters or songfests around campfires. Whiskey was distributed by the army itself and when it wasn't, the men found other ways to get it. Fights broke out. Pistols were brandished and shot, but no one was seriously injured. The day game of choice was horseracing on the roads leading out of Suffolk.

Pat remained aloof from the tomfoolery, not because he didn't want to join in, but because Tipping kept him at his side or sent him out on scout duty with his brother or an officer, looking for rebel movements.

In camp after reveille in late February, Captain McAnally singled out Sergeant Tipping and ordered him to lead a handpicked squad of men north to the Blackwater River. "George, General Peck is looking for information on Longstreet and his army, which our spies say is taking General Pryor's place. Your job is to conduct a Virginia loyalist named Jacob Benjamin to Petersburg. He'll go in and get whatever information he can, and then you get him back here, safe. The fewer men you take with you, the easier you can avoid being seen by rebel cavalry or militia."

"I think I'll take Pat and John Donohue and use them as forward scouts. They're both like Indians in the woods when they need be," said George.

"Take three more," countered Captain McAnally, contradicting himself. "In a fight, five men can stage a pretty good delay while one man and the spy run off. But remember, your job is to avoid contact and to record movements of Confederate troops around Petersburg and the Blackwater. In the best scouting, not a single shot is fired."

Tipping chose Billy Duffy and John Fitzpatrick to fill out his squad.

They spent the last night in camp around a fire with Jacob Benjamin, who had been a Unionist since before the war. Neighbors had burned out his home and barns and they tarred and dragged him through their Northern Virginia streets. He was eager to retaliate for the Union side.

Tipping decided to trade in their muskets for single shot carbines. The carbine was smaller and lighter than the .58 caliber musket rifle and loaded from the breech. He feared an ambush and wanted to avoid being overwhelmed without firing a shot.

Once underway, during daylight, the squad kept to the woods as planned. Pat and John took turns trudging 200 yards in front of the squad and then letting them catch up.

Three days later, Tipping's party moved along the south bank of the Blackwater, mouths agape as they watched whole divisions approach the river from the other side. George said to his men, "Longstreet is gettin' ready to cross the Blackwater with his whole corps."

"What do we do, George?" asked John.

"We're goin' to turn around and move as fast as we can back to the fort. The General needs to know this."

Later, at least thirty miles from Fortress Suffolk, Pat moved slowly out front, down a local road in the moonless night. He tripped and stumbled on a small branch and the crack resonated in the silence. A mounted militia group surrounded him before he could run into the woods. Pat immediately dropped his rifle and raised his hands into the air.

"O, what have we here? A Yankee boy, alone, or out front of more Yankees?"

"I'm alone," Pat said, perhaps too quickly. He swallowed involuntarily. "Been to the Blackwater to see what gives."

The militia leader, a large man, clubbed Pat across his back with his rifle. Pat staggered into a horse. Four other men jumped from their horses, stripped him of his knapsack, and probed his ribs and loins with the muzzles of their rifles.

"It befits yuh," the leader said in a loud voice, "to be truthful, Yankee boy, or we'll drag yuh at the end of a rope down the road a mile. Then we'll see if your tongue will lie like a snake."

Doubled over in pain and covering his chest and groin with his arms as best he could, Pat's voice quaked. "I tell you, I'm alone, or my men would have fired on you by now." The rest of the squad overheard the secesh leader and Pat.

The leader secured a rope around Pat's arms and chest and looped it about his saddle horn. "We need more light now, don't we?" he said. A second man threw a bucket of tar onto a small fire they had lit to warm themselves. The tar caught fire and he flipped it over Pat. Pat screamed in terror and pain as the tar burned his hands and face.

By the sudden illumination, George could clearly see Pat and the shadowy figures of four mounted men. He raised his gun and fired the carbine into the militia, as did the rest. All five horses reared up, neighed resoundingly, and galloped off. Pat was dragged 100 yards across a field until the rope jerked over his head, freeing him. He rolled into a shallow ditch and thrust his face into the water.

Pat yelled into the night and the squad rushed to his side. Tipping stood on a small rise and scanned the darkness, carbine reloaded and ready to fire. John and Billy cut off Pat's jacket and pants and ran him into the woods. George pulled out a blanket from his knapsack and wrapped him in it. John gingerly patted his brother down, exploring arms, feet, and ribs for possible fractures. As far as he could tell, nothing was broken.

When George asked him how he felt, Pat answered excitedly three times, "Just burns, thanks to all of you."

Pain surged from his burned hands and face. Dizzy from shock, he began to look around for his kepi cap.

John laughed, slapping him gently on the shoulder. "Are you drunk? We'll never find it in the dark. Don't worry! There's more at Suffolk!"

"Boys, the secesh will be out with men and hounds to hunt us down. We'll move into the woods, and at first light we'll find a creek and take it east toward Suffolk," said George. "Now, let's see if we can put together a new suit for our Patrick, lads. Look into your sacks for spares. I've got some ointment." John brought out a shirt and fresh socks; John Fitzpatrick offered a pair of pants, and Jacob, a jacket. George softly spread ointment over Pat's hands and face.

Off they went into the woods to await sunrise. Pat lay on the ground moaning, his burns, back, ribs, and groin throbbing in pain. John pleaded with him to keep his voice down. As soon as they were able to see twenty yards in front of them, Tipping rose and started jogging. The others needed no urging to match his pace. Pat stumbled forward, his hands covering his mouth to stifle his moans. The group came to a shallow stream heading northeast and ran into it. The cold water soothed Pat's burns and aches. He ran more easily. Tipping slowed his pace and they followed the stream for a mile or so.

In the distance, dogs bayed. The sound of the hounds and of a large group of riders grew nearer. Tipping ran toward a mass of cattails on the other side of the creek. He led his squad twenty feet into them and signaled 'down' into the cold water that rose halfway up the cattail stalks. The baying grew louder and nastier, then tapered off when the hounds and riders had passed. The scouting party waited but a minute, then climbed out of the creek soaking wet and shaking so badly they could not speak. They ran on stiff legs for a quarter mile or more, as much to restore body heat as to escape the hunting party, and then trudged through woods toward the rising sun.

Within a mile or so, the creek widened, becoming even more shallow. The men broke into a jog, running and jumping across water, slate, gravel, sand, and low banks.

Benjamin had a hard time keeping up. Twice Tipping called a rest to allow him to continue. After five hours of dodging across icy water, George ordered the shivering men to stop.

"I think we lost 'em, but no doubt they'll soon enough start runnin' the creek bed. Let's move into the woods 1,000 yards. We'll eat, dry out, and head south. We have to get back as soon as possible and let General Peck know

Longstreet will soon attack. Mary, Mother of God, if ever we needed your help, it's now."

The men made a small fire, ate rations, cleaned rifles, and turned in.

Tipping's prayer appeared to be answered three days later, as he and his squad, out of provisions, exhausted and stumbling along for the last day, slipped into Suffolk and relayed the news that Longstreet was on his way.

Pat headed straight to the field hospital, where an orderly dressed his burnt hands, face, and torso. Every day, John removed the bandages, cleaned the burns, and redressed them with fresh oil and wrapping.

Both brothers tried to put a good face on his wounds.

Holding up his bandaged hands, Pat said glumly, "I'm a picture, ain't I?"

John kidded him, "You look like one of those mummies from Egypt."

"Don't make me laugh! It hurts!"

At last, on April 6, the men of the 155th received their first pay and Pat used it to pay the sutler for whiskey he had previously bought, and to buy more.

On Monday, April 11, Longstreet's army appeared outside Suffolk's fortifications. Within minutes, 16,000 Federal troops manned their posts in Fortress Suffolk. Another 11,000 arrived that evening from coastal Virginia and immediately found themselves under siege.

The siege of Suffolk ended in early May. General Longstreet ordered a carefully planned and well-disguised retreat to start May 3 with the withdrawal of supply wagons. General Peck did not learn of the withdrawal until a day later. Union troops raced out the Edenton Road and other routes from Suffolk in time to make prisoners of 300 rebel stragglers, more casualties than the Union Army suffered throughout the siege.

While he held Peck's army in Fortress Suffolk, Longstreet foraged sufficient food—1,300,000 pounds of bacon alone—to enable Lee's Army of Northern Virginia to invade the North. What they obtained around Suffolk sustained 75,000 men for a month during Lee's campaign in Maryland and Pennsylvania, ending with his defeat at Gettysburg in July.

CHAPTER 9

Sangster's Station

M ost of Peck's garrison broke camp and moved to other assignments after the end of the siege. The Corcoran Legion and a few other units were left in place for two months as a minimum garrison to guard Suffolk. Many of its officers went north on furlough to visit families. John had saved his pay and did the same. He begged Pat to join him, but Pat refused by saying he had not saved enough to afford the trip, which was true.

John spent his time in Buffalo with family and friends, and while there met Johanna Mahoney at a St. Bridget's dance on his first night home. Throughout his one-week leave, after dinner with Theresa and Gram, John spent the evenings with Johanna.

Johanna had emigrated from County Clare with her parents as a young girl. She was tall, at five feet six and one-half inches, only half an inch shorter than John. Her long, luxuriously curly black hair, blue eyes, pretty face, and heavy breasts drew men's attention wherever she walked. She lived in the Ward and had gone to work as a domestic after the sixth grade. Because of her association with wealthy people, she had gained a worldly sophistication that contrasted well with other girls in the Ward and appealed to John. John considered her the complete woman. The week at home was personally satisfying and relaxing. He regretted having to return almost as much as Theresa, Gram, and Johanna hated seeing him leave.

On Friday, May 20, 1863, the officers and enlisted men of the Corcoran Legion gathered once again at Fort Suffolk.

Most units were transferred out and by June 22, Suffolk became a ghost town. Only the Corcoran Legion and a few other units remained.

The 155th was ordered to dismantle and set fire to whatever housing and fort structures the army had built in the area.

On July 3, the Legion transferred out and started its trek by rail and boat to Portsmouth, then to join General Rufus King's 22nd Corps guarding the Orange and Alexandria Railroad in northeastern Virginia, not far from the Capitol. The O & A connected Washington, D.C., to West Virginia, which on June 23 had become the only region to secede from a slave state, Virginia, and become a state of its own. The O & A linked with three vital rail lines and became one of the most fought-over railroads in Civil War Virginia. Company I was ordered to guard a ten-mile stretch near Sangster's Station, about twenty miles southwest of Washington.

At a regimental campfire on the night of July 5, Colonel Murphy announced that the Union Army led by General George Meade had defeated Lee's Army of Northern Virginia at Gettysburg, in Pennsylvania, two days before, and sent him reeling south into Maryland. Sadly, he said, some 23,000 men in blue were killed, wounded, or captured. That 27,000 rebels lost their lives, were wounded, or captured was small consolation. Satisfied murmurs spread among the men, but no one cheered. They had never heard of such battle casualties.

Murphy also reported that General Grant and his Army of the Tennessee, after a forty-day siege, had captured Vicksburg, Mississippi, and its army of 29,000 Confederate soldiers. Control of the Mississippi now belonged to the Union Army and Navy. The men cheered until their throats were raw. Was there a Union commander the equal of Lee? Indeed, it now seemed so.

At their campfire on July 6, Tipping drew his squad together and read parts of a New York newspaper aloud: "Headline . . . 'Irish Riot on West Side: Hundred Killed.' Below . . . 'Riot is finally calmed when Archbishop Hughes gets up from his deathbed, calls the riot leaders in, and tells them, "No blood of innocent martyrs, shed by Irish Catholics, has ever stained the soil of Ireland." 'The leaders went out and tried to calm their gangs the very day.'"

Tipping raised his eyes from the newspaper and looked at the men surrounding him. "Sure, you know why they rioted. We didn't have the money to buy our way out like so many Yankees. Word among our kind on the streets of New York was that the niggers were after takin' our jobs while we're off fightin' for their freedom." He failed to say that what really quelled the riots were several regiments of federal troops or that coloreds served in even larger numbers than did the Irish and that their casualties were just as great.

John remained quiet. He knew conditions in some parts of Irish Buffalo were the same as in New York City. Amidst the shacks of the Beach, alcoholism, gangs, murders, prostitution, and street violence flourished. They riot in Buffalo every day, he thought to himself.

Five months of utterly boring days passed, with the men of the 155th repairing rail track and fortifying the section they were assigned on the Orange and Alexandria near Sangster Station with a blockhouse that would serve as a miniature fort. Construction was hot, backbreaking work. Morale was low and discipline sagged. Sergeants resorted to violence to enforce orders.

That night, Tipping's squad gathered around one of several Company I campfires, warming feet and drying socks. John looked up as his brother arrived, noting it was the first campfire Pat had been at all week. He was about to question him, but decided to wait until they were alone.

Later, outside their tent with no one else near, John asked Pat, "Where have you been lately when you're off duty?"

Pat smiled slyly at his brother and said, "I been busy."

"What do you mean, 'busy'?" asked John. Then reading his brother's expression, he added, "Don't tell me you met a woman?"

"What if I have?"

John was puzzled. Had Pat met a woman from one of the nearby farms? His first thought was that a woman might settle him down.

"Who is it?" he demanded. "How did you meet her?"

Pat shrugged. "Does it matter?"

"What are you telling me, Pat?"

Sensing his brother suspected the truth Pat leaned forward and lowered his voice. "You're right. I did meet someone. She's a colored girl named Annabelle. She's one o' them contrabands always hanging around the camp looking for work. The men use her to do their laundry."

"Are you gone mad?"

"Come on, John, I miss bein' around women."

John was incredulous. "But a colored girl?"

Pat stared off into space. "It's not like I set out to do anything. I brought dirty clothes to her for washing . . . I haven't touched her, John. And she won't let me drink around her."

"How old is she?"

"Don't rightly know. Sixteen . . . maybe seventeen."

"Are you crazy, Pat? You go with a contraband, the guys won't have anything to do with you, in battle or out. I'm telling you. Break it off before you get in too deep."

Pat did not look at his brother. "Ah," he grunted. "I'll be okay."

The next morning, Sergeant George Quinn swore at John and struck him with his rifle butt when he was slow getting into line. The blow knocked John to the ground. He raised his arms to protect his head. Quinn poised his rifle to swing again. One of John's friends, Private Martin Gallivan, waved his musket at Quinn and shouted, "One more blow and you're a dead man, Quinn." Quinn backed off and muttered, "You'll get yours, private!" Gallivan heard him and replied, "You're a dead man, Quinn, the next time we go to battle."

Gallivan led John to the regimental hospital where a surgeon washed the blood off his head and from his left ear. He applied balm and a bandage and told John to come back if the pain continued for more than a day or two. The blow had hit the left side of his head, bruising his eye, temple, and ear. John remained dazed for the rest of the day, remembering little of the day's events.

Quinn was never disciplined, nor was Gallivan, as no officers saw the incident, nor did any Company I men report it for fear of recrimination from Quinn and other sergeants. When Captain McAnally heard of the incident, he transferred the sergeant to tending horses.

In their tent that night, Pat asked John, "Have you decided to do nothing about Quinn? It ain't right, brother, and you know it. That Quinn is one sick bastard!" Pat pointed his rifle menacingly as if he were going to murder the sergeant in his bed.

"Pat, I was glad you were out on picket duty or I know you would have killed Quinn. And do you know what that would have gotten ye?"

"Yah, I know. I would have been before a firing squad within days."

"So what does that get us? You know how things are. We're better off keeping our mouths shut. Quinn will get his one of these days, but it won't be from me."

"Yah, but maybe from me."

Pat asked for and received a short furlough and spent two days with Annabelle. John resigned himself to the relationship and, too weak from a mysterious illness to quarrel with his brother, said nothing.

Pat had spent much of his last pay on items for Annabelle, among them a red scarf. He pulled a sack of small household goods, food, and blankets from behind his back as he entered her shack, which was on the outskirts of Sangster Station, clustered among many other makeshift contraband dwellings and their horses and wagons. Surprised by his armful of gifts, Annabelle squealed and leaped into his arms. "Oh Mista Pat, I cain't thank you nuff." Pat said nothing, just held her, beaming at her obvious appreciation. "No one evuh done this for me. You diff'rent from the other soldiers, Mista Pat."

Pat chuckled. He knew most soldiers talked down to her as though she were still a slave. He had seen a few try to grab her breasts and buttocks and silently applauded her when she rebuked and slapped them as hard as she could.

"Mista Pat, you a good man. You treat me like a free woman." Pat choked up and smiled as she raised the items one by one from the sack, greeting each present with a gasp or a squeal. "Oh! Ah kin use this surely!" she exclaimed at the sight of a fine-edged knife. Overwhelmed as she lifted a hatchet, she merely shook her head. "Howdja know I be needin' things like this?" When she raised the last gift, an iron pot, she hugged him as though he were her only friend. Pat could not have been happier. No woman had ever responded to him with such genuine affection.

He joined her in washing clothes, gathering wood, and building a porch onto her shack, even though his wounds had not healed completely. Duties demanded by the army were nothing compared to the sense of purpose he felt helping this young girl.

At the end of the second day, before he returned to camp, she allowed him to hold her before the fire they had built in her crude fireplace. Her dark skin shone in the firelight and drove him mad with passion. They sat together, held hands, moved closer still, and began to clutch and paw one another. He wondered what it was like to kiss a colored girl. He had kissed a few white girls in the Ward. Hesitantly, he kissed her lightly on the lips. She kissed him on the cheek with a quick impulsive gesture. He kissed her back, pressing his lips against hers, and she made a smacking sound. Pat suspected it was indeed her first ever. Her mouth tasted of the onions they had just eaten. Pat sucked gently on her lips, savoring the tangy flavor. Their petting continued, becoming passionate and eager.

Back at camp, there was little to do. Most of the officers and many enlisted men were off on leave, including Tipping and Mooney. Camp discipline became irregular. Pat took full advantage, sleeping as long as he wished, walking to Annabelle's shack in the evenings. He spent hours adding support beams to the shack frame, tarring the roof, and nailing on an outside layer of board as protection from winter's cold. There was still time to fold her in his arms and make love to her before dashing in the dying light over village dirt roads back to his own shed. Their lovemaking was passionate. Annabelle was uninhibited in bed and now as madly in love with Pat as he was with her. Their time together excited and delighted them beyond anything either had ever experienced.

While working on her shack, Pat asked, "Annabelle, how did the master and his men treat you? I bet they were all over you."

"Dey was, but you know sompin, Mista Pat, I forgives dem."

"You do what, Annabelle? You forgive those rotten creatures. Why, you should have poisoned them and their women. They were pigs."

"Dat not de way Jesus be. He forgive everybody and bid us do da same. Didn't he say, hangin' dyin' on da cross, 'Forgive dem, Fadder, for dey knows not what dey does?'"

Pat shook his head. "Well, he wasn't talkin' to me, Annabelle. And not to you, either. There was only one way to teach those slavers to keep their hands off you. Maybe get a gang of your men and beat them till they were senseless or worse."

"Not true, Mista Pat. Dat only make it badder."

Pat could see she believed in Jesus and that was that. As she washed soldiers' clothes, she sang hymns like those he had heard at the Michigan Street Baptist Church: lilting, haunting melodies about her Lord. Pat knew that his grandmother, like many Catholic women, prayed silently several times a day. He had often heard her use a phrase or a sentence addressing God or the Blessed Virgin. Catholics, in general, were shy about talking about God except in phrases everyone was familiar with. Besides, Pat could not imagine forgiving the rebels for the way they treated Annabelle and for killing so many of his friends.

On many nights, Pat explored every inch of Annabelle's torso. How surprised he was when his hand moved upward over her expanding lower belly. "Annabelle, I believe you are pregnant with my child."

Annabelle's brow wrinkled at his words. "Is dat okay, Mista Pat?"

Pat nodded. "The most wonderful thing in the world, my little lady!"

Annabelle smiled a great broad smile. "You mean dat, Mista Pat? You ain't foolin' me?"

Pat shook his head. "No, siree. I ain't foolin'. It's the best news I have heard this whole war."

The girl placed her left hand on his where it rested on her stomach and snuggled against his chest.

In the quiet that followed, Pat thought for a while and then said, "I love you like I've never loved anyone. I promise you I will return after the war and marry you." Pat was so in love, he meant what he said, and so she believed him.

"Oh, Mista Pat, I never be so happy," she told him.

One day, Pat said to his brother, "I'm thinking back to Suffolk, John. If the secesh there didn't think us devils, they sure did after we destroyed everything we built and half of the village with it."

"Yah, Pat, the way this war is being fought in the South, we'll have to kill women and children alike. They all feel nothing but hate for us. They'll kill us if we turn our backs to them."

Their talk turned to their parents. They had died when the boys were so young that their parents stood as giant, if shadowy, figures in their imaginations. They talked about them often, as dormant memories came to mind like pieces of a puzzle.

"I have to think Dad would have been proud of us, Pat."

"Or a little jealous that he couldn't be here fighting the rebs right alongside us. How old would he be?"

"Forty-three or so, I imagine. Yah, even at that age he'd be commanding either I or K. What a thought, eh Pat? Fighting for the old man. Wouldn't yuh love it?"

Pat choked up and nodded. "Wouldn't that have been something?" When he gained control of himself he said, "Maybe that's why God sent Tipping."

They stopped talking for a while. Then John suddenly said, "Our mother was the heart and brains of the family. I think Da was a bit of a wild man and a fighter. You get that from little things Gram says, too."

"And wasn't his father just like 'im? Isn't that how Gram describes him, too?" asked Pat.

"True, he was, no doubt."

The boys often turned to talking about their parents and home, as a respite from the miseries of soldiering.

A shot rang out from an outpost, 100 yards from the Company I blockhouse.

"Grab your rifle, Pat. We're under attack!"

The brothers grabbed their rifles, took off in the rain without throwing on their gum blankets, and joined Mooney's squad. Mooney had led twenty men through a small wood and began to pepper a squadron of 7th Virginia Cavalry running up Company I pickets. The rebels dismounted, set up a line, and began rapidly to advance.

A second squadron on horseback charged, ignoring fire from a squad formed by McAnally. Officers shouted orders above the cries of men as rifle bullets tore up their bodies. McAnally and his men retreated and returned fire from within the blockhouse stockade.

In the face of unexpected and fierce resistance from Company I, the Confederate commander, General Thomas Rosser, sent in reserves from the 11th Virginia Regiment who waded through a ditch east of the rail line, ran up the embankment, and carried the stockade.

McAnally and most of his men slipped out the rear gate and ran down the drainage ditch on the other side of the track. Some were wounded or captured. The rest of Company I dashed in the opposite direction down the same ditch or into nearby woods. Pat and two others set up sharpshooting positions that looked back over a long farm field 300 yards out, hoping to pick off Rosser's pickets whom, they surmised, would soon be standing guard on the rail line.

Seven hundred rebels scrambled to scavenge what they could from the blockhouse and surrounding fortifications. Sensing their preoccupation with securing supplies, Pat skirted the field and moved up to within 100 yards of the enemy. Anger and hatred pushed him forward. Hidden ten feet up in a lush oak and aided by lightning that flashed across the rail tracks, he put three bullets into rebels moving in and out of Company I's old fortified positions.

The shots and wounded men brought a squad running across the field, somewhat angled away from Pat. Pat let one more shot fly before he quickly descended from the tree, jumping the last six or seven feet, and scampered off into woods. The rebel squad was now catching fire from Company I men who had watched from a safe distance, hidden among the trees. The sergeant leading them soon thought better of their uneven chances 100 yards from the main body and hastily retreated.

Rosser's raiders hustled up blankets, rain gear, and ammunition. What they could not carry they burned. They set fire to the blockhouse and to a nearby trestle over Pope's Run, a creek that flowed beneath the railroad. Then they remounted and galloped off. Company I men quickly extinguished the fires first on the railroad and then on their small fort. The company had taken heavy casualties: of the eighty men who had engaged the enemy, four had been wounded and nine were captured and carried off to Richmond prisons.

The next afternoon, Company I assembled to bury four of Rosser's raiders. With no chaplain present, Captain McAnally asked Corporal Mike Casey to conduct a small service. Casey had studied briefly for the priesthood under Bishop Timon and was known to read Scripture alone evenings in his tent. He read a verse from Revelations, observed a moment of silence, and then prayed, "Lord, may the souls of these brave men and the souls of all the faithful departed rest in peace."

All the men murmured, "Amen."

A detail of four soldiers serving brig time threw the four bodies on a wagon and buried them in the small church cemetery near the county courthouse in the village of Sangster Station.

That night Company I, all sixty-seven of them, gathered around a campfire led by McAnally. "Gentlemen, you have my admiration for the way you conducted yourselves. You fought as well as any group of men outnumbered ten to one ever has. You were 80 against 700 of them. I deeply regret the terrible wounds suffered by four of our men and maybe even more the nine herded off to prison camps. But I was especially proud of those of you continuing to fire on the raiders, even after they had captured the blockhouse."

Everyone knew to whom he was referring. Pat saw himself now as an invincible fighting machine.

A week later, Pat and John sat glumly around a late-night fire. The rest of the squad had gone to their tents or sheds. They had just gotten the sad news that General Corcoran had been killed in a freak riding accident. During a visit from General Meagher, it was said he was riding the General's horse, was thrown from it, and broke his neck.

"I don't believe a word of what they told us. Gen. Corcoran could ride wild stallions, two at a time. Who's going to protect us now? We'll be in the front lines in a month, Pat."

His brother nodded in agreement and the two lapsed into silence, lacking words to explain the whole affair.

Pat longed for Annabelle. The whole contraband camp had been destroyed by Rosser's Raiders and most, including Annabelle, had fled to Maryland, just outside Washington. Her sudden departure before they could even hold each other left him feeling lonely and guilty. Pat became quieter around campfires and less prone to acting out. His behavior was not lost on John, but he believed that in time Pat would return to his old pre-Annabelle self.

On Wednesday, April 20, 1864, the Corcoran Legion of 2,000 men was transferred to the 2nd Corps of the Army of the Potomac, which totaled 28,000 men and was commanded by forty-year-old General Winfield Scott Hancock. The 2nd Division, to which they were assigned, was commanded by General John Gibbons.

The Corcoran Legion had crawled quietly in a state of silent exhaustion into the front lines outside Spotsylvania Courthouse by midnight. They had marched forty miles from Belle Plain, near Fredericksburg, Virginia, on the Potomac Creek, a tributary of the Potomac River. Many slept in the open air with knapsacks at their heads, oblivious to flies and mosquitoes feeding on their unprotected flesh. Some had half a pup tent to match up with a friend's.

Others had discarded their halves as backpacks became too much to carry in the heat and humidity.

All through the three-day march, Pat could not get Annabelle out of his mind. He was dead tired, but at the same time, excited and eager to kill Johnnies the next morning. His head was full of alternating images of Annabelle and battle scenes surrounded by butternuts.

John had seen his brother jettison pieces of equipment as they marched. He was content that at least Pat had kept up with the unit when many were straggling behind. Looking ahead as usual, John had picked up an extra half tent. At least they would not sleep in the open on the last night before their first major battle. They were now part of Grant's Army of the Potomac and his Overland Campaign.

CHAPTER 10

Spotsylvania Courthouse

The 155th and 164th had three hours' sleep before they were ordered to prepare to assault the rebel lines on the morning of Wednesday, May 18. Tipping awakened his squad at 3:00 a.m. Only seventy men from Company I were present to answer their sergeants' calls. They were wet, cold, stiff, and tired from the long forced marches of the past days. They had slept in the same clothes for a week. Still, they crawled obediently out of their tents with little hesitation, barely conscious of where they stood. The sound of occasional rifle fire immediately reminded them they were on the front line, 1,000 yards from the enemy.

John shook Pat out of his blanket. "Pat, get your wits about you. We're going into battle in an hour."

Pat struggled to understand what he had to do. "John, I can't move my feet. They're sore and swollen. I'm not sure I can get boots on."

"I found you some fresh clothes and shoes. So get moving," said John. John had been up for half an hour and gone to the quartermaster whom he knew from the Ward and who, like John, worked with the bishop's maintenance crew. Only one of his wagons had made the trip thus far with the rest of the 155th. John requisitioned fresh uniforms, shoes and socks, and a few other items he and Pat would need.

Pat wondered how his brother and Tipping were always an hour ahead of the rest of the company. They were the world's best soldiers. Pat pulled off his clothes and put on the clean uniform and boots. His body tingled and he shivered in the cool morning air. The clothes had the fresh smell of brown soap that reminded him of Gram's newly washed laundry. His feet responded to the clean, dry socks with renewed vigor and he started to think about what lay ahead.

The unit ate a breakfast of hardtack and coffee. The remaining food and supplies were on wagons struggling through the mud somewhere between the James River and the army's current position. The men quickly cleaned their rifles without breaking them down, ran to the latrine, and were in formation within a half hour.

At 4:00 a.m., Company I stood at attention facing the enemy's line. Captain McAnally appeared in fresh uniform in front of his troops, his lieutenants to his left and right. Newell Moot Smith advanced a step or two forward of the main formation, the company flag in his hands, a green silk banner with the Harp of Erin in the center.

Tipping stood alongside John. Pat took what little confidence he had from the two of them. He was tense and voiceless. Fear gripping his heart and lungs, he found it hard to breathe. He couldn't wait to charge and start killing rebs. The air was cool and humid. Not a breeze stirred. The ground was soft, mushy. Ugly smells drifted up from the latrines, so McAnally moved the formation ten steps forward to fresher air.

"Pat, stay with me and cover me. Hold your fire unless you actually see the enemy. When we get outside their earthworks, wait until you see a reb firing at me," said John. "I'll do the same for you."

Captain McAnally addressed the company. "Men, we are about to attack an area called the Mule Shoe. General Meade thinks we should be able to break through where the rebel line sticks out like a sore thumb and slice it off with a massed charge where it connects to the main earthworks. March easily in formation through the woods and open field until we get to their sharp stakes, their abatis. Save your fire until then. Now, fix bayonets and follow the lieutenants and me. Once we get to the open field, be as silent as you can and we'll overrun the first line of their pickets, hopefully without their firing a shot."

The officers led off at a brisk pace. Some of the men exploded with reckless energy and ran ahead. Others straggled behind looking for a gully to hide in. Sergeants in the rear cursed them and prodded them back in line. Pat started moving out front, but a gentle poke from John's rifle pulled him back in line.

The four abreast formation broke apart as they entered the woods. They passed through it for 300 yards before picking up the pace of their march again as they entered an open field. Men stumbled in the dark over rocks and holes and brush. The formation slowed to allow the unit to stay together. Five hundred yards into their charge, they overran rebel picket positions. The first rebels to rise ran and fired into the air to give warning of attack to their main line.

Some rose too late and raised their arms in surrender, only to meet a bayonet in the chest. The 155th officers would not spare a man to run prisoners back to their lines. Hatred blocked remorse. It was to be a killing field. Kill every reb in your path. Union dead outside Suffolk had been stripped of their clothes and left to rot. The indignity inflamed Yankee hatred. Word from escapees of Andersonville atrocities reinforced it.

McAnally raised his arms to halt the advance before a long clearing. He sent Mooney to his left to see if the 164th in their new bright red and blue zouave uniforms was with them and ready for the run through what every man feared would be a wall of lead. He sent Lieutenant McCabe right to assure that Captain McConvey and Company K were ready. Both were in place. Major Byrne sprinted before the regiment. The signal was given to charge and the flag bearer stepped proudly forward. A shout went up and the men ran fast and low through a stand of trees that broke up their formation. They reformed their lines before open fields and crossed them on a quick march. This last clearing was nowhere on the maps given to officers the night before. The men were out of breath and their charge slowed to a walk.

Rebel artillery blasted the air. They were now within 200 yards of the rebel earthworks. The first shells passed harmlessly overhead. Confederate spotters adjusted downward. An artillery shell exploded the earth on Pat's right and blew three men from Company K into a twisted heap. The second line of rebel pickets and sharpshooters, hidden amid abatis along the front of their breastworks, fired volleys thirty seconds apart, one line loading and a second firing, as the Union men reached the last 100 yards. Shrapnel and minie balls tore apart the limbs of three Company I men. The 155th's formation dressed center to fill gaps, but then fell apart.

John slowed and moved from tree to trunk to bush to pit to swale, whatever meager cover presented itself.

"Pat, stay with me!" he yelled over his shoulder.

William O'Brian grunted and fell alongside John, begging John to help him. John hesitated for a moment, but then kept on running as trained. There was a thud and Billy Keefe slumped silently to the ground two men to his left. John's face was now splattered with blood. All he could think was keep moving . . . run run run on legs rapidly losing strength and speed. He could see the shadowy outline of trees in front of him.

The 155th entered a sparse stand of woods and dove for cover. A minute later, officers renewed their calls for attack. Without hesitation, the men rose and rushed forward through scrawny saplings and patchy clearings. With a sigh of arrival, they threw themselves on the ground in a shallow swale fifty yards shy of the earthworks. A constant stream of rifle shot passed above their heads.

The stench of putrefied bodies of Union soldiers who fell in the May 12th attack choked them. John told Pat to fire. Timing incoming shots, he rose up and fired a second after one buzzed above him. His was one of only three guns firing. Rebel sharpshooters were picking off those who exposed themselves.

Major Byrne counted his men and shouted to McConvey, "How many you got?"

The word came back, "Sixty-five men made it. Five down!"

With that, an officer yelled from the rear to stay where they were and the word passed quickly through the ranks. Unexpectedly, rebel fire lessened, perhaps to save ammunition.

Then Byrne stood before them and shouted, "Stand and charge! Charge, men!" Almost immediately, he fell with a wound to the head.

Pat hung two yards behind his brother, who methodically smashed rows of abatis, swinging his rifle butt back and forth. He then followed John running through with the rest of Company I. The earthworks loomed over them in the dark, only yards ahead. They climbed against guns firing down and bayonets stabbing from above, but the resistance was surprisingly light. The men took courage and rapidly mounted the earth and logs. The rebels broke and ran as the 155th reached the top. With half of its men still standing, the brigade had taken the breastworks.

As soon as they landed inside, concentrated fire poured in from a second line of earthworks 200 yards in front and squeezed off their cries of victory. The company had carried the high fortifications only to find them empty. The men fell to the earth stunned, exhausted, low on ammunition, and frantic. Then rebel artillery opened up from the new Confederate line of earthworks.

As they landed, Pat and John took three steps left and dove into a deep shell crater half-filled with shattered logs. Running, PM dropped in alongside them. Companies I and K often fought side by side. Their men mixed as circumstances dictated.

For five minutes, only two Union muskets fired along a 100 yard expanse of the old Confederate line. Three and then more men joined until ten men were mounting a token defense. Confederate artillery blasted away at the embattled group. Logs flew into the air and shards of wood plowed into two men's heads and shoulders. Men pushed logs in front of them and bravely fired while partially exposed to enemy fire.

Within an hour after the attack started, General Meade signaled through drummers to retreat. Wearing spyglasses and watching the battle from an upper barn door at a safe distance, Generals Grant and Meade decided continuing the attack was suicide. It would cost them most of two regiments.

For 12 hours, the 155th and the 164th flattened against whatever protection they could find: shallow indentations in the ground, logs blown into jagged piles by artillery fire, anything. Rebel sharpshooters angled for better shots and picked off exposed limbs. Sensing the direction of scattered Union musket fire, rebel artillery fired from 200 yards away, smashed into logs, and sent splinters through more bodies. Through it all, John loaded two muskets while Pat fired at overconfident rebels.

At last, darkness came. Under the protection of nightfall, all able-bodied soldiers stood and ran through holes blasted in the earthworks, leaving wounded, pleading friends behind. There was no formation now. Only run for your life pell-mell toward your own line. Rebel artillery fired a few shells over their old earthwork defenses. Thirty seconds after Union firing stopped, rebel soldiers raced forward, shooting into the noise of fading feet. John, Pat, PM, and all the other men stumbled and fell over bushes, rocks, and holes rising as fast as they could to keep on running. Pat passed comrades looking for John, whom he had lost sight of.

As he entered a clearing, rebel artillery exploded randomly across the field. He found John holding up Eddie Burns, who was bleeding from a hole in his right leg. Pat grabbed Burns by the other arm. They ran only a few steps when a partially spent shell fragment sliced through John's right shoulder. John released his grip, moaned, and stiffly fell backwards in slow motion to the earth.

PM appeared out of the dark and pulled him to his feet. The four continued a tripping, stumbling shuffle to the trees, then slowed to make their way to the Union lines.

Suddenly, from their lines, Union artillery guns targeted the Mule Shoe. Six- and twelve-pound shells crashed into both lines of Confederate earthworks and everything in between. Quickly, rebel fire ceased all around them.

They stumbled over bodies of dead and wounded men in blue. Limbs and heads were torn from torsos in gruesome configurations. Pat's attention jerked momentarily to a Union soldier who, an unspent artillery shell lodged in his belly, weakly begged for someone to shoot him. As artillery fire ceased, moans and cries for help could be heard across the acres.

Once behind Union lines, while men from Company I took care of Burns, PM and Pat stripped John of his blouse and shirt and stemmed the bleeding with a makeshift bandage cut from a rubber tarp, pulling it tightly around his upper chest and back. Pat then carefully replaced John's shirt, as John lay writhing in pain. Pat decided he could lie there for a day before receiving any attention. Hundreds were awaiting evacuation. He ran 500 yards to the quartermaster's shed and with help from an assistant quartermaster pulled out a stretcher. He, PM, and two other Company I men carried John to the regimental field hospital 300 yards to the rear of the main line.

Pat and PM pleaded with orderlies to take John inside. While they waited, Pat stripped him down to the waist and washed his upper body and head.

Pat could do little except massage the middle of John's back in hopes of distracting him.

John spent four hours of agony outside the mobile field hospital before he was taken in and looked at by a surgeon. After a cursory examination, he was bound in a bandage and transported by wagon a mile behind the lines to the divisional field hospital, which consisted of nine large fourteen-foot-high tents. Three tents had teams of surgeons standing around tables busily operating on wounded men. The remaining tents held up to ten beds in which lay wounded and gravely ill veterans.

Wounded men dulled by ether and chloroform were awake, agitated, and screaming throughout their surgeries. Chloroform by this time in the war had become the anesthetic of choice. It was applied by pouring it into a conically shaped towel or handkerchief held over a wounded man's nose and mouth. Nurses and ordinary soldiers held the patient down while surgeons operated. Bloody limbs overflowed a wagon and spread onto the ground ten steps from the back of the hospital.

The air was filled with vile smells as wounded men undergoing surgery or those ill with smallpox, lockjaw, and typhoid fever released urine and feces. Not enough personnel were available to keep patients clean or even to change their dressings. Very sick men lay alone, uncared for, infected by their doctors, and abandoned to their own waste.

After examining the wound, an assistant surgeon told John, "I think we can help you, private. I can feel the fragment lodged eight inches down your back from the wound. We gotta take it out right away or infection will set in and kill you." It had already been six hours since the shell fragment penetrated John's shoulder.

In a weak voice John replied, "Okay, doc, do it."

An orderly put a chloroformed towel over his nose and mouth. John, still on his stomach, slipped into a less agitated state of semi-consciousness. The orderly administered ether from a bottle and John became less agitated still. The surgeon cut deeply into his back. Pat held his brother down with every bit of pressure he could muster. In five minutes, the inch-long shell fragment was in a pile of garbage outside the hospital tent.

Immediately after surgery, two husky orderlies removed John from the operating table and carried him to a ward tent. The next day, a painful one for John, an assistant surgeon removed his bandaging and examined both wounds. His assistant, a colored boy named Henry Woods, spent the next half hour carefully washing out the wound and re-bandaging it.

When the surgeon returned to John's bedside and was satisfied with his condition, he said, "John, we're going to transfer you to St. Elizabeth Hospital in Washington. We'll take you overland and put you on a steamer."

"That'll be fine," John groggily replied, dropping back to sleep. Pat, on picket duty, never saw his brother after surgery.

At daylight, sharpshooters were ready to pick off anyone who ventured out to help the living, so no one did. Two days later a truce was called to allow recovery of bodies. Some were in pieces and defied gathering. Those in one piece were bloated and black. A sickening, sweet odor hung over the battlefield.

Squads, noses covered with bandanas, dug shallow trenches wherever half a dozen bodies were piled, distinguishable only by the remnants of their uniforms. Of the 410 men of the 155th regiment who charged, 60 were casualties. The 155th lost more men at Spotsylvania Courthouse than in the two previous years of war. The Corcoran brigade lost 209 killed, wounded or missing, including their commanders, Colonel Murphy, Lieutenant Colonel Flood, and Majors O'Dwyer and Byrne. A minie ball had entered Byrne's skull and removed his left eyeball.

For the first twenty miles of the trek to Washington, John lay on straw with five other wounded men in the back of a covered wagon bouncing over rutted trails. The wounded men moaned, cried, and cursed. The day was bright and mild, but they never noticed. They called for water repeatedly. The attending nurse, a smallish woman and volunteer from Connecticut, ran out of water twice. Once she had the wagoneer stop at an inn to use a water pump; the second time, at a creek to refill canteens.

The wagon halted for the day at a small crossroads hotel as darkness fell. One of the wounded was able to get out of the wagon with assistance and enter the inn. The rest, including John, propped themselves up, or were propped up by the nurse, where they lay. Those able to feed themselves did. The nurse helped those who could not. They ate cold meat and vegetables supplied by the innkeeper. The nurse redressed two men's wounds. The rest were told they would have to wait until they entered the hospital. Covered by two wool blankets, the men lay where they were and shivered through a cool night. They slept little and scratched a lot due to the lice brought from Spotsylvania.

The wounded were fed oatmeal, bread, and coffee the next morning before the wagon continued over rocky roads to Dunn's Landing on the North Anna River. There they were transferred to a small hospital ship that sailed ten hours to the Potomac River and Washington. The mighty river flowed flush with spring waters that made navigation easy and allowed the men, who were not feverish and tossing about, to sleep for most of the journey. The weather was sunny and clear throughout the trip.

In two days of travel, John's wound reopened twice, bleeding profusely until, with no tourniquet available, another wounded man applied pressure on the bandage above the wound.

Two hours after arriving at a Washington dock, John lay weak in a comfortable bed in St. Elizabeth Hospital. For the first time in three days, he felt relief from constant pain and discomfort. He was given mild sedation, a bath, fresh bandaging, clean clothes, and all the food and water his body craved. *And no lice . . . praise God . . . no lice.*

"Perhaps because of the bleeding," a doctor told him, "no infection set in and thus no gangrene." Within three days, at his surgeon's urging, John was up and walking stooped and gingerly around the hospital. Beds filled the hallways with Union wounded coming up from the first battles of Grant's Overland Campaign.

Boredom and compassion trumped his natural shyness. He wandered through wards and halls, wherever veterans lay, and traded stories with those able to do so. He found many were grateful for the company. All had stories to tell of stupid officers and ferocious battles.

He befriended Peter Cassidy, a twenty-year-old Yankee from Portland, Maine. Peter came into the hospital with a grave wound of his left leg just above the knee. Most men with similar wounds had their limbs amputated at the field hospital to prevent infection. Surgeons had been able to save his, using a technique pioneered by Chicago surgeons.

John visited Peter often during the week. At first, there was little conversation as Peter fought pain and surgeons reduced his agitation using ether, chloroform, and then laudanum. On the third day, Peter became quite calm and the two exchanged stories about home.

The following morning, John began another daylong vigil at his friend's bedside. A surgeon lanced Peter's leg once again. This time John noticed dark green coloring in the leg, a sight too familiar to John. He choked back tears. The surgeon told Peter gangrene had set in and that they would have to amputate. Clutching John's arm, Peter burst into tears.

Within an hour, the amputation was complete. Peter's left leg was but a stump starting six inches above where his knee had been.

John watched in horror as his friend's face took on a sickly pallor and his voice a croaking sound, early signs of what John recognized from the battlefield. Within two days, Peter was gone. He had not regained consciousness.

John lapsed into deep melancholia. An orderly urged him to leave the hospital and take short walks outside on the spacious grounds and beyond into the surrounding neighborhood. For a few days, John, the object of stares in his hospital gown worn over pants, did the same tour. He ambled slowly across the lawn, down Alabama Street, and through the neighborhood. He would find a bench and sit enjoying the sunshine, the flowers in bloom, and the brightly dressed women with their flowing skirts and broad hats of many colors. A few smiled at him and one stopped to chat. *Funny how the smiling face of a pretty girl can make such a difference*, he thought to himself. He continued to watch the people strolling by long after his buttocks ached from sitting on the hard bench, trying to imagine what they were thinking, where they were going, what their homes and families were like, anything to pass the time.

Each day he bought a Chronicle and read about the terrible battles of Grant's campaign. The papers carried long lists of local casualties. Images of what must be happening to the 155th tortured him. Some days after reading the paper, he walked with vacant stares into the evening, shuffling through the neighborhood like a vagrant.

Soon after arriving at the hospital, John had written Johanna a brief note telling her he had been wounded but was mending rapidly. He said he was thinking of her all the time and hoped she would write. A letter arrived a day later as if in answer to his wish. She wrote that after she heard the bad news from Gram—who had heard it from Carrie, who had read it in a Buffalo paper—she went door to door in the Ward and begged money from relatives and friends to purchase a train ticket to go to him. She closed saying she hoped she would soon have enough money.

Without further warning, a week later in mid-afternoon, Johanna appeared at John's bedside. She moved close to hug him, but hesitated. He sensed her reluctance. "I'm much better. You won't hurt me." She warmly embraced him. The smell and feel of her hair stirred him. She stepped back and scrutinized him carefully.

"John, you do look well, I'm happy to see. You seem to have gotten good care."

"I have, Johanna."

"Where exactly is your injury?"

"Shrapnel caught me just below the right shoulder and plowed downward into my back." At this revelation, Johanna winced. "They removed it a half day later in the regimental hospital and then sent me here to recover. There has been no infection or I'd be a dead man."

He assured her that his wound was healing fast and would leave no permanent weakness.

Satisfied with his answer, she drew near his bed and began telling him news of home. "Gram and Aunt Theresa, all the boys from the Travelers baseball teams, my family, friends at St. Bridget's, all of them send their best wishes for your recovery and are keeping you in their prayers."

"Jo, have yuh been to see Gram and Theresa?"

"Indeed, I have. Every few days to get word of you and Pat. Your letters meant everything to us. We three women gathered for supper at Gram's after work two or three times a week."

"How are they? Gram says nothing about herself in her letters. Probably doesn't want us worrying."

"Gram is okay. She stays active. Walks to mass every morning all the way to the cathedral. She does her own shopping with a little help from neighbors, especially Carrie.

"Theresa is working in Fillmore's law office. That lady is a saint. Helps Gram clean her house. Goes shopping with her. They are very close. You come from good people, John."

"I know. Not every orphan is so lucky."

"What about you? Where are you working now? How do they treat you?"

Their talk refocused on themselves and whatever came to mind. Her visit lifted John out of a deep funk. Conversation flowed effortlessly. Toward nightfall, he asked her, "Where will you stay tonight, Johanna?"

"Oh, Sister Mary Veronica set up a room for me at a pension run by the Sisters of Mercy not far from here. I can walk there or take a hack."

John replied, "We'll take a hack and I'll see you to the pension . . . if you don't mind being seen with an invalid."

Over the next several days, they spent much time walking outside, sitting holding hands, speaking little, looking for private places to embrace. By the end of the fourth day, they were confessing their strong feelings for each other.

Then on the last day, just before she had to leave for the train station to return to Buffalo, he asked, "Johanna, would you think you might ever, someday, when this war is over, think of marrying me?" Lifting her hands to her face, she nodded, whispered "Yes," and kissed him tenderly on the lips.

Over the next two weeks, Grant ordered flanking maneuvers first to the North Anna River and then to Totopotomoy Creek to roll up Lee's unprotected right side.

Each time, rebel cavalry scouts observed the Union flanking moves and alerted Lee. Lee immediately ordered his army eastward. Within a day, they lay in new defenses awaiting Grant's ponderous army.

The long forced marches and above all the sight of rebels finishing massive earthworks as they arrived at their destinations mocked Union leadership and destroyed Union morale.

The one relief came Friday, May 27th, when vanguard elements of the 155th reached Littlepage Bridge on the North Anna River at dusk after days of forced marches over eighty miles of alternately muddy and then dusty roads, usually with little to eat or drink because supply trains did not keep up.

On the other side of the bridge, Companies I and K turned left. After a few hundred yards, they came upon the gate of a large plantation, thus far undisturbed by the war. Captain McAnally and Captain Kelly, who had replaced Captain McConvey, stepped onto the mansion's wide porch, accompanied by two sergeants, and banged at the door. They drew their pistols and poised them before their faces. Behind a massive cherry door appeared a middle-aged mistress of stately bearing, average height, and robust build. Her well-groomed brown hair set off a long, flowing, pleated dress, which almost hid two female black servants who were standing behind her. With a forced smile, she addressed the soldiers, "Gentlemen, I beg you. We all are women here. Our men are gone to war."

Captain McAnally lowered his weapon, and smiling and bowing slightly, said, "Ma'am. We regret this unfortunate intrusion, but have no other recourse to feed our men."

The woman maintained her composure and answered with grace. "I am sorry, sir, for your men."

McAnally stroked his unshaven chin, gave a deep sigh, and brushed her aside. The colored girls squealed and ran off into the mansion. "Gentlemen, I plead with you!" said the woman. "We have barely enough to last till the next harvest and are eating but two small meals a day."

Ignoring her, the captains and the two sergeants went directly to the kitchen, where they removed a half dozen loaves of bread, fresh and hot, from the oven. They proceeded to the root cellar, where they found dried vegetables. Out back in the smokehouse, they scrounged a small amount of pork. The cache was not sufficient to feed all the men, so two male servants were ordered to slaughter the last pig in the barnyard and roast it. Then McAnally politely but firmly demanded the woman and her slaves serve supper to his eighty men.

Two cows in a pasture behind the barn provided milk. After consuming their first hot meal in twenty-three days, the officers relaxed with the cigars and peach brandy they had relieved from the absent master's private stock. They warned the woman and the colored servants to remain on the third floor of the mansion or they would shoot them on sight. Then officers occupied rooms on the first and second floors. Enlisted men took refuge in the cellar, the barn and in tents.

The next day the two companies continued on to Totopotomoy Creek, having exhausted one large household's food supply for the next year.

"Lee's done it again," grunted Tipping as he gazed across the creek. Rebel soldiers had barricaded the northwest banks with logs and earth. There must have been 1,000 of them and several had raised makeshift flags of white and were yelling across. "Hey Yankees! You take a bath and we'll take one. No shootin'... what d'ya say? Agreed?" Company commanders agreed. And it was understood that no one was to raise a rifle till the last man was done. It had been twenty-four days of continuous fighting and marching without a change of clothes or bathing. Both sides stood panting before the pure green waters of the Totopotomoy.

CHAPTER 11

Cold Harbor

On Wednesday, June 1, Union commanders realized that Lee was sliding his army south, occupying heights around Cold Harbor and posing a threat to their supply lines from the east. They ordered Hancock to lead a counter-move of the whole Army of the Potomac toward Cold Harbor. The 2nd Corps, including the 155th, pulled out of earthworks on the right of Grant's line and marched fifteen miles to the far left of the Union position around Cold Harbor. The roads were dusty. The night was hot and sultry. Pat stumbled along at the rear of the 155th without food or water, as provisions were late catching up with the 2nd Division. He found little to forage from the farms he passed. Farmers told him every farm animal had been plundered and roasted on campfires by the Confederates.

It was noon the next day before Pat straggled into camp, a half day after the rest of his unit. His weakness embarrassed him and he bowed his head and turned away from accusing eyes, as he walked through the camp.

Tipping could be severe on any man who straggled behind. Pat began to excuse himself before George could even raise his voice.

"Sarge, I just couldn't keep up. The piles are bleeding and raw. I have to rest every half hour or so."

"Go see the surgeon, Pat. Then get some food and rest. I suspect we'll be jumping off early in the mornin'."

Pat saw the surgeon, who examined him and gave him a balm. Then he walked to a nearby stream and bathed, washed his clothes, and dried off in the sun. He applied the balm and put damp clothes back on again, the same ones he had worn for two weeks. The balm was so smelly he knew every man in the company would know what his problem was. "What the hell," he laughed to himself. All that mattered was that he was moving with much less pain. He returned to his squad area, threw up a tent with Johnny Crowley, who had just straggled in, ate some hardtack, and fell asleep.

On Friday, June 3, the 155th mustered 330 soldiers at the center of the Union line between the town of Cold Harbor and Old Church Road. The men were rousted out at 4:30 a.m. to mount an attack on heavily fortified rebel positions. Pat had slept for ten hours and his piles were feeling somewhat better. He plastered on more balm and left his tent to join the rest of the company. With the men in formation, he sensed that they were facing another Spotsylvania. The Confederate army had been in place for two days, occupying high ground chosen by their engineers and commanders. They had been working between battles the previous day and night to rebuild their earthworks.

Pat missed his brother running interference, but thanked God that John was not here for another suicide charge. Before the attack commenced, Pat and a dozen pickets were ordered forward in the dark and fog to occupy rifle pits. They used pine torches carried near to the ground to find their way 100 yards forward of the main line. They dug pits or lay behind the few trees that remained standing.

"Pat, there is someone in the pit alongside me," whispered Crowley.

"Push him out. He's one of our dead from the battle on June 1," said Pat. Johnny nudged him with the butt end of his rifle and a rebel picket, not a dead Yankee, suddenly awakened and threw up his arms.

"It's a reb and he's alive!" said Johnny, as he turned and pointed his rifle at their lone enemy. "Jesus, look at 'im. He's an old man. Old enough to be my father."

"I'll run him back to our lines as fast as I can," whispered Pat. A golden opportunity to miss the first wave of the attack appeared like an angel in the night and Pat grabbed it before anyone else did. He pressed his bayonet into the back of the enemy soldier and yelled, "Move fast, reb, and you hold the torch. The whole Union Army is about to overrun us." They ran through the Union line and into the rear where two soldiers quickly took the prisoner in tow.

Just as Pat turned to rejoin his unit, a cannon blasted the fading night sky from the right and the world exploded with artillery fire. Thirty minutes later the regimental drummers beat out the attack order. Their new commander, rotund Brigadier General Robert O. Tyler, had arrayed the Corcoran Legion in one line of two ranks, nearly half a mile long. On the Legion's right, adjacent to Cold Harbor Road, was Colonel Peter Porter's 8th Heavy Artillery Regiment now being massed as infantry. A gun went off signaling attack and the 155th advanced with the 8th on its right and the 182nd New York and the 164th

New York on its left. The 155th moved forward at double-quick stride. In five minutes, they passed their pickets, who joined the assault.

Captain Doran led Company I, followed by his two lieutenants, across the field into a waist-deep, woody swamp formed by the headwaters of Boatswains Creek. The 164th veered left around the south end of the swamp and severed contact with the rest of the brigade.

Rebel sharpshooters, invisible behind trees and clouds of smoke, opened fire on the Union line and men began to fall. A cannon ball smashed into General Tyler's right ankle and command passed to Colonel Porter. General Colquitt's Georgians, hidden behind head logs in their earthworks, were firing from several angles. Blue-clad bodies began to pile up on the field. A bullet tore through Porter's neck. The Buffalo native was hit a half-dozen times and fell dead to the ground. The charge of the 8th was as dead, as their leader. Those surviving clung to the ground and waited for a bullet to end it all.

Pat was 200 yards to the rear. He barely noticed the shrapnel and spent bullets that fell around him. In minutes, he crossed yards of open hillside and drew within fifty yards of his unit.

Pat could see the stalled 155th was catching shrapnel and musket fire from the right and left and direct fire from above. In the first fifteen minutes of battle, half the regiment lay on the field dead, mutilated, or moaning. Captain Doran led the survivors behind a rise that partially hid them 150 yards from the rebel earthworks.

Just as Pat caught up, he heard Tipping's voice calling to his men, "Over here, men! And keep your heads down."

Pat sprinted with ten others to the indentation as 182nd soldiers rushed in as well in growing numbers. All dug furiously with bayonets, cups, and plates into red dirt, piling it in front of them with their hands. The smell of dew mixed with freshly turned earth brought images of farmers cultivating their fields to Pat's mind. He thought to himself, *I'm going crazy.*

A bullet raked up ground behind him. In front of him were legs that, he knew, belonged to Tipping. Shrapnel and rifle bullets splayed all around them. Pat pressed his body to the earth as hard as he could.

Tipping yelled to his men, "Keep your goddamn heads in the dirt!"

The rise protected them from Rebel fire, if they remained still as statues. The day dragged on. A searing sun desiccated them. Their heads began to spin. In a moment of quiet, Ritchie Egan raised his head just enough to glimpse rebel defenses. It was his last look. A sharpshooter split his forehead, spraying blood two men wide around him.

Night came sixteen hours after the attack commenced. The men broke for Union lines, leaving behind wounded begging for water or to be shot out of their misery. Cold Harbor cost the 155th Regiment 163 men killed, wounded, or captured.

On the Legion's left, Colonel James McMahon led the 164th over more protected terrain and reached General Martin's 17th North Carolina breastworks. The color bearer went down. McMahon grabbed the regimental colors and waved his men on. He fell dead, his body riddled with bullets. The charge ended with the first ranks either dead or mortally wounded.

Casualties for the 164th Regiment numbered sixty killed, forty-two wounded, and fifty-three missing. The entire Corcoran Brigade ceased to exist as a functioning battlefield unit. Its 900 casualties at Cold Harbor exceeded any other brigade that day.

Near rebellion broke out that night among the men of the 155th. Word spread that the number of Union casualties incurred that day was at least 5,000, maybe more.

On June 9, Grant ordered preparations to move the lumbering Army of the Potomac across the James River and on to Petersburg, through which passed five railroads supplying Richmond. It would be an immense operation, the largest of its kind in the Civil War: disengage over 100,000 men along a ten-mile front and march fifty miles, crossing a tidal river a half-mile wide and ninety feet deep.

The massive move began on the 12th. The 155th dropped off the front line and occupied a trench to the rear, guarding against a rebel attack until the roads around Cold Harbor cleared of Union soldiers. Then, they pursued Grant's columns heading south. After a forty-five-mile march over dusty roads and across the swollen Chickahominy and James Rivers, the 155th established its line a few miles outside Petersburg.

CHAPTER 12

Petersburg

G rant's army initiated its move so skillfully that Lee's scouts lost the whole Army of the Potomac for two days. By the time Lee caught on, federal units were across the Chickahominy River and well on their way to the James River.

On June 15, Grant's goal became clear to Lee. It was Petersburg, not Richmond—the habitual goal of Union armies since the beginning of the war in 1861—and the rail lines connecting the Army of Northern Virginia with its last ample sources of supplies in the Carolinas and the Deep South, especially Georgia. He telegraphed a message warning the War Department in Richmond and began transferring his troops by rail and road toward Petersburg.

Exhausted and hungry after a fifty-mile, three-day trek from Cold Harbor without food and with only the water they could find in creeks and rivers en route, the men of the 155th refilled their canteens and bathed in a creek near Petersburg.

Pat went out on picket with Tipping and his squad. They advanced 100 yards for a better view of the rebel line and stood in astonishment. Rebel breastwork logs were stacked haphazardly on top of low piles of dirt and not enough of that to withstand a modest artillery barrage. Pointing to the enemy's line, one of the men said what they were all thinking. "George, this is our big moment. We got to attack now and we'll take Petersburg."

Grant had left Petersburg to Meade, retiring to City Point, to coordinate the transfer of the Army of the Potomac and its vast supply network. Meade ordered General Baldy Smith's 18th Corps to attack the Confederate Dimmock Line, the outer defense line built in a ten-mile arc around most of the city and protecting it from the east, south, and west. It was a hot day. Dust filled lungs. Smith's army had marched fifty miles from coastal Virginia, much of it like the march of the 155th, without food or water. Nonetheless, his men jumped at the prospect of capturing one of the most strategically important Confederate cities, second only to Richmond in the East, and deliver a crushing blow to the Union's archenemy, General Robert E. Lee.

Smith delayed until 7:00 p.m. and then ordered a frontal assault. His men leapt over the defenses of the Dimmock Line and rolled back a mélange of rebel militia and soldiers three and a half miles. At that point, his resolve faltered and Confederate resistance stiffened with the arrival of a division of General Longstreet's troops brought in from Richmond the night before.

Had Smith engaged his reserves, the three divisions of Hancock's 2nd Corps, and continued the attack, he may have taken the city.

The army's morale descended into the dirt again as the men dug in and built breastworks all the next day.

On Friday, June 17, rations arrived at noon. After eating, the 155th was ordered out as skirmishers to probe the enemy's works and, if possible, to initiate a break-through.

The 155th led the attack. Company I went in with thirty men. They were to be supported by three regiments of the Corcoran Legion.

"Sarge, this looks like another exercise in suicide," complained one private as he looked across a field into rebel picket lines and main defenses. "Even their rifle pits are occupied in big numbers." By this time in the war, the men on both sides had perfected the art of creating earthworks that could be held by half the number of the attacking force. Defenders could inflict casualties three or four times what they would suffer.

"No doubt about it. We lost this battle yesterday," said Tipping.

With that, the signal came to form two lines in a field thought to be out of sight of Confederate sharpshooters and artillery, and to proceed to woods within 300 yards of the main rebel line. Rebel pickets and sharpshooters lay 100 yards off. They fired their rifles the moment they saw the formation developing, signaling back to artillery to open fire.

Pat heard thuds and cracking bones as men around him began to fall. Blind anger filled his soul. He hated the army and its brainless generals. His only comfort was Tipping. He moved alongside him and watched rebel pickets firing and sprinting back to their lines.

Tipping yelled, "Run to whatever gives cover, but keep moving and stay together."

It was now a drill practiced under fire since arriving with the Army of the Potomac on May 18. They crossed the field and entered the woods. It was porous and easily penetrated by rebel fire. The enemy was invisible, shielded by logs, earth, and smoke, pouring a solid stream of musket and artillery fire into the ranks of the 155th from three sides.

Shrapnel spread across the field and tore John Marr's legs from his body, his torso gushing blood like a mini geyser. A shell landed at their feet and blew Mickey McCabe and Billy Wiley five feet into the air. They sprawled spread-eagle on the ground, grievously injured but still alive. Captain Doran waved to his men to follow him. Johnny Parsons slumped dead in mid-stride. Timothy O'Brian and Billy Duffy fell still at their captain's feet as though forever refusing his command.

A spent shell or cannon ball whacked Pat a glancing blow on his left shoulder, dislocated it, and drove him to the earth. He rolled into a ball, clutching his shoulder and writhing in pain. Within a minute, the noise and mayhem of battle overcame shock. He struggled to reload his rifle.

He was now twenty-five yards behind his unit. He watched the last rebel pickets, occupying abatis in front of their earthworks, rise up and run for cover; he was only seventy-five yards from the rebel line. For once, he could actually see a rebel firing at him. A minie ball zipped over his head. The rebel soldier reloaded and started to raise his rifle. Bent awkwardly to his left, Pat could not hold his rifle tightly against his shoulder. Nonetheless, he brought it up alongside his chin and shot wildly over the man's head. The rifle recoiled and whacked his right shoulder. Pain exploded in his left shoulder once again.

Half of the 155th were dead or wounded. Men were scrambling for whatever cover the earth would yield thirty yards from the enemy. Supporting units were nowhere to be seen. The 155th lay directly beneath the enemy's earthworks, taking fire from above. Jimmy O'Connell yelped as a bullet ripped into a lower leg. Confederate guns were enfilading them, pouring a storm of lead and iron from three sides. Hugh Crane and Larry Reddy were hit in the arms as they tried to return fire.

Strangely, the rebel artillery ceased firing. Rebel sharpshooters continued their methodical work. Eddie Burns took a bullet in the thigh. John Burns rolled in agony, part of his skull blown open, blood and brains flowing across his left ear, then took a second minie ball in his left side and lay still. Tom Ryan moaned softly, sinking gracefully to the ground as a musket ball creased his skull.

Pat crawled back a few yards behind a providential boulder rising alone from the earth. Rebel fire was concentrated on the rest of Company I. There was nothing for them to do but conceal themselves with what little was available, including the bodies of comrades. Bodies literally blew apart, taking multiple rifle shots from close quarters.

Finally, after the men of the 155th lay exposed half an hour on an open battlefield, massed Union artillery guns repositioned and fired into the earthworks all along the attack front. Mortars lobbed shells just beyond the earthworks and spread shrapnel in wide arcs. Enemy fire slowed. Only an occasional sharpshooter raised his upper body from protected parapets and fired. At a second volley of mortar fire, they too took cover. The 155th withdrew, taking their walking wounded with them.

With head hunched over toward his left side, Pat staggered back to the Union lines. Pain drove him past stalled wagons of wounded toward the field hospital about a half mile in the rear. It seemed as though he would never get there.

In fact, he was one of the first wounded to arrive from the day's battle and received quick attention. An assistant surgeon spread him out on the ground, grabbed his left wrist with both hands, put his right foot into his armpit, and gave the arm a violent twist and yank. Pat's yell echoed through the valley. The shoulder slipped nearly back into place and most of the pain disappeared.

The surgeon would have done additional manipulation, but his attention was taken by wagons bouncing in and teamsters demanding care for their badly wounded charges. A muscular male nurse directed Pat to a bed and helped him undress. Pat lay quietly on his stomach. The nurse examined the back of Pat's left shoulder. Skin and flesh were severely bruised. A light layer of blood clotted over a broad area. The nurse cleaned and dressed the shoulder and back.

"In six weeks you will be as good as new," he said, motioning Pat to proceed to the wagon train about to leave for the City Point Army Hospital on the James River, twenty miles behind the Union lines.

The night was hot and humid. Pat lay against a sideboard, swatting flies and mosquitoes throughout the trip over pocked roads. He had no defense against lice and gnats that crawled up from the hay that was spread in a thick layer on the wagon floor. His shoulder ached in rhythm with bumps in the road. He dozed but could not sleep.

There was no sleep for the wounded and only a few stops for water and food. Just when it seemed they were to bounce in agony for all eternity, they arrived the next morning at the hospital, where beds, baths, and overwhelmed but compassionate nurses, more women than males for the first time in the war, awaited them. The Sanitary Commission had become more efficient in its care of the wounded and employed many more female nurses, Northern women, volunteers who labored like work horses day and night.

Pat lay on his right side and a surgeon examined every inch of his body.

"Are there any other conditions we should be aware of, Patrick?"

"I've had diarrhea on an' off for a month. I got piles like rocks and maybe rheumatism."

"Roll over all the way so I can examine your rear . . . Oh my, you sure do have piles. And what are your symptoms for rheumatism?"

"I've been coughing up some nasty stuff and flowing from the nose like a spring. My joints and muscles are so sore some days I can barely move. An' I have pains in my chest."

"Okay. That does sound like rheumatism. There isn't much we can do for it except rest you for a while."

"Can I join my brother in Washington? He's in St. Elizabeth's Hospital."

"Maybe so! Depends on their occupancy."

The next day another surgeon examined Pat. "Your wound is healing nicely, Mr. Donohue, but I don't like the sound of your breathing. How long have you been in the field?"

"Since November of '62, without a break," Pat answered.

"We're going to transfer you north for a month or so and see if we can clear up the rheumatism. Unfortunately, St. Elizabeth's is full. There's a good hospital in Philadelphia, the General, which has room. We could transfer you there." Pat readily agreed, thinking he could get a furlough and take a train home.

In City Point harbor, he boarded a navy steamer for Alexandria. From there, escorts led him to a military train bound for Philadelphia. Hospital personnel met him at the Philadelphia station and escorted him to a covered wagon, which they rode a few miles to the G. H. Broad and Cherry Street Hospital, also called simply "General Hospital."

During the day, Pat played keno and euchre with other veterans for no money, as gambling was frowned on by the hospital's Quaker administrator. When he wasn't playing cards, Pat visited with wounded veterans, playing dominoes and exchanging stories about their officers, battles, and the folks at home. He felt deep compassion for these men and found visiting with them the high point of each day. However, he was not comfortable with colored men and skipped by the Negro soldiers' ward on his rounds. He thought himself fortunate to be lightly wounded and was happy to be useful. He had no hankering for alcohol during his hospital stay. In bed at night, his thoughts and dreams, when not nightmares of war, were of Annabelle.

For two weeks, Pat enjoyed courteous care and time away from the front with its daily discomforts, boredom, and death. He stayed in a quiet wing of the hospital with other lightly wounded soldiers, where he was undisturbed by the moans of sicker patients. He slept soundly. His shoulder and other conditions improved.

He visited sick patients each day. Some had lost limbs on the battlefield. Others had suffered amputations a day or two after being wounded. These men needed someone to be with them, mutter a few encouraging words, and listen sympathetically to their fears for the future. During one tour of the ward, Pat accompanied a chaplain who talked to and prayed with a dying veteran. The chaplain moved on. Pat stayed, holding the poor man's hand until he died.

The next day, Pat visited a twenty-year-old Irish boy, who had only been in this country one year before signing up with the 20th Massachusetts Volunteer Infantry Regiment. Outside Petersburg on the same day Pat was wounded, a bullet ripped into the boy's abdomen and disintegrated. Surgeons could not remove all the fragments. Infection set in and then gangrene. His death was painful—almost as painful to watch—as he tossed in bed, vomited, and released bodily wastes. Pat took five-minute breaks, but returned to the soldier's bedside throughout the day and night. Finally, at seven in the morning, the soldier died.

Pat cried unashamedly. He said a rosary and the prayer, "May his soul and the souls of all the faithful departed rest in peace. Amen."

A surgeon examined Pat toward the end of the first week and advised that if Pat wanted a perfect shoulder, he'd have to perform surgery on it. Pat said thanks but no thanks. He had heard of too many veterans dying after being infected from minor surgeries. His left shoulder felt almost normal, and he was able to walk upright.

Groups of young women visited the hospital daily to keep the veterans company. Time cavorting with them was a welcome relief from his visits with soldiers. In their company, he thought of Annabelle. He missed her deeply and wondered where she was. Images of her shapely dark-brown body flooded his imagination. He should have gone with her, he knew, and pounded his pillow, cursing the war for separating them. "To hell with the army!" he cried.

Pat never got leave to go home. After two weeks in the hospital, he couldn't wait to rejoin Company I. An assistant surgeon examined him one last time and recommended Pat for light temporary duty in Washington with the Veteran Reserve Corps.

The army sent Pat by train to Washington with soldiers returning to their units. The group was nominally under the command of a Major Gruesbach. Pat could see no way to visit his brother until a conductor passing through their car announced in a loud voice: "Next, Washington Station."

"I have a brother, here in St. Elizabeth Hospital recovering from a shrapnel wound. I'd like to visit him."

"Go visit your brother. That's an order!" laughed Gruesbach.

Pat pulled his bag out of the top rack, thanked the officer for his kindness, and shouted, "Good luck to you, Major. I hope your unit does nothing but guard railroads," and ran from the train.

At 6:00 p.m., Pat arrived at the hospital. It took him a half hour in the mayhem of overcrowded wards and overwhelmed staff to find his brother. He sat quietly alongside John for a minute, but impatience got the best of him. He squeezed his brother's hand and called his name three times before John stirred from sleep.

As he focused his eyes, a broad smile transformed his face. "Pat, what are you doing here? The last I heard you were in Philadelphia."

Pat quickly repeated the story of the major he met on the train. "The VRC can wait a day," he said. "So, here I am. And how are you?"

"I'm getting better. The wound healed without an infection and I'm regaining my strength. You look well."

"Philadelphia was good, very good indeed. Lots of women around. I really rested up. Even my piles are gone. How was your care?" asked Pat.

"I will never forget the ride here from Spotsylvania," responded John. "But once here, the care has been good. The Northern nurses can't do enough for us. What about yours?"

"Same thing," answered Pat. "The wagon trip was pure misery. When we weren't tormented with pain and thirst, the lice drove us mad."

"And the hospital care in Philadelphia?" asked John.

"Couldn't have been better if I were home with Gram. You know what was the best? Sitting with some of our wounded comrades, the dying most of all. Maybe I should have been a priest." The brothers laughed.

"I had the same experience. A real privilege to sit with badly wounded and dying men. Some died with fear; some died like they were looking into eternity. I will never forget those men," said John.

John got out of bed and they wandered outside the hospital.

"Tell me first about Gram," said Pat. "What do you hear from her? Is she holding her own?"

"She is that. She has a hard time getting around. But she does get to church. Neighbors look in on her and fetch her groceries."

"Gram and Aunt Theresa are begging us to write more, even though they say it takes an interpreter to read your English." He chuckled a little.

"Johanna visited me here. What a woman! I met her at Bridget's while I was home. I'm going to marry her, Pat, when this miserable war is over."

"How long did she stay, John?" asked Pat. Pat was happy for his brother, but feeling pangs of envy over the way his brother's relationship with Johanna had blossomed into something permanent. His craving for Annabelle returned full force.

"She stayed a week. We spent all day together and really got to know one another. Johanna is a special lady. She works for rich folks and sees a side of life we never knew."

He paused and blew his nose into his handkerchief. "Hard to describe her. She's unlike any of the girls we traveled with."

"Wow, sounds like you're on your way to settling down and making a life for yourself," replied Pat.

"Maybe so. We'll see if she still feels the same way once I get home. If I get home."

"Are you returning to Company I, John? I think you could muster out, if you want to."

"I went in with you, brother, and if the Lord spares me, I'll muster out with you."

Late that evening they returned to John's bed. John lay down and they talked some more.

"Pat, what happened after I left the company?"

"Oh, God, how painful to talk about it. Massed attacks on rebs protected by huge earthworks. Hundreds of our friends killed or wounded. Almost all of our officers gone. They turned out to be brave men, John, but Meade and Grant are butchers. I choke up thinking about the horror of it all. If you think Spotsylvania was a slaughter, you should have seen Cold Harbor."

"How did you get wounded?" asked John.

"Well, Grant had us trying to outflank Lee four times, marching thirty, forty, fifty miles when we tried to take Petersburg. That's their big supply city, three or four railroads passing through to Richmond. And we could have. We half died to get there. We had two armies and outnumbered them four to one."

He sat in silence, thinking for a moment about the opportunity lost. "We lay outside the city without attacking it, listening to trains shuttling rebs in. We could have captured it easy when we first got there and the war would have been over."

He kicked at the floor in anger. "Men cried, begging their officers to let them attack. When we did finally get the order, the rebs were ready in big numbers and behind earth works ten feet high. I got hit by a spent artillery shell that blasted my right shoulder out of joint."

"Has it healed?" asked John.

"No, the surgeon didn't completely get it back in place. He didn't have time. There were hundreds of wounded men screaming for help."

After midnight, a nurse came by and told them it was time for Pat to retire. She offered him an empty bed in a wing of the hospital undergoing renovation. The abandoned space was spooky, hot, and humid. Pat undressed, made a pillow out of a blanket, covered himself with a sheet, and fell fast asleep. The next morning at six, the same nurse woke Pat. He had breakfast with John. "We'll meet soon back at the company," John said as the brothers turned away to hide their emotions. Pat picked up his bag, walked quickly out the front door, and hailed a hack for Fort Stevens and the Veteran Reserve Corps.

Pat reported for duty at the fort on July 4, just in time to witness parades and ceremonies celebrating Independence Day. He was assigned guard duty on a wing holding Confederate prisoners and given a shotgun. It was boring duty. Pat passed much of his time chatting with prisoners and playing cards with fellow guards.

Then on July 11, Confederate General Jubal Early decided the best way to pull Union troops from Petersburg was to attack Washington. He chose Fort Stevens as the most vulnerable point in the city's defenses. That day Pat became a line soldier.

General Early concluded after a two-day siege that his mission was complete. He had drawn off a corps and several regiments from Grant's command. Furthermore, the capture of the fort was not worth the price. He withdrew late on July 12.

The whole company cheered Pat as he returned to camp on July 18. Taunting him about his invisible wound, they grabbed him by the arms and shoulders and gently wrestled him to the ground. He didn't fight back.

Sergeant Tipping strode up. "Enough of your bollocks behavior or he'll have an excuse to return to Philly. Your brother is in St. Elizabeth Hospital in Washington. In the meantime, what a shame to mess up your clean uniform! Grab your rifle and see if you can find your friends out on the picket line."

Pat said nothing about having spent an evening with John. He did as ordered. After a night in a damp forest, his old rheumatism returned.

Grant had learned the futility of frontal attacks against strongly built and heavily defended Confederate positions. The battle for Petersburg became siege warfare: skirmishes, probes, sharpshooters sneaking up on pickets, troops building shacks for a winter in the field, band concerts, perpetual fatigue duty improving defenses, daily drills, insects, hot humid weather as the summer droned on, card playing, drinking—lots of drinking, mostly whiskey—and picket duty about every other day.

The day before John was to be discharged, July 23, a War Department representative visited him on the ward. He saw that John was awake and opened up his black notebook.

"John Donohue?"

"Yes, sir."

"I'm Lieutenant Stanfield." Stanfield was a few years older than he, John guessed, maybe twenty-five or so. He was tall, thin, and walked with a slight limp. His brown hair was neatly trimmed and his green eyes conveyed concern for John. "How are you feeling, John?"

"Better every day, Lieutenant. The care is great here."

"Well, I've examined your record and while your wound does not threaten your life, it is enough to make you eligible for permanent furlough from the army. You can go home."

"Lieutenant, if it is all the same to Mr. Lincoln, I'll be going back to my regiment as soon as I can carry a musket ten miles. I've a younger brother with the 155th who needs a guardian angel."

Stanfield grinned. "Mr. Lincoln likes the spirit of you Irish boys, John. He appreciates your desire to stay until the job is done."

"Well, Lieutenant, I take it from the Veteran Reserve Corps pin you're wearing you have stayed the course and not gone home when you could have."

"Thanks for the commendation, John. Got mine at Gettysburg. Like you, I felt I could still make a contribution and so I joined the VRC."

John returned to his unit on July 26. His fellow soldiers, especially Tipping and newly promoted Captain Mooney, appreciated his courage and loyalty. "Welcome back," they shouted, slapping him on the back and shaking hands. Pat hugged his brother, grabbed some of his gear with one hand, and held on to his arm with the other, as the four walked to the shed where Pat had prepared a surprise.

"You're a sight for these bloody eyes, John boy. Can't believe you chose to come back, except to protect this wild brother of yours from a Union prison or a rebel grave," George laughed. "I have to tell you, your brother is now a fine soldier. I depend on him same as I did you. We missed you and maybe lost a few men because you weren't here."

John chuckled. Pat opened the shed door. "John, it ain't home but it's as close as we'll come." John explored the shed, noting the comforts: a cast iron stove, bunks off a wooden floor, thick straw mattresses, an earthen jug of water. Wisely, he did not ask where Pat got the stove or the bunks or how he got them here, not in front of officers who did not want to know anyway.

Shaking his head, John dropped his gear and put an arm around Pat. Then he retrieved his musket and without being asked, left with his brother to go on picket duty.

As Pat sat beneath a giant fir tree, he thought about the big brother beside him. *Great to have John with me again. Felt naked out there without him. Just didn't know how naked till he got back.*

CHAPTER 13

Reams Station

The siege of Petersburg continued from the spring of 1864 into summer. Throughout the summer and fall, the pickets of the 155th and soldiers all along the Union line witnessed a welcome sight. Confederate soldiers were crossing in the dark and surrendering in increasing numbers.

Pat and PM walked seven rebels to the quartermaster's station. As they returned to picket duty, the two talked about how important it was to be alert.

"Their army is showing signs of falling apart," offered Pat. "The war could soon be over."

"We're most vulnerable to a rebel sneak attack when we're on picket duty. Don't forget, we got to expose ourselves as little as possible, even if it means refusing to advance," said PM.

On August 23rd, Meade and Grant decided to rip up a stretch of the Weldon Railroad around Reams Station, twelve miles south of Petersburg, to remove that railway from Lee's supply system altogether. The Weldon was one of two remaining railroads supplying both Richmond and Petersburg.

Lee, as usual received reports from his commanders and scouts on the likely intention of this Union Army thrust. He realized that, should Grant succeed in destroying the Weldon that far from Petersburg, Confederate government and military operations concentrated at the two cities would have to retreat south to North Carolina.

Three miles from Reams Station, the 2nd Corps began tearing up the Weldon tracks and continued right up to their destination. About 7:00 a.m. on August 24th, the 155th, with three hours' rest over two days, staggered into Reams Station, not much more than a hamlet on the line.

John and Pat were in Tipping's squad, building defenses. "Pat, don't you wonder when this goddamn war will end? The rheumatism has every limb of mine aching." He paused and then walked to a rise from which he could better see their line. "I've a sinking feeling the Johnnies will catch us right here at the railroad where we're weakest."

Pat grabbed his bedroll, kepi cap, and rifle and walked out to the line of rifle pits. He dug himself a pit and dragged a good-sized log in front of it. Pat lay in his pit, rarely raising his head. Snipers might be in the woods beyond. Union pickets were spaced twenty-five yards apart. Bushes, clumps of trees, and undulations in the land blocked their views of one another. Pat was feeling alone and vulnerable.

Suddenly, a shot grazed the log and dug deep into the earth a few inches beyond his feet. Pat jerked his knees up as far as he could and slowly moved his head to the left, one eye scanning the field before him. He gauged from the way the bullet had kicked up the ground that the sniper was not far off, but Pat could not see him.

It was hot and humid, not a breath of air circulating. Pat cursed the wool uniform he was still wearing after months of summer weather. A few ants climbed busily out of the ground and crawled into his clothes. They moved over his back and stomach and tickled him. He shook reflexively and tried to crush them against the earth. Every minute or so he peered around the log lest the secesh descend from his position and bayonet him before he looked up. They were bold and sneaky and survived because they knew the territory like their own barnyards and camouflaged themselves well.

Anxiety fogged and distorted his thinking. Beads of sweat rolled down his side under his uniform. By noon, he had no more water and his body began to crave it. Only fear kept him in his pit.

A bullet split the log in front of him, which told him his enemy had a bead on him, hoping to flush him out and send him running toward his line. It would then be a rabbit-shoot or even easier. He looked around the log with one eye again, panning a small stand of trees 100 yards in front of him for any movement. As his eye grew accustomed to the blend of limbs, leaves, and sky, he saw a patch of brown shake a large branch ten feet in the air. He reached down, pulled his rifle to his head, and looked around the log again.

A scrawny, motley-dressed man in a floppy hat slid down the backside of the tree and started toward him, bent low, stepping lightly in bare feet. He waited until the man was less than twenty-five yards off, then rose quickly to his knees and fired. The minie bullet sliced through the man's right side and sent him crashing to the earth. Pat moved quickly to reload his rifle. As he did, the wounded rebel got up and in slow motion began to square around to fire. He raised his rifle, fumbling to place the cap over the pin and to pull the trigger. Pat froze.

As the secesh readied to fire, a shot rang out from Pat's right side and blew the man into a motionless heap. Pat sank back to the ground, sweating and faint. He turned right and squeaked, "Thanks, brother," to John, who waved back with a smile.

At about 2:00 p.m. on August 25, rebel skirmishers appeared and traded fire with 155th and 164th pickets. A half hour later, several lines of Confederate troops in full attack formation came out of the woods. Lieutenant Wilson, in command of Union pickets, passed the word down the line to fire on order and then take fifty steps to the rear before firing again. Within two minutes, however, the pickets were racing back to their lines as fast as they could as the rebels commenced their eerie screeching and attacked on the run.

Pat was the first to reach the breastworks, 100 yards west of the Weldon. He fell in line with Company K.

Major Byrne was running back and forth across the backside of the earthworks, yelling to his men, "Only the front line fire! The rest of you wait until the rebs run into the dry creek bed below us. Fire together on command and fire low! Make every shot count."

The rebel lines burst into the field 200 yards from the earthworks, yodeling their high-pitched howl. Union artillery grape shot swept the field. The brigade's front line poured in a volley of rifle fire. Men fell, some without a sound, some screaming as limbs blew apart. Rebel soldiers scrambled for whatever cover a stump or a culvert provided. An officer called retreat. Rebels rose and ran to the rear.

Union soldiers let out a cheer that resounded down their lines. The field was littered with dead and wounded rebels pleading for help and water. No one ventured out from either line. Pat rose up and joined his company.

At 4:00 p.m., Major Byrne watched the rebel soldiers re-form west of where they first attacked at the edge of woods. "Right fifty yards," he yelled.

With the precision of a drill team, the Union line re-formed. The compact rebel formation, taking advantage of a forested rise, broke out yelling 150 yards from the Union line and threatened to breach it. Byrne spread the order to hold fire. Too long, it seemed to Pat. As the enemy reached within 100 yards, the major shouted, "Ready, aim . . . fire." The noise of artillery and 2,000 rifles drowned out every sound and thought. Fire from all across the Union line visibly thinned the rebel force in the same moment.

Their shattered line continued to advance, but then, as if hands from the earth were reaching up and pulling down struggling prey, the line wavered and fell to the ground. Pat stared blankly into the contorted face of a soldier who lay over a pointed stake not twenty yards off. He was just a boy, the red marks of scurvy plainly visible beneath the grey of his skin. Blood spurted over his blue jacket.

Then the rebel lines rose and ran back across open space, sped by bullets and canister shards from behind. Several more fell before they reached their lines.

At 5:00 p.m., mounted rebel scouts appeared on a hill overlooking the Union line. Pat could see two of them carefully scanning the length of Union fortifications. An hour later, Confederate cannons opened up concentrating fire on one section of the Union line, just west of the railroad track.

Two shells exploded five yards away and shocked Pat into a fetal position. He lay moaning quietly at the base of mounded earthworks, unwounded but cowering and crying like a newborn. The shelling continued for fifteen minutes.

The rebels attacked a third time. Lee packed most of his reserves, two regiments, at a single point just opposite the west side of the Weldon. This attack met the same fate as the first two and it seemed it would surely fail. Soldiers fell before the onslaught of canister and rifle fire. Then, a second mass of rebels held in reserve swarmed toward the Union position alongside the rail line.

The 164th and the 36th Wisconsin cracked and began running wildly to the rear. Hundreds of rebel soldiers pushed through the breach, and turned right and left across the unprotected rear of Union lines. More blue-clad soldiers threw their knapsacks and rifles on the ground and rushed chaotically to the rear or surrendered. Within seconds, the 8th Heavy Artillery Regiment came under rebel rifle fire and every man was killed or threw up his arms. Rebel soldiers trapped the left flank of the 155th. Colonel Murphy, running before his troops, saw the panic as it developed and ordered the 155th and the 170th to face left and fire on the rebels—but too late.

After a single volley, Murphy saw that his firepower was too light to stop the horde and shouted a retreat. Retreat became a mad rush to the rear. The vanguard escaped. The rear formation of the 155th stood and fired one more volley before being overrun. A few men attached bayonets and started to stab at the ragged mass, but then all were pushed to the ground, like pins before a giant bowling ball. For these men, there was nothing to do but release rifles and throw up arms.

John was in the forward formation. He ran to the rear, into the midst of the 61st New York Volunteers, led by its commander, General Nelson Miles. John joined them in fighting to recapture the 8th Artillery battery. Within minutes, however, Miles, too, saw they were about to be cut off, so he ordered a disciplined retreat down the Jerusalem Plank Road. The rebel attack slowed to take control of 2,000 Union prisoners, which accounted for the rather unmolested escape of the balance of the Union force.

With the end of the shelling, as screaming rebels advanced toward him, Pat regained his senses. He rose, still in a daze, and fired. A wave of grey overran his position and buried him in a pile of blue soldiers. All was darkness. Panic seized him. He could hardly breathe. As he was fading into unconsciousness, the weight of the pile eased and the sun spread across his face. He felt a rush of relief as he drew a shallow breath and then breathed faster and deeper.

A butternut-coated corporal kicked him to his feet and began running him back at the point of a bayonet to rebel lines. Pat frantically cast his eyes right and left. He knew the first minutes were crucial when the chaos of battle afforded an opportunity for escape, but none appeared. They moved farther and farther into enemy lines. They joined other grey and blue on a quick march in the same direction.

He fell out, hoping the prisoners and guards would run by, but he had barely hit the ground when a bayonet sliced into his right shoulder, deep enough to start blood but not seriously wound. He got up and ran for a while, then slowed to his captor's pace.

He felt peering eyes behind him. He looked back and saw PM. As his panic subsided a little, he slowed enough to let him catch up, but not enough to draw another bayoneting. They had plenty of company, half the 155th and 164th, it seemed. In a separate group were officers, including Major Byrne, Captain Kelly, and Captain McConvey. McConvey had been shot through the chest and was gasping for breath. Supported by his fellow officers, the captain was struggling to walk. Pat picked up his pace so that he wouldn't hear McConvey's wheezing. Finally, the rebel guard, equally uncomfortable, ordered the other officers to carry the captain.

Pat looked up. Before them was Petersburg. Prodded by a bayonet, he walked down the main street between a gauntlet of civilians and militia, who were spitting and yelling, "Welcome to Virginia . . . Goddamn nigger lovers . . . Starve to death, yuh Yankee bastards." Spit flew across his left eye and cheek.

CHAPTER 14

Prison Life

It was Saturday, August 27, 1864. Pat, PM, and David Smith sat glumly with fifteen other prisoners, silently bumping along during the twenty-mile train ride to Richmond, past rolling country, quite pleasant to behold. It reminded Pat of the countryside near East Aurora.

"Goddamn, you knew one of these times those idjit generals of ours would either get us killed or we'd end up in a rebel prison," said PM. "I guess we're damn lucky we're not rotting in red clay with many of our mates."

"We're almost certain to spend time in one of Richmond's prisons, probably Libby," replied Pat.

Smith listened morosely. At thirty-nine, the second oldest of Company I, he feared he'd never see his wife and four children again. Long since had he regretted enlisting. He was a dozen years older than the rank-and-file and reduced to a gaunt shadow of himself by constant campaigning since joining the Army of the Potomac. He was sure he had pneumonia.

The three lapsed into silence for the rest of the ride.

The train pulled into Richmond depot. Guards ordered the captives to get out of the boxcars, line up, and march. At first it felt good to march, but men soon began to straggle behind in the heat and dust.

"PM, the guards are beating any man who falls."

"Let's lift the two on the ground there, but do it quickly or the guards will beat on us," said PM.

Pat and PM grabbed two badly wounded prisoners under their arms and not-too-gently pulled them along. Their groans shook the whole formation. The air was heavy with heat and humidity. The sun beat down on them. They turned a corner after an hour-long, two-mile march, and there was Libby Prison, an old tobacco warehouse complex of three buildings.

Guards separated enlisted men from officers and led the enlisted men into the middle building. A flight of stairs took them to the Milroy Room, so named by inmates after its commandant. The room was crowded with hundreds of men standing shoulder-to-shoulder over others on the floor. Many were barefoot. Pat's jaw dropped in shock at the sight. Men's skull bones showed through their skin. Their mouths hung open, sucking air. Some crouched listlessly against the walls. A few lay in fetal positions on the floor. The stench caused the three to choke and vomit up bile.

The three men pushed through the crowd to the far end of the room. There, Pat approached a man leaning against the wall. "What's your name, sergeant?"

"Jeremiah Benedict, 15th Massachusetts. Captured on the Jerusalem Plank Road, August 10."

"Pat Donohue, 155th New York. Taken at Reams Station two days ago. This place is so packed we'll sleep standing up."

Jeremiah said, "I heard from one of the old guards that they're releasing prisoners to Belle Isle and Andersonville. Word is that Sherman is getting closer to Andersonville, so maybe we won't be sent there."

"What's the food like?" asked Pat. "So far, there's been none."

"Worse by the day. The rebs are on rations themselves, so we're lucky to get a little gruel once a day. You mix it with a cup of water and bake it in the big oven on a stone or in a cup, whatever you can find, or eat it as mush . . . or starve."

"Some of these guys look like thugs," observed Pat.

"Some of the inmates would rape their own mothers," replied Jeremiah. "They're escaped felons and deserters, Southern criminals, and Union loyalists. Keep with the men from your own regiment."

In the days that followed, the three watched "fresh fish," new prisoners, crowd into the Milroy Room. Like them, each was given a thin blanket. The room was sultry, not a current of air anywhere. To stand within three feet of a window was to be shot. Nights, Pat slept next to PM on the hard floor. They received a pound of uncooked gruel—kernel, ear, and husks milled together—which the men mixed with their daily cup of water. Pat was surprised and grateful when he was handed a yam toward the end of the first week and a day later a chunk of moldy meat that made him sick when he forced it down.

In the second week, a few of the men began to howl and attack other prisoners. Others grew quiet, feverish, and diarrheic. Negroes came infrequently to clean the latrines out in the yard, which overflowed with human waste and drove the healthy as far back as they could get. The very sick and the dying lay anywhere they collapsed.

Pat kept his calm by imagining how his brother would behave in these conditions. The stress of the place, however, played tricks with his mind.

One week into September, PM said to Donohue and Smith, "We've got to get out of here or we'll go mad or die on the floor shitting our brains out." They all had dysentery.

Smith replied weakly, "I've been talking to one of the guards, an older gent from County Meath. He may get us on the Belle Isle list. Says there's room there and tents."

"You're a godsend, Smitty," replied Pat. "I'm about to go mad if we stay here much longer."

"Let's push our way over toward the front gate. Believe it or not," said PM, "that may be the best spot in the joint. The guards force the new prisoners in farther and there seems to be more space there, maybe more air too as the gate swings open several times a day."

"You lead the way, PM. I'll move in front of Dave and make sure he makes it," replied Pat.

On September 9, after two weeks in Libby Prison, Donohue, Dolan and Smith were transferred to Belle Isle, a small island just yards across shallow water in the James River. It lay at the west end of Richmond and served as a prison for Union enlisted men. Shacks and Sibley tents accommodated 10,000 by late 1864.

"One more day at Libby and I would have charged a guard and been killed trying to strangle him," said PM. "At least we're out in the air here." They looked around, surveying the mix of tents and sheds overseen by guard towers. Once on the island, the prisoners were left to their own devices.

Pat nodded. "Right, but the nights are starting to cool, so we got to find a tent to begin with. Then make a shed. I can't see how, though. This place has been stripped of every twig."

"I'm weak as an infant, weaker every day," Smith said in a lucid moment. "Maybe there's a way to take a swim and end up in Union lines. You two could make it."

That night the three fell asleep in the open. Toward morning, a storm rumbled in the distance; within an hour, it began to rain hard. At a nearby Sibley tent, PM asked to be let in out of the storm. A shout came back, "If you open the flap, we'll beat you to death." After trying two or three more times, the occupants of one tent allowed them to crowd inside out of the rain.

As light dawned, Pat pulled on PM's arm and whispered, "Let's go down to the north end of the island and see if we can snag a log. Now is the time, before the rain stops and the men get up." Pat remembered tree trunks bobbing down the Buffalo Creek in spring floods. Smith saw them move out. He coughed harshly and dozed off.

Pat and PM found tree trunks and large branches in the swirling river, floating to shore in a small cove. Working quickly, the two men pulled out a dozen pieces of wood and piled them on shore. They gathered up smaller branches and twigs for firewood and then rested on the ground.

It began to dawn on Pat for the first time that he might not make it. In the two weeks since his capture, his strength was gone. He lay there thinking all he wanted to do was rest. He barely felt the rain.

"Stay here, Pat. I think I know where two other men are from the 155th. We need some help and some kind of tool." With that, PM walked off. A short time later, he returned with four men, Pat Kinnane and Pat McGowan from the 164th and Jim Beasley and Tim Nolan from the 8th New York, all taken at Reams Station on the same day they were.

By nightfall on September 8, they had built a lean-to that would sleep all seven, including Smith. A week later, they got half of a Sibley tent from two prisoners whose mates had died and threw it over the poles. Over the next month, they scavenged for wood and perfected their shack.

They saw how other prisoners had constructed crude fishing poles to catch trout and rigged up one for themselves, using minnows for bait trapped with a blouse. For two weeks, they caught nothing. Angry words and shoving matches developed among them over small issues.

Then a guard gave them a fishing hook in trade for a button Smith still had on his blouse. That day they caught two large rainbow trout. They cooked them on a stone slab with dried wood taken from the river, obtaining flame from a neighbor's fire. They devoured the fish. Immediately, their stomachs growled in protest. They learned, after periods of starvation, to eat a little at a time.

They looked for an opportunity to swim to freedom. On warm days, Dolan and Donohue bathed in the James, watching for one unguarded moment on the part of the guards. It never came. On October 10, a new influx of prisoners entered from battles around Petersburg.

After the Battle of Reams Station, John joined elements of several regiments under General Miles in an all-night retreat to Union lines. He entered the shed Pat had made comfortable while he was away. It felt empty. He tossed and couldn't sleep, worry running through his mind: "I can only hope Pat is alive. I saw a mass of hands go up when the rebs swarmed over them. I hope one was Pat's . . . I have to write Gram."

The siege of Petersburg continued. What remained of the Corcoran Legion was folded into other units occupying the front around Fort Stedman outside Petersburg.

Word came to John from Tipping that Pat, along with 2,000 others, had been captured and probably dispersed to prisons around Richmond.

Life in the defense line became more miserable through the fall. John did picket duty and repaired earthworks. It rained and rained. Rheumatic fever took hold of his joints once again. Supply wagons mired in the mud and rations did not reach them for days.

They foraged in the countryside. The first few days were glorious. They found farms with hogs, peaches, apples, potatoes, and brandy and whiskey. The sight of women, children, and old men begging, crying, and yelling at them left John shaken and guilt-ridden. He ate well for a few days and tried to stay busy in order to keep disturbing images out of mind.

Picked over and trampled farms yielded less and less. He grew weak as winter approached. Rebel deserters confessed that the Confederacy was not feeding its troops. He had only to look at them to see the truth of this. More were coming in every night, ragged and emaciated. John became depressed. For the first time since joining the army, he disobeyed army regulations and bought brandy from farmers. For the next week, he drank heavily to quell nightmares about a starving brother.

On Wednesday, October 12, guards walked through the prison camp, separated out 500 prisoners, and told them they were being transferred to Salisbury Prison, North Carolina. They ordered them to sit on the ground and wait for orders to march to the rail station. Gloom overtook Pat. He had regained a little strength from the fish they caught and was weighing ways to escape. He felt sure one would open any day.

"What do you think, can we lose ourselves in the crowd?" asked PM.

"The guards would shoot us before we took three steps," said Pat.

That night the whole prison was served salted codfish. PM cursed the commandant. "He knows what he's doing. This codfish will have us thirsting like we were in the middle of the Sahara."

"Yah, but what choice do we have?" said Pat. "This is the last food we'll see till Salisbury." Along with most of the other prisoners, they ate salted cod that night.

At 1:00 p.m. the next day, 500 marched under orders across the James River and formed four close columns. They continued on through the streets of Richmond. Downtown, guards stopped them. They stood over an hour exposed to cool temperatures, rain, and a jeering public. Men sagged to the ground.

Some fainted, falling heavily, among them David Smith. Pat and PM waited until a guard appeared next to them and then raised Smith to his feet. The guards ordered a march to the rail depot. There the prisoners were crowded so tightly onto rail cars they rode standing up.

Pat writhed in agony. He had known thirst before, but nothing like this. All around him, prisoners moaned and pounded on doors, begging for water. Guards, some touched by the prisoners' misery, others fearing a breakout, appealed to the engineer. The train stopped on the banks of the James and a few prisoners were sent to the edge with canteens. They lay face-down in the water and drank as much as they could and then brought water back to the others. Two days later, Saturday, October 15, weak and tormented by lack of food and water, the prisoners entered the gate of Salisbury Prison.

Salisbury Prison property was purchased by the Confederate government in 1861 for use as a military prison for disorderly Confederate soldiers and civilian Union sympathizers, as well as Union soldiers from the First Battle of Manassas and sailors captured on the North Carolina Outer Banks. The main building was a single brick structure, forty by one hundred feet, constructed as a cotton mill and abandoned ten years before the war.

During January 1864, Negroes had built a palisade stockade fence around a six-acre area that included the mill and a dozen smaller outbuildings to hold an influx of prisoners. Fifteen-foot-long logs were placed three feet into the ground. A platform was built three feet from the top on the outside of the palisade. There were thirteen sentry posts from which guards walked their beat day and night. Nine wells were scattered throughout the yard, but water was scarce and polluted. Inmates dug additional wells, only making matters worse as waste water drained into them and soon into all the wells.

At the northwest and northeast corners of the stockade, cannons guarded the interior space with the threat of canister shells. The guards dug a shallow trench called "the dead line" six feet inside the walls. Any prisoner who crossed that line was shot. The boundary was interpreted liberally by a few sadistic guards who shot prisoners for target practice. A new building, twenty by eighty feet and two stories high, was constructed to serve as a hospital. The prison was stiflingly hot in summer, bitterly cold in winter, and had virtually no ventilation.

Melancholia, panic, and determination to escape set in among the inmates as they learned from the guards that Grant had stopped all paroles and prisoner exchanges.

Confederate officials estimated camp capacity at 2,500. By October 1864, when Reams Station prisoners arrived, camp population rose to 5,000. About one third had tents. Wood was in short supply, so no cabins were built. The rest of the inmates lived outdoors and burrowed into the damp clay of that part of western North Carolina. They had only the clothing they were wearing when captured. Few had blankets. They slept in the holes side by side for warmth. Some, too sick to do otherwise, lay day and night on the open ground.

"Look at these men," PM muttered to Pat in disbelief. "This is about what we saw at Belle Isle and at Libby, an army of skeletons.

"They're not feeding them ... Mother of God ... those men are dead," PM continued as they marched by the dead house, an open building toward the front of the camp, to which the dead were dragged by other prisoners or Negroes.

Suddenly, their guards left them without a word. They were on their own to find shelter. That night the men received their first ration of gruel, a chunk of meat, and a potato. The men mixed the gruel with their daily cup of water and ate it like a gourmet meal; they were that hungry. The ground was wet and muddy from overnight rain and the stench of human waste piling up in open trenches near the walls assaulted their senses.

Dolan, Smith, Donohue, Kinnane, McGowan, Beasley, and Nolan had all made the march from Belle Isle. They sought out one another and made their way to a small area at the southeast tip of the stockade, where there were fewer prisoners. Four of them had half-tents and blankets wrapped around their waists under their pants. The seven scavenged for branches to lift the tent covers off the ground. They found none and spent half the first night wrapped in tent canvas and blankets, and then walked throughout the rest of the night when the cold drove them to their feet.

At 3:00 p.m. the second day, the guards distributed a half pound of gruel to each prisoner, but no water. The men gagged at first as they stuffed it in their mouths, then adjusted intake to a pinch at a time to let saliva catch up. They consumed every grain. Time was beginning to hang heavy. On the second night, the seven slept on the ground, again wrapped in tenting and blankets. Hundreds of prisoners had no covers and were compelled to walk during much of the night to keep warm. The six forced Smith to join them and had to hold and drag him around the perimeter of the prison.

By the third night, the six had hollowed out a hole four feet square with a case knife brought by Beasley and the jagged end of a branch. They dug a cave at one end of the hole sufficient for the seven of them to sleep, side-by-side, front end to rear end. Pat had ripped a loose board from the outside of the dead house for firewood when no guard was looking. Before they bedded down, he set it afire at the end of the cave over which a hole had been dug. Most of the smoke curled upward; some wafted back over the group.

To turn when a position could be endured no longer, one would order loud enough to be heard, "Turn left," and the seven would roll over onto their left sides. The ground was hard and cold. Smells of human waste drifted into their burrow.

Although he desperately craved rest, Pat lasted only halfway through the night. He struggled to his feet, bumping into PM, who slept in front of him, and went off on another tour of the prison. Confused and angry at the same time, he said a rosary and calmed down.

Salisbury Prison had no stream flowing through it. Waste flowed out of the camp into the nearby village of 2,400 people via a culvert dug by a squad of inmates overseen by a sergeant.

Sunday morning, October 16, dawned bright and clear. A light breeze caught revolting smells and floated them over the village of Salisbury. Villagers rose, angered by the stench, and formed a delegation to complain to the commandant. Church services were canceled.

Donohue remained with Smith and stood guard at their tent. Dolan, Kinnane, McGowan, Beasley, and Nolan walked around the camp seeking information.

"Soldier, can we talk to you for a minute?" asked McGowan. "What's your name?"

"Reg Price, 2nd Ohio, been here two months. Taken near Winchester."

"Who's the commandant here? What's he about?" asked Dolan.

"Major John H. Gee, the most inhumane bastard you'll ever meet."

He paused briefly and then continued. "One thing I warn you. You walk over the dead line, and they'll bury you the next morning. The young guys will shoot you without hesitation. The old guards are okay. They'll treat you like a man."

Dolan asked, "What about food and water? Do we get anything else but dust cakes?"

"Half the time we get a cornbread baked in the camp's new oven; sometimes a piece of meat served with maggots or a potato turning green. Otherwise, it's a dust cake, if anything at all."

He stopped talking for a moment and looked across the yard. Then he continued. "The only guys who stay alive are the ones who learn to trade for food."

"Who do you trade with and with what?" asked McGowan.

"The trick," explained Price, "is to join details that go out for water or wood. Be near when the guards are looking for volunteers. Civilians line the way to the creek and the woods, looking to trade souvenirs for food."

"Like what?" asked Dolan.

"Like a ring made out of rubber combs or your uniform buttons, any little keepsake."

Price nodded off and Dolan and McGowan went back to the tent to relay what he had said to Donohue and Smith. They stood around talking and picking lice off their clothes. The prisoners nicknamed it "skirmishing." It was the only way for prisoners to get rid of lice, as there were no pots to boil their clothes in.

At 1:00 p.m., the guards meted out the day's ration, dry meal—they had run out of bread—sorghum, no meat, no potato. That day the men made "Johnnie cakes" over a fire on flat rocks borrowed from other prisoners.

Pat had piles so bad they were like pebbles to his touch. He cried with pain when he walked. Wild thoughts of attacking guards rampaged through his mind. PM walked him slowly through the camp, calming him. "If the group is to survive, Patrick, you have to work with us and stay calm."

Smith had dysentery and pneumonia. Most of the time, he slept when he wasn't leaning his rear end over the "sink," as the latrine trench was called. He coughed till he lost his breath and gasped for air. Then he caught his breath and coughed again. The coughs were dry, but then he spit out wads of green phlegm and his coughing subsided.

The day was moderately warm, for which the men thanked heaven.

The next day, October 17, with trust built with neighboring inmates from New York, the six set out for the marketplace on the east side of the camp. Prisoners well enough to walk gathered there to exchange rumors and trinkets they made the day before. Donohue watched as a guard and an inmate bargained over a Bible carved from a bone.

"You're crappin' me, soldier, if you think I'd give this Bible to you for so little. As starved and miserable as I am," said the inmate, "I'll wait until I get a job on the outside."

"Look, Yank, you won't ever get out again, weak as you are. You can't carry a cup of water or a twig."

In time, the guard doubled his offer and the prisoner took it. Pat and the rest soon understood how the barter system worked.

As they walked through the camp, misery assaulted their senses. Wretched creatures lay sleeping against buildings or sprawled around holes, lice and flies picking at their faces. These men had lost all hope and desire except one: the desire to die.

PM said to his partners, "You can see what our lot is if we don't stay together. You can't lose hope. We're brothers and we can't forget it. None of that Buffalo versus New York shit!"

That night before falling asleep, the six compared notes, a practice they promised to repeat every night thereafter.

Smith lay in silence except to cough. Twice his coughing was so hard he woke up the whole group.

Kinnane spoke up. "We have to make something and find people to trade with. We'll volunteer for as many jobs as we can. We need tools to work with, too."

"That's it," agreed McGowan. "Another thing . . . The rebel convicts and Union deserters are stronger than the rest of us. Probably get a little more food and water. They come out like ghouls at night to rob the weaker Yanks lying off by themselves. We'll teach them not to come our way."

"You're right," said Pat. "Tie one up and stick something up his arse. Dump him outside the rebel barracks. They'll get the point."

"Yah, and it's not just rebs. Some of ours would steal from their own mothers," said Nolan. "We got to teach them the same lesson."

"I agree," said Beasley. "But what skills do we have? We're dumb chaws who never done nothin' but day labor in our lives."

Kinnane piped up. "I have an idea. Me and Magowan could paint small rocks with our names and regiment numbers."

"That might work," agreed PM. "There's only one place to find paint—the carpentry shop where they make furniture for the administration. I used to help my uncles make wagons and cabinets."

The next day, Dolan attached himself to a skilled carpenter from Salem, Massachusetts. In two days, he filched a drill, a bit, a clamp, a small piece of canvas, and red and black paints he carried out in broken canteen pieces. In the meantime, Donohue and McGowan volunteered as water carriers and filled their pockets at the creek with flat rocks no bigger than three inches across. Kinnane and Magowan were now in business and began to turn out a dozen brightly colored souvenirs a day. The water bearers carried a couple each on their trips to fetch water or wood and found a steady market. They brought back cornbread, yams, and an occasional piece of bacon. As miserable as the men were, they were eating better than most of the prisoners.

That night it rained steadily. The next morning the men crawled from their hole, coughing from deep in their lungs. Smith spent the day wrapped in blankets, shivering out in the sun where the men had dragged him.

CHAPTER 15

First Hatcher's Run

On Thursday, October 27, the 20,000 men of Hancock's 2nd Corps occupied the southwest section of the Union line surrounding Petersburg. The Appomattox River, which divided the city, formed its left flank and the Jerusalem Plank Road its right flank. The 155th was bivouacked near Fort Dushane, toward the middle of the 2nd Corps sector. Augmented by returning sick and wounded, it numbered 130 men. Company I had 20 men. Ideally, regiments numbered 800 to 1,000 and companies 80 to 100.

Second Corps moved out at 3:30 a.m. in a battle plan suggested by Meade to Grant, whose purpose was to tighten the ring around Petersburg by seizing the Boydton Plank Road and further cutting the city's supply line by capturing the South Side Railroad. The role of 2nd Corps was to outflank the Confederate line at Burgess's Mill over Hatchers Run, and march on to occupy the South Side Railroad. Their objective depended on a link-up with General Warren's 5th Corps.

At Burgess' Mill, Hancock found a well-entrenched enemy led by General Heth positioned on the west side of Hatcher's Run, overlooking Burgess's Mill and the bridge over the run. Confederate General Hampton's cavalrymen had dammed the creek days before and flooded the low-lying area on the east side of the run. If 2nd Corps men wanted to make their way north toward the railroad, they would have to wade across a flooded area and charge over a very narrow bridge. Meanwhile, three rebel brigades were driving from the rear under the command of General William Mahone to augment Heth's force. Warren's 5th Corps was nowhere to be found.

Shots sounded in the woods toward mid-morning to the north and east as Union pickets fired and ran from onrushing rebels. The 2nd Corps line had been outflanked on two sides and was now being attacked from what had been the rear.

New orders quickly came to company commanders to form a square a mile across in order to be able to fire in all directions. Two thousand men from Mahone's brigades burst through Hancock's right flank and into the square from the east. Second Division regiments closed in around the rebel brigades with a fierceness born of self-preservation. Mahone's brigades, sensing the trap, turned and rammed their way back out of the square.

Throughout the afternoon, Mahone's and Hampton's brigades slammed through Union lines only to find themselves beset from all sides. During intervals of rebel reorganization, Hancock's men rushed to build interior lines of logs and earth to avoid artillery and mortar fire from both Yankees and Confederates.

When attacks came, Hancock's soldiers crisscrossed the square to meet them wherever on the square they came. For three hours, the fighting raged as rebel regiments carried out assault after assault to exploit the advantage they were sure was theirs, fighting with the confidence and abandon of certain victors. Hancock's men held their position.

Tipping, seeing the situation before hearing orders, prompted his squad to be ready to about-face and fire. He had the best marksmen firing and the rest reloading to achieve maximum effect.

Toward the end of the day, a minie bullet tore into Sergeant Tipping and he slumped to the ground. John and the rest of the squad surrounded their beloved leader. They shook their heads in disbelief, anger, and disgust. Their sergeant had always seemed invulnerable to enemy fire. Blood was pouring from his left side. His face was ashen and his body limp.

After a day's engagement, Southern commanders pulled their troops from the field. Stillness descended upon Union forces. That night at 10:00 p.m., fearing a resumption of the Confederate attack, Hancock ordered a hasty retreat eastward to the main Union lines. Wounded men, guns, wagons, and horses lay in its wake.

John grabbed a loose horse. With help from Mooney, he loaded Tipping's body face down across the saddle. All that night, John led the horse through mud and brush back to their main encampment. He lifted the body into his tent and fell asleep.

The next morning, as soon as reveille sounded, John went for Father Gillen. He and Mooney raised the body onto a triangular ambulance wagon. Mooney led a procession of Tipping's old squad in sad silence to a knoll overlooking the James River where they had dug a grave. Father Gillen said the Catholic graveside prayers and they buried their friend.

Hundreds of still, crumpled blue and grey uniforms were left behind guarding Boydton Plank Road and Burgess's Mill, two of Confederate General Wade Hampton's sons among them. More than 1,000 of the 1,728 Union soldiers who died there were supplied by 2nd Corps. Nineteen men of the 155th died on the field. George Tipping was the lone soldier from Company I to meet his fate. After the burial, John went on picket duty. Lying behind a tree, he cried.

Two days later, John wrote Catherine Tipping a brief but heartfelt letter of condolence.

On Saturday, November 5, the prisoners at Salisbury were divided into groups of 1,000 men led by a sergeant major and squads of 100 men with a first sergeant in charge of each squad. Each sergeant was to report the presence or absence of the men in his squad and draw down their rations. As Beasley and Donohue were dragging up a corpse from two holes west of them to the dead house, an old plot wrote another chapter in Donohue's mind.

"Jimmie, we used to vote the dead in the Ward and pick up a few bucks. We kept them on the voting rolls long after we planted them. Why not keep the dead in a cool hole for a day before we drag them to the dead house? Then we'll gain a second day by having our squad leader wait a day to hand in their names. We draw the rations of two extra men."

Beasley went to the sergeant in charge of their squad and explained Donohue's plot. The sergeant liked the idea. Over the next weeks, twenty dead men helped feed their comrades.

The seven shared equally whatever food Kinnane's and Magowan's souvenirs brought in trade. Still, the conditions of the camp and the onset of winter weather drained their bodies and spirits. Their clothes were rags held together by string torn from canvas. Sleeping underground exposed them to the ravages of dampness and cold. Melancholia weighed heavily on all the men in the camp as every day they saw ten or twenty men dragged to the dead house.

Word swirled through the camp that the prisoners would soon be paroled. The men took heart, believing Grant had changed his policy. As days dragged on with no paroles, they realized it was just a rumor.

Pat walked daily through a wing of the main building, converted to use as a hospital, where he saw sick and poorly clad soldiers lying on straw on the floor, vermin crawling on them. Some men were too weak to slap the lice from their faces. Blankets were scarce. No medicine was available to control dysentery, the leading cause of death. Watching his fellow soldiers die from disease bored into Pat's head and left a permanent memory. There was not enough water for the nurses to wash their patients and no brooms or brushes to clean the floors.

Many patients were coiled up waiting to die in their holes or out in the open. Healthier prisoners visited friends to provide whatever comfort they could. Nurses drawn from among inmates returned to sleep with the rest of the prisoners. Pneumonia, typhoid, cholera, tetanus, tuberculosis, and smallpox raged through the camp like apocalyptic plagues. Almost every prisoner had dysentery.

Out of the blue, a guard approached Pat with a package from Gram that contained a variety of sausages, dried fruits and vegetables, and coffee. Pat ran back to his group to share his newfound bounty. Within an hour, the contents were gone. It was a miracle, they all agreed: "A package from heaven just when they needed something to heal their bodies and lift their spirits." Twenty other men received packages sent by their families through the Sanitary Commission. It was the first time such packages were released by the commandant.

Three of the six competed with other prisoners to haul water and wood. Since they were among the stronger, they were chosen to cut down pine trees in the nearby woods. They loaded small logs on flat cars that carried them to the northwest corner of the stockade. There, the logs were unloaded and dragged inside. Each squad was allowed to keep the amount of wood three men could carry.

Pat dug up blackberry roots, thought to be a remedy for diarrhea, according to what Gram had told him when he was a kid. The three poured a few pails of water into a barrel, all they could carry. Two men extended a pole through holes in the barrel and carried it back to the prison on their shoulders. What they brought had to make do for 100 men.

Along the way to the woods and creek, civilians continued to trade sweet potatoes and cornbread for Yankee souvenirs.

On November 13, another load of "fresh fish" arrived—about 300 colored soldiers and 1,200 white. Guards stripped the coloreds of almost every bit of clothing, including blankets and coats, and left them naked to the weather. Salisbury now held almost 10,000 inmates.

On November 15, word came through an older guard that Lincoln had been reelected. The news spread as though on a breeze. Cheers rang out from all sides of the yard.

On November 25, a rebel relief column of sixteen Senior Reserve guards entered the stockade at noon. A group of prisoners attacked the column with clubs and disarmed the guards. Three of the guards were killed, eight to ten slightly wounded. One thousand inmates then rushed the main gate in an effort to reach the arsenal. Few got beyond the gate. The Reserve guards' guns held only one bullet each. The remaining guards and two cannons fired upon the insurgents.

Soldiers from the 68th North Carolina Regiment who had just left their station at the prison were waiting for a train to transport them to their new assignment. They rushed back a short distance to the stockade and joined in the murderous fire. Sixteen prisoners were killed and sixty others wounded.

Pat and his friends remained in their burrow waiting to see which way the revolt went. Besides, they had other plans.

The aftermath of the revolt was worse than the revolt itself. Rations were reduced. Frail men soon began dying in twice the average daily number. Ultimately, about 250 men died because of the attempted escape.

CHAPTER 16

Escape

Nights in November, Pat dug a tunnel with twenty men who believed escape was the only way to survive. They chose as their starting point a cave in an area of the yard pocked with underground warrens and facing a woods fifty feet beyond the north wall.

The diggers worked around the clock, taking turns to create an opening about forty-eight inches in diameter that ran diagonally down and then once beyond the wall diagonally up. The clay was damp and solid, which, while difficult to dig, provided some safety from cave-in. They raised the dirt to the campground, where others spread it thinly into the mud, which was already red with the dirt dug from inmate holes.

The greatest danger of discovery came from other prisoners. A bribe of double rations and Confederate money to use in the sutler shop was being offered to turn in those digging tunnels. When one of the other prisoners did, guards investigated, but not always in time to catch the perpetrators, who abandoned the unfinished tunnels without a moment's hesitation. To be caught trying to escape was to be punished with withdrawal of rations, heavy work wearing a ball and chain, or being lashed with a cat-o-nine tails upon a bare back.

Conditions in the tunnel were extreme. The work was inherently strenuous and done in cramped quarters. Most of the excavation was done with a case knife and a piece of tree limb for a mallet. Workers tunneled around large rocks and tree stumps. Fortunately for them, there were relatively few. Tunnels expanded an average of six feet a day.

Of the six, only Pat dug the tunnel, so the rest could remain free to make souvenirs, fend for food and water, and care for Smith. Pat's health had deteriorated in spite of the extra food he received. He was able to dig the hard clay for only thirty minutes at a spell. Nonetheless, he took extra shifts. He found the exercise raised his body temperature and overcame the cold, which otherwise numbed his hands and feet.

When the tunnel was done on November 30, one of the inmates, driven by starvation, reported the escape plot to a guard.

Pat lay quietly in their hole, exhausted and frustrated. The guards had not caught him, only because he was not yet in the tunnel when the guards entered and because he was unknown to the betrayer. Those caught were forced into hard labor with scant rations. More than half died as a result.

The next morning, Pat returned from water duty and told the rest: "The guards and the locals are willing to pay more for our painted rocks. The word is the South will surrender soon and we'll be sent home."

Dolan said he heard the same thing in the carpentry shop. "It must be true. One of the guards gave me paint and an awl. He looked the other way and I made off with leather and a drill that Kinny says he can use to make watch fobs."

Kinnane's artistry steadily improved, but his health, along with that of his mates and the rest of the prisoners, was steady declining. By mid-December, the prisoner exchange rumor was dead. On Saturday, December 12, Pat made his usual rounds: the market place, the dead house, and the various regimental clusters. Kinnane took a break from souvenir making to walk with him. They passed the area inhabited by colored soldiers, who were lying stripped and motionless. Pat grimaced at the sight and he shook his head. One dead colored soldier's body was crawling with large white maggots.

He was silent for a moment; then muttered, "Let's get out of here."

As they continued their tour, they grew depressed at the sight of men breaking out with scurvy, red marks covering their necks; others moaned, unable to move because of Dengue Fever.

On December 13, Smith died. His mates said a "Hail Mary" and an "Our Father" over him, mumbled a few platitudes about his being in a better place, and dragged his body into the cool hole for a day. Then they carried him to the dead house and waited for the burial squad. They asked that he not be stripped and that he be buried by himself at the north end of the trench.

Later in the month, Kinnane, Pat, and a large group of immigrant Irish Catholics met a priest at the main gate. Father Custis, a chaplain appointed by the Confederate War Department to minister to Roman Catholic soldiers throughout the South, was the only clergyman who ever visited the prison. "Father, have you got anything for us?" asked Kinnane.

"I've got a few rosaries. Would you like one?"

"We would, to be sure," said Pat. "But, Father, can't you do anything about the conditions of this camp? We're all dying here. Most of us will never see our families."

"There is nothing I can do about camp conditions. The Confederate government has asked me to persuade you to join the Confederate Army. They call it 'galvanizing.' They'll give you a bonus and guarantee you $100 Confederate a month.

"If you won't take their offer, all I can say is let me bless you and remind you that the Lord Jesus suffered the worst pain ever known to mankind. Put yourself in His hands and He will help you bear your terrible conditions."

"Thanks a lot, Father," said Pat and Kinnane contemptuously. Pat was by this time even more bent on escaping.

Two hundred men did take an oath of loyalty to the Confederate government and quickly left the camp.

By December 20, a team of prisoners that included Pat finished another tunnel close to where they had dug the first. They had been at the exhausting work for two weeks in the dead of night in claustrophobic and dangerous confines.

On Saturday, December 24, in the middle of the night, PM and Pat wished their mates well, telling them they would see them again once they were all free. Fear and loss of companionship threatened their resolve to escape. They quickly left the hole and joined twenty others in the tunnel before they changed their minds. PM had prepared a pouch containing a pound of gruel, a flint stone, and a small, sharp-edged piece of iron. The two had discussed what they would do once free of the prison, but mostly they just wanted to get as far away as fast as possible and not to leave a scent trail. The rest of their crew remained behind in case the two were captured. If they weren't, they would dig a tunnel and attempt to escape, which was looked on by all six comrades as the only option other than death.

Once above ground outside the prison wall, they stood motionless until they heard a guard pass. As quietly as they could, they made their way through the small woods and out into the village. No one was stirring as they hurried down the main street and beyond.

An hour into their escape, Pat and PM heard dogs barking. Hoping to link up with Unionist civilians who were helping runaways escape into Tennessee, they found a stream they imagined flowed northwesterly. An overcast sky precluded any certainty. Fear of being traced by the bloodhounds kept them in the water for some time. When PM sensed it was safe, they left the creek bed and trudged on, faster than before in an effort to overcome frostbite and raise their body temperature. A steady rain washed away any scent they might have left.

Both men wore kepi caps and extra blouses they had taken from dead inmates. Their pants were wet. They were cold and weak from hunger and shivering uncontrollably. Driven on by fear and tension, they took a side road that crossed the creek. As day broke with heavy cloud cover, they moved off the road into woods keeping the road in view. Once again, they picked up their pace.

Pat sighed. "Hopefully we run across a farm along this road and either knock at the door or hit the chicken coop. I can't go on much longer without food."

PM rubbed his cheek before giving his opinion. "I say we look for a lamb or a calf in a pasture out of sight of any farm house."

"Sounds better to me. I wonder what direction we're going?" asked Pat.

"Northwest or we need a new plan," replied PM.

Silently, the men plodded along. Hours after the breakout, their pace slowed as their strength waned. After walking and stumbling another two miles, they came out of the woods facing a pasture laced with knolls, swales, and rocks. A few sheep grazed lazily in the midday sun. PM pointed to a lamb standing beside a ewe a hundred yards or so off in a meadow.

"I say we rest a while," said PM, "and then club that lamb and drag it off into the woods. You head for the ewe and I'll take the lamb. But first, I got to get a club."

After a short rest, Dolan found a thick branch about the size of his arm, broke off its small limbs, and away they went across the field. The ewe began to bleat as they approached. Somewhere in the distance, a hound bayed.

The plan worked. PM and Pat lumbered through the woods with the slaughtered lamb. After a quarter mile or so, Pat stopped to catch his breath. "I think we can cut up the lamb and roast it."

"Not a good idea, Pat. I'm starvin' the same as you, but I say we rest a minute and then keep moving until just before nightfall. We make camp, and only then eat the lamb."

They struggled on, taking turns carrying the lamb for several more hours before stopping. Veering deeper into the woods, they gathered enough kindling to last the night and built a fire. They pulled apart the lamb and used the iron used to start the fire. They roasted it and ate ravenously.

"Oh God, I haven't felt warm in months," said Pat. "That heat feels so good."

"Yah, me too," replied PM. "Let's see if we can keep it burning through the night." Heat even on one side of their bodies was a luxury and made them almost forget their many other discomforts.

After piling heavy branches on the fire, they fell asleep, huddled beside one another on the ground. Soon both began to toss and turn with aching stomachs. They had eaten too much too fast. Their bellies angrily protested. They piled more wood on the embers and waved a shirt over the pile until the wood caught fire, then rested against the nearby trees.

"Well, what do we do if we've been going northeast instead of northwest?" asked Pat.

"Probably gone too far not to keep on moving in the same direction. We got to find a railroad heading north. We been lucky so far, but it can't last forever, Pat."

"Agreed. We won't find Unionists in plantation country. So there's no other way to avoid the secesh if we've been going northeast."

The next morning, they rose to a cloudy day but with the sun clearly visible. Both men knew instantly they had been traveling northeast. "Well, Pat, that settles it," PM said, pointing to the sun. "Now we have to find a stream flowing northeast or at least due north. You agree?"

"You see it the same as I do, PM."

At the sound of hounds baying from the south, they each grabbed a leg of the lamb off the green spits they had suspended above the fire and wrapped them in the lower part of their shirts, which they tucked into their pants. Stiff from the cold Carolina December night they had endured without cover, they disguised the site and moved away from the sound of the hounds as quickly as weak legs could carry them, traveling north.

The woods bent to their right. They came across a creek, but they reckoned it was heading east. They walked another hour. The baying grew louder. They began running and soon crossed a second creek, wider than the first and flowing north. They jumped from rock to rock or gravel, where possible, and made their way upstream. The baying continued as before. They dragged on, slower and slower, cold and wet, pain searing their feet and legs throughout the day. As the sun faded, the baying stopped. An air of confidence returned and they slowed even more.

That night, deep in woods, they made a fire and feasted again on roast lamb. This time they ate more deliberately, savoring every bite.

The next morning, Pat talked about their situation. "Our chances ain't good. By now, the word has gone out to be looking for twenty Yankees. They've all got hounds for hunting, so what's the answer? Maybe we have to take a chance. Find a friendly person that'll help us."

PM mused, "There must be women living alone or with their kids, 'cause their men are off in the rebel army. I say if we come upon a house, we see if we can find a woman to help us. If we find a river flowing north, we make a raft and float to freedom." With a small stick, he made a few aimless lines in the soft soil. "If we come upon a train moving north, we hop on without being seen. Has to be a supply train, no guards on the last car, one with food and supplies."

"That says it all. Let's go," said Pat.

Later that day, they approached a hamlet. They continued to the far side until they came to an isolated house and hid in the woods with the house in full view. A low barn stood off a few paces behind the house. Alongside the barn, a vegetable garden lay fallow, two rows of old corn stalks standing stiffly against a light breeze. Beyond them, a single cow grazed in a hilly meadow. Chickens and ducks ran freely in the garden and barnyard. A turkey appeared from the far side of the barn, chased by two boys.

A thirtyish woman, short, thin, with scraggly dark hair, came out to bring up carrots and potatoes from a root cellar under the barn. A collie stood by and began to chase the boys, who were still tormenting the turkey. The woman went back in the house, apparently to cook dinner. The boys and the dog soon followed.

Pat whispered, "She appears to be living alone with her boys."

PM cautioned, "Let's wait a few minutes to see if anyone else comes out of the house."

A few minutes later, the two men approached the door. The collie bared its teeth, barked, and then growled furiously. The woman answered the door with her boys behind her, a shotgun held across her chest and fear spreading across her face.

"What do yuh want? Who are y'all?" she asked, staring at the shaking skeletons before her.

PM spoke softly. "Ma'am, we're Yankee prisoners of war." He watched the woman's face before saying more. Her expression did not alter.

With eyes narrowed to slits, the woman asked, "You from Salisbury?"

PM hesitated before answering. Almost instantly he realized, where else would they have been prisoners? "Yes, ma'am."

The woman remained stone-faced.

Dolan swallowed and looked down at his feet before continuing. The men took off their hats and bowed toward the woman. "Will you help us? We ain't going to hurt you. We're Irish men and have great respect for the Mother of God and all women."

For a few tense seconds, the three stood silent. Pat wanted to look at PM but kept his gaze on the woman, who was beginning to swing her gun toward them.

Finally, the woman lowered her gun and answered, "You may come in. Y'all put me in a bad way. My husband is two years dead, killed by a Yankee bullet at Malvern Hill. I am a loyal daughter of the South. But I am also a Christian woman."

"Ma'am, we won't stay but a day or two and we'll do what we can to help out as a man should," said Pat. The boys backed away and stood at a distance as the men entered.

Later that evening as they repaired a broken barn door, PM remarked, "The woman is boarding us when she and her boys are on the edge of starvation themselves ... Did you hear her tell her boys we were Yankee soldiers and they should stay clear of us? She warned them to say nothing about us or they'd all be killed by the militia."

For two days, the men stayed with the woman, whose name they learned was Miriam, and her two boys, ages ten and eleven, in the tiny hamlet of Springstead, near Franklin. The house was small, sparsely furnished, and badly in need of work. In return for food and shelter, Pat and PM worked inside the house and barn, plugging gaps around windows and doing other small repairs. She gave them some of her husband's clothes, which they accepted gratefully, especially the two jackets and fresh underwear, as the weather had turned colder. What they were wearing was unfit to be used as rags.

When the boys wanted to visit a neighbor's children, their mother told them, "You'd best remain to home." They watched the men work and began to help, fetching tools and finding nails and screws. Evenings, they ate dinner together and afterward in front of the fireplace, the men played jacks with the boys, who protested when their mother told them it was bedtime. The men were tense throughout their stay for fear a neighbor would wander in, but their hearts were touched by a home life they had not known in two years.

In the small barn with a goat, a sow, and five piglets for company, they threw padded comforters beneath and over themselves and slept one against the other in the hayloft.

The second day, the men showed the boys how to repair window sashes and holes in the walls of the house. Their mom watched, unsure that she approved of their growing relationship, but grateful that her boys in some small way were learning the role of men of the house.

By the time they left, the four males were at ease working and playing together. Pat felt he and PM had made up in a small way for the terrible loss of their father. Miriam smiled politely in their company, but said little as though the less she knew of them, the better she would be with nosy neighbors. At table, the men asked about Confederate army installations in the area, how active the local militia was, and other questions that would cue them on what to avoid. The boys started to answer, but their mother quickly interrupted and shut off the conversation. She reminded them that they were to say nothing to neighbors about the Yankee visitors or she would be beaten, tarred and feathered by both neighbors and militia.

The third day, the men thanked Miriam for her hospitality. She asked how they knew her name. Pat answered that one of the boys told them. In fact, PM had casually lifted an envelope with her name and address on it from the fireplace and put it in his pocket. Miriam gave each a biscuit, a chicken leg, and directions to the nearest north/south railroad and they left before sun-up.

The two felt stronger, their symptoms of dysentery and scurvy somewhat lessened. They were now some thirty miles north of Salisbury, she had told them.

After two days of stumbling through tangled woods and swamps adjacent to the road, they came upon the North Carolina Railroad running between Atlanta and Richmond.

"Pat, we'll find the right train, but we have to be patient. We need some food before we get on a flat car. It may be two days to Petersburg. I say we try to find another friendly widow before we hop a freight train."

The two walked until they found a small clearing in the middle of the forest, where they made a fire, ate the last of what Miriam had given them, and plotted their next move.

Pat said to PM, "Hungry as we are, the right thing was to stop and think. We got to have food before we continue our grand tour of the South." They fell asleep much as they had the night before, getting as close to the fire as they could.

Awakening within two hours, the men built up the fire again and talked as they walked around it.

"PM, there's something different about the farms we passed toward the end of the day, yesterday. They were larger . . . plantations, they call them."

"Yah, I see where you're going. We saw colored people in the fields who might help us."

"Well, they just might. They hate their owners and are the first to run off, I hear."

Pat and PM fell back into an uneasy sleep. At first light, the two set off, hidden from view but close enough to fields to survey them. After a half-day's walk still in woods, PM saw several colored men and women laboring in a distant field.

They hid themselves next to the field, stomachs grumbling again, until it seemed safe to approach one of the field hands.

With light steps, they made their way through the woods that ringed the field until they came to a spot close to some colored men digging out rotted tobacco plants. After what seemed an eternity to two starving men, one of the colored men left the group and headed in their direction. They were about to run when he stopped at the edge of the woods, opened his trousers, and peed. Dolan called out to him in a low voice. At first, the young man stood dead still and stared at them. They were dressed like Southerners, but seemed different. They were wearing kepi hats, not something he had seen before. He walked over and took down his pants as if to relieve himself.

"Yuh not from aroun' dese parts."

Pat and PM nodded, smiling. "We're Union soldiers escaped from Salisbury prison. Can you help us?"

"Stay here and I be back come dark."

With that, he pretended to wipe his rear with leaves, pulled up his pants, and ambled nonchalantly away.

Pat suggested, "Let's move away from the edge of this field to a safer place where we can hide for the rest of the day."

Dolan marked the spot so they could find it again by hanging a branch several feet up a tree. "Good idea. That darkie knows the area. We don't."

Some distance away, they came across two large fallen trees and hid between them. Saying little and taking turns sleeping, the two men spent an anxious afternoon in fear of betrayal. As the sun dipped in the sky, they crawled out from their temporary shelter and waited at the spot PM had marked.

The sun disappeared, taking with it the day's warmth. There was no moon. They scanned the field anxiously for the colored man.

"I can't see shit," Pat complained.

PM looked up. "At least the night's clear. The stars are out."

"I still can't see shit."

"Would we see 'im, anyway?" PM joked.

Almost at that moment, the man appeared. He held a small burlap bag and handed it to the two white men. Pat opened it and found carrots and potatoes and a skinned rabbit.

Pat and PM thanked him profusely. They knew this poor man risked being tortured and lynched in order to help them.

The man nodded, but said little. Pat asked if they were close to railroad tracks. The man pointed to their right. "That way," he said. "Not too far."

Without another word, he turned away from them.

That evening, they savored their feasts, stomachs no longer complaining, but saved some grilled leftovers for the next day. They found the railroad, slept beneath a trestle in the cold and damp, and rose before first light. Grateful for the jackets and woolen long underwear, they said a prayer again for Miriam, and for the slave and the food he had brought them.

"Let's find a grade where the trains slow and where we can hide until the right one comes," said Pat.

They stored the leftover food in the burlap bag and, keeping the track in sight, they walked for a long distance. Then they stood behind trees, watching a steady procession of trains moving north. Guards on the first and last cars afforded no opportunity to board. Pat and PM munched on carrots, but saved the rest. Toward nightfall, a long freight train approached at less than ten miles an hour. It was guarded by a few older men standing in a railcar behind the engine.

"This is the one," said Pat, and they both jumped to their feet. They crouched, ran to the rear of the train, and crossed to the other side. Seeing no guards at this end, they leaped onto a flatbed carrying crates of ammunition bundled in rubber tarps. The train moved slowly up the grade. Loosening one end of a tarp, they crawled under it. Rejoicing at the warmth, they thanked the Lord for their good fortune. They were on the road to freedom.

"I'm guessing this train supplies Lee's army in Petersburg," observed PM. "We could have a quick ride. If you remember, we were put on sidings every time an army supply train was coming through ... Cut a piece from this tarp. We may need it tonight."

In less than a day, the supply train was outside Petersburg where it stopped for another train broken down just ahead of it.

"I say we get off here and hide close by in some woods. This area is looking familiar," said PM.

The two men were elated, believing they were within a few miles of a Union line. About dusk, the train jolted forward, and the men jumped off as it slowed to climb a grade.

They moved into woods and hiked until darkness swallowed their path. They ate the last of the food provided by the field hand and again blessed him for helping them. Fearing a fire would be seen or smelled by rebel pickets, they did not light one, but fell asleep wrapped in the piece of rubber tarp, until the cold of the night roused them. They marched in place or propped themselves against trees until the sun began to rise. Then, using their hands as bowls, they poured the gruel from their pouches and licked it. With the sun at their backs, they strode off in search of the Union line.

The first people they encountered were some twenty colored men, women, and children in a field. Two women carried infants. Like Pat and PM, they too were searching for the Union Army.

"You know where the Union Army is?" asked PM.

"We heerd it be just beyond that road over yonder, but we also heerd the 'Federate cav'ry is round here, too."

The words were hardly out of the man's mouth when a Confederate cavalry troop appeared from over a hill. The colored women screamed and the group scattered.

The two Northern escapees bent low and ran along a fence rail. The rebels were much more interested in them than the blacks. They had been as visible in the crowd of black faces as fire in the dark. In the face of drawn weapons, Pat and PM quickly threw up their arms.

The Confederates took them a few hundred yards into a rebel encampment, bound their hands and feet, and left a single soldier to guard them. Later that same day, two cavalrymen returned and took off Pat's ropes. Pat and PM shouted good luck and God bless at one another as Pat was herded away.

The Confederates prodded Pat in the back with every step until he jumped onto a train heading southeast with a dozen Yankee prisoners, who had been given no water or rations since capture. When the train stopped alongside a creek, they were allowed to get off under guard. Pat knelt and drank at will. He thought, *God knows what punishment PM will get if he returns to Salisbury. We were so close to Union lines. I can hear John saying, "The war is almost over. Don't do anything stupid!"*

Feelings of loss at being separated from his best friend, anger at his misfortune, and fear of the unknown all swirled around in him as he lay silently against the wall of the car. Soon he became curious about the other prisoners, more recently captured than he, better dressed, and more physically fit. He spent the next twenty-four hours exchanging stories and dozing.

Early on Saturday, December 31, the train arrived in Florence, South Carolina. Local militia of the 5th Georgia Infantry Regiment met twelve Yankee prisoners at the station and marched them in tight formation four abreast from the depot down a long mud road.

A few fell and the younger guards cursed and kicked them or beat them with rifle butts until other prisoners stood them up. Those who staggered were prodded with gun butts until they fell and then the guards beat them, laughing and shouting every form of blasphemy and taunt. A rising sun tantalized the prisoners while crisp cold air invaded their scantily clad bodies.

Pat walked with mixed emotions. He was glad to stretch his legs and exercise his body, but he was weak and tiring fast. Twice he wanted to face off against sadistic guards, but could only muster the strength to take the next step and the next and the next. A few farmers stood in front of their homes and shouted to the guards, "Slap the damn Yankees a good one" . . . "Jab 'em in the balls." Otherwise, the streets were deserted along the half mile to the prison.

After going through intake outside the main gate, Pat commented to the prisoner alongside him as they looked around the camp, seeing thousands of enlisted men in blue standing about or sitting in the dirt, "Well, there'll be no tunneling out of this place. Did you see the ditch they dug around the stockade?"

Indeed, the prison was a twenty-three-acre walled encampment, finished on the fly. As at Salisbury, the dead line was clearly marked by a line of boards the inmates were not to cross, otherwise they would be shot.

Florence Stockade Prison had 10,000 Union prisoners, swelling in number daily. Sherman's march through Georgia was thought by Confederate officials to have Andersonville Prison in his path, so its prisoners were being transferred to Florence and Columbia, South Carolina. The day was cool, but sunny. Prisoners were lying about, walking listlessly, or digging shelters in the ground. Many men in Pat's immediate line of sight appeared near death. Conditions here, he judged, were worse than at Salisbury.

Guards appeared from time to time. The prison was loosely organized: three dozen old men and boys, commanded by two officers, and deployed in two shifts.

Pat received the daily ration, a cup of water and a cup of gruel with a tablespoon of molasses or sorghum. He mixed and ate it slowly before a guard ordered him to join a water detail.

As the water brigade trudged to a creek outside the prison gate, Pat introduced himself to another prisoner. "Sergeant, tell me about yourself; how long you been here?" he asked.

"Sergeant William Trasker, 134th Illinois, captured two weeks ago in Georgia fighting with Sherman." Trasker was a broad-shouldered farmer whose frame no longer filled out his uniform. "Let me tell you, the guards are not to be messed with, especially the young ones. Some of the older guards are okay." He hesitated as a guard staring at the two caught his eye. "No one is eating around here, guards, locals, or us. Twenty to thirty men die each day and are thrown into a trench over yonder. If you can make a decent-looking souvenir you can sell it to the guards or outside when you're on detail."

"What's the deal on escaping, Bill? Seems like it could be done fairly easily when you're outside the walls."

"Well, Sherman is heading up the coast from Savannah. If I were to escape, I would head for Charleston and join the Union Army there. I'll tell you though . . . you got about 100 miles to walk. This state is secesh end to end. It wasn't the first state to secede for nothin'.'"

Wrapped in a pup tent, Pat slept with Trasker the first night in Trasker's hole, which they had enlarged, digging with broken tree branches all afternoon. The next morning, he walked among the prisoners, asking questions. As he hauled water for an hour, he saw several civilians asking prisoners if they had souvenirs to trade and concluded that the market for Yankee-made handwork was about the same as at Salisbury.

"If I get the materials and a few small tools and you get the stones, we're in business," Pat told Trasker with renewed enthusiasm.

"Yah, you're probably right, Pat. Our chances are good that Sherman will free us before too long."

"We just have to last that long," Pat said with trenchant seriousness.

"That we do," Trasker agreed. "The rebs'll try to move us again before Sherman gets here. In any case, the odds look better staying than escaping."

Trasker talked to a sergeant in charge of the guard, an older man who was himself seen to be suffering from a limited diet. He convinced the man that Trasker had been a master carpenter back home and could be more useful in the carpenter shop. The shop was being pressured to produce beds and small cabinets for Confederate officers, who had moved into an empty building on the road between the prison and the town after transfer from the Deep South. The commandant and regional commanding general accepted the offer, frantic to cope with the influx of thousands of prisoners and Confederate and civilian guard officers.

Trasker went to work in a shop run by another inmate parolee. When that man died of tuberculosis a week later, Trasker was offered a parole to act as the camp carpenter. He signed a promise not to attempt to escape under penalty of being shot on the spot—no questions asked—and was given a certificate signed by the commandant and the local commanding general.

Trasker told the commandant he needed help; the backlog was too much for one man. Given permission to add a man to his staff, he recommended Pat, who signed a parole and joined Bill in the carpentry shop outside the walls the next day. The two slept on gum blankets on the floor of a loft above the shop and drew their food from the commissary with Confederate officers. Their certificates gave them access to storage areas where they found dozens of Sanitary Commission packages not yet pilfered by officers. They opened packages and found clothes, shoes, small tools and utensils, and edible canned foods and cakes in the more recently arrived packages. Both men burned their old clothes and bathed in facilities reserved for officers. In their fresh clothes, they looked like officers, most of whom dressed in civilian garb with a slouch hat, an occasional butternut jacket being their only uniform.

Trasker was indeed a first-rate carpenter. He organized the carpentry shop with the best equipment and materials in the camp to turn out ten or twenty bunks a day. There was no time for cabinets. Officers groused at being forced to store personal items in backpacks, mostly taken from Union dead and prisoners. When the commandant saw the quality of Trasker's work, he asked him to increase production. Confederate officers were streaming into Florence, 50 to 100 a day, off trains from Alabama and Georgia. Pat was surprised. Many were strapping young men. Talking to him as they helped him set up bunks, they freely admitted that with their fathers' influence, state government officials appointed them militia officers. They were serving out the war at home . . . until Sherman appeared.

The commandant urged Trasker to increase his staff in order to produce more beds. He and Pat discussed exactly what type of inmate was desirable. Pat recruited two recent arrivals in good physical condition, mature men who would guard their tongues and who had elementary carpentry skills: two Illinois farmers, Johann Werner and Jacob Anstatt, both captured from Sherman's army. Johann and Jacob were given paroles and certificates as well.

Within days, the four had the freedom to move about outside the prison throughout Florence. It did not take them long to establish a black market of Sanitary Commission objects, which they sold for large sums of inflated Confederate dollars. In their new dress clothes, they were indistinguishable from the Confederate officers, who were everywhere in town and in the countryside. They ate not only in the officers' mess, but in Florence restaurants unbothered by military or civilian officials as long as they produced their certificates signed by the regional commanding general and the commandant.

Pat was suffering from diarrhea and piles and Trasker from a mild case of pneumonia, but they were growing stronger each day.

In February 1865, six weeks after they had arrived, guards cleared out the camp. Guards, officers, and inmates boarded trains heading north. Sherman's drive was about to hit South Carolina. The four had been listening to officers' conversations and had prepared themselves for the train ride north, carrying enough food and dollars to assure as comfortable a trip as possible.

It was a strange ride. There were guards, but they were not guarding. Outside Petersburg, their train stopped for water and 200 prisoners simply strolled away. With directions from the guards, Trasker, Donohue, Werner, and Anstatt walked one mile until they found a large Union encampment. The war was over for them.

When Pat had entered service, he weighed 155 pounds. The day he arrived at the Union lines and was taken into a field hospital, he weighed 100 pounds, fifteen of which had been gained in the last three weeks. He was suffering from dysentery, piles, scurvy, rheumatism, and cholera. He would survive the cholera because he had been exposed to it in both Rochester and Buffalo.

Union soldiers cheered the prisoners as they walked into the Union camp and slumped to the ground. Soldiers brought wagons and carried the four to the quartermaster. He welcomed and congratulated them for having survived and led them to the regimental field hospital.

An orderly had Pat undress and bathe, gave him fresh underwear, and led him by the arm to a bed. Never had Pat been in a bed that felt so good. He slept, woke to eat and relieve himself, and slept some more. After three days of rest and care, he sought out his carpentry shop mates and thanked them for the good times they had together. He bid them the best of luck and boarded a wagon and then a train to Belle Plain, followed by a ship bound for a convalescent camp near Washington.

CHAPTER 17

The Final Battles

On January 1, 1865, Captain Mooney promoted John to the rank of corporal and used him from that point on as a scout and flag bearer.

A dreary winter changed into a pleasant spring. Few flowers bloomed in the flattened fields, which became ankle-deep, boot-sucking quagmires when it rained. John looked across the wide expanse between the lines and saw red earth torn by shells, rutted by wagons, and trampled by the feet of marching armies. He longed and prayed desperately for an end to the war.

On April 1 at 9:00 a.m., Grant ordered a general assault. Feelings were running high all up and down the Union lines. Confederate soldiers were refusing the orders of their officers. Small groups raised white flags and gave themselves up. Union soldiers were attacking without orders and were carrying Confederate positions.

That evening after a full day's fighting and Confederate troops in retreat from positions they had held for months, John was as elated as any Union soldier. Instead of celebrating that night around the campfire, he visited with the chaplain of the 164th. He had visited with Father Gillen three times over the past three years. Tonight, he decided it was time to reload spiritually once again. The priest greeted John with a broad smile.

"Father Gillen, I can't tell you how grateful I am that you have time for me. It seems like this war is crowding out anything good from my head. The only thing I hold onto is my faith in God."

"John, you are fortunate. I've been seeing men who after three years have lost everything: the memory of their loved ones, faith in God, and whatever it is holds them together."

"The bodies of my fallen friends keep crashing in on my sleep, Father. Their faces won't go away. I can still pray the prayers my grandmother taught me, but they are nothing but empty words," said John.

"At least you still make the effort to pray, John. You are still in touch with God. Many other soldiers in the 155th and 164th are living in a world without God and Jesus. They talk to me about shooting themselves or running carelessly before an assault." He arose, took his breviary from a bedside table, and used a ribbon to open it.

"We Catholics don't read the Bible as frequently as we should, but I know of no better way to restore our faith. The breviary, which every priest is obliged to pray daily, is mostly drawn from Sacred Scripture, much of it from the psalms."

"I see where you are going, Father. Why don't you read one of the psalms? And please, read it slowly or my mind won't take it in."

Father Gillen read a psalm from the evening hour of prayer of the breviary, Vespers, and then explained what the psalmist was saying.

John leaned back in his chair, shut his eyes, and relaxed. Afterward, he did something he had never done. John prayed in his own words, letting the priest continue the prayer whenever he grew silent. When both men ran out of words, they were content to remain several minutes without saying anything. They finished by praying for all those on both sides who had lost life and limb in the war.

"Father, now I'd like to confess, if I may."

"Of course, John," The priest took a stole from the bedside table, draped it over his shoulders, and said, "May God give you the grace to make a good confession, in the name of the Father and of the Son, and of the Holy Ghost."

For the first night in months, John slept soundly until reveille the next morning. Near sun-up, he gathered with the other noncommissioned officers outside a Sibley tent where the officers of the Corps were to meet their new commander, Major General Francis Barlow. The weather was warm and clear. Everyone was in high spirits. They passed the time competing with one another over who had had the best officers over the last three years. They recalled the many officers killed, seriously wounded, or captured. John commented that he had changed his mind about his commanding officers. Other than one, they had all turned out to be valiant leaders.

As they talked, in rode General Barlow, only thirty and already a grizzled veteran of every battle fought by the Army of the Potomac. Twice wounded at Antietam and again at Gettysburg, his health betrayed him at times, but he drove himself like no other general the men knew. Beneath his officer's frock coat, he wore a woodsman's plaid hunting blouse. His boyish face was clean-shaven, unlike other generals and their adjutants, who wore carefully groomed beards. He stopped outside his tent and addressed the men briefly in a low voice that had them leaning forward. After he spoke, Mooney turned to the officers and bellowed loud enough that Barlow heard him, "That man is one of us. He'll lead us to victory."

In rode one of Grant's adjutants with orders from their commander. Barlow wasted no time. He ordered an attack of the whole Corps at Hatcher's Run and the Boydton Plank Road for 10:00 a.m. After a short fight, the 155th and 164th overran the positions of North Carolina and Alabama regiments and captured a rebel battery and three cannons.

John sat atop a huge, captured parrot gun, gazing upon the happiest scene of his life: Confederate officers losing control of their ranks, their soldiers surrendering or fleeing in disarray. More Confederate units retreated, and holding the city became untenable. At midnight, Lee called for the city to be evacuated.

Within a few hours, John sat once again on a captured rebel cannon and watched long lines of blue-clad troops marching smartly into Petersburg and smoke pouring from warehouses and mansions. Men and women jammed the streets, yelling and shouting, drinking and praying, cursing at the soldiers and wringing their hands in despair.

Petersburg had finally fallen after a ten-month siege. The mayor formally surrendered his city the next morning. That evening, Richmond fell, eliciting wild celebrations across the Union lines.

The 155th was held in reserve until April 7 and the Battle of Sailor's Creek, which was actually three battles occurring simultaneously on the north and south roads of Sailor's Creek Valley and at a battle line north and west of two high bridges over the creek. Rapidly pursuing and taking prisoner of hundreds of Gordon's men, the Corcoran Legion attacked the high bridge to Farmville on the north road. Fleeing rebels had torched it. Twenty men formed a bucket brigade and doused the flames with water from the creek.

Carrying the company flag, John led a squad to the creek, where they wet blouses and filled canteens. Companies I and K then charged confidently across the smoldering bridge. A few Confederate soldiers delayed 100 yards down the road to fire on the leaders, but they did not tarry long as 1,600 of the late General Corcoran's Legion poured through the smoke and rushed onward. Alongside the bridge, Union engineers quickly cobbled a pontoon bridge and more federal troops and artillery crossed with cavalry.

Most Southern troops wisely surrendered.

John acquitted himself that day just as he had throughout the war. He ran to protected positions, held the flag aloft, and waved the company on. Company I took not a single fatal casualty in the last week of the war.

The three battles of Sailor's Creek cost Lee twenty percent of his army, 7,700 casualties in all. Eight Confederate generals were captured, including Lee's oldest son, George Washington Custis Lee.

On Saturday, April 9, Lee, blocked by four Negro regiments and surrounded by the Army of the Potomac, sent a major under white flag to tell Grant he would accept the terms of surrender offered on the 7th. He had hoped to break through a Union line and link up with General Joe Johnston's army in North Carolina.

By early afternoon, thousands of Union soldiers encamped across the small village of Appomattox, awaiting their generals. Occasional shots rang out in the distance as a few die-hard Southern soldiers refused to accept the inevitable and paid with wounds or worse. The Civil War in Virginia was over. The 155th sat only yards away from the McLean House, where the surrender was to take place.

John sensed this was a privileged moment in American history, and he was there to take it in. He had never seen General Lee, but had felt his presence and admired the way he led his armies to victory, often against heavy odds. Lee was a superior general in John's mind, unequalled by anyone on the Union side, even Grant.

Suddenly, soldiers were standing, crowding the roadway, hoping to get a glimpse of this larger-than-life nemesis in grey. John craned his head. He felt a hand on his shoulder from the soldier next to him, leaning left to get a better view. Every eye stared forward.

There he was! General Lee, dressed in a splendid new uniform, bearing a handsome ceremonial sword, and accompanied by three aides. Erect in the saddle, he carefully guided his faithful mount, Traveler, through parted masses of blue. He dismounted and entered the McLean House. A half hour later at about 1:30 p.m., Grant, dressed in an old mud-splattered uniform and without his sword, rode in with three generals and his personal staff of over a half dozen.

At 3:00 p.m., Lee emerged, nodded respectfully to the Union soldiers crowded around the McLean House, and rode off with poise and grace.

Minutes later, Union soldiers began to fire into the air in celebration of their great victory. Grant ran out of the house and shouted orders that out of respect to the brave men of the Confederacy, living and dead, there was to be no show of triumph.

John admired the class and character of his supreme commander. Like Grant, he felt no triumph. He had witnessed many of his friends die or be maimed for life. He had also walked across hundreds of dead and wounded Confederates, some of whom no doubt he had shot himself. These images haunted his sleep and would, he thought, for the rest of his life.

On April 12, around their evening campfire with a New York newspaper in hand, John sat reading what went on inside the McLean House to members of his squad. Ely Parker, a full-blooded Seneca Indian from the Tonawanda Reservation near Niagara Falls and Grant's indispensable adjutant, had prepared the terms of surrender. When the book was written, Grant showed it to Lee, who read it and remarked that Grant's stipulation that Confederate officers could keep their side arms, horses, and baggage would have a very happy effect on the Southern army. He pointed out that Confederate soldiers often brought their own animals to war. Grant reflected for a moment on the need these men would have for their horses and mules once home and adjusted the terms to include them as well.

CHAPTER 18

Pat Comes Home

Pat convalesced in the spring of 1865 in a camp in Alexandria, near Washington, officially called Camp Distribution by the War Department and unofficially called Camp Misery by the thousands of veterans who passed through it from 1862 to 1865.

On the afternoon of March 1, a Fenian recruiter approached Pat, who was sitting outside his barracks alone on a bench, and introduced himself. He welcomed the Fenian's company.

"Someone over there," and he pointed to a group of veterans, "said your name is Donohue, private. My name is Thomas Carey from County Wexford. Would you be interested in hearing what the Fenian Brotherhood has planned for this year and next?"

Pat had watched the Brotherhood grow in popularity among Irish American soldiers during the war. Its rhetoric captured his imagination. He often dreamed of someday fighting the British, as his father and grandfather had.

"I would," Pat replied.

"Could you pass the word among others like yourself?"

"Gladly," said Pat. "There are quite a few of us in camp here."

"That would be grand." Carey was a short, stocky, red-haired Irishman. It was obvious to Pat from the man's red face that he certainly had not taken the pledge and a yellowed lower lip told him Carey was also a heavy pipe smoker.

Pat searched in the encampment where he knew Irish veterans would be lounging. Some had already heard Fenian recruiters, who had free access to army units in both the North and the South during much of the war.

Rebel prisons had released many like him in deteriorated health. Others were suffering from wounds in recent battles across Virginia during Grant's last push on Lee's depleted army. Still others poured in daily off ships coming from the Deep South, where Sherman was moving north through the Carolinas.

An hour later, twenty veterans of Irish heritage sat on blankets and campstools under a spreading oak that shaded them from a hot, mid-afternoon sun to hear what Carey had to say. It was a mixed group, mostly unmarried men under 30 from throughout the North, dressed in clean uniforms or in civilian clothes. Four had suffered serious leg wounds and had to be carried or supported by their friends. Two were amputees who came on a horse-drawn cart. Some, only partially recovered from their illnesses, lay listlessly on blankets waiting for Carey to begin. The men warmed up to Carey as he approached each man, shook hands, and passed out cigars.

His introductions finished, Carey walked to an elevated position front and center to the group. With head down, he paused as if pondering how to start his remarks. He introduced himself to the group and related the purpose of their gathering. Then he said, "I'm here to tell you, a great deal of progress has been made by the Fenian Brotherhood in just the past year alone! We're well organized, don't ye know now. Thousands of men throughout Ireland have joined the Irish Republican Brotherhood. They're making it very uncomfortable for Royal Irish Constables, British soldiers, and sympathizers every day now. Men are giving their lives daily to free Ireland from despotic rule, just as so many of your brethren gave their lives for the Union and Abraham Lincoln, our great president."

The men murmured their approval of what Carey had said. One of the men asked him, "I've heard it a dozen times, but what does 'Fenian' mean?"

"Ah, I'm glad you asked that. 'Fenian' comes from the word 'Fianna.' Fianna were ancient Celtic warriors who lived by themselves like monks and defended the Irish people when they were attacked."

Pat nodded knowingly. He had, indeed, heard Gram tell stories of Finn McCool and the Fianna.

"Let me say a word about the leader here in America," continued Carey. "John O'Mahony survived the rebellion of 1848 and escaped to America. He has organized circles in every big American city, with centers in those circles called IRAs that drive the circles and keep them on target. His goal is to supply the Brotherhood with the best American arms and to get many of you to join.

With the help of men like yourselves, we can throw out the British bastards after 400 years of domination."

Carey puffed on his cigar while his audience digested his last words.

"So, when you get home, I suggest you find the circle in your city, whether it be Chicago, Buffalo, or New York and consider joining it."

"What about New Jersey?" someone called out, eliciting laughter from the audience.

"Why, yes! Even if you live in New Jersey," responded Carey good-naturedly.

"You're a tough, hardened bunch now and you'd drive the goddamned Brits into the Irish Sea, if enough of you joined the Brotherhood in Ireland. Your government will be helpful, too, what with the Brits supplying the South with ships, arms, clothing, and everything needed to wage war against the American government."

He looked at each man as he relit his cigar. "Now, if you have any questions, I'd be happy to answer them."

The men spent the next hour going back and forth with Carey. Tremors of enthusiasm rolled through Pat's stomach.

He continued to rest beneath the oak for several minutes after the others left, thinking about his Whiteboy father and the great adventure that awaited him if he joined the Fenians and invaded Ireland. "Fekkin' Brits," he thought, anger overwhelming him.

After a few minutes lying still, staring blankly off into a blue cloudless sky, he muttered aloud, "I wish I could afford more of these Cuban cigars."

When the weather in Alexandria turned hot and humid in April, Pat volunteered for a warehouse job. There he worked in a cool basement where good Kentucky bourbon was stored. Pat became an expert at hiding a bottle in his clothes before heading to the barracks. Over the next four months, he drank freely every night with men from Ohio and Upstate New York, many of them Irish. Pat was a central figure in the group, a hero of sorts for smuggling out the best whiskey. He led them in singing, storytelling, and an occasional brawl. Some evenings they marched through downtown Alexandria, shouting and harassing secesh women. Twice, military police threw him into a paddy wagon and he spent the night in the brig.

Military provost guards showed convalescing soldiers enormous leniency. Deeds that would have been punished by court-martial were ignored. Pat took every advantage of lax military and civil discipline and had a great time for himself, but for only a couple of hours a day. He tired easily.

He grew to love bourbon. It hit the brain quickly, making him happy and daring at the front of a gang of veterans out for a good time.

Nights, relaxed in his bunk, his thoughts turned to Annabelle. He was still infatuated with her, imagined making love with her, and schemed to visit her. He was concerned about their child, who by now he figured was more than a year old.

While he had a great deal of freedom to move about in the Alexandria area, he was under orders to remain close to the camp. He asked permission to visit cousins in Sangster, but was refused when the story supporting his request was quickly seen as fabricated. To go as far as twenty miles away without permission constituted desertion. He would not risk dishonorable discharge so close to being mustered out and receiving a pension. Besides, he was broke as his back pay had not yet been cleared.

Patrick struggled to get out of bed. All the beer and booze he had drunk the night before was exploding his bladder. Staggering and unsure of the direction of the toilet, he leaned against a wall a few seconds until his brain cleared. Then he moved out into the corridor and through the outside door. He lurched into the colored men's latrine. Colored and white slept in separate dorms, ate in their own mess areas, and sat on garden benches which, though not signed WHITE or COLORED, were just as clearly understood. As he stood at the long ditch peeing, a man walked up beside him.

"Hello, Mr. Pat."

"Henry Woods! Where did you come from?"

"Appomattox. Now I'm one of the cooks."

"Thanks for the way you treated my brother. You saw he got good care and I know you did the same for other 155th men." Pat marveled at the size of the young man, a good four inches taller and much more muscular. The last time he had seen him over a year ago, Henry was just a boy.

"Yah, your brother was grateful. Some of them didn't talk so nice to me when I first joined the surgeons, but they changed. I even sang at their campfires some nights. When I seed CT units in the field 'round Petersburg, I joined the 41st las' October and fought through to the end."

"Well, glad yuh made it, Henry." Pat was thinking, *I'd like to ask him about fighting the rebs. The CT ran before the butternuts, I've heard many times . . . Maybe some other time.*

Henry sensed Pat was in a hurry to get out of the colored latrine. He had wandered in by mistake and did not want to be seen in it with Henry. *Dis is the las' time we goin' to talk,* he thought to himself.

Pat walked back to his bed, made it up, found a broom, and cleaned up some of the mud he'd dragged in. Then he picked up a glass reeking of whiskey and returned it to the cafeteria before heading off to the warehouse.

A week later, after more wild behavior the night before, Pat was cited for disorderly conduct and assigned to clean up the cafeteria with the colored help. Pat knew he would be taunted by other vets for what they considered the worst punishment of all—being forced to work with the coloreds—but he was secretly happy to have the excuse to talk with Henry. He moved in the dish line right alongside him.

"Henry, how you being treated?"

"OK, Mr. Pat. I be needin' time to find out where my family be. Meantime, I gotta eat and stay dry."

Pat was quiet for a minute wondering what it must be like to be colored in Northern Virginia or even Washington. There were thousands of contrabands like Henry Woods. He admired the way Henry handled himself, quite self-assured for his age and able to make his way among whites.

"Henry, did you see General Lee when he rode in to surrender?"

"No, but I see his men surrender when dey ran into a Negro wall of CT cav'ry. They had just scattered white troopers when we came along."

"You were cavalry, Henry?"

"I was, Mr. Pat. And we was as good as anyone. Fought against the best Confederate cav'ry. One of the first units into Petersburg and Richmond. Once Lee surrendered his army, we knew we was free. Wasn't only Mr. Lincoln freed us. It was General Grant." Henry picked up a tray of clean dishes, moved it to a nearby cupboard, and returned. "Long as that devil Lee in the field wit' his army, no nigger in the South ever be free. Appomattox was our big day!"

"I never thought of it like that," replied Pat. "I never fought with colored troops in the field. Were there many who were allowed into battle?"

"At first, all I do was guard the Center Point Depot. But in de las' year we be trained and fight jus' like you boys."

"And did you hold your own with the rebels?" asked Pat. "I know they hated you coloreds and killed you rather than take you captive. Or if they did put you in prison, they murdered you there."

"An' don't you know, we knowed sure 'nough, Mr. Pat. So we fought like the sun was never comin' up again if we get taken by them bastards."

For the next few minutes, Pat and Henry traded questions and answers about colored troops.

Finally, Pat asked Henry, "By chance did you know Annabelle Lee? You joined the regiment at Sangster. Was that your home?"

"That be it, Mr. Pat. I run from the baddest master you ever did see. But I's no idea what become of Annabelle after the Union Army lef'. I be mustered out tomorra' and go lookin' for my family. You leave me yuh address and if I find her I write yuh straightaway," said Henry.

"I sure will, Henry. I wish you well and thanks again for all you did for my brother and the other soldiers. I would have liked to have seen you in full uniform and gear on your cavalry horse." They shook hands and parted.

On Monday, July 10, 1865, Pat was formally mustered out of the U.S. Army. With his final pay, a large sum that covered his time in captivity, he bought a few souvenir gifts for Gram, Jack, and Jo, but saved most of the money. He caught Northern Central trains from Washington to Elmira, where he waited three hours before boarding a New York Central to Buffalo. Boring stretches were made pleasant by a few pints of whiskey he had pilfered. Whiskey was becoming his tonic for dealing with melancholia and boredom. "Nothing wrong with that," he reasoned. "I've suffered enough these last three years."

At 6:00 p.m. the next day, thirty hours after leaving Washington, he walked from the Exchange Street Station to Louisiana Street, conspicuous in his uniform. The day before, he had telegrammed Gram to expect him. Although he passed several taverns with old friends waving from the front doors and saw numerous neighbors on Elk and Louisiana Streets, he went straight home with only passing waves and greetings.

Maire was waiting at the door, telegram in hand. He grabbed and hugged her. How he had missed this lady! Then he hugged his cousin, Jo, who was now twenty-six. "Jo, what a good lookin' woman you've become!" he said. Pat shook hands with her husband, Harry, and warmly embraced his uncle. "Uncle Jack, you're a sight for sore eyes, that you are, and I can't tell you how much I missed you all."

Gram saw at a glance that her grandson was thinner by far than when she had last seen him. He also smelled of whiskey. Jack and Jo noted his condition as well, but like Gram, said nothing

"Oh Pat, I was so afraid I'd never see you again. So many of our boys are not comin' home, bless their poor souls. I'm so thankful to God that He kept you alive, one of His favorite few."

"And John!" interjected Jo.

"And John," repeated Gram, nodding to her niece, "the both of ye, thank God and His Holy Mother!" She shook and laughed and hugged her grandson once more, crying tears of joy and relief.

"And John, indeed ladies!" roared Pat. "John was my guardian angel! Gram, you'll never know how many times I thought about desertin'. It was your smilin' face that kept me goin' for another day." He coughed to gain control of the deep feelings that were threatening to show on his face. "I'm so grateful for your letters and boxes. One even reached me in the Salisbury prison. You had angels and Luke Blackmer carting that one, Gram. Luke was a man in town who tried to help us prisoners."

Gram beamed proudly that God had answered her prayers and seen her package through. Jo had done just as Pat had asked in the single letter of his that reached home while he was in Salisbury.

She had worried over her cousin throughout his time in service as she too read the papers daily. "Pat, we couldn't take a full breath until you got home," Jo interjected. "Carrie Duggan read your telegram to Gram, but I had to read it again and again waiting for you to come."

"Tell me what you all heard from John," Pat pleaded. "He wrote a brief note in March before the last battles at Appomattox and I heard the 155th was there at the end. So John must have been there too. But no mail from him reached me in Alexandria after March."

Gram hesitated for a second to gather her thoughts. "Maybe it's because the regiment was busy rounding up stray Confederates, as he said in his last letter. Jo, you tell the rest."

Jo was caught off guard. "Well, John wrote that in May they were in a grand march through Washington before all the generals and congressmen and the like. The letter ended saying he'll be home before the end of July. He says he was amazed that you survived the prison camps, a testament to your endurance. The Union Iron Works was the best training for you, he says, and he can't wait to see you."

The five sat around the dining room table with coffee and cake talking like there was no tomorrow. Even usually laconic Jack was bursting with questions. "Pat, how was it?" asked his uncle. "I heard you fought in some awful battles!"

"I was lucky to survive at that," Pat replied. "One reason was John and George Tipping. Whenever I got into a tight spot, there they were to save me. God be good to George. How we missed that wonderful man!"

He paused and the three waited for him to continue. "Did you ever hear of grape shot, Gram?"

"What, they were shootin' fruit at you boys?"

Pat laughed. "Yah, but the grapes were made of iron and shot from a big artillery gun that spread iron across the field like rain coming sideways. It would wipe out a whole squad of men, arms and heads blown off. We lost fifty men, half our company, in ten minutes at Cold Harbor."

Gram and Jo grimaced at Pat's descriptions. Men did not ordinarily speak so graphically with their women present. Gram pulled out a whiskey bottle from the cupboard and poured Pat, her brother, and Harry a double shot each, Jo a single. Jack brought in a tankard of beer and Jo put a big box of chocolates in the center of the table.

Pat asked Jack about the new elevators he had seen on the river as he walked home from the depot, but the family brushed his questions aside.

Gram grasped Pat's hand in both of hers and peered intently at her grandson. "You and John were both wounded. What happened?"

"Well, Gram, we were wounded just bad enough to leave the field. John was hit the second day we joined Grant and his Army of the Potomac, a year ago in May. A shell exploded behind us and John caught a slug of iron in the back.

"I bet he didn't tell you when he wrote, but he could have stayed home with the wound and all. Truth is, he wouldn't abandon his Company I mates. Gram, you know, most of all he came back to look out for me."

A broad smile lit up Maire's face. "That's our John!"

Pat nodded, grinning. "It wasn't a month after John got hit that an empty shell hit me and busted up my shoulder." With that, Pat unbuttoned his blouse and slid it off his back.

"Oh, I see the place." Gram pushed aside his loose shirt and moved her hand softly over the wound. The scar tissue was visible, but it seemed to have healed well. "The shoulder looks a bit out of whack. Does it hurt, Pat? Can you do your old job at the Works?"

"Ah, it ain't much now, but I was in a world of pain when it hit me. The shell slammed into my back and blew my shoulder out of its socket." Although she'd seen more than her share of injuries here and in the Old Country, Maire winced at his words. "Oh my God, Pat, t'was the work of Satan, to be sure."

Jack nodded and recounted having seen a man suffer the same way when a boom snapped at the elevator.

"Exactly, Uncle Jack. Stunned and staggering around was I. I seem to remember someone grabbed me and threw me to the ground, 'cause there were shells bursting all over the place and minie bullets thick as flies."

"What kind of war was it that they were shootin' little bullets at you guys? Were their soldiers little fellas, too?" asked Gram.

Pat laughed so hard tears came to his eyes. "No, Gram. That's the name for the bullet musket rifles shoot."

Suddenly, Pat slammed his hand on the table. "I almost forgot!" Reaching into his breast pocket, he produced an article wrapped in a small square of linen. Handing it to his uncle, he said, "Here, Uncle Jack. I picked this up just before I left Washington."

Unwrapping the package, Jack withdrew two oval grey bullets, less than an inch long, that had collided in flight and fused together.

"It's two minies that hit each other, probably shot by opposite sides, one by a Confederate and the other by a Union soldier," Pat announced.

Now it was Jack's turn to look dumfounded. "Can ye believe that? My goodness," said Jack and he held the odd chunk of lead before the women. "Do ye see that, Maire? Jo? Isn't that somethin'?"

Harry asked to see it and rolled it around in the palm of his right hand and then across the table to Jack.

"Imagine what a swarm of flying bullets could do to flesh and bone!" said Pat. Gram and Jo shivered at the thought. Pat was about to describe what minies did to human flesh, but he caught himself in time.

Jack reached out to hand the souvenir back to Pat, who held up his right palm. "No, no, Uncle Jack. It's yours. I thought you might like it."

"Why, thank you, Pat." Jack smiled and rewrapped the gift in the linen cloth and deposited it in the pocket of his jacket. "Wait till the men see it at work tomorra."

Eager to end the grisly topic and realizing he had been too long in the company of men grown hard and crude, Pat gave the two women the gifts he had bought them, silver necklaces with images of the White House carved on light blue glass. They tried them on immediately and both kissed Pat on his cheeks at the same time.

Pat explained, "I bought them from a Cherokee Indian selling them on the street near the train station in Washington. I just liked them and thought they'd look great on both of you . . . and indeed they do!"

Pat waited until the women settled back and continued the story of his wounding. "One of the guys walked me back to the field hospital and a week later, I was in a hospital in Philadelphia. Gram, I tell you, life was good in Philly. Lots of surgeon's assistants and nurses to look after me, change the dressing every day. Good food. I was in no hurry to get back. No lice, that's what I liked most. Day and night in camp and in the field the lice attacked us. Lice are the best army in the world, even in the coldest weather."

The evening drew on with more questions and more stories. Pat noticed that Gram's eyes were drooping and her head nodding. Pat said they would talk more later. He was home for good, so Gram pulled herself up with a hand from Pat, hugged him for dear life, and told him she loved him more than all the saints and angels in heaven. He pushed a wad of bills, $90, into her apron pocket. Unconscious of her new wealth, she lumbered off to bed, using her grandson for a cane.

The evening's conversation was over. Jo said she and Harry had to leave. Jack said it was time he went to bed, too. They all had to work the next day. Pat decided to hold for another day the photographs he had bought for the three of them of President and Mary Lincoln before he left Washington. He felt like a new man, healed and well. He was so excited to be home that he knew he would not be able to sleep. Besides, he couldn't wait to see the boys at Kennedy's, so out he went and tied on a dandy.

CHAPTER 19

John Comes Home

PM was released by guards after a train ride from Salisbury to Danville, Virginia, in February of 1865 and hiked ten miles to a Union railroad. He spent the next two months in a Washington hospital before mustering out on Saturday, July 15, 1865.

He arrived home five days after Pat. After spending a day with his family on Tecumseh Street, he knocked on the door on Louisiana Street after noon on Sunday. Pat jumped for joy to see his old friend. "So, pal, what happened after they put me on a train? Last I saw you were still chained to a tree."

"And there I stayed for another day until they shoved me onto a train for Salisbury."

"You weren't ball and chained as soon as you entered the gate and made to clean latrines?"

"No, probably because the rebs knew the war was just about over and were changing the rules to meet the situation," PM replied. "Maybe they were afraid they'd be executed themselves if they kept up the old ways, shooting prisoners who got too close to the line and prisoners who tried to escape in order to survive."

"Tell me . . . Nolan, McGowan, Finnane, and Beasley, did they survive?" asked Pat.

"We all came out together. Finny was so weak we had to steal a wagon and pull him the last ten- miles. But he made it. I saw him in the hospital. He's okay."

Pat threw up his hands and cheered at the good news.

"What about you? Where did they take you?" asked PM.

"South Carolina, Florence Prison, and there I stayed until they set me on a train for Charleston. Was about the same as Salisbury, but because of a farmer from Illinois who was a master carpenter, I was put to work making beds and cabinets for Confederate officers who had run from Sherman. I pretty much lived the life of a rebel officer for the last few weeks before being set free." Pat then related the crazy tale of his last days in captivity.

When he had finished, the two stopped talking for a few seconds, both thinking about Smitty. "We gotta visit Smitty's widow and kids and see how they're farin'," said PM.

"We will. Let's go now. They must still live on Mackinaw," replied Pat. "It pains me to even think about Dave. He never should have entered," replied Pat.

Pat and PM visited Mrs. Smith and her four children. It was a stressful visit. She was still grieving, as was the oldest daughter. They answered Mrs. Smith's questions about the circumstances of her husband's capture and imprisonment as briefly as possible.

Pat told her, "Your husband was a good soldier and died telling the two of us he loved his wife and children more than anything else in the world."

PM added, "He prayed that God would have mercy on him and died shortly afterward. You all can be proud of your husband and your father."

"Have arrangements had been made for the full pension you were to receive, Mrs. Smith?" asked Pat.

"Yes, the pension payments are a big help and for the rest we're receiving support from Dave's brother and my family. We're doing ok."

Pat and PM pressed $10 each into her hand and backed out the front door as graciously as they could. It was an awkward time for both. She held their hands as they left and thanked them.

That evening, they made a tour of the bars in the Ward, telling war stories and renewing friendships with old pals. In the midst of their tales of army life, battles, and captivity, they remembered the people who helped them along the way, including the colored field hand who had given them food when they were starving. Not knowing who he was, they could do nothing except to pray for him. They imagined him a free man now, working as a lowly farm hand somewhere in North Carolina.

They decided the best way to show their appreciation to Miriam was to send her money. They pooled a purse of $25 each and agreed PM was to send it the next day. He had kept the envelope with her name and address sewn in a cuff in his pants all through the last months of the war.

Within the first week home, Pat returned to work at the Union Iron Works on Catherine Street as an iron roller, a semi-skilled position given him by the bosses because he was a war veteran. PM joined Pat there.

The Works occupied fifty-three acres and annually produced 25,000 tons of iron, mostly beams and angle iron used in the construction of commercial buildings across the country.

Both men barely survived the dirty, heavy, hot labor of the mill over a sixty-six-hour workweek. Two weeks into his return to work, Pat was suffering from dysentery and piles so bad he could not get out of bed. Early that morning, Gram walked over to PM's house to ask him to let the Iron Works Office know not to expect Pat that day, but that he hoped to return the next.

Pat lay in bed when he was not visiting the outhouse. He knew he could not keep missing work and worried that the bosses would fire him before the week was out. It depressed him to realize he could not work as he had as a seventeen-year-old before the war, and that some days he could not work at all. He had always been proud of his strength and endurance.

"What kind of man am I if I can't work?" he wondered. "Nothing like my da, who could work sun-up to sunset for years!" He remembered his father forcing himself some mornings to work at the grain mill or ride a wagon ten or twenty miles to set up a barrel shop. As usual, he was unsure what he remembered first-hand and what he recalled because Gram had told him.

Gram had given him a salve that reduced his piles, and he was soon able to move about. He sat in the backyard, enjoying the warmth of the sun. In mid-afternoon, he knelt on the ground. He pulled weeds in Gram's small garden and thinned out a row of carrots and another of beets. What he pulled he gave to their young pig, kept in a small shed and pen at the back of their lot. He remembered that in December, when the winds and snow blew off the lake, Gram kept the pig in a wooden box in her bedroom.

As a boy, Pat showed nothing but disdain for such work. Gardening was women's work. Now he no longer felt that way. Kneeling in the dirt in the warm sun, it occurred to him how close he had come to never again being able to do simple work like gardening or tending the pig. He was glad to be alive and home with Gram.

The next morning, Pat felt somewhat better and forced himself out of bed at 6:00. He met PM at the corner of Tecumseh and Hamburg and they walked into the plant at 6:30. He went into the office to apologize for missing work the day before. The superintendent demoted him on the spot from iron roller to common laborer, reduced his pay, made a quarter of it payable in goods at a local market, and sent him to furnace No. 1 to rake slag.

171

Pat's job was to pull slag from the furnace with a long, heavy rake to a mound near a narrow track, where other laborers shoveled it into a small hopper car. Mules pulled the laden car to a swamp on the river that the company was filling in. Other laborers were doing the same thing alongside him and at the other two furnaces.

In mid-July, the temperature in Buffalo exceeded 80 degrees and it was muggy. Near the furnace, the temperature was 120 degrees. Acrid fumes hung in the air from soft coal and molten iron. New workers like Pat choked until they almost lost their breath. The older men on the job were used to it. Many who had been at the mill for years suffered from lung diseases, were short of breath, and could work only brief periods before moving off to the river to suck in fresh air.

Within a half hour, Pat's clothes were soaked in sweat. He rested his rake and slipped off to the outhouse toilets a hundred yards away, near the creek. He was so weak he thought about quitting that very moment, but after resting for five minutes, he went back toward the furnace.

With lowered eyes, he looked around for easier work. He walked to an old slag pile men had raked away from the furnace the day before. It was cooler there and the fumes were less. He picked at the stiff slag with his rake and pulled it into small piles at the railhead. His co-workers saw what Pat was doing. Some resented his deception, but most excused him. They knew he had spent months in Confederate prisons and covered for him the same as they did for the older men.

Pat survived one day at a time, avoiding bosses and finding make-work around the three furnaces. Then a foreman caught on, panned him loudly as a labor faker, and made him return to work at the mouth of the furnace. The next day, Pat found a way to disappear again. His artful dodging made him the butt of jokes and harsh talk by the younger crew members. He appeared nightly at Kennedy's with PM to drink his unhappiness away.

Toward the end of April 1865, John marched through Richmond as a part of General Meade's victory celebration. He also marched in President Johnson's Grand Review of the Federal Armies in Washington on May 23. A third time after mustering out in Washington on July 15 and training to New York, he participated in a parade held to honor returning veterans from the Irish and Corcoran Brigades.

On the evening of July 26, he returned home. The next evening, he and Theresa made the short walk to Louisiana Street and visited with Maire, Jack, Jo, Harry, and Pat. Pat and Jack wanted to know all about John's escape at Reams Station, the battles at the end of the war, and Lee's surrender at Appomattox. John briefly described each.

Pat asked, "How did you make corporal?"

"Mooney pushed me to accept the promotion and I finally gave in," said John. "I guess he thought I should be earning a few more dollars to send home. He also had some special duty for me."

"And what was that, John?" asked Pat.

"Scouting."

"No surprise there, brother. You were as good as a Seneca on his best day. But didn't you also act as the company color bearer?"

"I did for three or four of the final attacks."

"I'm surprised you're not buried in some unknown grave. Those reb sharpshooters always aimed for the color bearers, unless they were boys. Most didn't last a month."

Disturbed to hear about how close her boys had come to death, Gram changed the subject. "John, I'm after supposin' you and Theresa talked about your lady friend. Yuh can't leave us out in the cold, now can yuh?"

John explained, "Johanna's visit to St. Elizabeth Hospital raised my spirits, and because of her I got better faster. I knew after her week with me at the hospital that she was the woman for me."

Gram excused herself and came back with a whiskey bottle and glasses. She raised a toast to John and Johanna first in Gaelic and then in English:

May God be with you and bless you,
May you see your children's children,
May you be poor in misfortune, rich in blessings.
May you know nothing but happiness from this day forward.

The four raised their glasses and cheered John and Johanna. Then Gram invited them into the dining room table where she served a dinner of roast beef and turnips, with apple pie for dessert. As they ate, Pat and John moved the conversation toward a subject they had often discussed in the field.

"Gram," John said in a serious voice, "we always wondered why you didn't bring us back to Buffalo right after Da and Ma died."

"Well, son, it was only right to give Conal and Margaret the time they needed to fold you two into their family." She then edged the conversation to goings-on in the Ward and the parish.

John would not be dissuaded from what was really on his mind. "Gram, hold on a minute. Pat and I often talked about our parents during the long days and evenings in camp. We were so young when they died and we remember very little about them."

Gram smiled, "Boys, the stories of your parents, they will take a month of Sundays to tell. I'll start when dinner's over and we're all resting on soft chairs with a cup of tea."

The brothers waited anxiously for dinner to end, then Pat and John rushed around the kitchen setting out teacups and boiling water, only to be disappointed when Gram begged off. "We'll do it next Sunday, boys. I'm a bit bushed, as they say around here these days." Jack turned in as well. Jo and Harry left for home.

Pat walked with John and Aunt Theresa to her flat on Mackinaw Street. "I'm going to work as a bridge tender on the Michigan Avenue Bridge," John told him. "That way I work through the winter. How are you doing at the Works, Pat?"

"Ah, I know the end is coming. The bosses are ready to fire me now," he replied. "The truth is I can't handle heavy work six days a week. I don't have the strength."

"Nor I to go back shoveling coal."

Theresa bade the two brothers a goodnight and went to bed. Pat sat for a while with his brother, chatting on the porch about their days in the war. Both men choked up when they recalled the many friends who hadn't made it.

"Pat, no one's death hit me like George's. The next time we stood ready to attack the rebs with him not there, I wanted to run back to camp and hide. He was my courage."

"I know what you mean," nodded Pat, "although I am surprised to hear you say it. You were always steady as a rock. I kinda took your place at his side," he added. "At Reams when I got separated from most of you, it was George and you I was lookin' for."

"Do nightmares still wake you from sleep? I'll tell you, and you only, they still do me," John said emphatically.

"Me, too! Probably will be with us for many years . . . maybe forever," added Pat. "I wake up yelling and crying, curled up tight in a ball many nights."

"And the worst one, Pat, is the image of George still as a statue, with blood all over his jacket."

The brothers sat quietly for a minute, looking blankly into the still night. Then John asked, "So . . . are you going with the Fenians, Pat?"

"Indeed I am. I've been giving a quarter a week to the Fenian Brotherhood since I started work. And they promoted me right away to the Circle."

John stared long and hard at his brother, but said nothing. He didn't have to. Pat knew John was thinking that he was crazy to throw his lot in with the Fenians.

THE FENIAN RAID AND MARRIAGE

CHAPTER 20

The Fenians Invade Canada

O n Thursday, October 10, 1865, Pat and other members of the Buffalo Circle boarded a Boston New York and Pennsylvania train at the Louisiana Street Station. The day before, he had told his bosses at the Works that his grandfather had died in Philadelphia.

The DL&W was not yet a single system with one set of standard tracks. With the various transfers and changes from station to station, the trip took forty hours. Pat did not mind the long trip. The Circle members had plenty of whiskey. They played cards, told stories, and flirted with young women. He slept fitfully, when at all. Meals were catch as catch can in depots along the way. Pat was groggy when he arrived.

Surrounded by 600 Fenian delegates, Pat experienced a rush of emotion at the very first session when they shouted for a new constitution like the American Constitution, and with little opposition, passed it by voice vote. When O'Mahony insisted on a narrow focus of invading Britain from Ireland with the Irish Republican Brotherhood, they booed him off the stage. In his place, they elected William Randall Roberts, a New York City dry goods merchant. With little urging from him, they drafted a new platform whose main plank was the capture of a region of Canada. Canada was a British colony and capturing a section of it would give them leverage to trade for Irish independence

Pat returned to work telling his foreman an elaborate story of his grandfather's funeral. The foreman replied, "A strange coincidence, isn't it, that the funeral should be in the same city as the meeting of the Fenians?" But he accepted Pat's excuse because the big bosses were not yet ready to fire him.

Monthly, Pat trekked downtown to the United States Pension Office to collect his $2 pension. He regarded the $2 as a pittance for what he had been through and when compared to what others were said to be getting.

In an emergency meeting of the Fenian senate in New York that December, Roberts had O'Mahony impeached and deposed. O'Mahony organized a second Fenian Brotherhood with its own governing body. "How very Irish!" remarked the *New York Times*.

President Roberts called a fourth Fenian Convention to be held in Pittsburgh in February 1866. Pat drummed up another excuse for his bosses at the Iron Works. He had to meet cousins coming in from Ireland, he told them . . . in New York.

The trip to Pittsburgh with two other Circle members took the better part of two days over railroads of different gauges. Pat and the others from Buffalo were a day late, but arrived in time to shout their votes for Roberts' proposition: "Men of Action will seize Canadian land and trade it for Ireland's freedom."

For another day, the Fenians clamored for a free Ireland, blasting the air with ancient Irish myth and oratory. The last evening, they drank until the wee hours of the morning, toasting the invincibility of the Irish Civil War veteran and cursing the British. Pat still had a hangover a day and a half later when his Erie Railroad train pulled into the Exchange Street Station. The next morning, he exercised his right as a revolutionary and stayed home from work. By 10:00 a.m., he was in Kennedy's Bar on Ohio Street, stomping, shouting, and drinking stout by the pitcher with a bar-full of men. His five-day absence went unreported at the Iron Mill. His foreman had been on a bender for the same period of time.

O'Mahony beat his rival Roberts to the punch. In April 1866, he led 100 armed Fenians, nearly all Union veterans, to the banks of the St. Croix River in Maine. From there he attacked Campobello Island, claimed by both New Brunswick and Maine, hoping by logic unique to him to touch off a war between England and America and free Ireland as a corollary.

Both the United States and Britain dispatched gunboats and scattered the Fenians across the New England countryside. Fenian leadership had made no provision for food or transportation for their members' return home. Caricatures of ragged Fenians begging in village centers throughout eastern Canada and northeastern United States filled newspapers around the world, mocking the Fenian movement and embarrassing every person of Irish blood, no matter how distant from Ireland. In May 1866, Roberts made his move. With Fenian Brotherhood dues, he purchased 15,000 surplus rifles in Baltimore, loaded them onto boxcars, and shipped them to Cleveland.

Pat walked to Aunt Theresa's and made a last attempt to entice his brother into the ranks of the Brotherhood. "John, I know you think Roberts and O'Mahoney and Stephens are daffy, but you agree with every Irishman that Ireland should be free of the British yoke."

"Pat, the Fenians are not the boys to do it. They mean well, but they're poorly led."

"Maybe so, but they have a lot on their side. Thousands of Irish veterans are out of work. They're angry at fighting a war for the Abolitionist Know Nothings who hate our guts the same way the British do."

"They're not prepared to fight the British army in Canada," replied John.

"I think we are. We could see 20,000 men ready to invade Canada. And we've got the arms: thousands of Enfields and Springfields waiting for us in Cleveland."

"Well and good! But where's your leaders? Where were they at Campobello?"

"I say the Brotherhood is organized and ready. It's learned its lesson. Generals like Sweeney and Lynch, who were heroes in battles in the South, have taken over. Join us, John!"

"You've got a lot on your side, I grant you, but I've got a tender's post on the Michigan Avenue Bridge and am about to marry. I don't see Johanna sitting around knitting while I play soldier once again. No, Pat, I'll not be invading Canada this year."

Pat had met a young woman, Mary Nagle, who, along with co-workers from her father's business, frequented a Washington Street bar, McSheehan's. Mary had begun life as a poor girl in Fermoy, Cork, and was raised in her mother's boarding house in New York City. When she came to Buffalo to live with her father, she lived the life of a well-to-do West Side business family. At first, Mary was reluctant to enter a serious relationship with Pat. His First Ward accent and conversational style were rougher and cruder than what she had become accustomed to. He lacked education and his work experiences were limited to poorly paid, dirty, heavy labor.

Pat had never met a woman like her and sought her out at McSheehan's every Saturday evening thereafter. In time, Mary was taken by his Civil War stories and the way he adored her. Then one night Pat told her that he had something to say that she might not like.

"Mary, I think we're getting along great and I want to be honest with you. I joined the Fenians after coming home from the war and we're about to invade Fort Erie."

"I like your honesty, Pat, but I don't like your joining the Fenians. It has me saying 'goodbye' to you right this very moment." She took a sip on her beer and continued. "I knew of the Fenians in Ireland. They had crazy men for leaders there and it's no different here. That calamity at Campobello proves it. How can you join such a witless group? I can't help but wonder when you Irish men will learn from your past." She turned to walk away.

"Mary, just listen to me for a minute. There are 20,000 of us and we're well led by generals who won battles in the war. We have arms and a plan to capture a region of Canada."

Mary looked at Pat like he was mad. Pat rushed on to explain the situation to her. "I'm to cross the Niagara River in a week or two with three others and collect the information we need to defeat the Brits." He hesitated before going on to see her reaction. "I'll be making maps to prepare our invasion."

"Pat, if I ever told my father what you're up to, he would forbid me to see you ever again. When Campobello hit the Chronicle, he came into my office angrier than I've ever seen him. We're done, Pat, and don't ever speak to me again." She started to stride off as she shook her head and teared up.

Then another thought came to mind and she turned back. "You think for one moment the bosses at the Works are going to take you back after a leave of God knows how long, a leave for which you have not asked?" she chided Pat. "No, you will not have a job once you get back."

Pat was stunned by her reaction and said nothing, but thought to himself, *They're about to let me go anyhow. I have to find something else.*

She stood silently for a moment, then went on shouting at him. "You're aching for another adventure. You just can't imagine yourself left out. Why, there's been no training of the lot of you! And do you think for a moment the British don't have their spies in bed with the Fenians, closer than their own wives?"

Pat pleaded with her. "Mary, please believe in me. This will all be over by the end of June and I'll be working come July. The time off will be good for me. I'll build strength and find work the day I return."

Mary could see there was no stopping Pat, so she made a firm decision. He was not for her, much as she cared for him; she took two steps toward him, kissed him lightly on the cheek, and without saying another word walked off.

In late May, Fenians by the thousands from all over the United States swarmed toward Cleveland, where they hoped to cross Lake Erie and invade upper Canada. They disguised themselves as railroad laborers. General Tom Sweeney, their commander, sent a message to the Cleveland Fenian Circle that General William Francis Lynch, who had commanded the 58th Illinois Volunteers under Sweeney, would meet them in Cleveland. Lynch was to rent boats to cross Lake Erie and attack Canada.

Incapacitated by his war wounds, General Lynch never showed up, nor had he secured boats.

The night of May 30, the Fenians slept in warehouses and whatever accommodations they could find. Sweeney sent word by an adjutant that they were to proceed to Buffalo. Fenians headed out in all directions from Cleveland to confuse police and federal military agents. By 10:00 a.m., the majority were on eastbound New York Central trains. In ten hours, the trains approached farmlands a few miles south of Buffalo and Fenians jumped off to avoid authorities waiting at the Exchange Street Station to arrest them. Small groups walked into South Buffalo throughout the afternoon and evening and were billeted in homes, barns, halls, and warehouses secured by the Buffalo Circle, many in the First Ward. At the same time, under orders from General Grant, the frigate *USS Michigan* steamed into Buffalo with a contingent of marines.

Buffalo Circle members unloaded boxcars of rifles in a freight yard east of Buffalo and carried them in wagons to a Black Rock jump-off point on the Niagara River.

In the course of May 31, 1866, the Fenian plan became clear to American and Canadian authorities. Fenians were massing in Malone, New York; St. Albans, Vermont; and Buffalo for invasions across the border. American and Canadian authorities alerted military units to move by train and boat to those points. Militias at Toronto and on the Niagara Peninsula were ordered to Port Colborne.

Some 16,800 Fenians were gathering in St. Albans under the command of General Samuel P. Spear. The invasion of Fort Erie by 5,000 Fenians was to be but a diversion.

Captain O'Neill, age thirty-two, had come up from Tennessee with a small regiment of 200 men. In Cleveland, he received word that General Sweeney had promoted him to colonel and made him commander of the Fort Erie invasion force. In Buffalo, Colonel O'Neill met with the Buffalo Circle's 7th IRA Regiment commander, Captain Bailey. He was impressed with the tactical information garnered by the regiment's advance group in Canada a week before he arrived.

The night of Thursday, May 31, 1,000 men proceeded north over Buffalo's radial street system without being stopped by Buffalo police and assembled by 5:00 a.m. at the Pratt Blast Furnace Landing in Black Rock. A second, larger group numbering 4,000 was to follow the next day.

Pat had sailed as a member of the 7th Regiment's advance scouting party from the foot of Main Street across to Fort Erie on May 24. The day had dawned bright, clear, and calm. Along with three other members of the 7th, he rode a ferry that sailed daily from Fort Erie, carrying passengers, fish, and British finished goods to Buffalo. Fort Erie was a small southern Ontario village of fewer than 1,000 residents spread along the shoreline at the eastern end of Lake Erie and the mouth of the Niagara River.

On arrival, the four Fenians split up. Pat climbed from a pier in the village to a high point where he could see most of the area. Ruins of a fort, captured by Americans in 1814, spread out to the south. Along the shore were piers as far north as he could see. A variety of fishing and freight boats lay at anchor, some propelled by large white sails, others by steam and sail. A line of pubs and inns extended from the village's lakefront harbor north along the Niagara River, broken only by a beach where children were running and playing ball. A few boys were diving off a pier, unfazed by the chilly spring water. Just beyond the village limits to the west, farms with green grain fields and fruit orchards in full bloom fell away to the horizon. The view mesmerized Pat. He wished he could stay right where he was for the rest of the day or, better still, join men he saw lounging in an outdoor café.

Captain Bailey had given Pat a generous allowance of British sterling, enough for him to move about and sustain himself for a few days in southern Ontario. Pat had never felt so carefree. He headed south and roamed through the ruins of the old fort, noting there were still a half dozen British soldiers lazing about.

He walked a few hundred yards into the village, a pleasant stroll over the grassy knolls of a waterfront park overlooking the Canadian shore. Buffalo lay clearly visible to the east, beyond green waters. He exchanged pleasantries with a group of old men and asked about establishing an Irish pub in the area. He told them he had migrated from Ireland to Niagara, a town thirty miles north at Lake Ontario, a week prior and made his way to Fort Erie on the train that ran along the Niagara River.

Indeed, now he took that trip in reverse from Fort Erie to Chippewa, about ten miles to the north adjacent to Niagara Falls, where, on foot, he scouted the British soldiers billeted there. He estimated that there were at least 3,000 and noted that they had heavy artillery. From there, he hitched rides on farm wagons and horse cars to Niagara. He sensed no air of impending danger, in fact, quite the opposite. The natives were tending their business as usual. He enjoyed his conversations with them, weaving in seemingly innocuous questions about the military and geography. These were people like his own in the Ward, good God-fearing, down-to-earth folks.

He stopped in a pub just up the street from St. Vincent de Paul Roman Catholic Church and talked to the Irish proprietor about finding work. He was told portions of the Welland Canal were being trenched along a new route, mainly with Irish labor from Cork. He made a mental note that the canal in such a state could be quite vulnerable. Seeding the canal with a half dozen mines that sank a ship or blew up a lock would put a real dent into British trade. He knew from friends in the convalescent camp that the rebels had done just that in Southern ports during the war. He thought to himself there might be among the Confederate Fenian members one who knew how to turn an artillery shell into a mine. Some of those butternuts were clever bastards.

He hiked toward Port Colborne, sixteen miles from Fort Erie. Detouring into Stevensville, he found a market in the center of town and bought lettuce, horseradish, sausage, and bread. He chatted with Canadian Irish, who were well established in southern Ontario with their own farms and had long since made their peace with Canadians and British alike. If the Fenians were counting on Canadian Irish to join them in capturing a slice of Ontario or Quebec, what Pat learned would give them pause.

He caught a train from Stevensville to Port Colborne, surveyed Welland Canal locks, and ate a tasty dinner of fresh walleye at an outdoor café alongside the canal. He conversed with wealthy farmers, a sea captain, and English immigrants on their way to establish a business in Windsor. Then Pat walked to a nearby elevator and hitched a ride working as a deck hand on a steam freighter loaded with Canadian grain bound on Lake Erie for Buffalo. It was clear to him from his conversations that Canadians were proud of their country and their British heritage and would fight hard to protect it from another American invasion. They were still smarting from the invasions of the War of 1812.

In Buffalo a week later, he joined the rest of the squad and briefed Colonel O'Neill about the people and the terrain he had just observed. O'Neill silently noted the natural way Pat had been able to blend in with the local population

181

and secure vital information across the whole area. Pat had also sketched a rough map with details of military significance.

"This is exactly what I need," said O'Neill as Pat beamed.

On May 31, Pat and a small group walked the five miles from downtown Buffalo to Pratt Landing in Black Rock. Along with a few hundred others, he labored through the early morning hours unloading and loading guns and supplies.

Under orders from General Grant, the U.S. District Attorney for Western New York had ordered the *USS Michigan*, an iron-hulled gunboat out of Erie, Pennsylvania, to head off the Fenians. It arrived too late to stop the first group.

A thousand men, the size of a Civil War regiment, had crowded onto barges in the early morning of June 1 and were towed across the narrow expanse of the Niagara River without being intercepted. Many were dressed in Union blue blouses and kepi caps, several in Confederate grey, the rest in work clothes and slouch hats. Some wore green shirts over their blouses. Five Civil War regimental banners flew among them. The men were excited and noisy. They sang Union and Confederate songs together. O'Neill had to quiet them several times, warning that their loud voices carried clearly across the river. If the British were waiting on shore, their artillery would blow up the barges and British riflemen would shoot them like ducks bobbing about helplessly in the water.

The *USS Michigan* steamed downriver at sun-up, eight of its guns—including a thirty-pound parrot rifle—pointed menacingly ashore, and prevented 4,000 Fenians waiting at Pratt Landing from crossing.

O'Neill had conceived a robust strategy with information from Buffalo IRA scouts. His plan was to establish a bridgehead interior to a line running from the Niagara River along Black Creek north of Fort Erie to the Welland Canal, and from Chippewa on the Welland Canal to Port Colborne. To achieve this, he needed all 5,000 of his men.

Upon embarking, officers had supplied the first group of 1,000 men with forty rounds of ammunition each. As the men disembarked on the Canadian side a mile south of Frenchman's Creek, they were handed rifles.

O'Neill ordered Captain Owen Starr, commanding Indiana, New York, and Kentucky regiments, to march along the Niagara River and its adjacent rail track, capture rolling stock, cut telegraph lines, and occupy the village of Fort Erie. Starr, in turn, was to have Captain John Geary lead his New York unit further west and disrupt the railroad running between Fort Erie and Ridgeway.

The New York, Ohio, and Tennessee regiments overwhelmed local militia with few casualties on either side, occupied the village, and posted pickets around it. Starr then brazenly ordered Dr. Kempson, the village council president, to prepare breakfast for his men.

Geary captured the fort and its complement of six British soldiers. By 7:00 a.m., the green Fenian colors flew over the fort. He then advanced west from Six Mile Creek toward Port Colborne, ripped up rail and telegraph lines, and destroyed the Sauerwein Bridge on his way back.

O'Neill ordered three scouts, including Pat, to commandeer horses and procure information from the locals about troop movements. This they attempted to do at farms near Fort Erie. The population relinquished horses only at the point of a rifle. A few shouted epithets about the invaders' original and current countries. Pat, with two horses in hand, turned his horse back toward these English Canadians. The other two scouts shouted at him that he was under orders to continue back to Colonel O'Neill, who needed the horses immediately. He pulled on the horse's reins and did as ordered, although with a few well-phrased statements about the farmers' colonial heritage and sexual proclivities. In all, the scouts returned with nine well-bred horses.

Colonel O'Neill ordered two scouts to ride along the Niagara River toward Niagara Falls and another pair west toward Port Colborne. Two hours later, they returned with word that three thousand British and militia troops were massing in Chippewa and two thousand Canadian militia in Port Colborne.

O'Neill marched the bulk of his army, about 800 men, north along the Niagara River five miles to the Newbigging Farm and set up bullet screens made from fence rails. O'Neill assumed correctly from scouting reports that British troops would, within the day, move south along the river from their encampment near Niagara Falls.

In the meantime, Pat returned to the village on horseback and joined members of the Buffalo IRA Regiment. One Buffalo Fenian joked, nodding toward the *Michigan*, a three-masted gunboat offshore, "No more of us will be coming across the Niagara, that's for sure."

"You're right," said Pat. "We shan't see another Fenian unless he swims across from the Ward." His brother's warnings about Fenian leadership and President Andrew Johnson's likely intentions flashed through Pat's head. He returned to the main force at the Newbigging Farm and repeated to Colonel O'Neill that the men he had were all he would ever have.

They walked together away from the body of soldiers. "Pat, I need someone to scout the Lake Erie shore for militia coming from Port Colborne by ship, rail, or foot to block off our escape route. If the scouting reports are accurate, over 5,000 local militia and British regulars could be after us by day's end. Ride along the shoreline a few miles toward Port Colborne. See what you can learn from the locals." With those simple instructions, he returned to address his soldiers.

O'Neill shouted to his men, who now numbered about 700. "We're outnumbered twenty to one. I find that encouraging. Scouts tell us the Redcoats will be marching from Chippewa ten miles north of here."

He pointed to a hand-drawn but accurate map. "They have scouts out and will know the instant we begin marching north along the river. Once they start moving upriver, turning that crowd around will be more difficult than reversing Lady Johnson's corset." The men laughed.

"As soon as we're sure British scouts see us, we'll swing inland at Black Creek and march straight for Limestone Ridge, which is no more than five miles distant. We will form a smaller perimeter than I originally intended, bounded by Black Creek and the Limestone Ridge running from Black Creek to Lake Erie.

"Should the British arrive unexpectedly, we will not advance to Port Colborne, but to a defensible position in the old fort. From there, we should be able to escape to Buffalo, if we have to."

Simple enough, thought Pat, *but where is he going to get the barges to get us home? There are a dozen tied up in Port Colborne, but I saw none in Fort Erie.* He gave it no more thought. Maybe some would tie up there later. O'Neill was his kind of leader. He'd get the barges somehow.

After dark, 700 Fenians broke camp, leaving their fires burning, and marched north on the river road. The crew of the *USS Michigan* continued to observe Fenian movements through field glasses. At 9:00 p.m., the captain on the bridge yelled that Frenchman Creek Bridge was on fire. O'Neill had stacked 300 rifles, for which he had no men, on the bridge and set them ablaze to attract attention. It did. The British in Chippewa got the news from their scouts shortly afterward.

An hour after starting up the Niagara River shore, O'Neill and his troops turned west at Black Creek. They did a forced march of four miles, occupied the only rise in the area—Limestone Ridge, a mile north of the Village of Ridgeway—and erected light defenses. He then strung out pickets 500 yards south at Ridge and Garrison Roads, directly in the path of the anticipated Port Colborne militia.

At dusk, 1,000 volunteer militia under Colonel J. Stoughton Dennis gathered at Port Colborne. Canadian authorities had ordered the militia to march toward Stevensville and catch the Fenians between them and Colonel Peacocke's British soldiers marching from Chippewa. Instead, Dennis decided to block a probable Fenian escape route. At 3:30 a.m. on Saturday, June 2, he led 80 men from the Dunnville Naval Company militia onto the tug, the *W.T.*

Robb, and steamed off to Fort Erie two hours later. The bulk of his militia, 900 men, Dennis left in Port Colborne.

Pat was driving a wagon he had commandeered in Fort Erie up the Lake Erie shore at sun-up, when he sighted the tug racing at full speed toward Fort Erie, loaded with red-uniformed men hanging on the rails. He unhitched the horse from the wagon and rode bareback to alert Captain Starr in the village that the Canadians were opening up a third front, probably from Fort Erie by ship. Starr ordered Pat to the Lake Erie shore to determine size and direction of the new force.

Pat watched about twenty militiamen disembark from the tug. They proceeded into the Village of Fort Erie and took fifty-six Fenian stragglers prisoner. Pat returned to Starr and relayed what he had seen. Ordered back to Fort Erie by Starr, Pat planted himself behind a giant maple, from which point much of the village center was visible.

After numerous delays, Peacocke finally ordered his mostly British army of 4,000 infantry and artillery from Chippewa south along the river to Black Creek. The Fenians were nowhere to be found. An hour or so later, he turned the column right toward Ridgeway and Stevensville.

The militia in Port Colborne boarded a train to Ridgeway. There they met up with Major James A. Skinner, who assumed charge from Booker, who was absent anyway. The militia had armed themselves with what was thought to be adequate ammunition, forty to sixty rounds per company, and sent the rest back on the train. One company took no ammunition at all and had to be supplied by the rest when fighting broke out. The Queen's Own Rifles Company, in brilliant red, white, and blue dress uniforms, carried breech-loading, lever-action Spencers and forty rounds each.

The Canadians marched from the Ridgeway Rail Station to a point a mile east on Ridge Road. As they crossed Garrison Road, Fenian skirmishers opened fire on the lead company, the Queen's Own, who rapid-fired their carbines and exhausted nearly all their ammunition within minutes. The Queen's Own skirmishers advanced until they ran into a second line of Fenian skirmishers behind bullet screens at Bertie Road, about 800 yards north of Garrison Road. The Canadians charged and drove the Fenian skirmishers back into the main Fenian line.

Somewhere a bugle sounded an enemy cavalry charge, or a retreat, the Canadians knew not which. Some ran back from where they had come. Others backed around into a square, a strategic maneuver used to deal with swirling cavalry assaults. Seeing the confusion, O'Neill ordered an attack. Retreating Canadians and charging Fenians slammed into the square and started a rout of militia all the way back to Port Colborne.

O'Neill's men pursued the Canadians 1,000 yards, then halted. He ordered a forced march into Fort Erie. The *W.T. Robb* was cruising just offshore, a floating jail for fifty-six Fenian stragglers captured by the Dunnville militia. The Fenians fired on the *Robb*, which quickly steamed out into the river, leaving seventy-six militiamen stranded on shore. Some escaped overland into farms. The Buffalo 7th IRA Regiment, which O'Neill had used to garrison the village, captured the rest. During the brief battle, a militia soldier shot his ramrod, knocking 7th commander Captain Michael Bailey from his horse and seriously wounding him in the abdomen.

Colonel John O'Neill was victorious in both encounters with Canadian militia, but the same good sense he showed leading his men in battle told him his victories were over. In only a matter of hours, twin columns with many times his force would attack—the British army descending from Chippewa and the reorganized Canadian militia from Port Colborne. The *USS Michigan*, with her picket tugs *Harrison* and *Farrar* and the US revenue cutter, *The Fessenden*, were patrolling the Niagara River and Lake Erie, watching his every move. With no reinforcements or additional supplies, his choices were few.

Late in the evening, O'Neill released his prisoners and moved his troops to the ruins of old Fort Erie to wage a last stand. Not only did the advancing enemy boast superior numbers—about 5,000—but they had artillery that could destroy his force from a mile away. Fortunately, a bit of Irish good luck appeared at this moment in the person of Fenian Captain Hamilton, who crossed from Buffalo to Fort Erie in a small boat. He informed O'Neill that a large barge, the *AP Waite*, was being towed across the short expanse of Lake Erie between Buffalo and Fort Erie by a tug commanded by Hugh Mooney. To both men's amazement, it evaded four US Navy ships and arrived just offshore. Within less than an hour, by 2:00 a.m. on Sunday, June 3, O'Neill loaded 500 of his men on this scow, all who could fit, and started back across the Niagara. In midstream, the *USS Harrison* fired a shot across the tug's bow and took it in tow.

Pat had joined O'Neill and his men in the Fort Erie ruins and spent the night with them, but did not leave with them. He decided he would wait for the ferry in a pub he knew from his scouting excursion on the north side of the village. He hid his rifle, his kepi, and blue blouse in the crawl space beneath the pub and went in. In his best brogue, he told the locals he was immigrating to Canada through Buffalo. For the rest of the day, he drank whiskey and told stories about Half Night O'Toole and other Cork characters. He had the locals in gales of laughter. He became quite drunk.

British soldiers appeared later that afternoon from Chippewa. The locals, who by now suspected Pat's true identity, told him they were most sorry to have to hand him over. Like any of the good men of Fort Erie, they would just as soon ignore the shouting and shooting going on around town and continue drinking. The soldiers put Pat on a train under guard on June 4 and sent him to Toronto.

Fenian infantry spent an exposed and cool night on the windswept barge docked near Fort Porter in Buffalo harbor. Officers appeared before a U.S. magistrate on Monday morning. A sympathetic federal court judge in Buffalo released all men below officer rank outright and released officers on their own recognizance, which was about the same thing.

One hundred seventeen Fenians surrendered to Canadian militia in various places around Fort Erie and were shipped by train to Toronto, courtesy of Her Majesty the Queen. There they were paraded down city streets before an outraged public who threw garbage at them. Pat spent the night incarcerated in a makeshift jail in the basement of a municipal building and appeared before a judge the next day.

No one had located Pat's kepi, blouse, and musket, so there was no evidence to counter his statement that he was simply enjoying a pleasant afternoon in one of Fort Erie's finest establishments. The Canadian judge found him not guilty for lack of evidence that he was, indeed, a Fenian soldier. The Crown fed him lunch and once again put him on a train without handcuffs or guard. He returned to Fort Erie that same afternoon; from there he hitched a ride to Buffalo with a Canadian fisherman delivering yellow pike.

The Fenian invasion of Fort Erie had been brilliantly conceived by General Sweeney and intelligently led by Colonel O'Neill. With only 800 to 1,000 men, however, the Fenian foray was doomed. Even had all 5,000 troops been able to cross the Niagara, the Fenian generals had made no provision to resupply them. They had also misgauged the willingness of Canadian Irish to support their forces once they landed on Canadian shores. Even with 5,000 men, O'Neill's army would have been outgunned and forced to surrender or face massacre at the hands of British regulars and Canadian militia.

Twenty-two Fenians were tried by the Crown in Toronto in the fall of 1866, found guilty of high treason, and by February 1867 sentenced to be hanged. All twenty-two eventually had their sentences reduced to twenty years' hard labor. Twenty Fenians were acquitted, forty-nine released for lack of evidence, thirteen released on bail, three held for trial, and six disappeared without a court appearance. The fate of four others is unknown. US Secretary of State Seward and the US Congress sought the release of those still in prison.

Pat met his grandmother on the stoop of her cottage on Louisiana Street. She cried and hugged him. "Oh, Pat, no more wars for you, please, lad!"

Pat told neither his grandmother nor another soul how he was captured. It was the type of uncourageous act that, if known, would get him labeled throughout the taverns of the Ward. He'd never shake it. It would shame him and his family for life. No man would work with him, if any boss would hire him.

CHAPTER 21

Mary Nagle

Garrett Nagle owned a small blacksmith shop outside Fermoy, County Cork that catered to tenant farmers. As famine conditions caused tenant farmers in the region to migrate, so in 1849 did the Nagle family—Garrett, his wife Ellen, and six children—to New York. A year after arriving in New York City, unsuccessful at starting a business there, Garrett left the family at age thirty-two and went to work in Buffalo, milling ships' hardware. He quickly saw the potential to supply hardware to the booming mercantile trade industry in Buffalo and persuaded his boss to capitalize a supply business that he would run. Business thrived. Each year thereafter for five years, Garrett bought out a portion of the equity investment until he fully owned the business.

Garrett had been a heavy drinker in New York. In Buffalo, he attended St. Patrick's Parish at the corner of Ellicott Street and Broadway. At one of the bishop's anti-drinking crusades, Garrett took the pledge never to drink again. He also adopted a disciplined lifestyle in imitation of his principal investor and other Protestant business owners. He was impressed not only by their personal lives, but also by the fact that a disciplined life appeared to translate into well-run and very profitable businesses.

He attended Masonic meetings and was invited to join the Lodge at Washington and Exchange Streets, where many of his Presbyterian colleagues were members. When he approached Bishop Timon about it, the bishop was four-square against such a move. He warned Garrett that he would be forced to excommunicate him, should he become a Freemason.

The Church placed no impediment, however, against joining the Odd Fellows. Garrett joined the Odd Fellows Lodge on Franklin Street, one of two Catholics out of 150 members. He bought a home on Niagara Street near

Porter in a neighborhood dominated by bourgeois Americans, whose families had roots in New England and, before that, in Britain.

In Ireland, he had sympathized with area Whiteboys and supported them financially. In Buffalo, he became frustrated with the poor work ethic of many of his Irish-born workers and joined Odd Fellow friends in condemning the Irish and their lazy and riotous ways. He noted that Bishop Timon himself was ashamed of the behavior of lower class Irish, who were mostly from the First Ward and the canal district.

Within two years of his arrival in Buffalo, Garrett wrote his wife, Ellen, about joining him. If she was unwilling to forgive him for leaving the family and refused to give up the successful rooming-house business she had built up over a decade, he suggested that she at least send two or three of their children to live with him. She refused to move, but offered to buy train tickets for any of their six children who wanted to live with their father.

Memories of their father's drunkenness dominated the thinking of all of the children except one. In 1853, Nagle's youngest daughter, Mary, age eight, joined him in the company of an older Irish woman whom Garrett hired as her nanny. Mary had lived with five siblings and her mother, with whom she had frequent rows as she grew older. She wanted to continue beyond the sixth grade, but her mother demanded she quit school and act as a maid in her cramped boarding house in lower Manhattan.

Mary looked on Buffalo as nothing short of the promised land of personal freedom. Her father gave her a spacious, well-appointed bedroom on the third floor of their mansion overlooking the river. She had no trouble accommodating herself to its Victorian architecture and pleasant décor or to servants who did the cooking and cleaning, to fine clothes, interesting and bountiful food, and good times with her father and his friends on weekends. Garrett's success in business assured that Mary never wanted for anything.

Her nanny remained with the household for the next nine years, doting on the girl. In time, Mary grew closer to her than she had been to her own mother.

After Mary finished eighth grade at St. Louis School on Edward Street, she spent two years in St. Mary's Academy and Industrial School next to the cathedral on Franklin Street. Upon graduation in 1860, her father brought her into the business. Mary was 15 and emerging from her teenage growth spurt as a pretty, if awkward, young lady. She was bright and had a penchant for math. Every evening, she and her father talked about the business over the supper table. Her father was elated that Mary had a mind for business. Having someone like Mary embedded in his office was invaluable.

After three years on the job, her loyalty to him and her administrative skills freed him to spend the day dealing with contractors and business owners. Buffalo was the hub of East-meets-West in America. Business owners, especially merchants and manufacturers, were expanding as quickly as they could secure capital. Buildings were growing out of the ground at every corner and all along the lake and riverfronts.

There was money to be made at Nagle Supply Company, but someone had to tend to the details of finance, taxes, personnel, and other administrative issues. Between 1860 and 1866, Mary matured into that person and not a day too soon. By 1862, the Civil War had doubled Garrett's business.

There was no way, however, that Mary could be confined to home, church, and office. Young people found plenty to do in the city's church halls, clubs, and taverns, and on waterways, beaches, and in picnic groves in the beautiful Buffalo summer. Social clubs formed along class, ethnic, and religious lines. Mary, however, was not limited as were other young Catholic girls to parish and neighborhood venues.

The center of the city's social life had spread several blocks north from the foot of Main Street at the Erie Canal. Local entertainers and New York vaudeville acts filled Buffalo's nightspots. Successful Irish were to be found in growing numbers in downtown clubs, on stage, and in the audience, drawn by the popular culture germinating in New York and captivating the nation. New York City had discovered the market value of Irish culture.

One establishment favored by up-and-coming young Irish was McSheehan's Saloon and Theatre on Washington Street. Davit McSheehan was from County Cork, as were many Buffalo Irish. He understood his customers and supplied the brands of whiskey and other beverages they most preferred. He traded across the Niagara River, importing excellent Canadian whiskey, which rapidly replaced Irish whiskey in favor. It was easier to get, cheaper, and suited the tastes of his clientele. He soon learned to pay off a few cops and smuggle it across the border to avoid the American tariff.

McSheehan's was one of the largest establishments of its kind in Buffalo. Davit had recently redecorated the premises in the style of a Dublin pub, with a carved dark oak bar set off by a thirty-foot spread of whiskey, gin, and other hard liquors aglow in gaslights before an equally long mirror. The back room was a statement in oak tables and chairs and snugs that shouted to couples and families that this room was made for special occasions.

At twenty, Mary was attractive, charming, and had money to spend. She was five feet seven inches tall, had dark hair and blue eyes, and was endowed with a lovely, full figure. She dressed in the latest New York and European fashions.

Mary had a wide range of friends, from people her own age to business associates from Nagle Supply and its customers.

Davit adored her, all the more so, it seemed, after his sister died. Very quickly, she became popular with his regular crowd of rising Irish Americans.

She also frequented the social scene of the elite American set at house and club parties, where her stunning appearance and ease of conversation over business and trade guaranteed her attention from males.

In November 1865, after a Fenian Circle meeting, Pat Donohue met Mary Nagle in the back room at McSheehan's and was taken by her beauty and outgoing personality. Pat was an inch taller than Mary, with a strong body and a happy and handsome face. He dressed in a three-piece suit, high-collar white shirt and bow tie, and top hat. He sported a turned-down mustache and goatee, much as he had seen officers grow toward the end of the war.

His self-confidence, Civil War exploits, and Irish stories attracted and amused Mary. He, too, had money to spend, having collected two enlistment bonuses since coming home. He was earning a steady wage, only half of which he brought home for his board.

They soon began to meet on weekends at McSheehan's. She could not bring him to her other social engagements. He simply did not fit with that cultured, educated, Protestant crowd.

In April 1866, they went on a date to McSheehan's for the opening of the spring entertainment season. Performing was Dion Boucicault, who, although his name hardly revealed it, hailed from Dublin. He appeared at McSheehan's, singing songs from his highly successful melodrama, *Pat Malloy*, which had recently debuted on Broadway. Buffalo was the last stop before taking the play overseas to Dublin, London, Manchester, and Paris.

After a beer in the back room, Mary and Pat passed through the dining room to a theatre seating 300. Arriving early, they found seats close to the stage that offered a good view of Dion and his musicians. It was important to be up front, insisted Pat, if he was to understand the singer's heavy brogue.

The thick curtain parted. Dion entered dressed in britches and caubeen, a tall, brimless hat. He was a small person, balding, and had a pleasant elfish face, set off by a mustache and beard. The crowd snickered a little at his appearance and then hushed. With no introduction, the five-piece band rolled through a stanza and then he began to sing. His tenor voice was surprisingly strong and filled the hall:

At sixteen years of age, I was my mother's fair-haired boy,
From Ireland to America across the sea I roam,
And every shilling that I got, ah sure I sent it home;
My mother couldn't write, but on there came from Father Boyce;
"Oh, heaven bless you, Pat," says she—I hear my mother's voice!

For ould Ireland is me country, and me name is Pat Malloy.

He sang several verses, always ending, "For ould Ireland is me country, and me name is Pat Malloy."

By the second verse, handkerchiefs daubed wet eyes. When the song ended, the crowd clapped tentatively. Slowly, the applause grew as voices and whistles filled the theatre. Then the crowd stood and cheered as though at a baseball game. Boucicault had hit a home run with this mostly Irish crowd.

As the crowd settled back into their seats, he was joined by an attractive young woman dressed in the short green jumper of a stage colleen, played by Mary Hogan. She sang in a high, sweet voice an answer song that Boucicault had just written, "Mary of Fermoy." It was a tale of her Pat, forced from Ireland by landlord and high rent. He had to leave his sweetheart behind to gain Columbia's "bless'd land of liberty." Again, there was nary a dry eye among the Irish in the house when she finished.

Dion and Mary Hogan sang ten more songs written by Boucicault before other acts, mostly Irish, replaced them. In all, the show lasted an hour and a half.

Afterward, they walked arm in arm down Main Street to the corner of Allen. Pat was thrilled to be alongside this stylish young woman. She wore a black overcoat over a dark green satin dress with an upturned collar that accentuated her delicate neck and a broad oval hat tipped up around the brim, articulated with an eagle feather.

They hailed a trolley heading west. He sat as close to her as he dared.

Mary clapped her hands joyously. Her eyes twinkled in the moonlight that passed though the parted curtain of the trolley door. "Oh, Boucicault has a voice that pierced my soul, Pat. His words brought back the sadness of leaving Fermoy and coming to America."

"Boucicault's characters could have been from the Ward," said Pat. "Indeed, I could put names to every one of them."

"What a big voice that small man has," commented Mary. "It blended well with Mary Hogan's little-girl voice. It was a great show."

"I was hurt by the way he talked about the Irish. Weren't you?" asked Pat.

"Not really. True, some of the characters he played cast the Irish in an unflattering light. Still you had to laugh, didn't you? We're a strange race of people," she sighed, and she slid her hip closer to Pat.

Pat was taken off guard, thrilled with the blunt way Mary expressed her feelings, a free woman like none he knew in the Ward.

"The show made me wish I had my parents again. Stories I heard from Gram came back as they sang. I'm proud to be Irish."

Mary nodded. "I know. I feel the same."

Pat paused before speaking again. "Most of all, I was proud to be with you. You made me feel like I stood above every man there."

As they neared the Nagle mansion on Niagara Street, Pat added, "I have to tip my hat to our own here in Buffalo, people like your father, how they've stood up to the Know Nothings." He grew silent and turned toward her, touched her face gently with his left hand, and kissed her on the cheek.

Mary didn't know what a Know Nothing was. They exited the trolley and she left him on the sidewalk saying, "Pat, thanks so much for the evening. I enjoyed being with you. You're the perfect gentleman."

Pat waited until she was in the door, turned, jumped, clapped his hands, and started the long walk home to the First Ward feeling light as the feather in Mary's hat.

A month later, Mary brought Pat home to meet her father. After a few preliminary questions about the show the two had seen the night before, Garrett Nagle began to interrogate his daughter's would-be suitor. "I understand from Mary that you served with the 155th in some of the worst battles in the war. I congratulate you for serving your country."

"Thank you. It was the experience of a lifetime."

"Pat, you can imagine that as her father, I am concerned whether the man she may be getting serious with can support her as she has been raised."

"Of course, I understand your concern."

"How far did you get in school?"

"There was no money to go past the sixth grade, so I began to run errands for sailors and shine shoes downtown. Eventually, I went to work for Bishop Timon and then for a year as a laborer at the Union Iron Works. I joined the 155th at eighteen and spent three years in service. I'm working once again at the Iron Works."

Pat told neither Mary nor her father that he had joined the Fenians and was about to cross to Fort Erie to scout for their invasion.

Garrett asked him about his family.

"My parents died in Rochester when I was five. My grandmother, Maire Joy, brought me and my brother to Buffalo and raised me. She's a wonderful lady, sews vestments for the bishop and many of the parishes in Buffalo. That's how she supported us."

Garrett remembered Mrs. Joy from a meeting at St. Patrick's. She was the one who inspired a successful Irish festival.

The next day, Garrett made inquiries about Pat with the Iron Works' purchasing manager. The manager feared that the very traits that probably made Pat a brave and fierce soldier also made him an unreliable worker. He added that Pat's stay in prison left him too weak to labor in an iron mill and others had to cover for him.

The manager regretted to add that Pat's tenure at the Iron Works was coming to an end. He simply could not keep up with the work. The Iron Works manager mentioned Pat's lack of education meant Pat would never rise above an unskilled laborer and his weakened constitution permitted not a full day of that. Hearing these statements, Nagle stroked his mustache, a habitual gesture he made when he was deep in thought. Garrett concluded that Pat was unstable and in the long term might be trouble.

Garrett had gathered enough unsettling information about Pat to call Mary into his office at the end of the business day. He closed the door. Standing erect, he gazed on his daughter with a serious expression and cleared his throat.

"Mary, Pat is a very likeable young man, but he has no future. I've checked with people who know him and know him well. I think you should find a way to break off the relationship and stop seeing him. He will make you very unhappy."

Mary's temper flared. "Who said things about Pat? What did they say?"

"Mary, you are twenty-one, bright, and beautiful, if I say so myself. I think Pat has a certain spell over you. As your father, it is my duty to stop you from doing something ill-advised. What else are fathers for if not to protect their daughters?"

Their conversation became increasingly angry. Mary stomped out of the office and went home. Garrett concluded his daughter was in love, or at least believed she was. That evening, after a supper without conversation, he forbade her to see Pat again.

That last comment was all Mary needed. She was an independent woman whose business responsibilities had grown over the past five years. By twenty-one, most women like her were already married, and these days educated women didn't ask anyone's permission.

She and Pat never missed another Saturday night together. They threw Catholic morality into the Buffalo Creek and made love after every date in a cheap hotel downtown.

Then in mid-May, before scouting Fort Erie, Pat told Mary about his Fenian involvement and she ended their relationship.

By the time Pat returned to Buffalo from Toronto, the Buffalo papers had covered the invasion and its aftermath. As it happened, Mary attended mass the next Sunday at the cathedral and heard one of Bishop Timon's more powerful sermons, very sympathetic to the Fenian cause. Mary and her father, who attended with her, left mass feeling guilty about their lack of understanding of the Irish cause and the justification for the Fenian movement after 400 years of brutal British rule. Foolish or not, the Fenian struggle for Irish freedom was right and good and they above all, Irish-born Americans, should be praising Fenian soldiers for their courage. That was the conclusion of Bishop Timon's message and they took it to heart.

Mary and Pat became engaged that August.

Despite his misgivings about Pat and his anger at his daughter's rebellion, Garrett Nagle was a realist. Mary could leave his family and his business, which could not run without her; or he could accept Pat and hope for the best. That was his only real choice.

Rationalizing Mary's relationship with Pat, Garrett's attitude turned 180 degrees. With the announcement of their engagement, he adopted the view— on the surface, at any rate—that Pat was Mary's choice and so the right choice it had to be. After all, Patrick was an engaging character. He came from good people. His grandmother was known throughout the Irish community and was a friend of the bishop.

Mary told Pat she wanted to talk to Mother Joy about their intended marriage and about the wedding. She knew many of the family's relatives and friends would have to be invited, but she did not want the excessive drinking and rowdiness that was a standard part of weddings in the Ward. The one ace in the hole she had was Bishop Timon. If the bishop were to be present at the festivities after the wedding mass, there would be very little whiskey, perhaps only wine and porter.

Pat set up the meeting with Mother Joy. Mary came by carriage on a Saturday evening in September. She had eaten dinner with Mother Joy and Uncle Jack twice before on Sundays and felt at home with them. They obviously liked her very much. While she clearly came from money, she had no airs about her. When she was with them, she fell into their conversational style.

"Mother Joy and Uncle Jack, I want to be a part of your family. So I'm asking your blessing on our marriage."

Maire beamed at the news. "Well, Mary dear, my brother and I welcomed you into our home when first you came. No regrets have we. You're a dream come true. We can't make your wedding a grand affair, but we know how to make a wedding spree."

Jack remained silent, but nodded his head.

Pat and Mary were wed at St. Patrick's Church on Seymour and Emslie in the Hydraulics on Sunday, October 21, 1866. The mass was presided over by Franciscan Father Bonaventure. Two hundred people gathered for the reception at McSheehan's. Both Pat's friends and Mary's attended and enjoyed themselves, as did Garret's Lodge brothers. Mary's mother and siblings did not attend because she did not invite them. It had been years since she had left New York and in all that time, she had not heard from them.

The wedding was carried off with fun, but also with deliberate sobriety. John and his fiancée, Johanna, stood up for the bridal party and sat at the head table. John toasted his brother with glass held high. "Pat, never in your life have you done something more worthy of praise than making Mary fall in love with you. May you cherish her all the days of your life, my dearest brother."

Maire, Garrett, and Bishop Timon all told old Irish stories that had everyone laughing. They sang, danced, and cheered on the rest of the family. Pat was thrilled to have won Mary as his wife, but resentful that the bishop had dictated the terms of his wedding. He wanted a wedding like his friends', a total bash.

Pat and Mary had known one another for ten months. She was twenty-one. He was twenty-two. They rented a downstairs flat on Kentucky Street in the Ward. From that day on, Garrett slipped Mary a $10 bill every other Sunday when they came for dinner, a sign of his affection, if not his wholehearted approval. Garrett had considered hiring Pat to work in his warehouse stocking and picking inventory, but thought better of it. The fact that he didn't was not lost on Pat nor Mary.

Maire had summoned up her best effort to celebrate her grandson's wedding. She was now nearly seventy-five. Arthritis in all her joints, severe in her hands, had forced her to give up sewing. Pat supported her the year before he married and then brought her into his home for the last months of her life. By this time, her brother Jack, nine years younger than Maire, was able to work only three days a week and could barely support himself. He too moved to the Kentucky Street flat.

Asthma from years inhaling grain dust constricted his lungs. Living with Jack and Maire brought Mary happiness and joy. Maire prepared meals. Jack took care of small repairs and improvements Mary sought in the apartment. Simple folk with no pretentions, they lingered with Mary evenings at the supper table, talking about her work and reminiscing about the old country. Mary enjoyed the first months of her marriage in part because of them.

On February 10, 1867, Maire passed away in her sleep after a final illness that had lasted but two months. Bishop Timon insisted on celebrating her funeral mass even though he was barely able to stand. While anointing a dying Sister of Charity, he had contracted erysipelas, a disease of the subcutaneous skin that in two years spread over his whole body, became increasingly painful, and restricted his movements.

The bishop controlled Maire's funeral and wake, every stitch of it. So ostentatious had Irish funerals become in this country, so rowdy were their wakes, that Bishop Timon was ashamed of his own kind before the city's Protestant clergy and leadership. He had promulgated a decree to all parishes that there could be no more than four carriages in any funeral cortege, and that wakes were to be celebrated in a sober manner, respectful of the Church's teachings on death, and the place God prepared for those who live and die in His grace. When Pat proposed to make a boisterous, lavish affair out of the wake and to appeal to the Friendly Sons of St. Patrick for funds to carry all family members in carriages, John had but to remind him that the bishop was in charge and that Maire would be buried as the bishop saw fit.

Pat cursed his brother for not supporting him, for being such a lackey of the clergy, and stalked off without another word. When he complained to Mary, her face became red and she spit out her words. "How can you be such a fool, Pat!" she shouted. Mary had the first inkling that her marriage to an uneducated First Warder might be a trap.

It was their first serious fight. Pat bolted from their little flat on Kentucky and spent the afternoon drinking at Kennedy's. The next day, he came half-drunk to his grandmother's wake, held in the cathedral at Bishop Timon's request, instead of in her home as was customary. Mary came to the wake with Uncle Jack and Jo. The following day at the funeral mass, not to bring shame to the family, she sat with Pat. The mass was attended by over 400 family members, friends, and parishioners.

As he began his homily, Bishop Timon came down from the pulpit and stood at the head of the casket. A face racked with pain gradually transformed into one of beatific calm.

"John Donohue and Johanna Mahoney, Pat and Mary Donohue, Jack, Jo and Harry, members of the Joy and Donohue families, you know I've spent much of my life studying the Irish people. I learned their ancient language and speak English with their brogue, even though I first visited that blest country with my parents well after my birth. The old Irish, like your grandmother, have been a source of courage and inspiration to my priesthood. There is in a few of them a rare strain, like a vein of gold, of that ancient Celtic race that could not be touched, let alone broken, by the British throughout 400 years of the most intense persecution the world has ever known. These people hailed mostly from the west of Ireland, hidden up in moors and mountains where no 'civilized man' would go. I read and dreamed about them until I could almost hear and see them sing and dance around their evening fires." He stopped momentarily and stared at Maire in the open casket. "However, they never became truly real until I met your grandmother. She was like the matriarch of a clan that had survived untamed in the Boggeragh Mountains until an angel lifted her whole into the First Ward. She was that genuine."

"It wasn't just her ancient ways that distinguished her. Maire Joy was a wise woman who knew how to bring life and love back to two scared little boys, just as she had to her brother, Jack, and her niece, Jo. She understood people, especially young people. Except for her height, everything about her was grand: grand laugh, grand voice, grand heart, and grand stories, stories that we'll never forget." At this point, a stray dog meandered down the center aisle, chased by an embarrassed usher. The bishop paused and quipped, "Now if Maire were in her pew as she was almost every morning, the poor creature would have sat down beside her and rested his head in her lap." The congregation smiled and nodded appreciatively at the easy way the bishop handled the situation.

"She was afraid of nothing, including this bishop. She treated me more like her son than her episcopus ordinatus. The presence of so many of her priest friends here today is powerful testimony to the deep personal bond she formed with those who wore her vestments.

"She got up early every day and breathed deeply the God who dwelled in and about her. She toasted the new day, and a great day she would say it was to be. She found ways to bless, give courage to, and do good things for all those she met. If you ever wonder how small, common acts can mound up to a grand big life, think of your sister, aunt, and grandmother, our Maire Joy. Her spirit filled every room she entered. It fills this church today, aisle to arches."

The bishop paused, staring up at the cathedral ceiling as though he might see Maire flying about somewhere up there. "May it release the pettiness of our hearts and transform them with the abundance of God's presence all the days of our lives!

"Maire lived in the Spirit and exuded joy and love, as she lay dying a painful death. I did not console her. Rather, she consoled me with her simple, natural faith in her God. She told me she loved me and I broke into tears, as I am about to do now. She prayed for God's blessing on this servant and sinner. She entered the home God had prepared for her as unselfconsciously as she did the cottage on Louisiana Street. God was that real to her. God was that present to her. He was her closest friend and she carried God in all His joyful abundance to you boys, John and Pat; to you, her brother, Jack; to you, her niece, Jo-girl; to me; and to all of us who knew her."

Throughout the bishop's eulogy, Pat held his head in his hands. He was so ashamed.

On Holy Week Tuesday, April 16, 1867, the Right Reverend John Timon, first Roman Catholic Bishop of the Diocese of Buffalo, and Maire Joy's friend and confessor, followed her in death. His last sermon had been delivered on Palm Sunday, two days before. Except for a handful of insiders, Protestants as well as Catholics were stunned by the bishop's death and were free in their praises of him: his character, his work, and especially the many kindnesses he had extended to them. The bishop was laid out for five days in the cathedral rectory and the doors thrown open to allow one and all to pay their respects. Over 90,000 mourners filed through. No one was as beloved in his lifetime by the bishops and laity of America, Latin America, and Europe as Bishop Timon. No bishop of Buffalo would ever be missed like its first.

On March 11, 1868, Mary gave birth to her first child, a girl, and named her Katherine, after an aunt and Pat's mother. Her daughter aroused protective and happy emotions that she had never felt before and could not even begin to share with her husband. Pat was initially disappointed that their first child was not a boy, but that quickly changed when Mary set his daughter in his arms. As the weather warmed, he proudly wheeled her through the streets of the Ward.

On Thursday, July 16, 1868, after a courtship of four years, John married Johanna Mahoney. Their wedding was small, celebrated by the Very Reverend William Gleason, Diocesan Vicar General at St. Joseph Cathedral. Msgr. Gleason was a friend of the bride's family. The reception was held in the parish hall with thirty friends present. They served a light buffet and port. The bride and groom paid for the reception themselves. There were toasts from Msgr. Gleason and Pat and Mary, who were best man and bridesmaid. Dancing was energetic, though accompanied by a lone fiddler. The wedding was over by midnight. John and Johanna skipped out unnoticed before the last dance and spent the night quietly in their flat on Alabama Street. The next day both had to be at work by dawn, she as a domestic for a family, John as a bridge tender.

CHAPTER 22

Worker and Father

On a Friday night in December 1868, Pat was late coming home from work. At midnight, he banged into the front door and staggered into the living room. Mary, dressed for bed, had been asleep on the couch waiting for him. She jumped up, dazed and startled. The baby wailed. She rushed to the crib, which was nestled in a dark corner of the dining room, cradled her daughter in her arms, rocked her, and spoke to her in calming tones. Within a minute or two, as Pat slouched on the couch and mumbled, Katherine fell back to sleep, and Mary placed her once again in her crib.

She walked over to her husband and in a low voice said, "Pat, it's after midnight. You're drunk. You reek of smoke and alcohol. You scared your infant daughter out of a sound sleep."

"Mary, love, I stayed too long with the boys. You can't begrudge me a few shots after a week in that hell hole."

"Let me help you get these dirty clothes off." As she took off his shoes, Pat fell asleep. She threw a blanket over him and put a pillow under his head.

The next morning, Pat was up at 7:00, ready for work.

"I'm sorry, love, for the spree last night. It won't happen again."

"Oh, get off to the Works and don't forget to come home on time. We're expected over at Dad's tonight to celebrate his birthday." She kissed him hard on the lips, shoved a lunch pail into his hands, and pushed him gently through the door.

"How is it I love him so?" she murmured to herself. "One thing gives me confidence. No matter how much he drinks, the next morning he's at work on time." Something else bothered her more—his chronic weakness. "He really hasn't recovered from the war," she murmured to herself.

Pat walked across the dirt floor of the factory through a large door to a field on the east side of the plant. One of the laborers leaned on his rake and yelled to Pat, "To the swamp, Bones!"—short for "Lazy Bones"—and pointed toward the creek. The other men nearby smirked. Pat dipped his head slightly, but said nothing. At the swamp, he began raking out a mound of slag into the creek. PM joined him, long-handled rake in hand.

Four men dumping gondola cars every five minutes shouted insults at the two and laughed. It was bitter cold this time of year. A westerly wind thinned the fumes from the furnaces and slag. Pat and PM bent to their work. The four prodded the mule and cart up and down the track as fast as the mule would go. By mid-morning, work had to be stopped, as slag mounded before the track. The gondola workers stood idle back at the furnace, content with the bottleneck they had created and barking their complaints out for all to hear. Within minutes, the foreman walked out to the swamp and gruffly warned Pat and PM to speed it up.

Pat's head was still throbbing at mid-morning. He turned to PM and asked him, "How are you feeling this morning? I caught some heavy lip from Mary."

"So did I from Bridgid, but she'll get used to it." Within the past year, PM had met and married Bridgid Donnelly. "The women in the Ward know we men are going to tip a few and come home a bit unsteady once in a while."

At noon, Pat dragged himself through the front gate and started with PM for home down Tecumseh Street. It being Saturday, work was through. The two men walked in silence. Then Pat said, "I think I have to find something else, PM."

PM nodded in rueful agreement. "The Iron Works is about to finish off what the Johnnies didn't," he said. "Besides, the bosses have about had it with us."

"I see it, too," said Pat. "Jobs are opening up at some of the new grain mills on the Creek. We'll keep our ears open at Kennedy's, though $2 a day at the Iron Works is tough to match. Rest up tonight. I'll see you at church."

Dolan turned onto Tecumseh Street. He was only 100 yards from his flat. Both of them had refused company housing within the walls of the plant. They had their fill of the company sixty-six hours a week.

Young men hanging on corners in the Ward shouted, "Hey, Bones," as Mary and Pat walked to the market that afternoon and to church the next day.

Finally, on the way home from noon mass, Mary asked Pat what they meant. Pat sloughed it off, saying, "Oh, it's just mates joking around."

When she heard it again from a group of young men on the corner of Elk and Louisiana, as she, Pat, and the baby were coming home from the market the following Saturday, she realized this was more than a joke. Deeply upset, she probed Pat more insistently. Anger flashed across his face and he told her not to worry. "They're just assholes, acting stupid."

A week later, Pat and PM were both fired after months of warnings. For three months, they found work constructing an extension of the Erie Canal called the Hamburgh Canal. Pay was less than at the Iron Works and part of it the contractor gave in store-pay, redeemable at a general store at Main and Genesee Streets. Mary asked her father for the use of a horse and wagon to move them to a cheaper apartment over a small grocery at Carroll and Heacock. After moving them, Garrett took his daughter home, where they sat and talked as they had not done since she married. They conversed about Nagle Supply, social events, and her friends at work and on the West Side. When he dropped her off late that afternoon, she found herself longing for the excitement of the life she once had and the company of educated business and social associates.

Garrett had considered giving them the money to remain where they were, but decided against it. He suspected the firing was due to Pat's drinking as much as to his war-weariness.

In the spring of 1869, the old Company I captain, Hugh Mooney, dropped by one evening. The Dolans and the Donohues were sitting on the Dolans' front porch over a few ales. Neighbors gathered on porches as long as the weather was good, May to October. Mary and Bridgid were both pregnant. Katherine had been put to bed in a side bedroom. Wisely, they each nursed a single glass of ale through the evening. The two Pats were on their fourth when Hugh walked up.

"I was hoping I'd find you two lads tonight. Mary and Bridgid, how are you? Looking lovely as ever!"

The women smiled, excused themselves, and went inside. Hugh had something to say to their husbands. They liked Hugh. He was tall, handsome, a bit overdressed, but a good man, good to his wife, Kate, and often seen by them walking his son and daughters down Ohio Street to the small park Ward residents had carved out of a field.

Hugh was a friend of the general manager, Michael Dillon, at the New York Central Freight Office. Dillon hung out at Mooney's Saloon and Boarding House below Mooney's flat on Ohio Street. A few years older than

Dolan and Donohue, Hugh Mooney walked deliberately and erect, with the air of the captain he'd become at the end of the war. Mooney was a hero to Pat. He reminded him of General Corcoran. Both were always at the front of their men in battle and were the last to leave campfires at night, sometimes on all fours.

Mooney, unlike Corcoran, cared little about discipline. After drinking all day at Fortress Suffolk, he stole another officer's horse and rode down the Edenton Road, shouting to the pickets that he was chief of the Grand Celts, a group within the 155th that invented new ways to raise hell. For that misadventure, he was demoted from lieutenant to private and served two months in the brig. Soon after his release, Captain McAnally, a friend of his going back to the Ward, restored his rank and position within Company I.

At the Battle of Cold Harbor, Mooney took a minie bullet through the left shoulder. He was out of action for three months, but returned to his company rather than accept a permanent furlough. There was no one in the city who Pat admired more.

"Pat and PM, it's always great to be with you lads. How the two of you made it through Salisbury is a monument to your manhood."

"Thanks, Hugh. We seldom think about it, but it left its mark," said Pat. PM grunted in agreement and offered Hugh a glass of beer.

"I know it did, Pat. That's why I came by. I thought of you two when I heard there were jobs opening at the Central as freight carriers."

Pat and PM could hardly contain their excitement. "Hugh, could your timing be any better?" said PM. Calming his voice a little, he continued. "There are plenty of jobs here in the Ward, but they're as bad as the ones we've got or are just temporary. Both of our wives are expecting. So we can't just up and quit like two young bucks." Pat nodded in agreement.

Hugh smiled broadly. "Well, let me first congratulate you. Being a father is the greatest experience of my life. Here's the story. The New York Central is buying up small roads all over the East and Midwest. It sees Buffalo as the biggest inland port in the country in just twenty years or so. There could be a real future for you with this company. Michael Dillon is the general manager from New York and a friend of mine."

Pat and PM nodded.

"Now, the job is unloading package freight from rail cars. You will be out in the weather, but that's nothing new for the likes of you two. And the bosses are reasonable. They let their men work at their own pace. The pay is the same as you're earning now, $2 a day, sixty-six hours a week."

He paused for a few seconds and drew on his beer. "You need to decide soon. I had Dillon put a hold on the jobs for now, but he has to fill them in a day or so. He likes the idea of hiring Irish, and hiring Civil War veterans is a real winner with him. He's a gentleman. I think you'll like him."

"Hugh, you have our answer now. Let's bring out the girls and let them in on this," said Pat.

Hugh nodded and Pat went to the door to call the women out. When Mary and Bridgid appeared, the two Pats began to speak at the same time.

Bridgid put her hands up and said, "Okay, just one of you give us the story."

PM looked at Pat and said, "You let them in on the good news." Pat quickly went over the offer. The ladies turned to Hugh and grabbed him by an arm. "Thanks, Hugh," said Mary. "I can't tell you how much we appreciate your thinking of our husbands. Thank you so much." Then Bridgid repeated: "Oh, bless you, Hugh Mooney. God bless you!"

PM looked at the two women and said, "Well it's settled then." He turned to Hugh. "Monday morning we'll quit and come over to the freight office and sign in, if that's okay."

"Yes, I believe it is. I'll let Mr. Dillon know to expect you."

The women went back in to cut a cake Bridgid had made and boil the tea. Hugh waited for the wives to move out of hearing distance and then blurted out the last thing on his mind.

"You won't embarrass me now, lads, will you? You have to give me your word you'll never come to work drunk or drink on the job."

Dolan and Donohue assured Hugh those days were a thing of the past. The two lapsed into a moment's silence. Done were the carefree days of their adolescence, but they weren't sure it was a good thing.

On Sunday, October 24, 1869, Mary gave birth to her second child, a son named after her maternal grandfather, Robert Joseph. The boy was small, seven pounds, ten ounces, measured eighteen inches with a full head of light brown, curly hair. He was healthy and his eyes shimmered with a clarity that bespoke intelligence.

Six months later, on the first warm day, Mary beamed with pride and pleasure when she took the baby for a buggy ride back in the old neighborhood along Louisiana. Her women friends up and down the street greeted her, saying how great she looked, not a bit of maternity bulge left. Kate, now two, struggled to keep up with her mother. Her mother's affection was shifting slightly and unconsciously to her son. "You're prettier than ever, Mary. Nothing like a baby to bring the best out of you," said old Mrs. Shea, the matriarch of the Flats where Pat and Mary lived.

"I imagine your husband is all over you every night. You send him to Father Hennessey for a talk. You don't need a third baby too soon."

Mary smiled demurely. She agreed with this wise old lady. Already, she was scheming how to handle Pat in bed. He wanted sex only a week after she gave birth. She liked sex, too, but she did not want a third pregnancy just yet. She wanted to enjoy her children.

While she cleaned and cooked, she pushed images of her old life as business partner and socialite to the back of her mind. Still, when the children slept, she sat at her front window drawing fashionable men and women cavorting, dancing, preening.

She found ways to put off Pat. One scheme was to get out of bed as soon as Pat moved his hands over her stomach toward her breasts.

She would say, "The baby is awake and needs nursing" or "The baby needs changing" or "The baby is upset." She had ten different lines, lest Pat catch on. Once out of bed, she would sit with the baby until her husband's snores signaled she could return to bed unmolested. Tension grew in him from the lack of sex and resentment as he felt himself odd man out among the children.

In November, Bridgid gave birth to a boy. She and PM named him Terence, after her deceased grandfather. The new parents doted on their infant son. PM fed him from a bottle when Bridgid went dry. He plunged into fatherhood. For Bridgid, motherhood was literally the answer to her fondest prayer. She felt even more complete sharing their son with his father. Bridgid and Mary communicated feelings they shared with no one else and grew closer than twin sisters.

At two months of age, Terry became feverish and began vomiting. His parents nursed and prayed over him day and night. The second day, with his son crying uncontrollably, PM ran for a doctor, who diagnosed the illness as diphtheria. He had no remedy, just advised keeping the boy bathed in wet cloths to control his temperature and praying he would have the strength to endure. He didn't and died within a week.

The Dolans were crushed. So were their best friends. After the wake and funeral, conversation among the four grew sparse. They cooked, played with Katherine, and took turns with the baby. They found any way to pass the time but talk honestly about how empty and helpless they were feeling. The Donohues believed they had to be near their friends every day. Often, the Dolans wished they'd go home so they could mourn openly with one another.

Mary bathed her children carefully, tenderly, and often. She looked on her son with anxiety after Terry's funeral. He was such a fragile infant, she thought. She held him through much of the day. She worried at the least sign of illness, sniffles or a light fever. So many children in the Ward never survived their first year. The Dolan child wasn't the only infant funeral that year; there was at least one every month, it seemed. Along with other women, she'd throw her arms around the grieving mothers, helpless to console them with empty words.

Catholics often repeated ejaculations throughout the day like "Jesus, Mary, and Joseph, have mercy on us." Hers was "Not Robert, Lord, please, not Robert." She prayed it a hundred times a day.

She spent time with Kate, reading to her, but she began to plot ways to make something more out of Bob than what she saw in the Ward. In reaction, Pat doted increasingly on his daughter.

The job at the Central unloading boxes of freight was cleaner and lighter than the job at the Works. The pace, as Hugh had promised, was within the ability of most workers to keep up ... except for the two most recent hires. Pat took days off when his rheumatism flared up in his knees and shoulders, or could not leave the house for dysentery, or walk for piles.

Mary borrowed home remedies from other women, but they were seldom more than palliative. Pat relished the care she gave him and at times feigned greater pain than he felt.

The bosses ignored his absences, as well as those of PM.

These were happy times at work. The bosses were indeed reasonable men. The company threw parties at Christmas and Easter. Pat liked most of the men he worked with. His friendship with PM was an anchor. There were supervisory positions he could advance to. All that said, Pat could feel himself slipping deeper into a fallow state. He wondered how long he could keep up with the work.

Despite his promise to Hugh, Pat began to drink once again with PM, both at home and at Kennedy's. He seldom spent time with his son. He took his daughter to mass on Sundays, and then walked downtown, as far as her little legs could go. Then he hiked her up on his shoulders and strolled along the creek, watching sailboats and freighters moving in and out of the harbor.

Mary became distant and unhappy. She and Pat, when they talked at all, never alluded to the growing gap between them.

One late summer evening, the vaudeville act of Grogan and Farrell, entertainer Ned Harrigan, and other headliners from New York played at the Richmond Hotel on Main Street. Michael Dillon bought tickets for all his workers and their wives. When Mrs. Shea offered to babysit, Pat was able to persuade Mary to leave her children to take in the show.

As they waited for the show to begin, Dolan asked the wives, "Mary and Bridgid, what do you hear about George Tipping's family?" He had seen both wives talking to Tipping's wife, Catherine, after mass the previous Sunday.

"A widow's pension is good and all, but raising five children on it has to be a struggle."

"Yes," Mary said, "but the family is getting help from George's brother and other family members. Catherine is, however, worried about her daughter Lizzie, who is deep in sadness over her father's death. She's not eating. She's not attentive in school. She's in another world with no family or friends. Seems like nothing will pull her out of her melancholia."

The theatre lights dimmed and the curtains parted. The performer, Ned Harrigan, in a one-man show, transformed himself from one stock Irish character to another in the course of forty-five minutes on stage. All were characters Harrigan took from the streets of New York, but who were to be found in any Irish ghetto in the East. Harrigan made them appear real.

Afterward, standing at the bar with his fellow New York Central employees, Pat started repeating Harrigan's lines. The group turned away from their side conversations and howled and clapped as Pat imitated Harrigan's delivery, mouthing one of his sketches, and adding a story from the Ward. Mary watched proudly a step or two away, a bit stunned by the showmanship exhibited by her husband. She was relieved because Pat drank only two beers in the course of the evening.

In 1870, one of Johanna's uncles, Edward Needham, visited Buffalo. While at a family reunion at the Mahoney house, John asked, "How's your coal mine going in Pennsylvania, Ed?" As part owner, Edward was very proud of the stature the mine gave him in the community and business world, and of his rapidly accumulating wealth. Fifty years old and heavyset, he wore a custom tailored suit from New York, sported a large emerald ring on his right hand, and now and again lifted a gold watch from the pocket of his vest. In response, he talked about himself and his mine nonstop for two hours, during which he mentioned that his manager had recently been lost in an accident.

Needham was impressed by his niece's husband, how he listened and asked the right questions. Family members told him later what a great husband and worker John was. They said he never missed a day of work and seemed to be progressing well at the Division of Weights and Measures, which controlled the lift bridges in town. They mentioned, too, that members of his old company held John in high regard. He was known as one of the best soldiers in the regiment.

On the second day of his visit, Needhan offered John the manager's post that paid more than John would ever make with the city. John and Johanna were ready to leave Buffalo anyway, hoping to escape the dirt, noise, accidents, and rowdy behavior of the gangs of young men who had taken over the street corners. John was disgusted by the way politicians bid out contracts to friends and received kickbacks in return. Indeed, First Ward politicians refined corruption in city government to a fine art. Life was often dangerous and city jobs were precarious.

A month later, John and Johanna, with help from family members, were living in Blossburg in northeastern Pennsylvania, fifty miles south of Painted Post, New York.

As they walked a half mile to the freight office at Chicago and Ohio Streets, Pat turned to PM and said, "I'm scared. I thought I'd have recovered by this time. It's nearly six years since we're back from the war, but I don't feel much better than when I entered the convalescent camp in Alexandria. And I haven't done any serious drinking lately, so it's not the drink. Mary is expecting again. I can't quit now, but I have to find some lighter work the bosses will let me do."

"Tell you the truth, Pat, I'm about the same. I'm short of breath. There's pains in my chest. It makes me think I've got the consumption. What'll we do, rob banks?"

"No, PM, we're too slow for that, but the government owes us for what we lost in the war. I hear some of our officers have gotten big pensions. They know the politicians downtown. That's the answer. We need a pension of at least $20 a month each, 'cause let's face it, we can only work a few days a week."

On Christmas Day 1870, during their first visit back to Buffalo, John and Johanna caught Pat after high mass. John wore a black topcoat and top hat, Johanna an elegant red jacket above a long white dress. Old friends crowded around them and stared enviously. Pat was flabbergasted to see them looking so prosperous. Their faces broke out in huge smiles as they grabbed Pat and pulled him away. Separating themselves from their friends, they hugged Pat between them. "Pat, I have brilliant news. Johanna is pregnant."

Pat grabbed an arm of each and began to swing them around and around in a circle, yelling and whooping there on Elk Street in front of St. Bridget's. "God is good. What'd I tell you two? Relax and it'll happen, and here it is! I can't wait to get home and tell Mary. Come over for dinner this afternoon and we'll celebrate."

Pat burst in the front door, shouting, "Mary, Johanna is pregnant. I invited them over for dinner. Theresa, too. I hope you got a roast or something good to celebrate."

On Saturday, March 18, 1871, Johanna delivered a boy named Michael. John and Johanna were overjoyed. They had waited so long for their first child. Pat and Mary shared in their happiness.

Four months later on July 18, Mary gave birth to a daughter, Minnie.

"This baby is the picture of you, Mary. She's beautiful," said Pat as he bent to kiss his second daughter nestled in the arms of her mother.

Within a week, Pat was back in the neighborhood, wheeling his newest daughter and showing her off to all who would stop and talk.

"Mrs. Shea, Bridgid, come look at the wee one Mary just gave us. Isn't she the image of her mother?"

Mrs. Shea picked up the infant and tipped her toward Bridgid Dolan, who was walking with her.

"Well, we know this one is Mary's, Bridgid. Her eyes are every bit as blue and the dimples are just like hers. You are a lucky man, Pat," said Mrs. Shea.

Bridgid, depressed by the death of her son, had failed to conceive another child, which pushed her further into despair and PM with her. He would, without apparent reason, suddenly break off conversations and become silent, then respond in clipped phrases when Pat tried to restart their conversation.

Neighbors and family talked behind their backs. "What's wrong with Bridgid and PM? Don't they want children? They must be using the pelt." The preferred form of birth control of the day, the pelt was a four-inch square of rabbit pelt inserted in the vagina. Inevitably, word got back to Bridgid and PM and only made them feel worse.

"Pat, I'm so happy for you and Mary. How is she feeling?" asked Bridgid, putting on a brave front. Still, there was no hiding her sadness, as she admired her friend Mary's third healthy baby.

Pat turned on Ohio Street to show the boys at Kennedy's what God had given him, while Bridgid hiked over to the Heacock Street apartment to visit with Mary. She found her playing with her two-year-old son, while four-year-old Katherine, amused herself alone with a doll in her bedroom.

In September, Baby Michael came down with pneumonia. As his condition worsened, John and Johanna made an anxious return to Buffalo and the Sisters of Charity Hospital. The attention of the doctors, their own prayers and those of their families and friends were not enough. Within a week Michael died, not yet a year old. Michael's funeral from St. Columba's Church left parents and friends emotionally spent and depressed. Mary's anxiety for her children deepened.

CHAPTER 23

Garrett to the Rescue

In late July 1871, Dillon called Pat into the office. "Pat, the Central is hanging on by a thread. The country's in a financial panic. The New York banks are not lending. Money's tight, so the bosses are telling every office in the country to cut expenses, lay off half the work force, lower salaries. Do you understand me? I hate laying you off. You are a recent hire, three years on the job, but your work record is the worst of your crew. The bosses at the New York Central never fire a war veteran without extreme cause. Pat, you have a lot going for you personally. You're well-liked by coworkers and bosses alike."

He went on repeating himself. "I'm sorry to do this, but I've got to end your employment with the Central. It hurts me. We all like you and will miss you, but I cannot defend your work record to New York any longer. They're saying I have to let you go."

Pat bowed his head. His body sagged. "Mr. Dillon, I forced myself to show up unless I simply could not get out of bed. I did the best I could." He nodded and went to his locker to collect his things. He realized Mr. Dillon had been more than fair with him. His resentment was toward the Central's executives. He thought he deserved better, given what he had been through in the war.

As he walked home to Heacock Street, he choked up. The sky was bright and clear as it often is in Buffalo in July, a perfect summer day, but he did not feel part of it. Dark clouds overtook him. He felt stripped of his manhood.

As he crossed Swan and turned onto Carroll, he wondered how he would break the news to Mary. Kate and Bob were playing in a neighbor's front yard and ran to their father the minute they saw him, shouting, "Dad, you're home! Can you take us for a walk downtown?"

Pat stammered a bit and told them, "Go play while I talk to your mother; then we'll see."

With shouts of "Okay, Dad," they ran back to their friends. Pat watched them play, hesitant to enter his house. He knew there was no hiding the fact from Mary. When he saw her he simply said it. "Mary . . . I've been fired."

Lines tightened on Mary's face as she took her husband's hand and led him to the couch. Then her words spilled out. "Pat, there were quite a few days you stayed home over the past year or two. You've never recovered from the war."

"Those Know Nothings in New York could have kept me on. They know us veterans."

"You didn't go to school long enough to get a good job. I could ask my father to take you on, but would you accept a job with Nagle?"

Pat ignored her question. "Mary, I will feed this family if I have to work around the clock." Mary's words stung. Going back to school was not an option for him, nor was taking help from his father-in-law. "I'll work two jobs if I have to, and I'll make the government pay for what the war did to me."

"What about PM? Was he fired, too?"

"I don't think so, or Dillon would have called us in together or said something to me."

"How will you work two jobs? The jobs you get require you to work sixty-six hours a week. Besides, when would you spend time with your children? As it is now, they barely know their father."

Pat said nothing.

"Maybe I should go back to work. Theresa could mind the kids. She's about to retire, you know." Her thoughts drifted to Nagle Supply, going back to work for her father, and enjoying a life beyond the Ward.

"Mary, I won't hear of you working. The children need their mother at home. I lost my mother at an early age, and I won't see that happen to our children. Besides, Theresa retired because she's not able to work. She's lost weight. Something is wrong with her insides. She told John she's feeling some pain."

"The other thing you have to face up to is your drinking. It drains precious dollars and weakens your health. It has always been the ruination of Irish men. Pat, I can't stand being in bed with a drunk. I won't make love with you when you've been drinking like a sot."

Their exchange grew more heated from that point on. Pat uttered a tirade of curses and left the house for Kennedy's, slamming the door behind him.

Humbling herself, Mary appealed to her father, who gave her $100 to pay old bills and buy food.

"I'm skeptical of Pat's excuses," he told her. "I know Mr. Dillon at the Central and I'll ask him what really happened."

Garrett confirmed his suspicions in a confidential conversation with Dillon, who laid out Pat's irregular attendance record.

Sunday dinner at Pat and Mary's was tense. Garrett was angry and barely spoke. Mary tried to fill the gaps in conversation with tidbits about the children, the neighborhood, the parish, anything that would ease the hostility that hung in the air. Pat said little. Garrett barely hid his anger toward his son-in-law.

Listening to his daughter and conscious of her limited choices, he softened and fashioned a plan to curb Pat's drinking and put him to work. As he rose to leave, Garrett asked Pat to stop by his office on Monday about finding work. Pat felt cornered. He wanted no help from his father-in-law, but how could he refuse it?

Pat arrived at Garrett's office at 7:00 a.m., dressed in his Sunday best. "Good morning, Pat. I'm pleased you're here so early."

"Thank you for being willing to help me, Garrett. I'm eager to work. I just have to find something I can handle. The war's still with me."

Garrett wasted no time. "I know the war was a terrible experience for you. I also appreciate what you did for our country. But be honest, Pat. Haven't you contributed to being terminated at the Central?"

Pat knew Garrett talked to other bosses in the city and suspected he knew more than he was letting on. He paused before answering. "Garrett, I know I shouldn't be drinking like I do. I promise you on my mother's grave there will be no more of this staying out all night or hanging out at bars. I hate what it does to Mary. That's my solemn promise, Garrett."

Pat's apparent genuine contriteness and the strong oath he took impressed Garrett. He was sure he meant it, but doubted Pat's ability to remain on the wagon. Pat had a problem. He just could not admit that he was an alcoholic.

"Pat, I'm asking you to talk to Monsignor Gleason at St. Bridget's and take the pledge. If you'll do that, I'll talk to a friend about a job. One other thing . . . I'm afraid that as long as you live in the Ward you'll be drawn to your old haunts. I've located a large flat off Clinton on the East Side. I'll pay the first month's rent and have a wagon help move you."

Garrett was proud of the plan he concocted and his ability to cause it to happen.

"Garrett, I'm speechless. What can I say about an offer like that? I'll go see the Monsignor and take the pledge. We'll move from the Ward and I'll stay clear of Kennedy's and the rest of the watering holes there. The only drink I'll have will be with you and Mary, I promise. No matter what, there'll be no whiskey."

Pat went to work in the Turner Printing warehouse at Emslie and Seneca streets, moving paper from the dock and from storage to the floor. The family moved to a larger, one-story house on Lord Street. The change in residence did make a difference. Pat controlled his drinking for the most part, drinking at home and only beer. Mary joined him in an occasional glass and they resumed their old happy relationship.

On Tuesday, June 22, 1875, Mary gave birth to their fourth child, another daughter whom she named Nellie after an aunt in Ireland with whom Mary was close as a child. After a long and painful labor, Nellie was born blue, but survived. Nellie's eyes were dull. Pat refused to believe Mary when she told him Nellie would not develop as a normal child. The older children heard their mother talk of her as "a bit slow" and became highly protective of their baby sister.

Four years into his job, despite his earlier promises to his father-in-law, Pat returned to the print shop warehouse and storeroom after spending his lunch hour drinking whiskey at a saloon on Seneca Street. Mr. Turner was standing inside the side door as Pat entered.

"Pat, come with me into my office. Have you been drinking? Your work seems to suffer mysteriously many afternoons."

"Oh, I only had a short one or two. It doesn't affect my work."

"I think it does. After years of good work and coming to work sober, lately you're not safe to work with. Besides, the quality of your work is poor after you've been drinking. Things get broken or lost. I hate to do this. Garrett is a good friend. You're a veteran and all, but I have to protect my business and my employees. I'm sorry, but I have to let you go."

The next evening, embarrassed and angry, Garrett was at the flat on Lord Street. Turner had advised him that he had fired Pat and recounted the circumstances. Part of his anger was with himself. He thought he could move people to act as he wanted them to. "Pat, you're not supporting your wife and children like a man. You're wasting what you earn on whiskey."

"Get the hell out of my house!" yelled Pat. "You'll not talk to me like that under my own roof."

Without a word, Garrett walked to the door and left with his daughter at his side. "His drinking is ruining our family," she said. "I can't take it much longer."

Mary was thinking the impossible for an Irish Catholic woman in the Ward—divorce! Her disgust for what Pat was doing overcame her pride. She was about to beg her father to let her come home.

"Well, you'll always have a home with me, Mary. We'll not let those grandchildren of mine go begging on the streets as long as I'm alive. I'm going on Jefferson now."

A half-hour later, Garrett returned, his arms full of groceries, and walked straight into the house. Daring Pat to stop him, he spoke only to Mary and the children and unloaded a week's worth of food into the pantry and icebox. Ensconced in his bedroom, Pat didn't come out until his father-in-law left.

Pat found temporary work on construction jobs dredging canals that extended the Erie Canal into the harbor area and the First Ward. Buffalo was becoming a miniature Venice. The work, however, was heavy and weather-dependent. Pat forced himself to go to work. He sloughed off the heaviest tasks on younger workers. When the harbor froze, he was laid off.

Without Garrett's help, the family would have starved. Mary could not face the women of the Ward, or the thought of separating her children from their father. Pat tempered his drinking and spent more time at home. Sunday dinners at Garrett's went on as ever and the two men acted civilly for the sake of Mary and the children.

Pat went to mass irregularly, but he said the rosary every night or when walking to or from work.

Following the death of Edward Needham in 1876, the new mine owner replaced the managers with his own personnel and gave the old team a month's notice. In a letter, John informed Pat that he and Johanna were returning to Buffalo. Patrick took a train to Blossburg and helped with the move at both ends. The family had accumulated furniture, a few paintings, and numerous knick-knacks. Johanna conducted a sale of some of the belongings that paid for the move. John used a company wagon, moved loads to the train station, and shipped them on to Buffalo. The family, now with three children—Mary, John, and James born to them in Pennsylvania—moved to 51 Alabama Street, only doors from where they had lived before. John returned to his old job working for the City Department of Weights and Measures as bridge tender at the Michigan Street Bridge.

Given his comfortable status in Pennsylvania, John had not thought much about increasing his veterans' pension during his eight years there. The wages at Weights and Measures barely paid for rent and food. The family was living pay to pay.

In 1879, eight years after moving to Lord Street, Pat decided to reapply for a pension increase. Late one afternoon, he wrote a letter, had Mary correct it, and handed it to his son.

"Bobby, be quick about delivering this envelope to Mr. Moore at his office downtown. He's the government pension office man. You have been there with me picking up my pension. It could mean more dollars to the family."

Bobby, at age ten, was expected to help his mother around the house and run errands for his father. He was a small boy, but was used to making his way across much of the city and downtown. Off he went at a fast walk. Within an hour, he was back.

"Pa, Mr. Moore said you need a birth certificate to prove your age."

"Well, I don't have one. All I know is what Gram Joy told me. I was born in Rochester on March 25, 1844. The family Bible was lost after my mother died in 1849 and with it the records of your uncle's and my birth."

"He also told me to say the doctors will have to examine you."

"All right, son, did Mr. Moore say anything else?"

"No, Pa."

Anger and frustration with the government pension program welled up in him. "Think hard now, Bobby. You forget sometimes what you're supposed to be telling your father." He grabbed his son by the shoulders and shook him hard, as though it would awaken some dormant memory.

"Pat, don't shake your son like that!" cried Mary, rushing to intercede. "He doesn't deserve that kind of treatment. He did everything you asked of him." Pat's behavior toward his son was a major source of conflict in their home.

"He needs it. He's such a mama's boy. If I don't toughen him up, the young German crowd at Emslie and Clinton will beat him silly."

"You've been treating that boy like an orphan since he was born, whipping him for nothing, some sass you imagine he gave you, something he didn't do fast enough. Pat, you're no loving father to that boy. You don't spend time with him like a father should and you show him no affection." When Pat did spend time with his children, it was with the girls.

He cuffed Bobby on the right ear. "What am I going to do with him? He can't play ball like the other boys. He's a little girl. That's what you've done to him." Bobby started crying and ran into his bedroom.

"Tell me, Pat, what happened to the pledge you took before Monsignor Gleason? I've asked you that before. Don't deny you're drinking again! I can smell the whiskey on you a block away. You're back at your old haunts and staying out half the night."

Pat rose from the couch, struggling to control himself. He put his hands in his pockets and walked away from Mary. "You've got Bobby doing housecleaning and shopping for you. You're making him into a girl!" Pat couldn't handle his son's close relationship with his wife.

Mary followed him and got right in his face. As she was about to chastise him for the way he treated Bobby, Pat pushed her and she fell into a soft chair. Bobby, who had come to the doorway of his bedroom thinking his father was about to become violent, ran at his father with all his might and bounced off his legs to the floor. Pat laughed at him disdainfully.

A minute later, to show his authority over him, Pat gave his son some change and told him to go to the corner and get him an ale. He did as his father asked without backtalk, remembering that his mother had told him that was his duty as a son. Besides, he was afraid of his father and his temper.

In June of 1879, Mary gave birth to a fifth child, Annie.

In July, Pat wheeled the baby buggy down Clinton to Jefferson to Hamburg to Elk and on to Louisiana Street on a Sunday afternoon. It was a day for relaxation and socializing. Kate and Minnie, wandering out in front of the buggy, often played together, though they were three years apart in age.

The less attention she got from her mother, the more Kate tried to please her, minding the younger children and helping Bobby pick up the house and run errands. Kate and Bobby grew very close.

Nellie was now four and found dogs and toys in yards to dawdle over. When she fell too far behind, the family would simply stop. Kate would run back, grab her gently by the arm, and bring her along. It annoyed Pat that his only son was not with them. He was proud of having a son and wanted to show him off. Bobby remained at home keeping his mother company and working around the house.

Pat found part-time jobs working for a contractor constructing rail tracks across the Hydraulics to plants on the far-East Side. The men labored through most of the winter, in spite of heavy snowfalls. Pat continued doggedly through long days. Just to show Mary and Garrett he didn't need the drink, he drank sparingly.

In late September 1882, both Kate and Nellie came down with cholera. Despite repeated calls for reform by public health committees, septic

217

conditions had not improved much in the city and were worse in the Ward. Mary quarantined the girls in a back bedroom and fed and nursed them for two weeks. The girls died painfully a day apart in October. Kate was fourteen, Nellie four.

Their deaths numbed their parents. Mary was guilt-ridden and depressed. Hadn't she promised herself she would protect her children from all evils? Pat and Mary barely talked to one another. Over the two days of the wake, friends and neighbors sent food and crowded into the flat. Pat sat in his rumpled suit in the kitchen, drinking whiskey with the men. In a glum stupor, he mumbled incoherently.

Mary sat quietly crying in the living room near the casket, receiving mourners. Her son sat next to her with his aunt, Johanna, on the other side holding Mary's hand. The room reeked of gladiola bouquets sent by people like Garrett, Kennedy, and Mooney.

Male mourners entered the living room, offered curt, barely audible condolences, and moved on to the kitchen. There they tried to talk with Pat about everything except his two daughters. Female family and friends stayed in the living room, approached Mary when no one was with her, and consoled her. Much of the time, they just cried together.

Garrett came on the first night of the wakes and sat beside his grandson. He stroked Mary's shoulder over and over, his face throbbing with sorrow. He did the same the second night, never venturing into the kitchen. The disparate behaviors of the two most important men in her life heightened Mary's resentment toward her husband and the low-class men of the Ward.

After the funerals, Mary weakened and remained in bed on and off through Christmas. Pat bought a tree on Christmas Eve for half price and put a baseball glove for Bobby and dolls for Minnie and Annie under it. He fed the family their Christmas dinner with help from neighbors. Then he sat with his wife. When she wasn't sleeping, they talked about the deaths of Kate and Nellie and shared their sense of guilt over their passing. Mary's hostility turned to love once again as in this period, Pat drank little.

⟡ SECTION IV ⟡
DESCENT INTO THE ABYSS

CHAPTER 24

Increasing Instability

On November 7, 1882, Theresa died at age seventy-two, a shadow of her once robust self. She had been close to John and Johanna and their children. Her long bout with cancer had been painful for them and they sighed in relief when she died. She had begged the Lord to take her. Nonetheless, they mourned her passing as bitterly as if she had been John's birth mother. She had raised him, stood by his family financially in tough times, and sat with all of them in their illnesses. She was the matriarch of their family.

Daily in 1883, weather allowing, Pat pulled four-year-old Annie in a wagon between Broadway and Seneca Streets looking for "Employee Wanted" signs and just people watching. Annie talked nonstop, asking her father questions about whatever she saw. Pat obliged, basking in the admiration and love of his youngest.

The near-East Side was the crossroads of the city where Irish, German, Jewish, Negro, Italian, Polish, and Ukrainian populations resided. Factories were going up. There were new open-air markets. Ground floors along every major thoroughfare converted to stores for blocks on end.

Over the years that he worked for Turner in the Hydraulics neighborhood between the First Ward and the East Side, he had watched the construction of two manufacturing buildings at 663 Seneca Street, which opened as J. D. Larkin & Co. and employed hundreds of workers.

For information on the company, he turned to Hugh Mooney, who had sold his tavern on Ohio Street and opened a saloon on Seneca Street that was patronized by many Larkin employees.

"His employees are very loyal to Mr. Larkin and the company is growing fast," Mooney told him. "It manufactures soap. Sells its products door to door."

"What do the employees say about working there?" Pat asked.

"They say it is like no place else. Larkin believes his business is a partnership with his employees and his customers. Work conditions are the best in America. I say you should walk into the Larkin Building and see for yourself."

A week later, with Mary's encouragement, Pat dressed in clean, Sunday-best clothes and walked to the main entrance. He asked a guard at the door if he could observe the factory floor. The guard took him to a spot on the mezzanine overlooking the manufacturing area and explained the operations below. Scents, some mildly foul and some pleasant, perfumed the air as workers were converting tallow and ashes into soap.

Men were working at a steady pace, but supervisors did not hover over them. The workers operated steam-driven equipment, which did most of the heavy lifting. The floor was well lighted and ventilated and the machinery spaced, so that workers were not crowded together. After fifteen minutes watching the floor, Pat decided this was the place for him. He entered the administration office on the first floor and approached a nattily dressed young man, who was seated at his desk among many other office workers. He was slim, with a boyish face, brown hair, and a well-groomed beard and mustache.

Pat introduced himself and inquired about any openings.

"Well, we're not hiring for the shop floor right now, but we always need salesmen to sling soap and to call on retail stores. Can you sell soap?" The man gave Pat the once-over, trying to size him up on the spot and determine what kind of appearance he would make on the street selling Larkin products mostly to women.

"I can sell soap to pigs." God's gift to the world was how Pat saw himself.

The manager decided to take a chance on Pat. He seemed to have a salesman's gift of gab.

"Anyone with that attitude can work for the Larkin Company."

The next day, Pat appeared at 8:00 a.m. sharp and joined a dozen men and two women for an orientation session conducted by the president of the company, Mr. John D. Larkin, the same man Pat had talked to the previous day.

"Ladies and gentlemen, I know you are eager to get started, so I will only take a minute to tell you about the Larkin Company.

"I learned the soap business from the ground up in Chicago, doing all the things men are doing on our shop floor. Three years ago, I moved back to Buffalo, where I was born, with my new bride and formed J. D. Larkin & Co. in a rented building, not much more than a barn, at 196 Chicago Street. It had one other employee, my wife, Frances. I made the soap and she packaged it. In the first year, Larkin Company lost $3,000. The second year we quadrupled sales and made a profit of $3,000, largely because of a sales program invented by my wife's brother, Elbert Hubbard. Today, we have nine product lines. Elbert, who recently turned twenty-seven, has a sales force in four cities east of the Mississippi. We have products women want and a unique method of sales called 'soap slinging.'

"We are thinking about placing small gifts in every box of soap. Eventually, we'll offer women premiums, that is, opportunities to buy goods they all want and need around the house at pennies on the dollar, including some of the best furniture American women have ever seen. We believe in sharing whatever profits we make with our customers and our employees." Larkin looked down at notes he had spread on a podium before him. "If you go to work with us, someday you'll own part of the company and retire to a prosperous old age. Now I'm going to take you on a tour of our factory to show you how we create quality in every bar or can of soap we make. Then we'll go into our show room, where you can convince yourselves these are the products every American woman needs and wants."

For the next hour, Mr. Larkin led the prospective employees through the premises. Pat came home excited and told Mary there was no telling how far he could go with his talent for chatting up women. Mary had to agree. He sure had the Irish gift of gab.

The first day, Pat walked ten minutes to the Larkin Building at 7:00 a.m. and picked up his sales kit, which consisted of nine soaps used daily in every household and had names like "Sweet Home Soap" and "Crème Oatmeal." He walked with Elbert Hubbard and two other new salesmen into the First Ward. They divided the Ward among them. Pat took Louisiana, South, Tecumseh, and their cross streets.

Pat talked to Mrs. Shea first. She lived on Louisiana and was known by all the women in that area of the Ward. They sat over a cup of tea talking about accidents at the Union Iron Works and Father Gleason's latest diatribe on the schemes of Buffalo Know Nothings, inserted at the end of the noon mass at St. Bridget's . . . just before the final blessing, when everyone was anxious to leave.

Pat chimed in patiently with short phrases that encouraged Mrs. Shea to go on with her tales and free associations. After fifteen minutes of near monologue, the old lady noticed the soap kit and asked Pat what he had there. He then uncovered the colorful packages and explained each one's uses in glowing terms.

Using leads from Mrs. Shea, he crisscrossed his territory, calling on women she suggested and then on those they suggested. In four hours, Pat sold more product than the other salesmen canvasing the Ward combined. His commission was $5, two days' pay anywhere else he had worked. The next day, Hubbard gave Pat the Ward, the Valley, and every street south of William Street from downtown to Fillmore Avenue, four square miles, as his sales territory.

By the third month on the job, Pat was clearing $50 a month. $45 he gave to Mary; $5 he put in his pocket. Mary was thrilled. She recovered from the melancholia brought on by the deaths of Kate and Nellie. She urged thirteen-year-old Bobby to spend time with his father. Pat came home most evenings before 6:00 p.m. His strength and stamina improved. He joined a men's softball team at St. Columba's Parish. The family ate supper together. Soon, Mary felt as optimistic as Pat. This was the first job Pat ever had that promised a life more like the one she had known in her father's house.

Pat could not have been more congenial toward his family. He taught Bobby how to throw and hit a baseball. He took the children to the park with their mother. The family picnicked in good weather on the lakeshore. Pat was never more proud of himself as husband, father, and man, and neither was Mary. Their sex life improved considerably.

When he passed a Catholic Church on his route, he always made a visit and said his rosary.

Still, he missed the gang at Kennedy's. Toward winter that first year at Larkin's, he turned in his sales kit and receipts at 5:00 p.m. one Friday. At 5:30, dressed in his Kleinhan's suit and blouse, Italian silk tie, and Boston shoes, he was on his old stool at Kennedy's. As his friends came in from work, they approached him, big smiles on their faces, shook hands, and chatted.

Jim Kennedy called to the bartender to set up one of his best Canadian whiskeys in front of Pat. Soon he had five deep waiting on him. His bar mates, mostly old pals from the Iron Works, grain mills, and construction projects told him repeatedly how good it was to see him on his old stool. The men kidded him about becoming so henpecked under Mary's heavy thumb. They admired his classy attire and poked fun at the Columbus watch he wore in his vest. How high and mighty he had become! One old friend asked him if he was running for office. He shook his head and laughed with the rest of his mates.

The next day, word got back to Hubbard that Pat was drunk at 7:00 p.m. in a bar in the Ward the evening before, telling tales about the Larkin family. He fired Pat Monday morning. Hubbard had specifically warned all new hires that good behavior, most of all sobriety, was expected of all Larkin employees on the job and in public view. He had warned them that Mr. Larkin was a deeply religious man and would allow no exceptions.

The letdown and embarrassment was too much for Mary. She stood erect and in a quaking voice told him, "For the past few months this family lived like the best American families. We actually could see the day when our grocery bill would be paid off. We'd be able to send Bob to school beyond the eighth grade. I'd be able to replace the broken-down furniture and buy a set of matching china. Pat, what in the name of all that's good and holy is wrong with you? Sitting in a bar drunk and telling stories about the family that pays your bills and feeds your children? How foolish I was to fall in love with a low-class chaw!"

Mary's words hurt Pat deeply. His face twitched in anger and he raised his hand to slap her in the face. Bob pushed between his parents and his father ran from the house . . . all the way to Kennedy's. Mary burst into tears. Pat spent the whole night on his favorite bar stool touting himself as the best salesman in the company, lambasting Hubbard for not recognizing the fact, and berating Larkin and all the elite British bastards in the Larkin family. That night he slept in a small room above the bar and the next morning he was on the same stool when the bar opened at 6. He returned home that evening drunk, dirty, angry with himself, and despondent.

Later that week, when his money ran out, he talked to Jim Kennedy. The next day he met with Jack White, First Ward alderman, whom he knew well. Jack was a regular at Kennedy's. At Kennedy's request, Pat had delivered cards for White across the Ward during his reelection campaigns.

Jack got him a job as a guard at the county penitentiary on Georgia Street. Pat understood that in return he was to contribute to White's next campaign and work to get him elected. His new job was to sit at the guard station, lock and unlock cells to let prisoners in and out, and bring prisoners their meals. It paid a little less than the print shop and far less than Larkin, but required no heavy work. Pat was proud to walk in his uniform along Main Street after work with his revolver strapped to his hip. Often, he took the trolley to the Ward and returned home late at night in a hack, too drunk to walk the mile to Lord Street.

Their home was a house of stress. Mary spent more and more time in bed with headaches, pains in her chest, and violent coughs. Her sister-in-law, Johanna, came over as often as she could, but she had three children and Lord Street was an hour's walk from their home on Alabama Street, so she could not come as often as she was needed. Garrett paid for a two-week hospital stay for Mary at Sisters of Charity Hospital.

Then in mid-1884, the American economy went into recession. Major banks failed. Businesses bankrupted or cut their workforces and expenditures. Garrett's sales dropped by half. There was no money to hospitalize Mary further. He paid for a physician to see her at home.

Dr. Hanley came once a week on a Saturday afternoon. "I don't like the way Mary looks and sounds. She has pneumonia and she should be in a hospital or sanitarium. I can put her in, but how will you pay for it?"

Pat panicked. Her illness made him realize how much Mary meant to him. She was the center of his life and that of his children. "I don't know, Dr. Hanley. We don't have the money. I'll see if I can borrow from Father Gleason, but he's not a rich man himself. Maybe Jim Kennedy or Hugh Mooney would be good for it. How much are we talking about?"

"She could be in the hospital for ten days, or she could be in for a month. One never knows with pneumonia. It will cost $5 a day at least."

Pat wheezed a sigh of despair, "Oh my God! Where will I borrow that much money?" He had no idea. Once again, he stopped drinking, entirely this time.

Happily, Pat did not have to test his friendships. During the day, Johanna, other women friends, and Bobby nursed Mary. Pat shared care duties after work and on weekends. Mary recovered sufficiently over the next month to resume her role of wife and mother, although still relying on Bobby for housework. Distrust and cynicism toward Pat had possessed her from the moment he was fired at the Larkin Company. Even though Pat tended her with affection, she resented having to submit to his care. She could not conceal her hostility, even in front of the children. After she was up and about, there were still days when she was very weak and had to return to her bed for hours or even a day. She blamed her condition on her husband

John had made his first claim for additional pension disability in 1879. The Buffalo Surgeon Board found no ratable basis for increasing his monthly pension beyond the $2 granted when he left service in July of 1865. The scar left by the wound was clearly visible on his back under his left shoulder. That was all the surgeons were willing to certify came from the war.

He encouraged his brother to file again. H. Bowen Moore sat on the Buffalo Pension Board. It was to him that Patrick filed his second claim in 1883, eighteen years after leaving service.

He sat in Moore's bare office, door closed to the reception area, feeling poorly dressed before this lawyer who wore a three-piece suit. He moved his body from side to side and stammered when answering Moore's questions. Believing a larger pension was his due in justice for what he had suffered in the war, he caught himself, straightened his posture, and spoke in a firm voice.

"Mr. Moore, I need an increase to at least $8 a month. I'm not able to work full time. I've never gotten over the years sleeping on the ground in rebel prison camps. I lived in a hole for six months at Salisbury. They starved me. I lost sixty pounds."

"Mr. Donohue, what specifically is wrong with you?" asked a bored Mr. Moore.

"My shoulder healed cockeyed from the shell blast it took. It wasn't reset right. I tried to tell the surgeons that in the hospital, but by then the muscles had gone stiff. I have rheumatism throughout my body, catarrh in my lungs so bad I can't hardly breathe. I never got over the dysentery, which comes back every year. The piles are so bad sometimes I can't walk. And I know something is wrong with my heart . . . I have pains in my chest when I do heavy lifting."

"Unfortunately, these are all difficult things for the surgeons to certify, and even if they do uncover them, they must swear under oath they came from the war. We'll set up an appointment for you to be examined by the Board of Surgeons again, but the law is very clear. It allows a pension for disabilities due to certifiable wounds. Yours are not even visible and probably cannot be certified."

As the interview went on, he could read Moore's contemptuous attitude by the tone of his voice, the way he posed questions in legal language that he knew Pat did not understand, and by the negative commentary he added to Pat's answers.

John and Pat took a Saturday off to attend the funeral of 164th Captain Timothy Kelly at Immaculate Conception Church on the West Side of Buffalo. The church was a three-mile walk for both. They met at Hengerer's Department Store and talked about Tim.

"Pat, I don't begrudge Tim the full pension he got. He was not wounded, just sick and weak for the rest of his short life. The war takes another one of us. They say he died of TB in him from his prison days."

"I didn't envy the man at all. He was one helluva captain, maybe the best in the corps. I saw him after he got out of Danville Prison. His own mother wouldn't have recognized him. I saw him again a month ago and he was back looking worse . . . dragging his body around the house . . . dependent on Rose and the kids for a drink of water."

The two men walked silently on, melancholic about a friend and heroic officer, his young wife and children, and about their own unhealthy states.

The following Saturday, as Mary was scrubbing the kitchen floor, Annie, to get a rise from her mother, skipped across the shining floor. "Annie, stay off the floor while it's wet," her mother warned. "You'll fall and hurt yourself, do ye hear me, child?"

Annie giggled and slid across it repeatedly. Then she fell hard on her right hip and cried in pain. When Pat came home, she was still shrieking like a cornered cat, so he rented a hack and took her to the Buffalo General Hospital. The doctor pushed into her hip with his fingers until she screamed loudly, pronounced it fractured, and with help from a nurse built a lower body cast. He told Mary to keep her in bed for the next six weeks. Mary was as unsuccessful in keeping her youngest quiet in bed or in a chair as she had been keeping her off the wet floor.

One month after her fall, Annie got out of bed. She walked without pain, but with a decided limp that would be with her forever. The sight of his daughter walking like a cripple tore at Pat. Annie became her father's pet. He carried her on his shoulders and in a wagon wherever they went. He bought her candy at expensive shops on Main Street. He invented games they played together in the park off the basin.

He defended her spoiled behavior before her mother, whom Annie delighted in taunting with every mischievous act that came into her fertile mind. She became yet another source of conflict in an already anxious marriage. After years of doting on and spoiling Minnie, now Pat neglected her.

On January 16, 1884, the local Board of Surgeons issued their pronouncement that Pat, as Moore predicted, had no legal disability that would prevent him from doing physical labor. Moore sneered after Pat left the board hearing and muttered out-loud: "That man is another of those Irish, shirking their duty to support their families."

John went before the board around the same time. Afterward, they exchanged notes. "Pat, did you hear that Tommy Sanders of the 164th was given a pension of $8 because of the wound in his right shoulder? He can only do a few hours' work a day. His lungs are bad, got catarrh, diarrhea on and off since '64, just like you and me."

Pat's face reddened in anger. "I say we march up to the Pension Board and demand to know how he gets $8 and you and I get $2."

"Pat, there are two things we must do first. One is to join the GAR. The Grand Army of the Republic is building homes for poor vets and fighting for us in Congress. The second thing is to hire a lawyer."

"I hate to give them even a penny of our pensions," Pat responded, "but we're no match for the likes of Bowen Moore. I know that bastard's a Know Nothing. No handouts for fakers the likes of us Irish Catholics.

"I'm with you, John. Look into hiring a lawyer and let me know how you make out."

The brothers parted for their flats, a mile apart.

On his way home with full uniform and gun of a Saturday afternoon, Pat stopped off at the Irish Bogrunner Tavern downtown. There was entertainment that night: the noted New York showman Ned Harrigan, whom Pat had seen perform before. His jokes were no longer caricatures of rural Irish living in big cities. He sang and told funny and sad stories about the Irish grown up in New York. He varied his act with clog and soft shoe dances. He was a hit with the clientele, mostly immigrant and first generation Irish.

Afterward, before a bar full of patrons, Pat grew loud and raised toasts to his Irish parents, grandparents, and himself as a Fenian Irishman. "More Irish than the last mick off the boat," he shouted. "Who's done more for the Irish and the nation than one of Grant's men? Who's spent months in Confederate prisons?" He stopped and raised his glass. "Who's invaded Canada to win Ireland's freedom, but me?" The people at the bar began moving away.

Later, still at the bar, he told stories about the chaws of the First Ward from the Beach and did a bit of a soft shoe. Only a few drunks remained to cheer him on. By the time he got home, it was 6:00 a.m. and the sun was just rising. His loud entry woke up Mary. She backed away as Pat weaved forward. As he slumped onto the couch, she began to question him about the pay he had received at noon the previous day.

"Now, Mary, hald yer nasty mouth, or I'll slap it. It's me money and I'll spend it as I will."

He closed his eyes and fell into a light slumber. Mary went through his shirt pockets in search of money he had not spent. Pat woke up, pulled his gun, and shot it into the floor at her feet. Her eyes bulged; she screeched and fell back onto the floor. Bobby and the girls jumped out of bed and rushed into the living room in shock, the girls crying and yelling, Bobby and Minnie ready to take on their father when they realized what had happened. Minnie had grown increasingly sarcastic toward her father as she grew into her teens. She grabbed a pan and was ready to attack him with it. Bobby clutched a poker and he too would have hit Pat over the head.

Pat stretched out on the couch and this time fell into a deeper sleep. Mary grabbed Minnie and Bobby and pulled them into the dining room, where they stood silently holding one another until they saw Pat was no longer a danger. Bobby then retrieved the gun and hid it in the shed. They talked angrily with one another about what was happening to their home because of their father's drunkenness. Finally, they toasted a few pieces of bread and heated the teapot in the kitchen. They nibbled at the toast and sipped tea until it was time to go to church. Minnie walked out of mass after communion, shaking in anger at her father.

A week later, Pat came home from Kennedy's, where he had been showing off his uniform. He was proud of himself after years of taunting from the regulars about not showing up at work. "Mary, I want my shoes off. My back is aching and I can't untie the laces."

Hoping to avoid a fight, Mary knelt down, untied the laces, and took off his shoes. She felt weak and wasn't sure she could get back up. She called her son for a hand to steady her as she stood up.

"That's it, Bobby, you mama's boy, help your mother up. What about your old man? He could use a hand from you once in a while. There's more respect for me at Kennedy's than in my own house."

In a loud voice, he exclaimed about the way his family treated him and slapped his son across the head. Mary burst into tears. Bobby was stunned but recovered quickly. It was not the first time. Minnie cursed at her father and told him she'd take a butcher knife to him when he fell asleep if he ever hit her mother or brother again.

Pat showed up for work at the prison the next morning looking as though he had slept in his uniform. The deputy sheriff in charge became suspicious, checked Pat's holster, found a bullet missing from his gun belt, and fired him.

A month later, Pat talked Alderman White into getting him a job as bridge tender on the Michigan Street Bridge alongside his brother, John.

"John, this is a good job for you and me. No heavy lifting or shoveling. All we do is pull the lever whenever we see ships approaching. We should be set for life. And the view through the harbor is the best in town."

"I agree, but there's more to the job than that. Your friendship with the boys in City Hall paid off again. Who got you the job?"

"Well, there were two men who worked it out with the alderman. One was Jim Kennedy and the other was Father Gleason. I owe them."

"Pat, I think you've already paid off Kennedy, a few times over. You owe him nothing. As for Father Gleason, you know what he wants."

"I do. I know I've got to curtail the drinking."

A month later, Bob came running up to John's house on Louisiana at 7:00 a.m. and banged on the door. John had worked second shift and was just getting up.

"What's the problem, Bobby? Is your dad down with rheumatism again?"

"He is, Uncle John. And he asks you to cover for him this morning."

"I can do that. Tell your dad not to worry. Now get yourself home and get ready for school, lad."

"I will. I never miss. This will be my last year. I've got a regular job lined up at the Elk Street Market, evenings cleaning the stalls."

"How old are you now, Bobby?" asked John.

"I'm fourteen and I want to start working."

"I wish you would finish eighth grade and go on to high school and not work in the terrible stuff your father and I work in. There's no future in it and it's hard on you. Let's talk about it next Sunday, okay?"

"Okay, Uncle John, I like our little talks."

With that, Bobby ran off home to get ready for school.

Two years passed before Pat applied for a pension increase again, armed with information he had picked up in the Buffalo Courier and at Kennedy's. He had returned regularly to his old haunt.

On Tuesday, February 2, 1886, Pat appeared in H. Bowen Moore's office. "Mr. Moore, I've brought two witnesses with me who will tell you what we went through in the war and the condition I was in when I came back from the Confederate prison camps."

Moore frowned. "Mr. Donohue, your friends will have to make out depositions, but remember the law is very clear. A Civil War veteran must prove, before a board of surgeons, he is unable to do manual labor as a normal man would, from causes that stem from his war experience. There's more and more of you men hoping the federal government will take care of you for the rest of your lives, just because you served in the war. That's not how the law reads."

"Mr. Moore, I'm not looking for a handout. Before the war, I worked at the Union Iron Works and kept up with the best of them."

"Okay, Mr. Donohue, wait in that room over there. You can take off all your clothes down to your drawers. I'll take statements from your friends here."

Hugh Mooney testified to the soldier Pat was. He described conditions in the field. He said he had seen Pat when he came back home. He had a hand in employing him at the Central and found him to be in a weakened state, unable to do heavy manual labor.

Pat McCabe had been with Pat in the 155th until his capture and saw him when he rejoined the unit after being released from prison. He said he was no more than skin over skeleton.

The board surgeons dutifully examined Pat's whole body, paying particular attention to his left shoulder. They had him stand, extend his arms toward his toes, rotate his head left to right, and perform a few other movements. They found no disability from their examinations.

Mr. Moore's written disavowal of Pat's claim indicated that this was a case of a flagrant malingerer whose witnesses were not credible.

Unable to do regular manual labor and reduced to fragile states of economic existence, both brothers returned several times in desperation to the local pension board. Pat's wound was not visible to some examining doctors and slightly visible to others. John's was clearly visible. Both men had a $2 pension for wounds inflicted while in service. Both continued to receive that amount and only that amount.

Mary had grown very thin. Her hair was turning grey, her face ashen. She mentioned to her aging father that she had come to the end of her rope and was going to seek a divorce. She was not feeling well and Pat's drinking, his constant bickering with Bobby, the outbursts between Minnie and him, and his spoiling Annie were driving her to the brink. "I can't take it any longer, Dad. In ten years, I haven't known a peaceful hour when Pat's home."

"Mary, we're Catholics. Talk to your pastor. If he agrees with you, I'll do all I can. Business isn't great, but it's improving."

Mary had little faith in Father Connery at St. Columba's. He was advanced in years and gave short shrift to the marital complaints of the women of his parish. She had heard good things about one of the friars at St. Patrick's just up Emslie Street and decided she would talk with him.

Mary knocked on the door of the rectory and asked the woman who answered to see Father Francis Toomey. Father Francis was a young Franciscan friar, ordained less than five years, tall, broad shouldered, with dark hair, and dark complexion for an Irishman. He was popular with the young people of the parish and conducted its youth activities. Several female parishioners had a crush on him. Some families had transferred from other parishes to St. Patrick's because of him.

Father Francis led her into a parlor and shut the door. "What can I do for you, Mary?"

"Father, I have tried to make my marriage work, but living with my husband is no longer possible."

"Mary, sit down and tell me about your marriage. There must be some way we can help. How long have you been married?"

"We married right here in October 22, 1866, Father, so nearly twenty years."

"And what's the problem? Is he unfaithful?"

"No, Father. I wish he were. Maybe he'd run off and I'd be rid of him. He drinks and when he drinks he's nasty to me and to the children."

"How many children are there?"

"There were five, but two died of diphtheria. I just can't stand going to bed with a drunk who wants sex almost every night. Imagine what it's like to make love with a man who's been drinking for five hours! When he comes home, he gets violent! He's even shot his gun at my feet. He's slapped me and hits his son. His daughter, Minnie, hates him because of the way he favors one sister and then the other. We're constantly on the edge of hunger. He's not a good provider. He's been fired several times for his drinking."

Father Francis then had Mary recount the history of her marriage year by year, child by child. Mary admitted there were good years and he had worked steady for two or three years at a time.

"Mary, the twenty years have not all been bad. I see hope to remake your relationship. He has at times controlled his drinking. He has been a good father when he held a decent job."

"But it doesn't last. Our home life has gotten worse and now it's in shambles. Nothing good lasts with Pat."

"Mary, as you have been taught since you were a child, Mother Church is firmly against divorce and frowns on separation. You made a vow to remain with Pat in good times and in bad. The Church did not consecrate your marriage or ordain me to allow you to give up on your marriage without making every effort to make it work."

"I have, Father, twenty years of effort, but I can't stand it any longer. He's driving me to an early grave."

"Mary, do you think he still loves you? If he does, there must be a way to reach him."

"Yes, he says he loves me and I believe him. I'm afraid he just can't give up the drink and hanging with his pals at Kennedy's."

Their conversation went on for over an hour. Father Francis ended the session by saying he would like to talk to the two of them together. Mary walked home desolate. She had hoped she could make this young priest understand just how miserable and impossible her marriage had become.

Sunday, Pat saw John after the noon mass. "John, thanks for covering for me again. The rheumatism had me stiff as a dead man."

"Like I told you, Pat, we need an attorney. All these guys getting big pensions have attorneys who know how to deal with the surgeons or they just go around them to the Pension Board."

"I know, but no matter the job, you got to be able to get out of bed. I'm thinking of putting myself in the Bath Soldiers and Sailors Home for a stay, but I don't know how I'd feed the family."

John saw an opening to say something to Pat about his drinking. He had become aware from Bobby that things were not going well at home.

"Pat, I'm concerned about your drinking. Do you have the same problem our father had, and our grandfather before him?"

Pat was taken off guard by John's words. He and his brother had made it a rule since they married to stay out of one another's personal affairs. His face flushed. His eyes flashed angrily. In a firm voice, he rasped, "John, I wish you would have kept your goddamn mouth shut. What I do is none of your fekkin' business." He did a sudden about-face and stormed off.

Chapter 25

Deep Shadows

Mary never felt the moment was right to broach the subject with Pat about seeing Father Francis, together or without her. In fact, they talked less and less about anything. He was moody and drank heavily, whether at home or at Kennedy's. Strange as it seemed to her, he had convinced himself he was now tempering his intake of alcohol. If he had, Mary couldn't see it. His face was puffy and red, his nose bulbous and rosy, and his mid-section had assumed the classic shape of a beer-belly. His attendance at work was sporadic. There were days each month he was too sick or weak to go to work. Twice, ships stood waiting half an hour before the bridge because Pat was not alert on the job. The blame, however, fell to the whole crew of six men.

Pat and John passed one another daily at the bridge without speaking. After two years of Pat's spotty attendance, the rest of the crew refused to cover for him any longer. Covering for one another was not an unusual practice. Pat's absences just grew too frequent and at times surprised and exasperated his brother. The foreman fired him. Pat had expected to be let go and assumed a devil-may-care attitude. He got up the next morning and left the house as though going to work.

Pat approached Jim Kennedy at the bar that morning. Kennedy was widely linked to Fingy Conners, who controlled the Buffalo waterfront, and increasingly, the manpower that unloaded ships—"elevating" as it was commonly called—across all Great Lakes ports. Altogether, he controlled some 7,000 men.

"Jim, I can still work," Pat insisted, "but there are days I can't. Maybe I should join one of the gangs that shape up here at the saloon. If I can't make it some days, there would always be plenty of other men to take my place."

Jim Kennedy liked Pat. He spent money freely at the bar and brought humor and color to Kennedy's. He helped in political campaigns, most of them plotted in his saloon. Jim had lent Pat money in times of dire emergency. He believed Pat had never been right since the war, but that he was a good worker when he was feeling okay. Best of all, he always paid off his loans.

"There's an opening in Joe Healy's gang. You know Joe. I think the two of you would get along and, as you say, on the days you can't come, there are always boys at the shape-up looking for work."

Thus began Pat's short career in the grain mills of the Ward. In the years since the war, Buffalo had become the grain-handling center of the country. It had surpassed Rochester, and was overtaking Minneapolis as the flour milling capital.

On Monday, June 20, 1887, at age forty-three, Pat became a scooper in the hold of a grain boat, unloading winter wheat from Minnesota. The work did not overly tax him at first. The worst part of the job was the dust, which hung heavy in the air. He could barely see men fifteen feet away on the other side of the hold. He tied a bandana over his mouth. By the end of the day, twelve hours of steady work, Pat was weak and gasping for breath. He struggled to climb the ladder.

That night after a bath, he described the new work to Mary and Bob at supper. "I felt good this morning and wasn't too bad at noon, but by 5:00, I was exhausted. The dust stirred up the catarrh again."

Bob was used to his father's complaints, but the sight of his dad covered in grain dust from head to foot troubled him. "Just what do you do, Pa?"

Pat liked to talk to his son about his work. It was one of their few common interests. Bob was eighteen and had just secured a job as a teamster, carrying men and material to construction sites.

"Well, son, they tell me years back the men filled up sacks with wheat at a port on the upper Great Lakes and carried them into the holds of the boat. That's what your Uncle Jack had to do when he started. Now we do it by machinery, thank God, or I couldn't do the job at all."

Because of its location on Lake Erie, Buffalo was now the largest Great Lakes port, measured by ships in and out and tonnage. Rail lines shipped in cheap Pennsylvania coal. Coal was burned in boilers that created steam, which powered machinery, which emptied the grain and ore from freighters. The prospect that steam would be replaced by electricity generated at Niagara Falls was close at hand.

Mary decided not to ask Pat why he no longer had the bridge tender job. She knew she couldn't ask John or Johanna, who'd only give her half-truths as well. She could guess why, so she asked instead, "Is it dangerous, Pat? Do men ever get their hands and fingers caught in the ropes or get hit by the buckets?"

"Indeed, they do. I see men with fingers missing. I think John Fahey had his arm broke today and he was lucky. Got his arm up just in time to protect his face from a rope that snapped and whipped across the hold. Grain dust explodes and causes fires that kill. All it takes is a spark from a bucket striking concrete or metal to cause an explosion. Yes, it's dangerous work and the pay doesn't cover what we're asked to do." He ate more potatoes while he thought about options.

"Problem is, if we pull a strike, they'll call in the cops, who'll crack our heads and clear us off the docks. The company will hire a new crew before we get halfway home. One thing I know after one day on the job is that I don't want to see you, Bob, working on the docks or in the hold of a boat. It's not fit for animals. I'm glad you're driving a team of horses outside in the fresh air."

Mary returned to her sick bed often over the next years. In 1888, her closest friend, Bridgid Dolan, died in childbirth. She was the same age as Mary, forty-three, and had been continuously sick and in bed from the third month of her pregnancy. PM quit drinking the last six months of her life and tended to his wife from the time he got home from work, often relieving Mary. Mary bore up in spite of her weak state and the mile distance between their homes. She was at Bridgid's side nearly every day. PM talked to Pat about reducing his drinking, but nights Pat needed a few whiskeys to settle down and finish the day.

Bridgid's death caught all three by surprise and sent them into their own worlds of mourning. Pat didn't go to work for five days. Mary struggled to get out of bed mornings and moped through the day in a fog. The house had a morgue-like silence to it.

After the funeral, PM nearly lived at the Donohue's, sleeping over nights on the couch. He often broke into sudden, uncontrollable sobs. It was a month before he moved back to his home on Tecumseh Street. The first night home had him walking through the night or drinking tea at the kitchen table, unable to return to the bed he and Bridgid had shared for twenty-odd years. He returned to work at the Central, but without any of the spark and energy that had been so characteristic of his presence wherever he was. He began once again to drink with Pat at Kennedy's.

In July 1890, Mary confided to her children, "I'm leaving. I think I'm dying and before I get so weak I can't move, I'm moving out. I want to die in peace."

Bob argued with his mother to stay in their home. He would care for her and keep the old man away from her. Most nights he was gone anyway. But

Mary could no longer tolerate living with Pat and moved into a boarding house at 175 Clinton Street downtown with money from a rainy day fund she had built up over ten years, pennies at a time. Only her children had kept her home in recent years. Leaving them told a tale of utter exasperation and hopelessness. Garrett was humiliated and begged her to move home with him, empty except for two servants, but Mary refused to become dependent on her father once again. She wanted to die as an independent, free woman. She still harbored resentment toward her father that he had not supported her bid for divorce. Besides, 175 Clinton was more accessible to family and friends who could attend her and to St. Columba's Church, where she had become a member and from which she desired to receive last rites. She had saved for this very purpose and now she conducted the last great act of her life.

When he discovered Mary had left him, Pat paced the house and backyard frantically, slamming doors and punching walls. He demanded, begged, and cajoled the children to tell him where she was. He promised he would end his drinking forever. They stood like a solid wall and told him in the strongest terms possible their mother did not want to see him. Pat was crushed. He worked and drank to forget.

In late September, Mary knew she was dying. Her father and her children visited her daily. Garrett brought Dr. Hanley in to examine her and he confirmed Mary's opinion. Her vital signs were flagging. Pneumonia had resurfaced. Bob and Minnie stayed the night sleeping on her drafty floor, wrapped in three heavy blankets. Garrett sat in a chair next to her bed, leaving the room only when his feelings were about to erupt and disturb his daughter. Minnie quit work and was at her mother's side continuously with her sister Annie, who came every day after school.

"Bob, girls, please do not let your father come to me. I want to die in peace. Bury me at Holy Cross." She wheezed and asked Bob to call in the pastor of St. Columba's to anoint her. Bob trembled uncontrollably as he left the room, went to St. Columba's rectory, and returned within ten minutes. Garrett and the girls sobbed into their hands, trying to stifle their crying.

In a halting voice, forcing herself to exhale the words, Mary expressed her love for each of her children by name, one by one. She begged their forgiveness for her many faults. Her children took hold of her arms and shoulders, hugged her tenderly, and cried a torrent of tears. In breaking voices, they told her they always knew she loved them with all her strength. They said they loved her like no one else in the world. They repeated over and over, "Ma, you were the greatest mother of all."

Garrett begged her forgiveness for not helping her to separate from her husband years before. Mary said she probably wouldn't have anyway and thanked him for the care he had lavished on her since she was a girl.

Every muscle in her body relaxed. She closed her eyes. Her work was done. Her mind was at peace. That night, as all four watched over her, Mary became delusional as she fell in and out of consciousness. Father Connery, the pastor of St. Columba's, came and anointed her. The next day, October 5, with her children surrounding her, Mary Nagle Donohue drew a last long breath and her head slumped to one side.

The wake was held from John and Johanna's house at the request of the children. They would have preferred Garrett's house, but they wanted it held in the Ward, where all Mary's friends could attend.

John thought long and hard about how he would receive Pat into his house. When Pat appeared through the front door, John immediately moved from the casket toward him and took his arm. "Pat, I know how you cherished Mary like no one else. I'm truly sorry for your loss."

Pat sobbed and fell into his brother's arms. He said nothing. His anger at his brother died that moment.

Garrett contained his hostility toward Pat out of respect for Mary and his grandchildren, but anger dominated his countenance. He clenched his fists and thought to himself that he would shoot Pat if he had a gun.

The day after the funeral at St. Columba's, Pat went to the rectory to see Father Connery and pay for the funeral service. He had requested a low mass because that was all he could afford. That lowered him in his own eyes as much as anything he had ever done. He could have let Garrett pay and she would have had a high mass, but he refused.

"How are you doin', Pat?" The priest knew the whole story of their relationship, how Mary had moved out on Pat and then refused his presence when dying. "How are the children doing?"

"Father, Minnie is nineteen and she's been working downtown, although I hear she quit to be with her mother during her last days.. Bob is taking it very bad and so are the girls."

"Pat, the best way to handle their sorrow is to ask a question or two and hear them out. Say little. No advice, no words of consolation! Just comfort them with your presence and listening."

"I think Minnie is about ready to flee the coop for New York City. You know me well, so I can't fool you. It's too late now, but I'm going to swear off the drink. I wish I had treated Mary better."

"Oh, that's grand, Pat. The children need a strong father presence in the home, especially Annie. I see her in the school every day. She is a bright young lady, but a bit strong-headed. She could stray if you don't watch her closely. She'll need a lot of love and guidance, Pat."

"I know. I'll do my best. You can count on me, Father."

The priest knew Pat and many others like him in his parish, but decided to say nothing further. He had grown to view these men as hopeless.

That night Pat lay in his bed, aching like he never ached before, even in Salisbury. He began to sob softly. He could not accept that his wife had excluded him from her deathbed.

Pat promised the family that he would purchase a gravestone for Mary's grave and swore to himself he would keep his promise.

Garrett never forgave himself for not supporting his daughter when she wanted to divorce Pat. He went into work most days, but remained moody and depressed for the rest of his life. His only joy was dinner at home every Sunday with his grandchildren. He retained nothing but loathing for Pat and never invited him. Garrett died at age seventy-seven in 1892.

When his estate was probated, his will read that he left the business to a faithful manager who had loyally served for thirty years. He bequeathed small sums to two house servants who had been with him for decades and $2,000 each to his grandchildren. Bob used it to purchase a house at 52 Marvin Street in the Ward. Annie lived with Bob and put her money in a savings account. Minnie left for New York and married Abraham Davis, the son of a Jewish tailor. She invested her inheritance in his business.

Without Garrett's monthly gift to his wife and working only a few days a week, Pat was forced to humble himself and ask his son to take him in. Pat told his son everything in the old flat was his to move and keep, which he did in a construction company wagon.

When Pat learned that Minnie had married a Jew, he penned one of the few letters he wrote after the war, disowning her as his daughter. "You are no longer welcome in my home," his letter said. "No Catholic should ever marry one of those Christ-killing kikes."

Pat worked on and off over the next few years as a scooper and laborer on the docks. His health worsened. He became stooped and developed a constant cough. He looked old and frail, even though in 1894 he was only fifty. Pat applied for residency in the Bath Soldiers and Sailors Home in south central New York and was accepted.

On June 10, 1895, Pat left on a Delaware Lackawanna and Western local that took eight hours to reach Bath. It stopped at nearly every small village along the way, but provided a scenic and comfortable ride. Pat was able to move among the five cars through vestibules, a recent innovation, attached at both ends of each car. In the dining car, he drank tea and ate nothing, having only $1 in his pocket. As he rode, he gazed out the window mindlessly. His thoughts ran to sketchy memories of his first train ride with Gram and how much he missed her. She was the anchor of his early life.

The Veterans Home, opened in 1879, was set back from the main gate on 295 acres of land, between the Cohocton River and low hills to the southwest and the Erie Railroad to the north within the town of Bath. Its acreage was divided into three sections: the mowed grounds, which held over fifty structures, including an administration building, barracks, a canteen, an amusement building, and a hospital; the farm, with barns for animals and equipment, an orchard, and fields that grew a variety of vegetables and grains; and a cemetery. The Home's leadership consisted of retired members of the military who imposed an army regimen on the residents. Administrators believed that kind of discipline was what those who ended up there lacked.

After all these years, military life felt strange to Pat and he bristled from the day he entered. He ignored the presentations given at the initial orientation session. In fact, he walked out halfway through them. He resented the lack of freedom to drink and socialize as he wanted. He volunteered for cafeteria duty, waiting on tables and receiving nothing in return. He spent most of his idle time sitting with one or two equally negative residents bitching about food, sleeping quarters, and especially the director and his adjutant. He refused a medical exam and was told he would soon have to submit to one.

The Home staff helped him apply for a pension increase from $2 to $6. With $6 a month in his pocket, he could subsist in the Ward.

In the spring of 1895, Buffalo Pension Board special examiner J. M. Foote wrote a scathing condemnation of his peer, Bowen Moore, to the Board. Moore had been Pat's examiner over the past fifteen years. "I have observed that Moore as special examiner went out of his way to throw a cloud upon claims of honest and deserving men who chanced to be poor and without influential friends," Foote said in his report.

He recommended the increase and Pat was approved for $6 a month on August 28, 1895, retroactive to March of that year. Of that amount, the Home took $2 a month. On September 1, he received $28.

The Bath doctors made it clear to the veterans that their health was the number one concern of the whole staff. Pat laughed at much of what they said. Nonetheless, he was eating good food three times a day, sleeping seven to eight hours each night, imbibing only three beers a day at the canteen, and working on the farm caring for its Belgian draft horses. He stood more erect. His skin color returned to deep olive under the Bath sun and he felt and looked better.

In spite of all that he now had, he missed the Ward, its pubs, and his mates. He missed Kennedy's above all, its owner, its regulars, and just the familiarity of the place. It was his second home.

There was no place like the Ward. He longed to go home. He missed his daughter, Annie, who had turned eighteen in June 1897. His hostile feelings toward Bob waned and he was confident he could straighten out their relationship. He applied to the Bath board, which released him a month later without prejudice, which meant that he could apply for readmission whenever he needed to. He left in November 1897, two years and seven months after entering, and returned to the only residence he could afford, 52 Marvin Street. There he lived with Bob and Annie.

Bob continued working for construction companies as a teamster, joining the Cataract Power Construction Company in late 1897. He remained unmarried. Annie kept house for him. At first, Pat got on well with both. It was a great arrangement for him; Bob asked for no board.

Two days after arriving in the Ward, Pat walked to Kennedy's, where he celebrated his newfound freedom by buying every man at the bar a drink. There he learned that the Great Northern Elevator, a 187-foot-high mountain of a building, would open at 250 Ganson Street.

The Great Northern represented a revolution in elevator technology. It was constructed in rising stages of cylindrical bins, made of steel with a brick skin to control the temperature of the shell of the bins. Construction started in March 1897 and was completed in September. It was one of the first to be powered by electricity from Niagara Falls and had three marine legs on the Union Canal side that could elevate or load two ships at a time. For a year, it was the world's largest grain elevator, with a capacity of over 2,500,000 bushels.

Pat applied through Jim Kennedy, who provided the labor in a contract he held with the Great Northern, and was hired on as machine tender in December of that year. The Great Northern was but a quarter-mile walk from his Marvin Street home, but 40-mile-per-hour winds soaking up warm water over the 400-mile sweep of Lake Erie and creating deep, drifting snow across the shoreline made the walk in winter to and from work a chore.

Pat's job was to rig the marine legs with thick hemp rope and keep them running when a freighter was unloading or when boxcars were being loaded from the other side of the house. The marine legs moved along the top of the walls of the elevator. Electricity propelled a long leather belt with buckets fastened every sixteen inches along the belt. It was a responsible job and Pat took great pride in it. Within a month, he mastered the many knots required. The pay was modest, $.25 an hour, or $3 a day.

Pat returned to Kennedy's nightly with the elevator crew. To continue working, drinking at Kennedy's bar was a requirement. It was where Pat was paid by Jim Kennedy, who took ten percent of his earnings. Pat missed work occasionally, but kept his job because of his friendship with the bar owner.

On Pat's first day home, Annie received a letter from Minnie and began to talk about it. Pat objected strenuously. "I don't want to hear anything about her," he said. "She is no longer family and should be treated like a stranger." To punish her father, Annie read Minnie's letter out-loud to her brother after supper. Pat stomped out of the house and drank whiskey at Kennedy's for the rest of the evening.

After a month of steadily escalating tension and quarrels with her father, in December Annie left Buffalo at age eighteen to join her sister in New York. There she met Isaiah Davis, the brother of Minnie's husband, and married him, as much out of convenience and spite for her father as out of love. Pat repeated in a letter to her what he had written to Minnie before. "By marrying a Jew, you are no longer family."

A half year went by during which Bob and his father barely talked. One Saturday around 11:00 p.m., Pat came home drunk, spoiling for a fight. He stumbled into Bob's bedroom, waking Bob, and started right in on him.

"Robert, your mother's been dead for seven years, but you still act as though she's in the house."

Bob struggled to focus and respond. "Pa, what the hell's the matter with you?" He rubbed his eyes, sat up, and in a loud and angry voice that could be heard through the thin walls of the house, yelled: "You're right. There isn't a day I don't wish Ma was still alive. Every time you come home drunk, it reminds me how you treated her."

Pat slapped his son in the face and slurred: "Don't you ever talk like that to your father! I loved your mother all the years of our marriage." Feeling the urge to destroy his father, Bob pulled back and left the house.

The next day, when Pat returned home from the elevator, he found a small suitcase containing his clothes on the doorstep and the front door locked and bolted as it had never been. Shamed and embarrassed that his son had thrown him out before the whole neighborhood, Pat picked up the suitcase and moved to the Lighthouse Lodging, a squalid rooming house at 113 Commercial Street, near the canal. It was all he could afford: $.40 a night.

In April 1899, Buffalo grain shovelers and handlers went on strike over basic issues: elimination of saloon contractors like Connors and Kennedy who did the hiring and took a cut of wages; recognition of the International Longshoremen's Association as the sole bargaining unit for all grain workers;

and maintenance of the original wage scale. Pat was out of work for two months and lived on his pension and a little money he begged from his son. He was opposed to the strike at first, but attended union rallies and listened to men like Bishop Quigley and ILA President Keefe. What really changed him, though, was the presence of strikebreakers brought in by Connors from Cleveland. Fight them he could not, but he certainly wanted to. Through Keefe's leadership and support from civic and religious leaders across Buffalo, the strike was settled peacefully and the men went back to work on June 28.

After work the next Saturday, Pat cleaned up, put on fresh clothes, and walked into the Ward to visit his brother, John, as he often had done on Sundays since Mary died. John was sick with pneumonia and was under the care of a doctor. He was in bed when his daughter Mary greeted Pat at the door.

"Mary, you are looking spectacular. You're the prettiest girl in the Ward. Are you working now or are you still in school?" Mary was taller than Pat, with dark hair, fair complexion, and a slim, shapely figure.

"Oh, Uncle Pat, you always say the sweetest things. I'm working downtown in Hengerer's Department Store, don't you know."

"How old are you now, Mary?"

"I'm eighteen. I'm working in merchandising and buying clothes. One of these days, I might get to go to New York with our buyer."

"Ah, I can see you're excited about your work."

"You bet, Uncle Pat, and I'm well paid."

"Well, my dear Mary, you should be, and I'm sure the Hengerers are excited about you. I know I would be if I had a store and could hire such a pretty young lady as you. Now tell me. How's your dad?"

"He's doing better now. He's in bed. Can't stay up long. Mom is out shopping at the Elk Street Market with the other kids. Let me look in on him and see if he's sleeping."

A few seconds later, Mary returned to say Pat should go in.

John's face was sunken. His beard was scraggy. His hair had greyed and was unkempt. He coughed hard and often and brought up a wad of rust-colored phlegm. The room was dark and stuffy, the windows closed, and curtains pulled. It smelled of the bed pot, which John had recently used. Pat grimaced as he entered, but made up his mind to ignore the strong smells.

"Well, John, you're looking pretty fair. I was expecting worse, to be honest."

John grinned, pleased to see his brother although even after all this time, he still felt a strain and distance between them. He weakly extended his right hand. Pat took it and held it. "Dr. Hanley put me in bed a week ago." John began to cough again, grimacing from the chest pain.

"How do you think you got it?"

"I think I've had it on and off since we were in the service. Remember when I spent a week in the field hospital in Suffolk? But enough about my pneumonia. I hear you got a job as machine tender at the new Great Northern. And are you able to keep up with the work, Pat?"

"Barely. The dust is a killer. John, can I empty the pot?" John nodded and Pat took it to the outhouse out back, emptied it, and returned.

Johanna, John, James, and Katherine walked into the house from the market, their arms full of fresh fruits, vegetables, and meat.

"Uncle Pat," squealed sixteen-year-old Katherine, throwing her arms around Pat's waist. "I miss you. You don't come often enough."

She squeezed him, muttering a string of ums and ahs. Johanna and the boys were amused at the normally reserved Katherine's spontaneous show of affection for her uncle. As much as they all disliked his drinking, they loved his merry spirit, his stories, and the playful way he related to them. He generally came to the house sober and never in an evil mood. They had little idea of how he acted with his own children. They waited for Katherine to finish her greeting and then each hugged their uncle.

"Pat, your brother tires easily. Maybe we should let John rest and take a nap. Come on out back, sit down, and have a beer with me. We haven't seen you in ages," said Johanna. "John Junior, run to McCarthy's and get us a pail of ale, will you, son?" Pat gave his nephew a quarter.

"John, don't go back to work too soon. Pneumonia can be a killer. By the way, I hear there's a new pension law just passed. No need to apply based on war-related injuries and the like. I'm hiring an attorney, just like you said. Join me. Put in a new pension application."

"Gladly. Just get me the application and I'll help pay for his fees."

John was still receiving only $2 a month. With sons John, fifteen, and James, fourteen, working on the docks, the family was able to get by.

Johanna and Pat walked into the backyard and sat on a wooden park bench that had floated down the creek to the foot of Alabama Street. "Pat, what do you hear from Minnie?"

"Nothing from either of them. I can't tell you the pain it brings me. I warned them not to marry those yids."

Johanna knew as much from talking with Bob. It was one of the few things Bob had told her about Pat's behavior at home.

"Oh, Pat, how can you feel like that? Jews are no different than the rest of us. If your girls marry in the church, what do you care whom they marry as long as they're good to your daughters?"

"Johanna, I told them I'd disown them if they married kikes. And I don't think they married in the Church.

"Now, let's talk about John. He seems to be getting over the consumption, but don't let him go back to work until he's up to it." Pat slipped Johanna $2. As humbling as it was, she took it.

"I won't, Pat. I hear there are more elevators to come after the Electric. Is that true? Buffalo is booming. But the ordinary family in the Ward seems no better for it, you know what I mean?"

"You're dead right."

"Did you hear there's a group looking to get Bishop Quigley to build a second church in the Ward?"

"I did. Are you involved?"

"Indeed, I am. We want Bishop Quigley to appoint a priest to help us. Bridget's is overcrowded and getting Poles from the Valley. We're meeting with the bishop next week, and you know who's leading the delegation? Father Francis Toomey."

"My God, you women sure know how to pick your leader. The lot of you are in love with the poor man and now you got him building a church for you! In competition with his own, no less!"

Johanna laughed loud enough to be heard in the next yard. It felt good to laugh; it seemed as though she hadn't laughed in a long time. "Well, he is the handsomest man in the Ward, you have to admit. He's also one of the nicest and one of the brightest. What would you have us do, tap one of you boys from Kennedy's to lead us? Your gang can barely find its way home nights."

"Ah, Jo, you're being hard on us poor lads. We're only cleanin' the pipes."

They laughed a little and Pat stood up. He was choking up. Johanna brought back the pain of a long-gone wife.

CHAPTER 26

Bath Soldiers Home

At age fifty-six, toward the end of 1900, Pat's health had deteriorated so much that he was working only two days a week and that only because other scoopers were covering for him. It was common practice for younger and healthier scoopers to cover for their older and less able coworkers. His $6 pension was barely beer money. Bob had taken his father in once again, after visiting him at 113 Commercial Street and seeing firsthand the condition of this flophouse.

Pat hated sponging off his son, believing that at thirty-one Bob was still single because of him. After living with his son for a month, he cut his drinking in half in order to buy a ticket to Danville, Illinois. He had applied for Bath, but it was full.

Carrying only a single small piece of luggage, he boarded a New York Central for Chicago. The fifteen-hour ride was smooth and pleasurable when compared to past train rides. Pat slept when he was tired and conversed with other travelers when he wasn't. He spent much time in the dining car. There it was easy to initiate conversations, and it served some of the best cooking he had ever had.

The local rolling south out of Chicago was a six-hour struggle to cover 120 miles. It stopped in almost every village along the way. Pat got off several times when the conductor announced the train would be in the station for ten or fifteen minutes, bought a sandwich or an apple, and watched the crowd

245

of plainly dressed farm folk moving unhurriedly through the station. The landscape the train passed through varied only by the crops grown, tall corn or knee-high wheat.

The Danville Soldiers Home had opened in 1898, a mile from downtown. Its layout reminded Pat of the Bath Soldiers Home, with a cluster of buildings, spacious grounds, and a farm. The cemetery, hidden behind a grove of trees, had fifty-three headstones. Except for the woods and tree-lined road to the administration building, the place had little aesthetically to recommend it: plain institutional buildings and limited landscaping along roadways. Most of the 1,000 residents were veterans of the Civil War. A couple hundred men in their eighties were survivors of the 1846 Mexican-American War.

Life at Danville was much like life at Bath. The men lived in dormitories with bunks placed side by side, five feet apart. The day was regimented army style, reveille at 6:30 a.m., taps at 9:30 p.m. Drinking alcohol was strictly limited to what was served in the recreation hall: beer, three glasses a day. For diversion and pocket money, the men volunteered in the cafeteria or on the farm. No one was allowed to leave the Danville grounds except on supervised tours of local places of interest, which consisted of fruit farms, two picnic groves, and a hotel restaurant.

The Home's health care was good and Pat gained enough strength to work two or three hours a day, three days a week in the officers' mess hall, serving and cleaning up after meals.

A year later, Pat was bored. He had not made many friends, hoping soon to get a transfer to Bath or to return home. He missed the Ward, his family and friends there, and his drinking mates at Kennedy's.

Once a month, he received brief notes from Bob concerning the construction of new elevators in the Buffalo harbor and news and gossip about old friends and St. Bridget's Parish. Annie, Bob said, was still living in New York, although one or two notes hinted that she was thinking about ending her marriage. He said Minnie had divorced her husband and was living somewhere in Hell's Kitchen. Most of his notes devoted long paragraphs to labor strife on Buffalo's docks.

After two years at Danville, Bath notified Pat that there were now openings at its facility and that he should apply if still interested. He did and was approved. Bath was so much closer to home. On April 2, 1902, he said goodbye to his few friends at the Danville Home and headed for Buffalo.

Pat spent four days in the Ward staying at his son's home. Annie had initiated divorce proceedings and come home to live with Bob. Pat resumed his favorite stool at Kennedy's. He staggered home drunk and argumentative the very first evening. Living with Bob and Annie became as tense as ever, even though he had told them he would leave within the week for Bath. They could not wait for him to go; on Sunday, April 6, they shook hands with him and breathed a sigh of relief the moment he was out of sight for good.

Pat walked downtown with his same small suitcase and boarded an Erie Railroad train. Five hours later, he arrived in Bath, was assigned to Company D Barracks, and ordered to visit the surgeon's office. A volunteer greeted him with a polite smile. "Well, Mr. Donohue, I see you served with the 155th out of Buffalo. I'm Bill Slattery and I served with the 69th out of New York. Someday, we should chat about our service days.

"I have your records ready for the surgeons. You've been through this before, so you know what to expect. You'll be examined by Surgeon Babcock and Assistant Surgeons Burrows and Potter. Please enter the examining room and strip to your drawers. The doctors will see you shortly."

Pat did as he said and after a short wait, the three doctors entered the room.

"Well, Mr. Donohue, welcome back. Remind us. What was unique about your army history and how did it affect your health?" asked Dr. Potter, a tall, thin man in his fifties.

Pat gave his well-rehearsed account. He concluded by saying, "I've lived in Buffalo ever since 1849, raised a family of five children. My wife died in 1890. Had many manual labor jobs, but didn't keep them for more than a few years at a time. I've never really lost the catarrh, dysentery, and piles of the war . . . sometimes so bad I couldn't walk."

"All right, Mr. Donohue. May we call you Pat?" asked Dr. Potter.

"Yes, certainly, sir," he responded.

"All right, Pat, please get up here on the table and let us examine you."

Over the next half hour, the surgeons conducted and recorded a minute examination of Pat's body, which showed signs of kidney sclerosis. His ankles were slightly swollen. He had a high belly and his muscles were softer than the surgeons expected of a man who had worked at hard labor all his life.

"Pat, we generally agree with what you have been saying. What's your current pension rate?" asked Dr. Burrows, who appeared to be about the same age and height as Potter, but heavier and balding.

"Six dollars, sir."

"Were you ever turned down for an increase while at Danville?"

"Yes, the Danville surgeons recommended $8, but the Chicago Pension Board turned it down."

"We will see to it that your case is transferred back to the Buffalo Pension Board. Is that okay with you, Pat?"

"Yes, sir."

"Please make the necessary arrangements. Will you do that?"

"I will, sir."

He recoiled at the idea of writing his attorney, Willard H. Peck, to set up the appointment, and Bob to let him know he was coming home for a few days. His handwriting embarrassed him, but he wanted the money. Six dollars was an insult! He believed he deserved more. It angered him that so many others who had less disability were receiving twice as much. He was angry for his brother also, who was in the same straits.

Before they let him go, Dr. Burrows asked Pat if he drank. Pat bristled and retorted that he drank periodically, but did not drink every day and didn't need it. Questioning him more, the doctor added, "The reason I ask is that we see signs in your body that you're suffering from excessive use of alcohol." Without being dismissed, Pat got up and walked out. Babcock, whose final word to the patient was cut off by Pat's sudden departure, muttered to his colleagues, "That man is going to be trouble."

Pat walked to a bench and gazed over the tree-lined lanes, vast lawns with benches, tables, fountains, well-designed flowerbeds, a fruit orchard on two side hills, a hillside cemetery, and hundreds of acres of animal and grain farm. The scene mesmerized him. Massive improvements had been made in the last two years. Pat said to himself, "I think this time I'm ready to be here."

The next morning, he attended an orientation held in the newly constructed amusement hall, already in use while awaiting final installation of its heating and ventilations systems. It was an ornate, gothic-style building that seated 1,200 and was used as an overflow facility to house new inmates for whom no barracks had been completed. Pat took a seat in the second row; he really wanted to take in what the big shots were saying.

The men turned, whispered, and stared as Colonel Davidson, the director of the Home, entered the hall and made his way to the front row where other administrators were seated. On stage, his adjutant, Major Shillings, standing behind a podium, called the men to order. Both Davidson and Shillings were striking figures in dress blue uniforms, trimmed in black. The sun shone brightly on Shillings's left shoulder through the windows of the south wall, as though heaven itself confirmed his authority and what he was about to say.

Major Shillings was of medium height, with grey-brown hair cut short on the sides but hanging down to mid-forehead in front. It gave him a certain boyish look. "Good afternoon, gentlemen. My name is Major Shillings. I am a local boy from the Finger Lakes Region, a graduate of the University of Rochester in 1857. I worked as a civil engineer before entering service. I served three years as First Lieutenant in Company I of the 50th New York Volunteer Engineers, building bridges from the Battle of Fair Oaks to Appomattox.

"On behalf of our very dedicated staff, I wish to welcome you to the New York State Soldiers' and Sailors' Home, founded by the Grand Army of the Republic in 1876 and transferred to the State of New York two years later. The first meal was served to twenty-five Civil War veterans on Christmas Day of 1878. The formal dedication of the Home was celebrated January 21, 1879. Call me a blowhard if you will, but I believe it is the most unique and progressive institution of its kind in the country. The Home has about 2,000 men in residence on an average day.

"Our superintendent, Colonel Davidson, served as First Lieutenant, Company H, 30th Regiment, U.S. Colored Troops. He was decorated for bravery at the Battle of the Crater at Petersburg. He is a modest man who never mentions the deeds that won him that medal, but we are all very proud he is our superintendent, a man who works tirelessly to improve the Bath Soldiers' Home."

Colonel Davidson removed his hat, rose from his seat, and proceeded up a few steps to the stage. He dominated the podium with his size. He was muscular, trim, and still in fighting shape, although nearing seventy years of age. "No medal has been a greater honor than serving you men who saved the Union by your valor. If you find anything amiss with the Bath Home, I would like to know about it, and I assure you I will take whatever action is necessary. I wish you a pleasant stay and increasing good health."

Major Shillings then gave the men the schedule they were to follow each day: Reveille at 6:00, Formation at 7:00, Breakfast at 7:30, Inspection and Roll Call at 8:00, Fatigue Duty immediately after, Dinner at noon, Fatigue Duty again at 1:00 p.m., Recall and Retreat at 5:30, Supper at 6:00, Tattoo and Lights out at 9:00, and Taps at 9:30. Shillings called it "a schedule still firmly etched in your brains, I am sure."

The audience murmured in agreement.

"There are a variety of volunteer opportunities, depending on aptitudes, health, and skills. You will hear more about this from Doctor Babcock, Surgeon of the Home, and Mister Drummer, Superintendent of Grounds.

"We expect you to keep your barracks area and yourselves clean. The Bath Soldiers' Home is run much like the Army. We will respond with military discipline to drunkenness, disorderly conduct, or disobedience to the reasonable orders of staff. Such conduct will be reported to the Board of Trustees, which ordinarily dismisses the person in question from the Home. You will be allowed three glasses of beer or ale a day in the canteen. Passes to Bath and furloughs home will be granted quite freely.

"We warn you not to over-indulge in alcoholic drink on the premises, or in the bars that line Belfast Street from the Home, or in Bath. *Any abuse in the way of unmilitary behavior will be met with swift, certain, and appropriate punishment and most often with discharge.*" He paused looking straight out at the throng to allow his words to sink in.

When he spoke again, he introduced Dr. Babcock. "Dr. Warren L. Babcock is a graduate of the College of Physicians and Surgeons at Baltimore, Maryland. He served before his appointment here as assistant physician at the St. Lawrence Hospital for the Insane. He assumed the post of chief surgeon of the Home on April 1, 1902."

Dr. Babcock addressed the men. He was very tall, gangly, with an oversized nose, and thinning, dark blond hair turning grey at the temples. He was attired in a three-piece, dark blue suit. "Gentlemen, the Bath Soldiers' Home provides daily medical care in the hospital and in our clinic. Upon entry, you men are given a thorough medical examination, in order to determine the care you need. Thereafter, we give you an annual, more limited, follow-up exam.

"We are crowded for beds. As you know, men are sleeping in basements and hallways. Barracks L, when completed later this year, will do much to relieve that overcrowding. I have also recommended that an enclosed corridor be constructed to connect the second floor of the new barracks to the hospital. This and other improvements can only be made if the state legislature appropriates the funding. Please write your representatives in support of our budget request.

"I strongly urge that all men in residence be vaccinated for smallpox in July. We have thirty men quarantined with smallpox. There is no reason any longer for such suffering or the mortal danger to both staff and residents that smallpox poses.

"I encourage you men to be honest with examining surgeons. Your care will depend on it. Please do not be afraid to talk to me. Make an appointment and come in.

"We in the hospital are dependent upon you healthy men to volunteer as nurses and orderlies. I ask you to consider serving in this way.

"One last word! Bath provides the best health care in the country, I believe, but no one can make you a healthy man except you. You are more likely to live a long life if you follow these simple rules: good nourishing food, sufficient sleep, regular exercise, and positive meaning for whatever days God gives you. Otherwise, there is little any doctor can do for you. I look forward to serving you men who have served our country so gallantly."

Major Shillings then introduced Mr. Drummer. "Mr. Henry L. Drummer was born in Canandaigua and raised in Elmira. When he was twenty-three, he was appointed Superintendent of Grounds. His work has been recognized nationally by General W. W. Averell, Inspector General of the National Home for Disabled Volunteer Soldiers. No one can explain the wonders of nature with the clarity and passion of Mr. Drummer. Consider joining his nature class, as well as volunteering to work on the grounds, which are equaled by no other in the country."

Henry Drummer took his place at the podium, attired in brown pants, high button blouse and tie, and a black sweater. He was a small man. His whole body jerked this way and that, as though trying to enlarge the space he occupied. It made Pat nervous just to watch him.

"Gentlemen, this afternoon we have organized a tour of the hospital, the grounds, and the farm. Transportation will be available. You will become acquainted with the variety of tasks performed by your fellow residents. Mr. Edwards Smith, supervisor of the farm, has 200 acres to tend, hundreds of animals to feed, and their stalls and pens to keep clean. It is all healthy, physical work. Come, volunteer, and labor at your own pace at tasks of your own choice. We believe you will find real satisfaction in serving your fellow soldiers and grow in appreciation of nature."

Major Shillings spoke once more. "Gentlemen, our orientation is concluded. We invite you to proceed to the canteen for refreshments and to get to know one another and the staff." He saluted the men and left.

Pat's head was spinning. The whole session took ten minutes. He did what was suggested and headed to the canteen for a drink.

CHAPTER 27

Finding His Place

Pat felt a hand on his shoulder and turned around, staring into the face of Patrick Dolan. Dolan laughed. He had surprised his old pal.

"PM! I heard you were at Kennedy's last week. What a kick to see you! Somehow, we missed one another. Are you drinkin' mornings, lad?"

"Not one, me boy. I've taken leave of Kennedy and the saloon bosses."

Pat understood well PM's feelings toward Kennedy and the saloon owners who controlled Buffalo waterfront labor and cost Ward families money they needed to clothe and feed their kids. But Kennedy's was home to him, no matter what. He decided to let PM's remark pass.

They hugged, their embrace rekindling experiences going back to boyhood.

"Donohue, you're not looking bad for the shape of you, you old fart, ye! Looks like they treated you well in Danville. You've lost a little of your gut and you're almost trim enough to take on a rebel company."

"That I am, me lad, so watch your step or I'll throw you to the ground and put the boots to ye."

"Well, let's not get carried away, old boy. Our fightin' days ended long ago."

The two men laughed as PM waved to the bartender to set up two beers.

"Pat, you're going to like the Home this time," said Dolan.

"What's the word on Dr. Babcock and his staff?"

Dolan cocked his head slightly and thought for a few seconds before replying. "Health is number one for this whole outfit. It's all about doing what's best for the men. And that's true of the whole staff, believe me. You heard Dr. Babcock. He understands more than just your body. When did you ever hear a doctor talk about how important it is to be positive?"

"The grounds are like walking into one of those Delaware Avenue yards with their flower gardens and pretty shrubs all set out in fancy designs," commented Pat.

PM swung his right arm in a semi-circle, saying, "Take this place in, will you, Pat? It's an example of the concern of the staff for the residents and keeping them active year round." The two of them stood silently for a few seconds, turning toward all sides of the canteen, its card tables, ping pong tables, and dart targets, not to mention the long bar they were standing at, with its polished brass kegs and full wall mirror.

"Pat, Dr. Babcock has done great things for me. I never got over losing Bridgid until I started talking to him. I miss her, but I look to the future. I'm okay now."

"I'm happy for you, PM. I know what a loss Bridgid was for you. What do you have to say about Drummer boy? Is he just a nature nut?"

"I can tell you, Henry Drummer is the brains and the push behind all the flowers and tree-lined boulevards you see. That little man loves nature and believes that involving the men in flowers and trees and gardens is good tonic for what ails them."

"Yah, a lot has changed on the grounds since I was here last. Are you going to his nature classes?" asked Pat.

"I am. We're learning more than flowers and bugs. He teaches us modern science, all about Darwin and evolution. Kind of at odds with how we Catholics were brought up," added PM. Then they walked outside and PM commented on the things that came into view.

"Mr. Smith, the farm director, knows his plants and animals.

Look at those fields and vegetable patches. For years now, the farm has made money. You'll see. We eat pretty well, better than we ever did at home." PM paused to let Pat grasp all he was hearing and seeing.

"Before you commit yourself to any one duty station, take the tour this afternoon, walk through the hospital, poke your nose in all the farm buildings. You'll find me in one of them. I'm nursing piglets and cleaning the sty. Spend a few minutes with Mr. Drummer." Dolan threw down the last of his beer and ran off.

Pat was taken aback. *PM had been a pretty heavy drinker back in the Ward. Work was something to avoid. Now he was working with pigs and can't wait to get back to them. What happened?*

That afternoon, Pat did as his old pal suggested. The tour started at the hospital. He left the group and walked through three wards to get a closer look at the care. The wards were as clean as Mary's kitchen on a Saturday afternoon. They were airy with high ceilings and fans. The walls were freshly painted white.

Dr. Babcock was on the floor, making rounds. He seemed to know exactly what was going on with each patient. There were plenty of nurses, some older men like himself who had volunteered, and young women, probably hired from the region.

Pat hailed an attractive young nurse, "Young lady, can I ask you a question?"

"I can't talk long, sir, but I'd be happy to answer your question," she responded.

"I was just wondering how you feel about your work, ma'am. Are you treated well by the staff and the residents? Are you happy with your pay?" asked Pat.

"Sir, they pay the male nurses more than the female nurses, and that's not fair, is it? Was a day when female nurses couldn't touch a male patient, but these days we all do the same work and the men are glad for the care. Other than the pay, I love the work. The doctors are very respectful of us and most of the men are like my own father. Once in a while, I have to deal with a real crab, but not often. The whole bunch are a lovable lot."

"Wow, that's quite a statement. Thanks for the honest reply," said Pat.

He sat in as Babcock explained to a group of men in the ward how calming down their reactions to negative inner voices improved their health. He advised them to "breathe deeply and think positively!" Pat did not understand all that he was saying, but calming down made sense to him. He sometimes got mad over things he later thought stupid or silly. And he stayed mad for weeks, months, even years.

He spent the rest of the afternoon visiting the grounds and the agricultural operations, sometimes with the tour, sometimes wandering off by himself. The flowerbeds were massive; the ponds and walkways were well laid-out and cared for. He was amazed by the size of the farm. It had hundreds of animals: cows, pigs, goats, cattle, calves, geese, chickens, ducks, and two dozen horses, among them Belgian draft horses. It was to these awesome creatures that he was most attracted.

The tour ended at the canteen. The canteen was a recent addition, open all day from after breakfast until tattoo. It allowed the men to recreate throughout the year, organized by Henry Drummer, with input from Babcock and the rest of the staff.

As the days went on, his first impressions of Drummer, Babcock, and Smith grew only more favorable. Working for any one of them would be an experience beyond anything he had had before. He volunteered to work with the Belgian horses. He joined Drummer's science group to learn about Darwin and his controversial theory of evolution.

During the first class, the guest lecturer, a Presbyterian minister and Home chaplain, said that the stories of creation in the first book of the Bible were never meant to be science. They were stories of God and God's love for his creation. Why couldn't God create humans over many millions of years by a process of evolution from lower forms of life? Was not nature even more magnificent when we people can see how connected we are to all created things?

Pat was shocked by what he heard. How could he still believe in the Catholic faith, which taught that God had created the world in 6 days and that the world was 6,000 years old? Pat began to question other things the church taught. Gradually, he stopped going to mass every Sunday, which he had more or less resumed after Mary died. Once or twice, he attended Protestant services and talks given by Protestant ministers. Still, he wanted to worship with a community, and the Catholic Eucharist held a mystery and specialness for him that the Protestant services did not.

On the second Saturday in June 1902, the weather turned warm and sunny and trains from Buffalo, Rochester, Syracuse, and even from New York City brought crowds to visit the veterans and stroll the grounds. Pat had never seen so many fine-looking ladies. He donned his GAR uniform and kepi cap and mingled with the visitors along the main right of way. He stopped at a bench occupied by three middle-aged women.

"Ladies, can I give you a tour of the grounds? My name is Patrick Donohue and I'm from Buffalo."

"Well, Patrick from Buffalo, that is very kind of you," answered one of the ladies who extended a gloved hand. "My name is Gladys and these are my friends, Dorothy and Gertrude. We're from Bath."

Pat was excited to be in the company of women. Over the course of the afternoon, they walked the grounds. He showed them the horse stables. With the permission of Mr. Smith, he led out a nervous Belgian mare named Pattie from the barn. Pattie was deep red brown, with a well-combed mane that hung to her shoulders. She had already been bridled and exercised. With a smooth and gentle touch, Pat walked her slowly over to the women. They recoiled before the huge animal, seventeen hands high, or five feet eight inches. Pat encouraged them to come closer, pat her, stroke her head, and talk to her.

While not totally comfortable, they stood for some time and admired, petted, and talked to Pattie.

He led them into the cemetery and told a story of a veteran buried there, a story he heard Drummer tell on the tour. Pat could see the ladies were enthralled. He made a promise to himself to learn more about the men of Bath, living and dead, so that he could add to his stories. He had always liked being the center of attention and had a knack for remembering tales and making them come alive, knowing that his slight Irish accent added a certain charm.

The ladies asked for his address so they could write him. This worried him a little. Would he have to write back?

In mid-September, a great deal of work had to be done in the flowerbeds and in the greenhouse before winter set in. Women from Bath often came out on Saturdays to work on the beds. Pat walked the grounds and noticed three women digging out bulbs and roots. He picked up a wheelbarrow and introduced himself. He offered to cart away to the mulch heap the weeds the women dug out and the stems they cut off. His offer was readily accepted. In between trips, Pat dawdled with the women.

"What's this that Mr. Drummer has you doing, ladies?"

He was answered by a woman named Abigail, middle-aged, fit, with graying, dark-blond hair, dressed in a high-collared long dress and wearing gardening gloves and an apron.

"In the fall, flower beds have to be pruned just like fruit trees. Flower roots spread out and sprout stems and leaves. Gardeners who want space between their stands of flowers have to prune them back."

A second woman introduced herself as Millicent and explained further. "You see those baskets we're filling up with bulbs? Well, those bulbs have to be planted again later in the fall or they won't grow in the spring. We think flowers add beauty to our lives like nothing else."

"Indeed, they do," said Pat admiring this very attractive, middle-aged woman. "I guess I never took the time to really look at them."

Pat spent the next hour carrying plant cuttings to the waste heap and conversing with the four women. He enjoyed the day like no other thus far at the Home.

Pat met PM every evening at the canteen. They drank liberally and reminisced about the Ward and the war. No one kept track of the number they drank, as long as they remained orderly. They managed to cram in a half dozen before tattoo. Pat became bored with the same routines every day and looked for a change. He and PM got passes, skipped dinner, and went into Bath. They found the Bath Hotel, an old three-story, Victorian structure on the main square. They sat down to an evening of inexpensive food and drink, well presented on a linen tablecloth, with polished silverware and English china. They could afford it with their pensions and pocket money from volunteering.

"This isn't bad, now, is it?" said a smiling Pat, raising his glass to his lifelong friend.

PM responded with a gesture of his own toward Pat. "Here's to good food, good beer, and good friends!"

"Aye to that, me lad!" They sipped and returned to cleaning their plates of the remainder of their meal.

Dropping his fork onto his plate, PM leaned over the table and said quietly, "We may not be able to do this much longer."

Pat looked up from his plate to his companion. "Whatd'ya mean?"

PM sniffed. "No more drinkin', for one thing."

"I don't getcha," Pat said and dropped his own fork to the tabletop. "What're you talkin' about?"

PM shrugged and with a knowing air continued his statement. "There are people who want to take away a man's right to have a drink now and again. To make"—and he held up his glass of beer—"what we're doing illegal. You ain't heard?"

Pat frowned. He'd heard it all before and he said as much. There were always groups, religious or otherwise, who were out to curb him and his pals from having a drink, who urged him to take the pledge. "They can't do anything."

"I dunno," said PM with a sigh. "They might, if the Double-yuh Cee Tee Yoo have anything to do with it."

The question on Pat's face led PM to go on. "The Women's Christian Temperance Union, the WCTU."

"I've heard of them," Pat said. "I've seen 'em, too. A bunch of old busybodies with nothin' better to do."

"That's easy for you to say. I hear they have their bowels in an uproar over the canteen serving beer."

"The hell ya say! Goddamn 'em, every last one!" Pat said in jest, refusing to take PM's concern seriously.

"The worst of them is that Millicent Hastings," said PM.

"I've seen her," Pat said into his glass as he took a sip. "She is a fine-looking woman. That bosom of hers cannot be hidden, no matter how much cloth she drapes over it. Any time she wants to talk to me about the evils of the divil drink, I'll sit right in her lap and snuggle my head up to her chest."

"Donohue, get serious. I tell you, that woman is poison. She's got a law going through the state legislature right now that will eliminate beer in the canteen. The woman is sick, but she's got more influence than the superintendent. I think we should hoot her off the grounds."

"Ah, PM, you're taking the bitch too serious. She doesn't have a chance in the legislature. Why, all those fellows drink enough to drown their districts. Remember Sullivan back in Buffalo? And he's no different than the rest of them. They wouldn't vote to eliminate beer from a brothel, let alone from a home of old soldiers."

Within the hour, Bill Slattery and two other residents from Brooklyn entered the hotel and took a table near them. Slattery remarked to his friends in a loud voice something about the rowdy 155th soldiers from Buffalo.

Raising his voice slightly, Pat taunted him. "Well, Slattery, I have to give it to you. You're a good nurse, but you boys in the 69th were just what the rebels ordered. They found out where you were in the line before every battle and attacked right there. They knew you'd run like girls . . . and you did."

Pat settled back in his seat, smirking and waiting for his words to do their work. They never failed. Insulting words flew back and forth. After both tables had impugned one another's manhood, Irishness, mother, and anything else they held dear, Pat staggered from his chair and smashed Slattery in the face with his fist before he could get to his feet. That set off a brawl that ended with a broken table, shattered dishes, spilt food, and an unconscious bartender sprawled on the floor.

Two Bath policemen cuffed the five residents and led them to the village jail. The jail had two cells, built to hold one prisoner each. Stretching out and sleeping comfortably was impossible. PM slept on a hard bunk first, then switched with Pat, who had been lying on the floor on a woolen blanket. The next morning, they got up stiff, sore, and hung over, when a policeman brought in a breakfast of oatmeal, milk, and toasted bread and roughly shook them from their half-slumber.

CHAPTER 28

Millicent

Major Shillings appeared in court the next morning to pay their fines and bring them back to the Home. The five were required to reimburse the Home the full amount of the fine, $5 each, and put on probation by Superintendent Davidson. Davidson was angry at them for disgracing the Home before the Bath public. He sentenced the three New Yorkers to shovel out pigsties and ordered the two Buffalonians to clean toilets. Both sentences were to last at least one month and would not be commuted until he was satisfied the five had learned their lessons.

Pat and PM cringed at the work before them. The toilet floors were messed by veterans who could not control their bowels. The stench and the thought of what caused it gagged them so badly they wrapped their faces in towels and did their work before breakfast. They were also under orders from Davidson to appear on an indefinite basis at WCTU lectures given by Millicent Hastings in the fall at the Bath Home.

On Friday, August 22, 1902, at age thirty-three, Bob Donohue married a woman he had met through friends at work, Mary Alice Driscoll, called by family and friends "Mame." He had fallen in love for the first time in his life, swept off his feet by this fun-loving woman, who transported him to a different world. Mame was from The Beach, a shanty district on the lake. Her parents were alcoholics. She was farmed out to a family named Coughlin, who boarded her during her teen years. School was an on-and-off affair that lasted through the fourth grade. She began working at ten for whomever would hire her downtown, and then as seamstress in wealthy homes. By fifteen, she was living the life of a single woman in the bawdy bar scene near the Canal.

Bob and Mary Alice were married at St. Charles Church on Ridge Road, just yards from the Lackawanna Steel Plant. St. Charles was a mission to the Italian population located in that area of West Seneca, later Lackawanna. Bob's pastor at St. Bridget's set up the wedding at St. Charles to avoid scandal. Mame already had two out-of-wedlock children, John, age four, and Alice, age one. Bob did not invite his father, as he had no desire to see him, and more than that feared his father would only get drunk and start fights at the small reception held at his Marvin Street flat.

Mrs. Hastings entered the lecture room met by sullen stares from all twelve veterans present. She wore a conservative, well-tailored fall suit, a matching shawl, high-black boots, and a tight curtained hat with a feather hanging from the back. She set her shawl on a chair and introduced herself and the purpose of her lecture. Pat muttered, "This shit is for no-balls Protestants." The men laughed.

Millicent did not change her tone or facial expression. Pat continued his occasional taunts throughout the hour they were together. When she asked for questions, he asked her in a hostile manner, "Do you think anything you say will stop my drinking?"

"My hope is that over the course of the lectures, Mr. Donohue, you will see for yourself what an evil impact drink has had on you," she responded in an even tone. "Fighting in the Bath Hotel and a night in jail must have been one of the low points of your life."

She stopped and turned away in disgust. Then after a few seconds, she lowered her voice and glowered at him. "Clearly, it was a terrible embarrassment to the superintendent and could have gotten you ejected from the Home. Is that what you want out of life? To be known as a common bar brawler?"

"Ah, that fight was nothin'. I've been in jail before," Pat responded nastily. "No one was hurt. PM and I would have paid for the broken furniture. We both like a good fight."

After the first lecture, she asked Superintendent Davidson to assign Pat to work with her on the grounds. He had heard Babcock predict at a staff meeting that Pat would be trouble after he cut short his physical and stomped out. Davidson admired her courage in taking on such a difficult person. He believed nothing she or anyone else said or did would change Pat. Nonetheless, he gave her permission to try.

During the first session working together, Millicent said very little beyond pleasantries, asking Pat painless, non-personal questions. They worked rearranging the flowerbeds edging the cemetery. She gave him a shovel and asked him to dig out a row of tulips opposite her. She ended the session after an hour in order to make the work as easy for Pat as possible. Pat enjoyed being out in the bright sunshine and complied with her requests with little hesitation. Although not conscious of the fact, he lost some of his hostility toward Millicent while working with her that very first time. They continued working together a day or two a week throughout September.

Pat attended her weekly lectures as ordered by the adjutant and never used coarse language or rude sarcasm in her presence again. But he could not altogether refrain from making smart remarks in class and getting guffaws from the other veterans. She ignored him, which at first annoyed Pat, but then caused him to remain silent throughout her classes. He could not help but admire her self-control.

On a sunny, cool day in early October, with leaves of red and gold on nearby hardwoods lining the road, Millicent decided to venture further. After working with Pat twice, she was confident he would receive what she said in the spirit it was given. The challenge he posed intrigued her. She wanted to know more about this Irish male's relationship to women and alcohol.

The two stood opposite one another, digging out bulbs with small spades in the ten-foot-wide tulip beds that separated the road from the cemetery, cleaning them with gloved hands, and placing them in a steel pail.

"Mr. Donohue, are you annoyed, just a little bit angry, at being lectured by a woman on the dangers of alcohol? Please pass me the pail."

"Truthfully, I am a bit. I heard it all before from my wife."

She said nothing for several minutes, but went on unearthing bulbs.

"Last spring, these tulips shouted the resurrection of Jesus, a fact that shed meaning on the lives of the men buried here and hope for us," she said as she pointed to row upon row of headstones. "Drummer did not plant 1,000 tulips to attract old ladies from Buffalo. But one has to be sober to see it."

Pat's head and shoulders shook and his face grimaced. "Mrs. Hastings, I do drink a bit, but these tulips dazzled me the moment I walked up the main road. They were not here seven years ago when I first came to the Home, and I don't think many were here when I left, because Henry Drummer wasn't here."

Sensitive to any inference that his drinking was a problem, Pat changed the subject.

"Ma'am, do I call you 'Mrs.' or 'Miss'?" She had been introduced to the men attending her lectures as "Mrs. Hastings," but she had never mentioned anything about a husband or children.

"'Mrs.' will be fine, Mr. Donohue."

He stood up straight, tossed his shovel aside, and stalked off toward the barracks. Millicent continued digging into the earth without looking up or acknowledging Pat's leaving. She realized she had been a bit preachy. It would have been better to ask Pat questions that did not impugn his character. Fearing she had lost Donohue for good, she reported the incident to the adjutant.

At dinner, Pat was told by Shillings to return to work with Mrs. Hastings or find a train to Buffalo. The next day, Millicent motioned to Patrick to grab a spade and do what she was doing one row over. Again, the day was glorious. Bath was in the midst of its Indian summer. Trees were at their fullest and brightest colors. Working face to face in silence, they dug rows and removed bulbs. The earth was dark, soft, and rich smelling. It dug easily. After a half hour's steady labor, she sensed from Patrick's breathing that his endurance was low and slowed her pace. He put down his shovel and walked slowly to a woods nearby to relieve himself. When he returned, she had slowed her pace so he could keep up with her. After an hour's work, she called for a break. Pat sat down in place. She walked a short distance among the gravestones and returned ten minutes later.

When two long rows were done after two hours' labor, he said, "I have to give you credit. Working in all those clothes and being a woman used to the finer things in life, you are no shrinking violet." In truth, he had become interested in a very masculine way in this unusual woman.

"Are you married, Mrs. Hastings? Do you have children?" With sweat draining down her face, a wet bodice beneath a heavy sweater and smelling a bit musky, Millicent smiled politely, paused, and then answered his question without giving sensitive personal information. She did not want to open up her private life to him. "I like physical work, Mr. Donohue. I was born in the Beacon Hill section of Boston, a neighborhood of mansions inhabited by some of Boston's oldest families. I went to private schools in the city as a child and was raised in the Presbyterian Church.

"There was little love for Catholics in my family, especially for Irish Catholics.

"I was sent to a girls' private boarding school outside Newton when I was fourteen and graduated at twenty-one from Wellesley College with a degree in biology."

"Well, I see now why your English and manners are so good. Tell me more about your family."

Millicent continued the conversation in the same bare-facts-only manner. "My father ran a shoe manufacturing and distribution business that sold boots all over the world. My mother had roots in English aristocracy; her mother's ancestors came to this country in the 18th century. She had an excellent education for a woman of her time, spending years in England and Switzerland in private schools. When did your family come from Ireland and how did they get to Buffalo?"

"My parents came to Canada in 1842 and two years later moved to Rochester. My brother was born in Niagara, Ontario, and I was born in Rochester. My parents died of cholera in 1849 and my grandmother brought us to Buffalo." Following her lead, Pat answered her questions as briefly as possible and then asked her, "Did you marry after leaving college?"

Seeing where this might lead, she cut off this line of conversation. "Mr. Donohue, I think the intimate details of my family life are none of your business."

"Well, you asked me about my family." Pat was annoyed by her retreat into secrecy, but remained unshaken in his resolve to learn more about her. He was fascinated by her life story, which was like none he had ever known. He put his questions aside for now and took a different tack. "You're a strong woman, Mrs. Hastings. I had a hard time keeping up with you."

Millicent was again caught off guard by his directness and said, "Thank you. I think Mr. Drummer will be very pleased with the good start we made today. He wants to vary the beds with flowers that will bloom all summer. The tulips are a glorious sight for three weeks, but then their leaves and flowers wilt and they leave a rather drab sight for the rest of the season."

She took his shovel from him and said, "You are quite strong yourself, Mr. Donohue, for a man your age. I was surprised at your endurance. Not many of the veterans could do what you did today."

Pat was pleased at her remark. He was gaining strength and his ability to dig for a few hours restored a little pride.

Pat sensed that the work for the day was done. The sun was low in the sky. The air chilled his sweaty body as they parted and he walked back to his barracks.

Later that afternoon at the canteen, Pat had one beer, made an excuse, and slipped away from PM. He walked in the dusk toward the cemetery. As he sat on a bench and went over the conversation with Millicent, he became suspicious of her motives for seeking him out, for praising him in a move calculated to blind him to her real intentions. Millicent was an educated, rich

English Protestant. Hadn't she confessed her prejudice against Irish Catholics? She was clever, but did not fool him. She just wanted him to stop his drinking.

He had to admit she was one fine specimen of a woman, with soft facial features, broad hips, thin waist, and a bosom that excited his imagination and made his hands itch to touch it. How delightful it would be to lie in her arms!

The next day, Millicent had Pat summoned to the same flowerbed. He dressed slowly and waited for a while. He did not want her to think she could summon him as though she were an officer, although the commanding officer certainly did whatever she asked.

As they continued to dig up the tulip beds, Millicent remarked, "Mr. Donohue, I'm somewhat surprised you continue to come back to Mr. Drummer's science group."

"I never had any science in school. It's interesting to learn what men like Darwin have discovered."

"You told me once what Darwin says causes problems for your faith."

"It does, indeed."

"Well, there's a priest in Elmira who is very much up on all the latest science. He may be of some help. His name is Father Hogan. We'll be going to Elmira one of these days. Why don't you act as our driver and go see him?"

"Thank you for the offer. I would like that."

She had become more confident of their relationship and ventured a more delicate question.

"Patrick, how old were you when you had your first drink?"

"I don't really remember; maybe twelve or so." Pat was thinking, here she goes again. This broad will be the witch of my life if I don't back her down.

"Have you had a day since then that you have not had alcohol?"

"Plenty of them! The Confederates barely gave us a cup of water a day, let alone beer or whiskey."

"Could you do without it?"

"Of course! And as I said, I did." The tone of Pat's voice became more combative and his replies more abrupt, but Millicent continued.

"Mr. Donohue, I notice a difference in the way the Irish drink from the way Germans or Italians or French do. Alcohol is an Irishman's humor and joy. Did you know, Mr. Donohue, the Irish have the highest rate of alcoholism in our country, right up there with Indians?"

He thought for a while and then decided this was an opportunity to put her in her place. "I don't think you understand the history of the Irish. Your people had us living like pigs for 400 years. My parents died before they were thirty from what the Brits did to them in Ireland and what the bosses did here.

I did the same kind of work as my father. So did my brother and all my friends. A few clinkers of whiskey is the only joy many of us ever know."

Mrs. Hastings was not put off. "Mr. Donohue, what you say is all true and makes me ashamed of my English ancestry, but think for a moment what alcohol did to your families. How many of your marriages were dominated, not by the British, but by alcohol?" At that moment, she lost control and picked up a verbal cudgel. "Your wife is dead, is she not? I wonder how you feel about how you treated her when you were under the influence of alcohol."

Pat choked up and sulked. The two of them lapsed into silence and continued their work. He repeated to himself what he had said 1,000 times before. "I can control my drinking any time I want to. Besides, Mary was a strong woman. Like all the women in the Ward, she knew how to deal with my drinking; she put me in my place when she needed to."

As his anger waned over the next hour, he found himself aroused by this strong and accomplished woman and the movements of her body beneath layers of clothing. He caught himself looking at the curve of her chin, the swell of her bosom, her hands, still delicate despite many hours of gardening.

Guilt overcame him as he remembered the sermons of Bishop Timon and the priests at Bridget's and Columba's against impure thoughts as the slippery slope into fornication and adultery. He tried to put these thoughts and images away by thinking of other things, but images of her body reemerged and dominated his imagination then and after. He dreaded having to confess such thoughts the once a year he went to confession. While he no longer went to mass every Sunday, he was conscience-bound by the Church's commandment to confess his sins at least once a year during the Eastertide. No sin brought greater condemnation from the priests than sins of sex.

Through the rest of October, Pat attended Millicent's lectures only because both Davidson and Babcock ordered him to. The more she lectured, the more resistant he became.

In early October, Henry Drummer consulted with Millicent regarding a new layout for the gardens. In the area ringing the cemetery and then surrounding the gate entrance, she and Patrick began planting rows of tulips and then rows of colorful flowers that would bloom throughout the summer season and into the fall: asters, carnations, coneflowers, delphiniums, foxgloves, hibiscus, liatris, rudbeckia, blackeyed susans, and other sun perennials. The two worked together throughout the month, whenever Millicent was not away doing WCTU presentations. The work was varied and physical, but seldom overtaxing. Pat divided his time between the horse barn, the greenhouse, transporting plants on a flatbed wagon, and digging and planting. His strength continued to improve and his spirits even more.

In the first week in November, the air was cool and piles of leaves covered the ground; wrinkled leaves still hanging on limbs were a drab brown. The sky was grey. Over the past month, Millicent had used their time together probing Pat about his military and work experiences, but especially his home life with his wife and children. Pat spoke about them in unrevealing statements. She concluded he had never really thought about the profound experiences of his lifetime. He just lived day to day doing what had to be done without reflecting on life's deeper meaning.

She decided to limit their conversation to what he wanted to talk about. They talked about growing up on the streets of the First Ward, laboring at the Iron Works, the grain elevators, and the Michigan Street Bridge. Patrick talked freely about his parents, his grandmother, his brother, his wife and children, Tipping, and PM. His real personality slowly emerged.

She was fascinated; how isolated her life had been from the lives of common people! She had to admit to herself, she enjoyed the company of this man. When they talked of ordinary life, his conversation was direct, earthy but not vulgar, and descriptive. She noted he did not look deeply into his most important relationships. She concluded his life was not unlike her own. Probably like her father, there were multiple factors that contributed to his drinking, like the example of his father and most of the men he knew, the early deaths of his parents, and then two of his children. The Civil War and especially the eight months in captivity had nearly destroyed his ability to do heavy work, the cornerstone of his manhood.

Even though he lacked endurance, the physical prowess he carried so unassumingly aroused feelings she had not known in years. The image of his rakishly handsome face and muscular body emerged in her consciousness when she least wanted it, usually when she was trying to fall asleep.

After talking about his father, Pat decided to ask her about her father. "Mrs. Hastings, tell me about your dad. Was he a good father to you?"

Millicent was caught off guard once again and was not clever at hiding the truth. She wanted to discuss Pat's use of alcohol once more and thought if she admitted alcohol had done much evil in her family, she could move Pat to talk about alcohol in his family. She had often used examples from home in her WCTU lectures, but had only alluded in passing to the effects of alcohol abuse in her own life.

"My father drank, but for years he seemed to have it under control. As my brothers grew into young manhood, they all drank scotch whiskey as soon as they returned home after work. My father took to having several drinks, and by nine in the evening, he was drunk. He abused my mother. He died at sixty. She feigned sorrow, but I could see she was a freer woman after that.

"Unfortunately, my brothers followed our father, especially Calvin. His wife has now divorced him and she and the daughters live in New York."

"I take it there were at least three of you at home. You never mentioned brothers."

"Yes, there were three of us. I was the oldest and alcohol was a problem."

"Is that why you've become so involved in the WCTU?" asked Pat.

"Well, partly. I married a man who was a professor at Harvard. I divorced him after twenty years of marriage. I know personally what alcohol can do to a marriage and a family."

"The WCTU held its annual convention in Boston in 1889 and I went to it. I was divorced and became very involved in its program. With a few other women, I began going into taverns in Boston, demanding that they stop serving alcohol. The worst receptions were in Irish taverns on the South Side. Men often became violent and literally threw us out bodily."

"I am not surprised, even though I do not approve of such behavior toward women."

The topic was squarely on the table. Millicent had come clean on the destructive effects of alcohol in her family. Now she looked for a way to cause Pat to open up. She had Pat assigned to accompany her and two other WCTU women, Kirsten and Abigail, on lecture trips in the Finger Lakes Region; they were generally short trips by carriage to surrounding villages, as well as less frequent trips in the southern tier of New York State, reachable by train connections at Bath. Pat actually wanted to go. Babcock made it an order. He decided Pat either stopped drinking or the Home was of no use to him. In fact, Pat would soon be dead.

Pat was in his glory driving a team of horses. When he stopped to water and feed them, he had the women get out of the wagon to stretch their legs. Then he showed them how to feed the horses out of cupped hands full of grain. He chortled a little derisively when they closed their eyes and extended shaking hands to the horses' mouths.

As they passed through narrow village streets, men who were gathered at taverns saw the WCTU flags flying from their carriage, jeered, and cursed the women. Some made lurid remarks. The women ignored them. At first, Pat enjoyed seeing the women a little uncomfortable. The third or fourth time, however, he had had enough. *The women were good people. They were working hard to get men who were ruining their lives to stop drinking. Many men needed that.*

When they reached their destinations, instead of helping the women out of the carriage or train and carrying their luggage and presentation materials, Pat jumped down from the horse or train car and walked to bars he saw on the way in. He did not want the women to think they owned him like a slave. Abigail and Kirsten complained to Millicent, but she decided to grin and bear his unmanly behavior for the moment. The drink had not affected his driving. She would wait to see who won this "get-your-goat" game he was playing with her.

Winter came. The women stopped traveling. Pat's work was confined to the care and feeding of the Belgian draft horses and driving wagons of grain from storage barns to the gristmill and food to cafeterias.

A persistent ache grew in his soul. He missed the company of the women, especially Millicent. He approached Major Shillings, told him he wanted to speak to Mrs. Hastings about being more useful to her on future WCTU trips, and asked for her address. Mr. Shillings hesitated but, knowing from conversations in the fall that Millicent had taken Pat on as her personal project, he gave him her address.

On a clear morning, Pat dressed up in his Sunday suit, walked a mile from the Bath Home to the village square, and hitched a ride on a farmer's truck to Millicent's home. She lived in a modest Dutch Colonial, set on a large, treed lot on Keuka Lake, six miles northeast of the Soldiers' Home. As he approached her door, he realized it was her company he was craving.

Millicent was surprised to see Patrick, but showed him in. "Patrick, welcome. Unfortunately, this is not a good time for me. I was just about to go to an educational session at church."

Standing just inside the door with hat in hand, Pat quickly explained his reason for coming. "Mrs. Hastings, I won't take your time. I just wanted to say I was sorry for the way I acted on our last trip in the fall and on other trips. I should have helped you women unload the wagon and set up the materials you were about to use. I do want to accompany you three and I promise to act like a gentleman, if you can see it in your heart to forgive me."

Pat turned around and began to leave. Millicent called after him. "I wonder if you would be interested in going with me to church. There will be no preaching or service. It is a lecture followed by discussion."

He quickly jumped at the offer. It meant she was accepting him again into her good graces and he could spend time with her. He had wondered to what denomination Mrs. Hastings belonged. He hitched a horse to a sleigh in the small barn behind her house. Millicent asked Patrick if he would like to drive. He said it would be his pleasure.

He sat up very straight, pulled on the reins gently, and clucked to the mare to go. It was a bright, sunny morning and the snow sparkled before them. Pat relaxed the reins and asked Millicent about the church and the lecture. For five miles, they rode over rolling hills cushioned by a fresh snowfall, which created a majestic white backdrop to farms and forests. As they neared the village, they passed residents walking into town. Several waved, greeted Millicent, and turned to companions to ask who the gentleman might be. Pat could see he was causing a stir among her friends and neighbors, which added mirth to the pride and joy he felt sitting beside this highborn and lovely woman.

The Bath Unitarian Church was a converted mansion. Chairs were arranged in semicircles around a podium. The décor of the previous owners remained largely unchanged. The interior walls were papered in brownish wallpaper, originally off-white, accentuated by dark oak crowns. Light flooded from large windows on two sides of the living room where they held their meetings and services. Electric lights suspended from the high ceiling in copper and glass fixtures illuminated the area below, one of the few improvements the mansion had seen since the Unitarians had purchased it ten years before.

Millicent sat toward the rear, where she thought Patrick would be more comfortable. Pat was used to Protestant groups and studied the people as they gathered, especially noting the women's shapes and faces.

The pastor introduced himself. "I am Reverend Jed Darlinghouse. I want to welcome all of you to the Bath Unitarian Church. My topic is 'Mundus Vult Decipi—People Want to Be Deceived.' I use the Latin, drawing on one of the most noted Unitarians of our time, the Reverend Sylvester Judd, and the discourse he delivered to the people of the Unitarian Church in Augusta, Maine, in 1842. The title of my lecture could also be called, 'Myth, Its Misuse and Abuse in the Church and Secular World.'

"As you know, a myth is a story with a deeper message, sometimes religious and oft times political. It is perhaps the most powerful form of storytelling known to man. Much of the Bible is myth. The Jewish and Christian religions, like all the great religions of the world, are based on stories not meant to be taken literally. Those myths were passed on by word of mouth from generation to generation down through many centuries. Eventually, they were incorporated into doctrine and law by those in power. They did it, I believe, to control their people.

"Science from the Renaissance on and most convincingly in the person of the late Charles Darwin has refuted the biblically based belief that the world was created in 5,000 or 6,000 years. That's what you get if you read Genesis as science. In fact, Darwin's, and later Huxley's, research indicates human life is a product of evolving forms of lower species over millions of years.

"With that introduction to the topic, I turn the floor over to you."

An hour of discussion then ensued between the audience and Rev. Darlinghouse. Pat sat fidgeting, looking around at the people, the room, and its munificent appointments. He was reminded of Mary's home on Niagara Street. Pat had not understood much of what the minister said, but enough to further shake his most cherished beliefs, especially his understanding of the Bible. He had been taught and believed without question that the Bible was the word of God, spoken directly to the biblical writers. His head was spinning as he drove Millicent home.

"I take it you are a Unitarian, Mrs. Hastings. Many people at the church knew you very well, it seemed. You told me you were raised a Presbyterian?"

"Yes, Mr. Donohue, I was a Presbyterian all through my early years. At the age of thirty-five, I converted to the Unitarian faith. Its principles fit my way of looking at God and religious doctrine. I was a Unitarian long before I joined, if you understand what I mean."

Pat did not, but nodded in order not to look stupid. All he knew was that he enjoyed her company and felt a spark of delight each time she said his name. That she would be with him and talk to him as her equal was the most wonderful thing in the world. The rest of the way home passed quickly as they discussed the principles of the Unitarian Church.

Pat unhitched the mare and fed her while Millicent stood aside, making small talk. As they parted with a prolonged handshake, he told her he had enjoyed the lecture and most of all her company. Millicent smiled and said something that she later realized made no sense. Pat again hitched a ride back to Bath and walked to the Bath Home, the time passing unnoticed.

Chapter 29

Breakdown

C hristmas Day 1902 was a welcome break from the Home's usual routine. Pat went to mass, which was celebrated in the chapel built on the grounds by the Catholic bishop of Rochester. He then made the long walk to visit Millicent, as previously arranged, to exchange season's greetings and bring a gift, a pot of red roses he had bought from the Home's greenhouse.

Pat felt immediately welcome as he looked into Millicent's smiling face and the graceful sweep of her right arm motioning him in. She had captured the spirit of the season in her living room with a spruce tree decorated with candles and large, colorful, round glass ornaments. Beneath the tree was a manger set with a dozen or so glass figurines imported from Germany and laid out on a sheet of white cotton. A large fireplace with a crackling fire warmed the room and exhaled the smell of apple wood. Any strangeness he felt disappeared. What a perfect setting in which to celebrate Christmas!

"Mrs. Hastings, I hope this gift tells you how much I enjoy our friendship."

"Indeed it does, Mr. Donohue, and I am most grateful for both the gift and the friendship." She hesitated as if about to say more on that subject, but then said, "Now tell me how you will spend Christmas? In Buffalo, I presume? Tell me about it while we enjoy a glass of fruit punch and a piece of fruitcake, taken from a recipe of my great-grandmother." Millicent poured Pat a generous glass of punch and then cut a large piece of cake, laid it on a crystal dessert plate, and passed it to Pat. He waited for her to do the same for herself. She motioned him to sit with her on her stuffed couch. They each cut into their slices of cake with sterling silver dessert forks.

"Oh, this is special. Drenched in juices," he exclaimed, "that create a heavenly taste and a wonderful chewiness. I've never had anything like it."

Then after a few more bites, he raised his glass and said, "A salut to your great-grandmother and to the baker!"

"Believe it or not, I made this in September. That allowed the juices to become solid and as you say, 'chewy'. Some of the best things take time—lots of it. Now tell me, how are you spending Christmas?"

"I truly miss my family and friends in the First Ward in Buffalo. For the next month, I'll stay with my son, Bob, and his new wife, Mary Alice. She has two children by a previous marriage. They're quite small, so I suppose I'll spend much time on the floor playing with them."

"Don't you have a brother in Buffalo, too? Are you close to him?"

"Oh, I'll certainly spend time with John and his family. I owed my life to him in the war. His wife Johanna could not be more kind to me. Their four kids are like my own. In fact, I get along with them better than I do with my own." The two lapsed into their own thoughts. Millicent decided not to pursue Pat's statement about his relationship to his children.

To break the silence, Pat blurted out, "The Ward has a hold on me like no other place in the world. I can't wait to get home." He took a sip of the punch and concluded, "Christmas is my favorite time of year and we celebrate it like the world's coming to an end the following spring. So it'll be fun. Now, what about you? Are you going home?"

"No, two friends are coming from Boston, old WCTU colleagues. They come every year at Christmas time. One's a widow and one's divorced. I look forward to their coming. We won't do much, just sit and talk about what we're doing with the WCTU." She took another bite of cake and then went on. "It's one of the highlights of my year. They are dear friends and they bring news from the East. We have so much to talk about. The week they're here just flies by."

"Do the Unitarians do Christmas, Mrs. Hastings?"

"Yes, they do, pretty much the same as any Christian church. They believe Jesus was the messiah that the Jews had been awaiting for hundreds of years. They just don't believe he was God." That led to more questions from Pat about the Unitarian Church.

"We really do love and admire Jesus just as you do, Mr. Donohue. One day we can talk about what and why Unitarians believe as they do. For today, let's just share a beautiful Christmas together in the few minutes we have left."

"Well, Mrs. Hastings, I agree with you," replied Pat.

A half hour after arriving, Pat rose to take his leave, seeing that Millicent had a busy day in front of her, much of it at the Unitarian Church and with her local WCTU companions.

Millicent was about to ask him to avoid alcohol while he was at home in Buffalo. Then she thought about it and said, "Pat, please take care of yourself, and be moderate in your drinking. Maybe only drink beer and make sure you eat something with it." Millicent broke her own rule never to advocate drinking in any way. She cared for Pat and was realistic about what he would do back home.

Late in the evening, Pat arrived in Buffalo and rented a room in a boarding house on Seneca Street near the foot of Main Street and the Erie Canal. He paid $.50 cents a day using money he had saved from his pension. He climbed to the third floor, resting on each of the two landings. His room held a twin bed, a nightstand, and a chamber pot. It was a stuffy, windowless room in the center of the building. Wincing at the smell of stale air and tobacco smoke as he entered, he thought, *At least it's got more heat than the outside rooms and their rickety windows.*

As he lifted a beer at Kennedy's, he remembered Millicent's parting words and committed himself to having but a few. By 10 p.m., engrossed in conversation at the bar, his commitment to Millicent forgotten, he was drinking whiskey with the best of them.

He spent a few hours with John's family on the day after Christmas. John was well and back to work. Later that evening, he walked the half mile to Bob's home at 52 Marvin Street. For the first time, he met Bob's new wife, Mary Alice. He had not been invited to their wedding and felt more distant from his family than ever. Her son, John, and daughter, Alice, both by her relationship with barkeep Michael Cavanaugh, were also there. He had no presents. He gave John and Alice a quarter each and wished them a Merry Christmas. He soon retreated to Kennedy's.

His drinking at Kennedy's and with friends throughout the Ward returned to its old level. After all, it was Christmas and everyone he met asked him to stop by for a drink. PM joined him occasionally at the bar. He was drinking less these days, but still enjoyed hanging out with old friends.

In early February, Pat returned to the Home in time to see Dr. Potter for a quick physical. After examining Patrick for five minutes, the doctor, sighing deeply, waited for Pat to re-robe so that he had his full attention. Then he began his commentary.

"Pat, your health is in serious decline. Perhaps we should transfer you to one of the national homes in the South, where it's warmer."

"I think that's goin' too far, Doctor," replied Pat. "I'll be back in shape in week or two."

"I doubt it. Your face is yellowed. Your ankles are swollen. You have a rash on your stomach that you scratch. Pat, do you understand what these symptoms mean? They exist as a result of a lifetime of heavy drinking and they will not be reversed in a week or two, I guarantee you."

He paused, and then asked, "Are you having difficulty urinating? Do you have pain in your back or side? Have you been vomiting recently? Do you feel cold much of the time?"

Pat nodded yes to all of Dr. Potter's questions.

"These are all signs that your kidneys are diseased, and perhaps your liver as well." He took Pat's hand. "Pat, you may not live out the year.

"This is particularly distressing to me because when I saw you last, working with Mrs. Hastings and around the barracks, you looked better than when you entered. You have received a great deal of care here. Has it all been for nothing?"

Dr. Potter put his hands on Pat's right and left side, feeling for his kidneys once again, double-checking to be sure he was correct.

"Patrick, where did you stay in Buffalo and what did you do?"

"Well, I stayed in a rooming house in downtown Buffalo. It wasn't the best, to be sure, certainly not like here. I ate most of my meals at a tavern in the First Ward. I visited my son and brother there a few times. It was a long way from the Ward to downtown and the rooming house. Maybe I tired myself out with all the walking and staying up late, visiting family and friends."

Dr. Potter was even more dubious. "Patrick, there is one thing that has been a problem for you: your drinking. You promised me you would curtail your drinking. Were you true to your word?"

"I did drink a bit, just a few beers and an occasional shot, doctor."

"You will pardon me, Pat, if I'm a bit skeptical. One easy explanation for your weakened state is abuse of alcohol and all the other abuses of the body that go with it. Be honest with me, because if I find out you are storytelling as you are well able to do, I will see to it you are dismissed from the Bath Soldiers' Home. I really had hoped you were at that crucial point in your life where you would admit that you cannot drink at all."

Pat got up and pounded his fist on Dr. Potter's desk. "I can handle the drink any day I want to! A few beers of an evening with my mates won't kill me. I can tell you that." And he stomped out of Potter's office.

The next morning, Pat recounted the episode to Dolan. "I won't let Potter treat me like some boy. I can still drink with the best of them."

Dolan listened in silence and then slowly turned away, shaking his head.

Given the press of hundreds of vets entering Bath, Dr. Potter and the other surgeons did nothing further to curb Pat's self-destructive behavior, nor did Potter act on his threat to dismiss Pat. And because he returned to a disciplined regimen once more, Pat's health did improve over the next three months.

In late February, Pat heard through PM that John Cavanaugh, the five-year-old son of Mame Donohue, had died when he slipped through ice playing on the Buffalo Creek. As bitter as his feelings were toward his son, who had not written to tell him, he wrote a brief letter of condolence.

Dear Mary Alice,
How terribele to lose your son! I almost feel your pain these many miles away.
My prayers and best wishes are with you. Please give my son and daghter my best. I
wish I could have been at the funerel to share your sadness.
Love,
Dad

Nearly the whole Ward had turned out for the boy's wake, which was held at the house, and his funeral at St. Bridget's. John Cavanaugh was buried on a bitter cold day in wind-swept Holy Cross Cemetery. Mame sank into deep and untouchable sadness. Throughout this period, Bob doted on his wife, rubbed her neck and back, bathed her, and kissed her even when she would not lift her lips to him. Eventually, his affection wore down her sadness and cemented their relationship. They never talked of the drowning again. Their daughter, Alice, never knew where the boy was buried.

In early May 1903, Pat gladly accompanied Mrs. Hastings and her companions, Kirsten and Abigail, to Elmira. Both women were short, grey-haired widows, Kirsten heavier than Abigail. They looked to Pat like sisters. The two laughed at Pat's jokes and imitated his Buffalo Irish accent when they wanted to get a rise out of him.

As in the past and in keeping with his Christmas promise to Millicent, he helped the women unload their materials and told them he was going to a Civil War cemetery, but would be back in time to help them load up again. He rushed off, somewhat excited about what he might find. He had heard from veterans at the Home that there had been a notorious Union prison in Elmira, perhaps the worst Civil War prison, North or South. He wanted to see it for himself.

There were no signs to direct visitors, so he stopped at St. John's Rectory and asked to see the pastor, who introduced himself as Father Hogan. Pat recognized the name, even though he could not remember where he heard it. They talked for a while before Pat told the priest of his interest. Father Hogan asked Pat if he would like to take a walk to the old prison site and see its cemetery.

It was a pleasant day and the priest seemed to be in no hurry. As they strolled over the tree-lined streets of Elmira, he described the prison. "Most young folks hereabouts don't even know such a prison existed. Truth be told, treatment of prisoners here duplicated what the Union Army learned about treatment of Northern prisoners in the South."

They walked about a mile through a pleasant residential area, past spacious lawns ribboned with daffodils and narcissus, before coming to a vegetable farm.

"This was once a Union assembly camp, Camp Rathbun," Father Hogan explained, "at which many Western New York regiments received their training before being sent south. In 1864, the camp was converted to a prison called 'Hellmira' by the inmates. Some 12,000 prisoners were held here between July 1864 and September 1865, when the prison was closed."

They walked on to get a better view. "It occupied thirty acres," continued Father Hogan, "and held at its most overcrowded peak 10,000 men in horrible conditions: meager food, unheated shacks, open latrines, and inadequate medical supplies and doctors. Smallpox and dysentery, one of the worst winters on record, and a Chemung River flood ravaged the prison population. Some 3,000 prisoners died and were left to one man, John W. Jones, a runaway slave, to bury in a cemetery a short distance east of here."

Arriving at the far side of the farm, Father concluded, "The prison was razed shortly after the war and sold to a farmer. It was a national disgrace and everyone wanted to wipe it off the earth. In large measure, they have. You can't find it in history books. It was as bad as Andersonville."

"Or Salisbury, where I was."

They walked on to the cemetery. "The federal government declared this a national historic cemetery in 1877 in a political trade-off with Southern senators for federal designation of cemeteries in their states." Pat listened quietly throughout the account, articulated knowledgably by the priest.

They walked up and down the long rows of grave markers, only the chirping of birds breaking the silence. Suddenly Pat straightened up and pointed to a tombstone. "My regiment may have captured this man at Cold Harbor. I may have run that poor bugger back myself," he said, as he pointed in surprise at the gravestone marked, "Silas Perkins, 17th Virginia CSA."

"We fought against the 17th there and captured several of their pickets."

The priest and the Bath veteran walked back to the rectory and sat out on its spacious white veranda. The midday sun shone warmly upon them and a gentle breeze puffed at their faces. Father Hogan asked Pat if he would like a beer, which he gladly accepted. They walked to a neighboring bar to get it and then returned to the rectory. The priest drank a tall glass of water and asked him about his Civil War experiences. He himself wove tales of Galway and coming to America into a two-hour conversation in which both men, with unusual honesty for men, explored one another's lives.

Father Hogan drew their conversation to a close. "Pat, in recent years I've spent more time alone thinking and praying, meditating on the banks of the Chemung River."

"I've heard monks do that kind of thing, Father, but I always thought it was foolish, a waste of time," replied Pat.

"I had a terrible time with loneliness and celibacy. I sometimes mistreated parishioners and neighbors. You know why, Pat? Because I used alcohol to douse my feelings."

"Maybe I have also, especially when my wife died. That was a terrible time for me. But I always got control back again and often stopped drinking for months at a time."

"Besides giving up the drink, Pat, I learned over the years to meditate on each incident in order to mine from it my hostility."

"What did that do for yah, Father?" asked Pat.

"Well, reflection calmed me down and made me more accepting of people." He concluded, "I think I've become a better priest: less judgmental, critical, sarcastic. And believe me, Pat, I was all of those."

He hesitated before going on. "Lastly, let me tell you, it took me years and many sad experiences to realize that alcohol was not for me. I did not give it up all at once. Only after it made a fool out of me and hurt my people did some of them come to talk to me courageously and honestly."

Pat brought up the issue of Darwin and evolution. The priest explained how easy it was to reconcile that theory with a doctrine of a good and generous God, once one accepted Sacred Scripture for what it was. In fact, God came out the better for it. Their conversation lasted the rest of the afternoon.

"What a once-in-a-lifetime day it had been," Pat said to himself, as he walked back under a clouding sky to meet the WCTU women, just in time to board the evening train for Bath.

Millicent knew where Pat had been and asked him if he had met with Father Hogan. Kirsten and Abigail stopped talking and listened. Pat gave them a short version of his meeting and then lapsed into silence for the rest of the ride. The women let him be.

Pat resolved to spend time alone on the banks of the Cohocton. He walked to the river often over the next months, weather permitting, and found favorite spots—a sandy beach, a large rocky outcropping, and a dock—where he thought about fights he had had with his wife and children, the way his anger had hurt those he loved. Still, he was not convinced he needed to do away with his drinking, even though the worst things he did were often after he got drunk. PM might have needed to, but not him.

Gradually, time spent alone became a habit and something Pat relished. He brought his newfound calmness to the Belgian horses when he tended them or plowed. He not only drove the WCTU carriage and carried in presentation materials—large boards with phrases and charts—for the women, he remained with them throughout the day. He used his mechanical ability to help set up and stage presentations. He entered into their conversations when eating together. His mildly sarcastic sense of humor leavened their discussions with brief stories of Mallow, the Ward, and the war that kept the women from taking themselves too seriously.

The women, for their part, felt more secure having him along. Taunts from tavern doors ceased after Pat stopped the carriage, got down from the driver's seat, and addressed the men. In a firm but respectful fashion, he asked them to curtail their vulgar language and show respect. They didn't have to agree with the work the women were doing, but they should act civil toward any woman.

The three women looked forward to their time together. He knew how to claim their attention and then build a ladder of events before bringing his stories to a sharp and poignant climax. He never drank when he was with them and seemed to be learning that he did not need it to enjoy himself.

The WCTU women returned to Elmira a year later in 1904. Pat brought the presentation materials into the local Baptist Church hall and rushed off to see Father Hogan. When he knocked on the door of the rectory, a young priest answered and told him apologetically that Father Hogan had died almost a year ago. Pat was stunned, his expectation of a unique and intelligent conversation dashed. He had so looked forward to seeing him. He wondered to himself, *Did Father know he was dying? Was that why he revealed so much about himself?*

Pat found a pub and drank whiskey before returning to the hall. On the train back to Bath, he was quiet and stayed to himself. That evening he left the station and went to a tavern. He was melancholic at the loss of this unusually spiritual, honest, and human priest and drank to ease his feelings.

The day after, the women were to travel by carriage along the Cohocton River to nearby Savona. Inside, they talked about how moody Pat remained from the day before. At the Savona Free Methodist Church, he carried in the materials and spent the afternoon in a tavern to douse his hangover. After their presentation, the women stored their materials in the rear trunk and seated themselves in the covered carriage. Kirsten, seated at a window, saw Pat stagger as he mounted to the driver's seat. She sounded an alarm to the other women. Pat pulled awkwardly on the reins, one before the other and the horses took off in confusion. He fumbled while trying to gain control and dropped one rein. The four horses careened across the countryside. Twice the carriage wheels slid over the edge of the road toward a ditch. The women screamed at him to slow down but by now, he was hanging onto a railing himself for dear life. By the time the horses slowed of their own accord, the women were frantic. Two horses had broken legs and had to be destroyed by a farmer who happened upon the scene. The farmer hitched their wagon to the two remaining animals and drove the women to Millicent's house. Pat straggled back to Bath and on to the Home, arriving in the wee hours of the morning.

The next morning, Major Shillings sent word that Pat was to come to him before breakfast. When Pat got there, not only was Major Shillings present, but also the farm director and the horse barn manager. They chastised Pat angrily for the way he had endangered the women's lives and the inhumane way he had treated the horses. They demanded he repay the Bath WCTU for the cost of the horses. Pat promised he would, but all knew how unlikely that was, given his income. Shillings finally said, "Despite repeated warnings about your drunken behavior and in view of this most recent transgression, you leave us no choice but to dismiss you. You will have to leave the Home at once."

Pat had no defense, nor did he want any. He was crestfallen by what he had done to the women and the horses and began to choke up. "I know the rules of the Home well. I know my drinking screams to heaven for punishment and I'll take whatever you mete out. But I am begging you not to throw me out of the Home. I can't do heavy labor. The Home is all I got. I'll die like a dog on the streets. Please, I promise I will never drink again. I will never see the inside of a tavern if you will let me stay. And I'll work hard to pay for the horses."

Dr. Babcock intervened. "I would like to give Pat one more chance to see if we can come up with a program to help him overcome his abuse of alcohol." The room went silent for several seconds. Then Major Shillings relented, saying, "There will be no compromise with Bath policy the next time."

The next day, Pat went to the barn, intent on apologizing to Millicent, Kirsten, and Abigail when they arrived. He was supposed to drive them to their presentation in nearby Hammondsport. Millicent met him in the barn as he was hitching horses to the carriage. "I no longer trust you," she told him; her words rushed out of her mouth in a torrent. "Let me say I was horribly hurt by your lack of loyalty to me, to Kirsten, and to Abigail, who I thought had become your friends, as well as to our mission. Once again, you gave in to drink in spite of your promises to me and Dr. Babcock and to yourself. You nearly killed us all. I had to replace the two horses myself. They had carried us faithfully for over five years and I was very fond of them. I feel totally betrayed by you.

"I've found another veteran to drive us, and I demand you stay away from me wherever I am and whatever I am doing. I never want to see you again as long as I live." She pivoted and left the barn.

Pat turned away in despair born of self-hatred and disgust over the immense impact of his actions.

Major Shillings summoned him the next morning. Millicent had recounted to him every word she had said to Pat. The director forbade him to go within sight of the woman and re-assigned him to work with Henry Drummer every day from after breakfast till noon.

Drummer gave Pat his work-order first thing each morning and then left him. Usually it was to clean out the horse stalls. He returned at noon, inspected his work, and dismissed him. Pat spent afternoons petting the Belgian draft horses or sitting quietly in the cemetery. His sense of guilt declined over time and in its place reigned self-pity.

CHAPTER 30

Rock Bottom

By Christmas 1905, after two years spent at the Home without reprieve, Pat was bored, resented the Home's regulation of every aspect of his life, and missed the Ward and Kennedy's. He would have quit the Home altogether, had he the wherewithal to live on his own. He left by train on December 14 and stayed with his son, Mame, and Annie, who had divorced her husband and returned from New York.

In addition to the historic sources of conflict that marred his relationships with his son and daughter, he annoyed them endlessly by forgetting things just said, repeating himself, and by his lack of hygiene. He sat all day in a soft chair, arguing and criticizing when he wasn't nodding off. He consumed his food with offensive noises and spilled it on the table and floor. Nights he returned home from Kennedy's drunk, loud, cursing, and hostile. Bob was torn between anger and pity seeing how feeble his father had become; finally, at Annie's insistence, he pressured his father to leave his home two days before Christmas. Pat took a room in the same ramshackle boarding house on Commercial Street that he had stayed in before, the Lighthouse Lodging, a stone's throw from the Erie Canal.

The atmosphere at Kennedy's was the same as ever. Pat clowned. He told stories. His imitations of chaws from the Ward drew laughs and new stories from his mates. Within minutes of arriving, he was one of the old gang. His drinking soon caught up to and, in most instances, surpassed the Kennedy regulars. Pat could hold his whiskey, they all said, better than ever, at least for the first few hours. Then he was drunk, slurring his words, staggering to the toilet, and after the closing-hour weaving his way back to the Lodging, where he stumbled up the stairs to his room.

There, he fell onto his bed fully clothed and immediately fell asleep. Slamming doors and loud arguments jarred his rest and jerked him into semiconsciousness throughout the night. The same routine went on for two days.

On Christmas, he was roused out of bed around noon, too late to go to mass. Christmas afternoon he went first to see John and Johanna and their children on Alabama Street. He brought no presents and made no excuses for his failure to do so. Instead, he made a grand show of giving each of the children half dollars and wishing them a Merry Christmas. Not wishing to embarrass her uncle, Mary, the oldest at thirty, accepted the money. John, James, and Katherine followed suit, despite the fact that all four were employed, paying board, and proud of the adult status they had achieved at home and among friends and coworkers.

They could see he had been drinking heavily and was suffering from a hangover. He hadn't bathed since Bath. His smell repelled them. His clothes were disheveled and dirty. They sat as far away from him at table as they could. His stature as their father's brother, the memory of many happy times together, of his stories and jokes and the games they had played together kept the family from simply showing him the door. He spent an hour with them. He toyed with the food Johanna placed before him, rambling nonstop about Bath, the Belgian horses, and his trips around the Finger Lakes region. He barely mentioned PM or asked them what was happening in their lives.

Instead of imploring him to stay on and spend more time with them, the family was silent when, after dinner, he excused himself and left. Johanna was in tears the moment he was out of sight. John couldn't hold back his disgust at his brother's derelict state and his sadness as he remembered better days in this very house. The girls cried with their mother. The boys shared some of their father's feelings. They all sensed a deep sadness underneath Pat's gay banter. They drew deep breaths of regret to see him walk out into the bitter cold of a Buffalo winter and its piercing winds in just an old suit coat. Yet they were relieved that he was gone.

He walked north on Alabama and crossed the tracks that split the Ward. A half hour later, he arrived at the home of his son. Mame had prepared a traditional dinner: ham dotted with cloves; cabbage, carrots, and potatoes all cooked together; Irish soda bread; and apple pie.

The family was still sitting around the table over glasses of porter and whiskey. Most of the leftovers had been removed to the kitchen. Pat paused before entering, summoned up his courage, put on a smile, and burst in the front door.

He was met with polite coolness by Bob and Annie. Bob, at thirty-six, still sported a full head of wavy brown hair. Annie, ten years younger, was in the full bloom of her womanhood. Mame was still mourning young John's death and at Christmas time, her pain was the keenest. Carrying her youngest son, Robert Jr., on her lap, while four-year-old Catherine played at her feet, she nonetheless bade Pat sit down and poured him a glass of whiskey. No presents were passed to him or vice versa. Pat repeated the same tales he had told at his brother's, but he could see he was unwelcome even on Christmas in his own son's home. Deeply hurt once again, he left for Kennedy's within a half hour.

Fortunately, Kennedy's was only five minutes away on Ohio Street. Three old timers shouted Merry Christmas as though he were a long-lost brother. In effect he was. These men had spent more time together over many years than they had with their own brothers. Many had spent more time together than with their wives.

By mid-January, he returned to Bath $10 poorer and with no more in his pocket than a punched rail ticket.

The next day, Doctor Potter summoned him in for his annual physical. Potter greeted him cordially. "Good morning, Patrick. Tell me, how did you spend the holidays?"

"I went home to Buffalo and spent a few weeks with family there."

"Would you please walk out in the hall and climb the steps to the second floor?" Pat did as he was asked, struggling to lift his legs going up and holding on tightly to a railing while taking one tread at a time coming down. He was breathing heavily as he reentered the office and his face was flushed.

Pat disrobed and stretched out on the examining table and Dr. Potter looked him over from head to toe. He listened to his heart, pushed his fingers firmly into his side, stomach, and back. He peered into his eyes, ears, and throat. He then stood silent for a few seconds, totally exasperated, and at a loss as to what to say.

"How old are you, Pat?"

Unprepared for such a question, he thought, "Surely, the doctor knows how old I am." Still, Pat answered, haltingly. "Um . . . sixty . . . uh, sixty-one in a coupla months."

"I would have thought you were at least seventy." Pat had no answer.

Potter continued. "Pat, you are in an extremely weakened state. You have the appearance of a very old man. Your heart and digestive system are diseased. You no doubt suffer stomach pains after eating, and more than likely you eat little. Your stomach, arms, and legs are swollen. Do you notice yourself becoming confused at times, forgetful, maybe even thinking about taking your own life?"

Pat did not answer.

"What has happened to you?" Potter was barely holding his anger in check. He had been seeing many men just like Pat and could not believe the extent of alcohol abuse among Civil War veterans. He was particularly struck by the rate of alcohol abuse among Irish veterans, who made up a quarter of the Home's population.

"Well, I stayed downtown and ate meals back in my old neighborhood with family and friends. Maybe all the walking did me in."

"You told us the same thing once before. Now again, your vital signs are poor. Your face is ashen. Your flesh is pale and your eyes jaundiced. Your ankles are swollen and make it difficult for you to walk. You reacted sharply to a poke in either side.

"I suspect you went back to drinking a great deal, even though you promised otherwise. Tell me the truth! Were you drinking heavily in Buffalo?"

Pat angrily rolled off the examining table. "Sure, I had a few beers, but nothing I couldn't handle," he said, storming out while tugging his coat on as he went.

At the canteen that evening, he ran into PM and complained about catching hell from Doctor Potter. "That doctor is like all the rest of those WASP bastards. They think they're better than us and can tell us how to live our lives. Well, Potter is full of shit and can't tell me what to do."

Dolan shook his head and stared hard at his old friend. "No, Donohue, you're the stupid shit, if I ever saw one, and I'm not about to stand by anymore while you drink your life away."

Dolan glared at his old friend, turned on his heels, and left without finishing his beer. Pat was stung and shocked. His best friend had never talked to him like that. He spun the events of the last day around in his head, growing more hostile toward PM and Dr. Potter as he did.

Pat spent the next four days in bed. He got up only to go to meals and use the toilet. He was too sick to work and did not visit his beloved Belgian draft horses, which he had combed down almost daily for years. Evenings, he walked to a bar just off the campus on Belfast Road, which led into Bath. He sat alone in a stupor and drank six whiskeys before the bartender cut him off. Finally, after a few evenings of this behavior, Pat fell off his bar stool and could not stand up. He lay on the floor, muttering curses and inanities.

The bartender notified the Home administration. Two orderlies were sent to carry Pat to the hospital and into a ward reserved for long-term alcoholics. Pat fell into a fitful sleep and woke up not knowing where he was. He got out of his bed, started yelling obscenities and banging into his neighbors' beds.

Orderlies grabbed him and threw him in bed. While one held him down, the other forced a dose of ether on him, attached restraints around his wrists, and fastened them to the bed frame. In that forced sleep, Pat settled down and the restraints were removed late the next day. For three days, Pat behaved well in spite of suffering withdrawal symptoms. On the third evening, however, in the middle of the night, he began to sweat, tremble, and scream at devils he saw standing over him.

He was moved to a private room and restrained once again. Shouting violent curses and talking gibberish, he pulled with all his diminished strength against the restraints and kicked at invisible objects. His legs, arms, and stomach swelled and his heart weakened. His skin turned pale grey and his breathing became deep and irregular. Feverish, he suddenly suffered extreme pains in the chest and left arm and could do little but whimper and whine.

Dr. Potter wrote on Pat's chart the next day that he was suffering through delirium tremens and had probably had a heart attack. He had no medicine to counteract either condition, except laudanum.

PM was not allowed into the alcoholic ward, but he talked to the hospital staff several times in this period. Shocked at what he heard from the nurses, he went in to see Dr. Potter.

"Dr. Potter, what is happening with Pat Donohue? Is he going to live?"

"Mr. Dolan, I don't know. I've seen many cases just like him. Some live; some don't. His illness is complicated by his heart condition. He's getting the best care we can give him, but it isn't much."

"Has anyone notified his family?"

"Yes, last night, but they were told there was little point in coming to see him. He's not conscious and can't talk."

For three days, PM returned twice a day to inquire about his friend. Pat's condition changed little over that time. Then on the fourth day, he rallied. The next day, to make room for another critical case, he was transferred out of his private room and back into the alcoholic ward, where PM found him unable to carry on a conversation. One of the few things Pat could say was, "I'd like a beer."

Each day thereafter, Pat grew stronger. After two weeks in the hospital, he asked to be released. Dr. Potter and Dr. Haskell, who had replaced Dr. Babcock, conferred together and called on him.

Pat was sitting up in bed. Dr. Potter began the conversation. "Well, Pat, you are one of the lucky ones. Somehow, you survived the DTs and a heart attack. We would like to release you, if you feel well enough to take care of yourself. Are you at that point?"

"Yes, doctor. I am walking to the toilet without any help from the nurses or orderlies. I'd like to get out of here, maybe go home for a while."

Dr. Haskell weighed in. "I don't think you are ready to go home yet. You are confined to the grounds. The guards will not allow you onto the Belfast Road. We'd like to bring your family here to visit you. Would that be alright?"

Pat nodded.

Dr. Haskell and Dr. Potter had come up with a strategy they wanted to try on Pat.

Dr. Potter called Pat Dolan in. "Who might have the most influence getting your friend to make a positive decision about his life?"

"That's a tough one. He's a real bullhead. Let me think about it for an hour and come back, if you don't mind." Dolan had hesitated to answer as he usually did to his friends, half-cocked and with a smart remark. He was not used to talking to educated people, especially doctors, whom he viewed with awe and shyness.

"Let me say with all the authority I have as a physician, Pat's heart has degenerated to the very point where any further drinking will close it down altogether. His mind is confused and he will descend into total senility if he continues drinking. His liver is not filtering alcohol. Any intake of alcohol will poison his whole system and he will die a horribly painful death." He stopped and drew a deep breath. "Have you ever been with a dying alcoholic? Your friend is at death's door."

Shaken, Dolan left and returned after lunch, naming "Robert Donohue and Millicent Hastings." As Potter wrote down the names, PM continued his commentary on his best friend. "Pat destroyed his relationship with his son long ago. In fact, his son threw him out of his house a few years back," he explained.

Then he paused to recapture the words he had prepared before returning to Dr. Potter. "Millicent Hastings brought Pat as close to giving up the drink as any person I know. Not even his wife, Mary, could pull that one off. He likes Millicent a lot. If anyone can convince him, she and Bob are as close as it comes in this life. But she too has been hurt badly by Pat."

"PM, will you contact Robert and ask him to come to Bath as soon as possible? I'll talk to Mrs. Hastings. I'm including you with them. Perhaps the five of us—you, me, Dr. Haskell, Bob and Millicent—should get together and work out our approaches."

Within a week, Doctors Potter and Haskell convened the group in a sitting room near their offices. Robert entered the room dressed in topcoat, a two-piece suit, high-collar dress blouse and tie, and hair parted down the middle, as had become the style. He was a small, husky man with a shy, relaxed demeanor. Millicent was present but unsure that she wanted to be.

PM and Robert greeted one another awkwardly. Sensing Robert's coldness toward him, it occurred to him that Robert was blaming him for much of his father's drinking and hanging out at Kennedy's. Though he had not seen Robert in years, he silently acknowledged that he had some right to feel as he did.

Potter welcomed and thanked all for coming. "Let me get right to the point. You know why I've asked you to come. I am certain all of you share misgivings about Patrick. No alcoholic leaves family or friends without negative feelings toward him. I know his drunkenness has gone on for many years."

He paused for a moment, reminded by his description of Patrick, that his father had been alcoholic and abusive. The memory of it was still somewhat unsettling.

"You may not have wanted to see him ever again. But we have a human life here; one that I, and I hope you, believe has much to give if he is sober. His sobriety is the crucial question."

Dr. Haskell interjected. "Let me say something at this point, and I apologize to Dr. Potter for breaking in. I think I know what you were going to say, Dr. Potter, since much of the burden of caring for men like Patrick falls disproportionately to you. We have an enormous problem of alcohol abuse among veterans here at the Home. We have used the WCTU, and in certain cases they have been successful in convincing a few of our men to give up drinking altogether. We are still searching for new methods for curbing this abuse. What you are participating in with Patrick could, if successful, become another weapon in our arsenal."

Dr. Haskell stopped and Dr. Potter continued. "Let me start by describing Patrick's condition. His heart has weakened considerably over what it was just three years ago when he entered Bath. While in the alcoholic ward, he suffered a heart attack three weeks ago."

At this point, Dr. Potter looked down and read from Pat's medical chart. "His blood pressure is low. His eyes and skin are yellowed and his whole body swollen, signs of cirrhosis of the liver. His muscle tension is flaccid. He is eating little but has gained weight from all the liquid that his body has produced because of cirrhosis. His head has shrunk, so perhaps his brain has lost mass. He is often confused as to time and place. His color is ashen, which indicates a slackening of metabolic processes."

Then he looked up once again and continued. "He was rescued from death's door by two nurses, who attended him eighteen hours a day and hand-fed him."

Dr. Haskell spoke up. "Your friend is in what is being called these days 'a severe state of depression.' If he begins drinking again, he will die a tortured death unless a heart attack or pneumonia takes him first. The question is, does he have the will to live? Can he stop drinking altogether?"

Dr. Potter concluded. "Robert, you may have some doubt about your ability to reach your father and in truth there is reason to believe he can no longer be reached by anyone. Millicent, you may have similar thoughts.

"Here is our reasoning. Robert, Mr. Dolan has told me that your father has always wanted a closer relationship with his only son. I believe he is profoundly disappointed that he has never had it. I think he sees himself as a dismal failure at being the head of your childhood family."

Bob had been looking at the floor throughout much of Potter's discourse. He drew in a long breath before responding. "I'm not sure what my father believes." Shaking his head, he went on. "He is very proud and headstrong. He was not a caring father to me and was very jealous of my relationship with my mother. He caused many problems for my sisters. They are badly confused women and failed at their marriages, I believe, because of him." His voice rose and cracked with emotion as he spoke.

"My mom was deeply hurt many times by my father's drinking. He was abusive to her and to me when he was drunk. In her last year, she left him and nearly died in an apartment house before we were able to bring her home to die." Dolan knew this was the lie her children made up to cover the embarrassing break-up of their parents and his mother's death in a second rate rooming house.

"She was buried in a pauper's grave in Holy Cross Cemetery. I think he sent her to an early grave and I find it damn difficult to forgive him." Millicent and PM were stunned by what Bob said and the deep emotions flowing from him as he said it. No one spoke for several seconds. Then Bob broke the silence with words that surprised them a second time. "But still, I'd like to have a father worthy of the name."

The doctors took his statements as no worse than what they had heard from many other such cases, maybe less.

Dr. Haskell, who had a degree in psychology as well as medicine, spoke. "Robert, it may well have been that your mother found in you what she sought in your father, and so grew very close to you. Mothers often become close to their first-born sons. He resented you and felt hostility toward you that he could not fully admit to himself. Can you understand what I am saying?"

Robert nodded. "I do, but above all it was the drink that drove my father out of control and made him act the way he did. When he was sober, he really wasn't a bad father. He was easy-going and full of fun. It's hard for outsiders to understand how attached the men of the Ward become to their saloons."

"I am sure you are correct, Robert. If you can, over the course of a couple of days here, start to establish a filial relationship with your father; it might help pull him out of his depression. I know that is asking a great deal, for as you said, alcohol has a terrible grip on him. Let me add forcefully, your relationship must be honest. Your father must seek forgiveness from you and your sisters for what he did to your mother and you three, and he must renounce drinking for the rest of his life."

Bob stood silent and not a little dubious about what the doctor was asking of him. His face expressed his pain and reluctance to risk another attempt at relating to his father. He was there, but he wasn't sure he wanted to be or that his father would or could respond positively to him.

Dr. Potter broke in. "Millicent, you worked many hours with Patrick and a genuine friendship seemed to arise for a period between you. There is no doubt in my mind Patrick likes the company of attractive women. He has often flirted with nurses here in the hospital. That's why I chose two female nurses to provide him with individual care. Is there anything you might say to Patrick that would appeal to his manhood?"

"Perhaps there is, Dr. Potter. I've been thinking more about Patrick these last days after hearing he was close to death. He was a big help to me while gardening and to our WCTU group when we were off making presentations. We all hoped that coming with us, hearing our presentations, listening to other men like himself, he would see what alcohol was doing to him. We were deeply disappointed when he didn't."

Haskell thought to himself, *She is saying "we" when, I sense, she really means "I."*

She lowered her eyes and seemed to be looking into the past. "He's a charming and engaging storyteller, I must say. He is most gentle with flowers and with his Belgian horses. So he can still make a contribution to the Home if he wants to."

"But obviously no one needs a drunk, Mrs. Hastings," Potter interjected. "So what Dr. Haskell said to Robert, I repeat to you. He must renounce alcohol whole and entire for the rest of his life and mean it."

Potter turned now to the last of the three people he had brought to the Home. "Patrick Dolan, thank you for persuading Millicent and Robert to appear today. You may have the most difficulty remaking a relationship that is honest and enjoyable and yet does not depend on drinking. You and Donohue have been, as you said, 'drinking mates' all your lives. If you are going to continue your friendship, it cannot include alcohol. Your one advantage is that you seem to have made a break with your past. You might be able to show him the way."

Later that day, the five of them crowded around Pat's bed while the two nurses gently awakened him and propped him up with pillows. They had separated his bed at one end of the ward away from the others and partitioned it with screens. He was clean but gaunt and had grown a scraggy, two-inch beard. Millicent and Bob did not recognize him at first glance.

The object of all this attention looked up and whispered weakly, "Saints of God, where am I?"

"You are still with us, Pat," said Dr. Potter with a smile.

"We will leave you with your son for a while. The rest of us will be in to talk to you as your strength allows."

They said good-bye and left father and son alone.

Robert stood awkwardly for a moment and then sat down in a chair vacated by one of the nurses. "Dad, how are you feeling?"

"Not so great, son. I'm weak as a kitten. It's great to see you." Then he paused, searching for the right words to say to a son who was showing great concern for him in spite of the terrible way Pat had treated him over half a lifetime.

He reached for the heart of the matter. "I still miss your mother. I know you don't think I treated her the way I should have and I didn't, but I loved her very much."

"I know you did, but your relationship went from bad to worse over the years. That's hard to understand, Dad, because Mom was a beautiful woman, a good mother and wife, as far as I'm concerned."

"It hurts to hear you say it, but you are right. I made all kinds of excuses for the way I treated her; they were as empty as an old grain elevator. How I'd like to have those years back! Your mother was a gift from God."

"How did you replace her once she was gone?" asked Bob.

"The same way I did when she was alive. With Kennedy's and whiskey. How stupid! I wish I had died in the war."

"How could Kennedy's and whiskey replace Mom? How did that work for you?"

"I'm embarrassed to even think about it," replied Pat. "I have no answer. It was dumb and only made me worse to you three. And I treated some really wonderful people here at the Home the same way, people who were only trying to help me."

Then the two lapsed into silence and tears came to Pat's eyes. "I even treated my brother like he was shit." He paused and then blurted out, "Right now, Bob, I'd just as soon end it all."

"Dad, you've got plenty of reasons to live if you want to make things right, plenty of ways to help others. You have talent and love you could give us all. You're only cursing God and all he gave you when you talk suicide."

"Can you stay for a day? I want to talk to you more, about us and your sisters, but I'm so tired I can hardly keep my eyes open."

"I'll be here when you wake up."

"Thanks for coming, Bob. I feel a bit better already." The obvious concern of his son coming from Buffalo in spite of Bob's hostile feelings toward him moved Pat deeply. That night, Dr. Potter arranged for Bob to stay at the Home.

The next morning, Pat ate more than he had eaten in weeks. Just as Nurse Gibson was leaving, Bob walked in.

"Hi, Dad, you're looking a bit better! How are you feeling?"

"I'm feeling stronger this morning."

Nurse Gibson added, "You were just the tonic to bring him around."

Pat finished his breakfast with a few pleasantries before speaking in earnest. "I want to talk some more about you and me." He began and then faltered. Breathing heavily and choking back strong emotions, Pat asked, "What do you think I could do to make it up to you in some small way for the lousy father I was?"

"Dad, I was thinking about that last night and this morning. Mary Alice was crushed by the loss of her son, John. She was lost in melancholia for two years. Two years! Well, God has His ways. A new baby's coming. We're going to name her Katherine, after your mother and our Kate, my sister, if it's a girl; Patrick, after you and your father, if it's a boy. Isn't that the old Irish way, Dad?"

"That is great news," replied Pat. "I'm so happy for the two of you."

"You get well and I will bring the children and Mame to see you, or you can come home to see us. But I have to be honest with you. Why do you think we fought over the years?"

"I think the drinking had a lot to do with it. I know I wasn't myself when I was drunk. I wasn't close to your mother, and you were. I'm really embarrassed by what I did and I'm sorry for it.

"Her dying without me alongside her, her refusing to see me on her deathbed fills me with guilt. To lose her love . . . well, I'll never get over it. All I can do is to ask you to forgive me."

"Nothing would please Ma more than to hear you say what you just said and to see you and me become friends," said Bob. Big tears welled up in Bob's eyes and in his father's. The sight of his son's compassion for him overwhelmed Pat.

"I know, son. I know I should have made your mother happy. She deserved to be, but I just would not give up Kennedy's."

Father and son were quiet for a minute, sharing grief for what was lost in their lives together and for a woman who had suffered a shortened lifetime with a drunk.

"I have to be leaving soon if I'm going to catch the train to Buffalo. I'd stay if you think we have more to say to one another. I want you to get well and I'd do anything in the world to make it happen."

"No, I want you to go home and get to work for that beautiful wife of yours and my grandchildren."

"Dad, I suspect I have deeper feelings for you than I ever knew I had. I would love to have my children come to know their grandfather, but I have to say, it can't happen if you go on drinking. It's that simple."

"Son, I'm going to get control of myself, above all—above all—no drinking, not a drop. Please pray for me, son, and write. I'll write back, I promise. I mean it, even though I never really learned to write very good. I do want to see my grandchildren and get to know them and Mame."

"We didn't get to talk at all about Minnie and Annie. I know I'm the reason their lives are so messed up."

"Annie asks about you, Dad, but I think she feels you disowned her and want nothing to do with her."

"It's true. I did disown her when she married that Jew, but I've met a lot of different kinds of people here at Bath and I'm learning to accept them. I would love to hear from her. Please tell her for me."

"I will, Dad."

"And Minnie? What about her?"

Bob grimaced and shook his head. "I hear nothing new about Minnie."

Pat sighed and looked down at his lap. "Does that mean she's still on opium?"

"Yah, I'm afraid it does."

"I feel like I'm the cause and I hate myself."

Neither could think of anything else to say.

Nurse Gibson reappeared, shaking both men out of their momentary funk. "I dearly hope I'm not intruding," she said as she entered.

Bob sighed and his face relaxed. He smiled gently. "Not at all," he said. "I, um, must be going, anyway."

"Son," Pat said as Bob stood up, "thanks for coming. I can't wait to see the grandchildren." Just before leaving the room, Bob turned, raised his hand to his forehead, and with a hopeful smile, saluted his father.

"Goodness, Mr. Donohue," Nurse Gibson said as she busied around the bed. "You finished everything on your tray and you kept it down."

"I guess some of my appetite is coming back," Pat declared.

"Sleep awhile, Mr. Donohue. Mrs. Hastings will be around shortly," said Nurse Gibson, whom Dr. Potter had put in charge of showing visitors in to see Pat when he was able to receive them. A smile came over Pat's face as he slipped into a deep sleep.

Millicent came in an hour later and sat by Pat's side, wanting to hold his hand, but not wanting to at the same time. She gazed on his bearded face and watched him breathe. She admitted she had been deeply hurt by this man, more deeply because she cared for him. He had betrayed her trust and affection, something she did not extend easily to men.

She spent the time in thought about the way she had acted toward Patrick. *I say the Our Father every night at bedtime, an old habit learned from my mother, and the words 'Forgive us our debts as we forgive our debtors' haunt me. I need to forgive not only Pat but my son as well. Oh Lord, loosen the bonds of hate around my heart so I can truly love,* she said to herself.

After a time Pat awoke. "Mrs. Hastings, how long have you been here?"

"An hour, Mr. Donohue! You slept well. I hope you're beginning to feel a little stronger."

"I am, indeed. I'm surprised to see you here, but there's no one I would want to see more."

Millicent blushed and changed the subject. "Mr. Donohue, it was always clear to me how fond you were of the Ward and Kennedy's, but I never saw how many things you covered up with your drinking. I learned a lot from your son."

"I'm afraid I was hiding a whole lot of stuff I collected like a ragman over a lifetime, things that happened, things I did, people I hurt, hurts I imagined. I just threw them all in my wagon and carted them along."

"So," said Millicent, "what caused the wagon to stop so suddenly and bury you under its junk?"

"Mrs. Hastings, alcohol just gets to a man after he drinks a long time. I know one thing. I told myself I could drink because I was Irish and had to work in such miserable conditions. I'm too ashamed to tell you how I treated Mary and Bob and the girls.

"I told my son that I was never going to touch a drop again in my life. It will be my way of making up a little for all the harm I did."

"Sounds like you are about to make a break with your past."

"I've wasted a good part of my life. If you will let me, maybe I can do something to help you the way I used to. Most of all, Mrs. Hastings, I want you to be my friend. Could we do that?"

"Mr. Donohue, is it time we become a bit less formal? Would you call me Millicent from now on?" "I will, Millicent . . . if you'll call me Pat."

Millicent leaned over, pulled Pat into her bosom and gave him a long and tender hug. Pat blushed and mumbled it was the best medicine he'd ever had.

That afternoon, when PM visited his friend, Pat was sitting up in bed.

"You've made a remarkable recovery, Pat. What's got into you?"

Pat smiled, relieved that he had not lost his best friend. "Well, you're looking good." PM's hair was neatly cut and combed and he was clean-shaven, except for a small mustache and goatee, the new look he had adopted for the new man.

"What are you thinking, Pat, after talking with Bob and Mrs. Hastings?"

"I'm thinking I've got some real friends and if I want to keep them and go on living, I need to make a break with the past."

"You wanna talk about it?" He removed his hat and sat at the end of the bed. PM wore a clean, pressed uniform and had polished his shoes. He leaned back, wanting to hear all about the change coming over Pat.

"What you said to me weeks ago hurt bad, but I know you meant it for my own good. I am a real shit. I've done a lot of harm I gotta undo"

PM laughed a little at Pat's reaction. "Let me tell you, Donohue, me lad, I did a lot of thinking about what I said to you. If you need changing, so do I."

"PM, I need your friendship. You're my other leg. Are we a sad pair of chaws, or what?" The two sank into silence.

Then the PM that Pat knew so well exploded. "I want to shave that ugly mug of yours. Who do you think you are, Moses on the mountain? Can I come back later with me brush and shaver?"

Pat smiled and nodded. "That would be good, but hone it a bit first, lad."

Chapter 31

The Storyteller

Four months later, at 8:30 a.m. on Wednesday, August 18, 1905, Patrick Donohue made his debut at the Bath Soldiers' Home assembly hall. Millicent Hastings sat in the rear, the only woman there. She had helped him write his speech and rehearse it. Mr. Drummer made his way onto the stage, where he introduced Pat, neatly groomed and dressed in his clean, pressed blue uniform.

"Gentlemen, let me introduce to you Private Patrick Donohue of the 155th New York Volunteer Infantry, an all-Irish regiment formed in Buffalo. He served three years and fought at Spotsylvania, Cold Harbor, and Petersburg with General Grant's Army of the Potomac. He was captured at Reams Station and spent eight months in such lovely garden spots of the Confederacy as Libby and Belle Isle, Virginia; Salisbury, North Carolina; and Florence, South Carolina before escaping." The men snickered knowingly. They had friends who had suffered grievously in Confederate prisons. Some had died in them. A number of residents knew these prisons first hand.

"Pat, as many of you know, is a resident here at the Soldier's Home. I believe he has a story you might find interesting." Drummer took his seat again on stage.

The sun was shining through the six floor-to-ceiling windows of the south wall. A hundred men clustered in seats on the north side of the center aisle to avoid the heat of its rays and toward the front to better hear the speaker. Hall capacity was rated at 1,000. The windows were open and the room was cool and comfortable. Those who came were there because they wanted to be and their mood was receptive. They knew only that Pat, who was known among the

295

residents for his antics in Bath and for his care of the Belgian horses, was to recount his own personal story.

"Good morning, gentlemen. I'm honored to be on stage with Mr. Drummer and to have so many of you come to hear me. I know you have other things to do and I'll be brief." He paused to phrase his opening remark. "Did I tell you sorry old soldiers the story of Peter O'Toole?"

A craggy vet in the front row yelled, "No, you dumb mick. This is your first time on stage or are you into the drink already this mornin'?"

The crowd laughed. Pat laughed, too, good-naturedly. "No, indeed, I'm not." He paused and then added, "Not that I never drank in the morning." The men laughed again. Then Pat waited for quiet and began.

"Peter O'Toole was a short little man in Company I of the 155th, barely five feet tall, with one leg an inch shorter than the other. You've heard of rich men who paid someone like us to serve for them. Well, O'Toole had to pay off a recruiter to join the 155th." Some of the men snickered at the irony of O'Toole's behavior. "For the first year, every time we got into a skirmish, O'Toole was nowhere to be seen. He was always straggling in the rear of the regiment. He complained his Springfield was too heavy for him, so the captain requisitioned a carbine from a navy friend and sawed off half its barrel.

"In April 1863, Longstreet laid siege to Fortress Suffolk in southern Virginia. He picked out Fort Dix and the 155th to probe Union defenses. If the rebs could have broken through there, they might have captured the whole coastal Virginia Union Army, 30,000 men." The men became quiet and leaned forward. "But O'Toole, from high on a tree, firing a rifle not much bigger than a revolver, mowed down the butternut lines three times when they attacked on the first day of the siege.

"At Sangster's Station in August of '63, our company was attacked by Mosby's crack cavalry. Imagine, one company about to be overrun by two regiments. O'Toole ran up a tree and shot the front rank of the cavalry, including a captain, like he was shooting tin cans off a fence. That slowed the cavalry charge enough for most of us to escape.

"O'Toole was our hero. He was our secret weapon. We got so used to his marksmanship that the moment the enemy attacked, the captain would count sixty and we would counterattack. We just knew within the first sixty seconds O'Toole would have the field bleeding Confederate red." Pat paused to observe the expressions on the faces of his audience.

"One night, the company carried O'Toole on their shoulders to the middle of the camp and raised him up on a tree stump. Every officer toasted him and gave him a drink of the best Kentucky bourbon. They wrapped a full bottle in a gold cloth bag and gave it to him for his very own. Over the next month, they fed him bourbon at every campfire and toasted his exploits.

"In March 1865, outside of Petersburg, three regiments of rebs, massed in just 100 yards, charged our flank. Our captain counted to sixty and the 155th, 500 men, stood and counterattacked, confident of their secret weapon. The rebel regiments didn't waver a bit. O'Toole had never made it up the tree. He lay drunk at its base."

The audience took a deep breath, anticipating what came next.

"The 155th lost a dozen men killed in the counterattack and twice that number wounded and captured. Fortunately, General Gibbon had moved two regiments into position to support us. The rebel attack was turned back.

"O'Toole should have ended the war a national hero and received a gold medal from the president. Instead, he sat two weeks in the brig and was treated like an outcast by the regiment for the rest of his service. His shame will outlive his grandchildren."

Pat bowed to the audience and walked off stage. A bewildered look came over the faces of the crowd, then cautious applause.

Pat remained faithful to his pledge to have not even one beer. He drove carriage for the WCTU women and helped them with their presentations. He spent many hours with the Belgian horses, exercising, feeding and combing them, and meticulously cleaning their stalls in bad weather and in good.

He accompanied the WCTU women to Rochester and, at Millicent's request, made a presentation in the downtown Odd Fellows Lodge. Pat spared no detail in telling his story. "I rioted on the streets against coloreds and used a club on them and ended up in jail. I came to my grandmother's wake drunk and to her funeral so hung over I had to hold my head with two hands. I had a beautiful, educated, loving wife and beat on her. Once, as a prison guard, I brought home my pistol and shot it at her feet. I slapped my son around because he got close to my wife and I mocked and abused him for over thirty years. I favored one daughter and then another and made their lives so miserable they fled my house. One of the two is lost today in Hell's Kitchen on opium. Because I talked maliciously and drunkenly about the Larkin Family in a local bar, I lost a job at the Larkin Company that would have sent my children to college. I wasted my whole adult life and God knows how much money because of alcohol."

His story led a few men to come forward and swear off alcohol.

From then on, he became a regular part of WCTU presentations wherever Millicent scheduled them.

Over the next two years, Pat spent many happy hours with Millicent on and off the Home grounds. He cared for the Belgian horses and, with other residents, tended flowerbeds, worked in the greenhouse, and placed flags on the plaza parade ground every Fourth of July and on graves every Decoration Day. He joined Company H's funeral honor guard and accompanied residents to their final resting place in the Home cemetery. He attended numerous funeral services conducted by Home chaplains and gradually came to grips with his own mortality.

His heart strengthened and his overall health improved to a state he had not known since his youth.

A letter arrived from Johanna in November 1907.

Dear Pat,

It is a sad time in this house. I felt I had to write you. Our John Joseph has come down with the consumption and is very sick. We had no choice but to bring him, his wife, Amelia, and their three children into the house and nurse him as best we can. Amelia is a strong woman and takes on most of the load. Katherine and I occupy the grandchildren.

John Joseph asked for you and would love to see you, as would we all. But we would understand if you decide not to come.

Your brother sends his best. He is pretty much recovered, thank God, and is back to work on the Michigan Street Bridge.

Our Lady of Perpetual Help has become a very active parish in the ten years since it was built. Our pastor, Father O'Connell, died in February. We miss him, as he was most kind to all. Father Lynch is the new pastor. He is full of life. We see him visiting families and bringing communion to the sick. We'll tell you all about it if you get home.

Lots of love . . .

Pat arrived from Bath at the Delaware Lackawanna and Western Depot and walked to the Michigan Street Bridge. It was 6:00 p.m. and dark. He met his brother just as he got off work. This was the first time he had been home since he had sworn off the drink. He had not seen his brother in four years. John spun around in surprise at hearing Pat's voice. Pat had greyed, but was trim and cheerful. John grabbed Pat by the shoulders, smiled, and shook him gently.

"I knew you were coming. I can't tell you how much I missed you."

"It's great to see you, too." Choking with strong feelings for his brother, Pat asked, "What's the word on John Joseph?"

"It doesn't look good. He's barely able to breathe. The consumption is destroying his lungs. We need another miracle like mine. I don't think you should enter the house."

"Ah, I'll wear a mask and say my prayers."

They continued in silence. The house was crowded with family and neighbors. Like most of the houses in the Ward, it was a four-room cottage. Pat was used to the spaciousness of Bath and felt a bit uneasy. He stood for a moment at the door and sucked in a deep breath. The heat and smells of body and kitchen odors bothered him. For all the people crammed into it, the house was subdued, so unlike the noise and laughter he remembered was a natural part of John and Johanna's home. James, Mary, and Katherine rushed to him. The rest followed. Soon he was surrounded with family grabbing his arms and hugging and kissing him. He was overwhelmed and struggled to hold back the tears. Johanna introduced Amelia and her children to Pat. Pat leaned in and kissed her gently on a cheek. He held each one of the children, making silly remarks that had all around them smiling. Pat was a natural with kids.

He entered John Joseph's bedroom, where Johanna sat leaning toward her son. Her dress was messy and stained from feeding John Junior. Streaks of grey in her hair and a haggard expression told a tale of long days and nights at his side.

She, too, had not seen Pat in years, clutched his hand, and held it to her face with obvious affection. "Oh, Pat, you are looking so much better than that last Christmas home. I don't think you should be in here, but you're a sight for sore eyes and we're so glad you came."

A pall settled over the group gathered outside the bedroom. Pat grew conscious of John Joseph's labored breathing.

"Ungle Pat . . . Ungle Pat . . ." His voice barely wheezed out the words.

Nodding to his brother and sister-in-law, Pat fumbled to cover his mouth and nose with the linen cloth she had given him. John stayed at the door, as there was little space inside the cramped room. The room was lit by a single kerosene lamp and was warm and stuffy. John Joseph was covered by two comforter blankets. Gaunt and pale, his breathing was deep and irregular. He emitted low gurgling sounds. Pat had heard the sounds of death before and his thoughts flew back to the General Hospital in Philadelphia. He bent over toward his left ear and in a low voice said, "John, lad, how are you? Your mom wrote and told me you were sick. But I know you'll be well again soon."

Time stood painfully still as John Joseph pushed out a few phrases, mostly just single words. "Ungle Pat . . . Ungle Pat." The rest Pat could not understand. He leaned down to his head again and said, "John, I'm with you. Rest a minute. No need to say a word, just rest."

John was a strapping young man when last Pat saw him, a hoisting engineer. Now his face was ashen and his head and neck stuck out of the covers, skin over skeleton. Memories of Salisbury and of his parents' last days flashed through Pat's consciousness.

John coughed weakly, but could not clear his throat. "John, let's just rest a minute." Pat pressed John's hand. His nephew's choking was disturbing. John's flesh was cool, clammy, and trembling. The longer Pat held it, the more he sensed a life easing away. Johanna wiped her son's cracked lips with her wetted fingers and wept openly. Pat motioned to his brother to take his place and stood in the doorway. After a half hour, John lapsed into unconsciousness and died moments later. The three adults hugged one another and cried aloud. The sound of deep sobbing spread like a wave through the rest of the house.

Pat stayed in Buffalo at the home of his son. Bob, Mame, Annie, and Pat openly shared the grief they felt for John, Amelia, and their children, for his parents and brother and sisters as well.

Throughout the wake, which began the next day and lasted two days, Pat stayed in the front room with his brother and Johanna, greeting mourners, most of whom he knew. The smell of whiskey wafted in every time the kitchen door opened and eventually brought on a strong desire to join the men in the kitchen. Pat left the front room about midnight and poured a shot without thinking. His niece, Katherine, now an adult of twenty-four, walked up to him, leaned toward his ear, and whispered, "Uncle Pat, I thought you weren't supposed to drink."

Pat touched her cheek with one hand and said in shaky voice, "Right you are, my dear one, and I thank you for reminding me." He poured the shot back in the bottle and left.

He stayed for the funeral and then returned to Bath. On the train trip, as he reflected on the death of his nephew and on his own mortality, peace spread through him like sunshine emerging after a month of March greyness. He sighed in relief that by the grace of God and his niece he had not given in to the temptation to drink. He reminded himself that it would not be the last. Other temptations would follow.

A deep desire for confession came over him. He had not been to confession for two years. He wanted to make his commitment firmer and his quest for inner peace stronger. He resolved to find another caring figure like Father Hogan, but he did not have to be Catholic. Pat's opposition to some Catholic teaching and rules, his attendance at many Protestant funerals and other services, and Drummer's classes had opened him up to a broader spirituality.

On quiet evenings before heading back to the barracks, Pat stretched out on Millicent's couch, his head in her lap. On a May night in 1910, he told her, "I feel strangely free, like just released from prison. Since you and the rest of the Bath crew came into my life, I don't need the Ward, Kennedy's, and drinking. I have a new life and you're at the center of it all, Milly."

She smiled. Her eyes moistened. She took her glasses off and cleaned them with a handkerchief. She leaned down, put her lips on his, kissed him, and said, "I have a surprise for you."

Taking his hand, she led him outside to the barn.

"I drove it yesterday from the showroom in Buffalo. Isn't it a beauty? And you didn't even know I was away."

"Let me tell you what happened while in the Pierce Arrow showroom ten days ago. I told the salesman why I wanted a Pierce Arrow. He warned me that while the Pierce Arrow Touring Car was the best car ever made, driving a car long distances was something women did not do. Rough roads make for perilous driving and frequent maintenance, he said."

"That only made you want one more," Pat grinned.

"How right you are!"

"Did he ask you what you could afford? I bet he did."

"Not in so many words, but he found out nevertheless. He walked me onto the shop floor and showed me the car they had built for George K. Birge, the famous Buffalo wallpaper designer and maker.

"Mr. Birge took me for a ride in his car the next day and had me drive it to Niagara Falls with his wife.

"A week later my car was finished and I spent two days being trained on driving and doing simple repairs like changing tires or spark plugs."

"This car shines in the dark and it's a monster. It must have cost you a fortune!" exclaimed Pat.

"Ten thousand dollars! Am I gone mad, Patrick? What else would I do with the money I inherited if not invest it in the work we're doing?"

She opened the car door and jumped up on the running board with an energy that belied her advancing age. She was now sixty-one, and Pat was sixty-six. "Pat, we'll hook a trailer to it and carry all we need to present our case with pictures and graphs wherever we go. The Pierce Arrow will take us to cities we've never visited."

"You're willing to try out new things, Milly, but I don't know if I'm up to it."

"Pat, a Pierce Arrow car won the New York to Bretton Woods Race. It's the best there is. President Taft owns one."

Pat had never ridden in a car. "And to think it is made in Buffalo!" He shook his head and smiled proudly.

"Friends have lined up a presentation in Boston on the 28th. Will you come? We need you. Your stories hit the men in the audience between the eyes. They have little but scorn for us women, but they listen to you."

"Of course I will. 'Twill be grand to ride with you ladies, as long as I don't have to drive that machine, Millicent."

The two-day trip to Boston with Millicent, Kirsten, and Abigail delighted him, every bouncing mile of it. The Pierce Arrow made it in style and relative comfort in spite of few paved roads, just as Milly thought it would. She was so proud of herself for buying the Pierce Arrow. She prized no material possession like it.

They rehearsed their act in a hotel on the Hudson and performed it in the Boston Downtown Masonic Temple. It was homey and fun. The women sang popular ballads with lyrics they had rewritten. They moved among the crowd and involved them in refrains and responses to their simple one-act musical. The moral was that real men and women didn't need alcohol to enjoy themselves. The crowd laughed at their corny jokes, sang the refrains, and cheered at the end of each song.

Then Pat got up and stood silently looking down at the stage. The audience stilled. Deadpan, he recounted the story of his life. Two men interrupted his talk with loud and scornful shouts in the middle of it. Pat smiled, kept silent while he calmed himself, and responded with humility and humor. The crowd shushed the hecklers into silence. Soon the whole audience was with him.

Men empathizing with the tragedies he brought to his wife and children bit their lips and fought back tears. Women freely broke down.

That evening after their presentation, Kirsten and Abigail returned to the hotel to give their friends time alone together. Millicent took Pat to the English Manse, an expensive restaurant seating 300 people, decorated in Victorian reds and blacks and frequented by Boston's elite. It rested regally above the Boston Harbor, electric lamps and candles shimmering out onto the open porch and waters beyond. Seated at their table was a well-dressed man in his late thirties.

"Pat, may I introduce you to my son, Thurman?" He rose: tall, dark-haired, bright-eyed, handsome, an imposing man. Pat shook his hand energetically and then mother and son embraced tenderly for a long moment. The night was revealing a side of Millicent that Pat had not seen: mother of an adult son.

Millicent chose dishes from an elegant menu for Pat and herself. Thurman ordered lobster. They ate while Millicent and Thurman talked about his new post at Northeastern University. Thurman was proud of his appointment as an assistant professor in the English Department and told Millicent about his students and his research into the works of early American poets. An hour later, Pat went off to the rest room, which at his age took a little more time. He stopped at an empty bar on his way back when an Irish bartender greeted him and started a brief conversation.

When he came back to their table, Milly was standing alone and angry. Thurman was gone. She gave a curt explanation that they had quarreled over his drinking and he had cut off their conversation and left the restaurant. Later on, in the car returning to their hotel, Pat asked her what she said that angered her son. She raised her voice and told him it was none of his business. Her words hit him hard, but he calmed himself and said nothing. Before they parted for their separate rooms that night, she apologized and gave him a sweet kiss on the lips.

On the ride back to Bath, Pat thought about the WCTU gatherings he had been part of and how they had changed him. He relished the experience and thanked God for having met Potter, Drummer, Hogan, and especially Millicent. Change in him had not come evenly or easily, but it had finally come, nonetheless.

He noted to himself the one thing all four had in common: their education. He no longer resented educated people, but sought their company and appreciated the way they thought about life and the world around them. He had begun reading books that Millicent suggested from the libraries on the Home campus. Reading had always been a struggle for Pat, but with coaching from her, it was becoming easier and less something he had to force on himself to please Millicent.

He continued attending classes given by Drummer and listening to speakers Drummer brought in. Learning excited him and new worlds were unfolding. He wrote to his brother about what he was doing. John replied in his neat handwriting, "Wow, I can read your writing and understand it. What's going on?"

That August, Milly took Pat to the Chautauqua Institution on the shores of Lake Chautauqua in Western New York during its annual summer program, which focused on the arts, religion, education, and recreation. They stayed at the Hotel Athenaeum for a week. It was her belated gift for his sixty-sixth birthday. The two attended as many presentations as they could cram into each day. At the end of the week, Pat surprised Milly by revealing that he was thinking about becoming a Protestant. Milly counseled him to wait a while and think about it, as he had deep Catholic roots.

In the early days of his second stay at the Bath Home, Pat had volunteered to plow fields behind two Belgian horses. They bucked and pulled apart when he first took the reins. After several minutes of struggle, he lashed out at them with a whip. They bolted, dragging him across the deep furrows of recently plowed ground. Pat was badly shaken and suffered broken ribs and multiple bruises.

G. Edwards Smith, the farm director, saw it all, but was powerless to prevent Pat from his fate. Days later, when Pat was able to walk, Mr. Smith called him to the barn. He led the two Belgians out of their stalls and harnessed them to a plow. He talked to them gently and stroked them across their broad shoulders, down their noses, and behind their ears. Then he led them out of the barn, took the reins, and clucked for the horses to draw the plow across the field. After a half-hour of plowing, he stopped, fed them a handful of oats, and let them take long draughts from a tub of water. Then, with a relaxed grip on the reins and constant patter, he began to plow again. He never used a whip.

Pat understood what Smith was saying. To whip a Belgian draft horse sent a message to the animal that the driver was not its friend.

Every year in April thereafter, for the month of spring plowing, Mrs. Hastings and the other women did their WCTU presentations alone. They missed Pat and he missed them, but once he put his hand to the plow, he would not turn back. This was sacred time. The Belgians and Pat morphed into a perfectly synchronized team and plowed daily, dawn till dusk with only breaks for dinner at noon and supper at five. Pat came to understand how easily these intelligent beasts would follow calm words and gentle touch. They plowed tirelessly and obediently without rearing up, kicking, or pulling off-line.

In 1909, Pattie, a mare whom Pat had often shown to women visiting the home on Sundays, died of old age. The Home's Michigan-born superintendent as of December 1902, Colonel Joseph E. Ewell, replaced her with a pair of Belgian geldings from Michigan State University. Pat adopted them and cared for them like sons.

The next year, Mr. Smith invited neighboring farmers to come by and watch Pat plow. They were amazed at how the Belgians responded to Pat after plowing, neighing and nuzzling him as he washed and combed them down. As one said, "Pat and his horses belong in church. They are more spiritual than a Sunday service."

At sixty-seven, Pat found the work of tending the horses too much for him alone, so he took on a delinquent fourteen-year-old from Bath named Perry Stedman. Perry was short, stocky, with dark hair and a sneering gaze. Over the next year this young man, whom neither father nor judge could control, worked with Pat driving the Belgians and accompanying him on WCTU trips. Pat let Perry try his hand at all the jobs the horses performed on the farm, modeling each task so that Perry could see how it was to be done. Then he had him do the tasks alone, but under his supervision. Finally, he turned Perry loose. Perry failed at times and learned there were consequences to every action. Mr. Smith hired him the day he turned sixteen.

Pat enjoyed his relationship with Perry. He saw the boy make real progress and thought perhaps he, Pat, could make a similar contribution to other problem adolescents. Pat talked to local judges about sending him other troubled youth and for two years, judges sent him delinquents from their courts until Pat grew unable to teach them first-hand any longer.

In 1913, at age sixty-nine, Pat relinquished plowing and care of the Belgians to younger men, Perry above all. Still, he could not absent himself from the opening of spring plowing. Standing at the edge of the grain field leaning on a cane, he coached and encouraged.

In the summer of 1913, in addressing veterans and other men at the Broadway Masonic Hall in New York City, Pat related this story: "Ronald Cleary was a New Yorker whose father, Jeremiah, emigrated from County Cork, Ireland, in 1842. Jeremiah was a clever tenant farmer who tended his farm and paid his rent even after it doubled. But he refused to pay it when it doubled again the next year. In the dead of night, he burned cottage, barn, and yard and walked thirty miles to Cobh, leaving his intended behind with her family.

"In New York, he bartended, learned the ways of American business, and saved every cent he could. He paid for his fiancé's passage to America and married her soon after arrival. They moved to Buffalo, rented space in a new hotel on Main Street, and imported New York stage acts and plays.

"Jeremiah sent his son, Ronald, to the University at Buffalo to study medicine, the only Catholic in his class. He overcame prejudice from his professors and fellow students and graduated first in his class four years later. Ronald set up practice on Pearl Street in downtown Buffalo. Within ten years, he married, had a family of five, and moved into a mansion on Delaware Avenue, where the rich and famous of Buffalo lived. With his father, he bought a dozen rental properties.

"Every night, Ronald's wife prepared a tumbler of bourbon on the rocks. It had been a long day of surgeries at Buffalo Sisters of Charity Hospital where he was chief of thoracic surgery. The whiskey relaxed him. Ronald found that two glasses relaxed him more. Then three . . . four . . . five . . . Over time, he changed character completely, began abusing his wife and children, fought with his father, frequented brothels on lower Main Street, and invested heavily in a horse ranch in Florida and a gold mine in California.

"Doctor Ronald Cleary went bankrupt in the crash of 1893. He lost his home and family, was reduced to panhandling, and died in agony of cirrhosis of the liver. Think about it. Like a thief in the night, alcohol brought down in a decade all that a father and son and their wives and families had accomplished over five decades!

"Be honest. Have you convinced yourselves you can handle a few drinks? Are there signs the drinks are handling you? That's what it did to me." Then he told his own story.

When they arrived home from New York, Pat sat quietly with Milly in her living room. The sun was passing into the horizon of a clear, warm evening.

"Pat, our next trip is to Rochester. That story you told in New York will go over well with that crowd. I know them." Milly was trying to make small talk and to subdue her affection for Pat, which had overcome her suspicious nature and past bad experiences with her husband and Pat. Pat took her hand and squeezed it firmly to stop her from talking.

"God is good, Millicent. I know He is because you are so good to me."

"So why do you look so sad, Pat?"

Pausing, his brow furrowed, he took a deep breath and looked into her eyes. "Millicent, I want to tell you something I've never told anyone. I abandoned someone I loved. I've never forgiven myself. She was an ex-slave girl I met while guarding the Orange and Alexandria Railroad at Sangster Station, Virginia in 1863. She was pregnant with my child. After we left Sangster Station that summer, I never dared to find out what became of the child. The memory torments me. I never told anyone about her, not my brother, not a priest in confession, no one. Her name was Annabelle Lee."

Pat went on to tell Milly the whole, long story in as much detail as he could remember. She listened silently, holding his hand with barely a hint of shock on her face. She waited to speak until she could see he had said all he wanted to say. She looked down at the floor and pressed Pat's hands to her bosom. Then she kissed him on the forehead firmly and said, "Pat, let's go find them."

Milly took a day to rearrange two presentations. The next morning, they packed the Pierce Arrow with suitcases and left early for Virginia.

The drive down rutted dirt roads crossed four states through sunny valleys and rain-swept mountains. The further south they went, the rougher the roads became. Milly drove cautiously until Pat, in exasperation, urged her to take a few long straightaways at speeds of thirty-five or even forty miles an hour.

Maps were often inaccurate and out of date. The two targeted small cities, towns, and villages, stopping at hamlet shops to ask locals about the best route to Washington.

From Washington to Sangster Station the road was flat and smoother, the weather hot and humid. People reacted to them with a mixture of awe at the Pierce Arrow and hostility toward two Northerners. Milly was tired at the end of each day from driving, but her excellent health stood her well.

Pat's side and back continuously pained him. He asked Milly to stop frequently so he could urinate in bushes along the road. Since it had not rained in days, dust filled their nostrils and coated their hats and oversized goggles.

Milly talked with Pat about his feelings as they neared Sangster Station and how he would speak to Annabelle, if they found her. During the long daytime rides, Pat thought about it and decided he would just do it—with respect, with gentleness, with honesty above all.

They arrived in Sangster Station shortly after noon, bought a few supplies and gifts at a general store, and asked directions to St. Luke's African Methodist Episcopal Church in the colored section of town, the church Pat remembered Annabelle attending. He knocked on the door of the rectory, which was set back alongside the church. It was an old, modest, two-story, brick building. As the door opened, a mild smell of mold and old furniture mixed with stronger odors of fried cooking. An elderly colored woman invited them in to a heavily curtained parlor. Streaks of bright sunlight striped the carpet. The minister entered, an imposing, athletic man about sixty years old, with a threatening demeanor. Pat and Millicent stood up to greet him, a bit taken aback at the height, size, and scowl of the man.

"Yes? What may I do for you? I am Reverend Pastor Simmons," he said curtly.

Pat stumbled over his words as he started. "Reverend Pastor, my name is Patrick Donohue and this is Millicent Hastings, my good friend, who drove me here from New York State. I won't trouble you with a long story. I am trying to find a woman I met while fighting with the Union Army here in Sangster Station. Her name was Annabelle Lee."

He paused waiting to see if the name meant anything to Reverend Simmons. He could see it did. "We were both young. I was nineteen and she was seventeen. She was tall and very beautiful. We fell in love. When I left, she was pregnant." He paused and sighed. "I do not have long to live and would like to find her and ask her forgiveness. I never tried to locate her and I didn't help raise our child. Can you help us?"

Reverend Simmons listened. He asked Pat and Millicent a few questions of a personal nature. Then his face softened into a smile.

"Mr. Donohue, I believe I can. Annabelle was a member of this parish until her death, over twenty years ago now." Pat had told himself that Annabelle might no longer be alive. He imagined she had lived a very difficult life. Still, the fact of her death hit him hard and he expressed his sincere sadness to learn of it.

After a few moments' pause to let Pat regain his composure, Reverend Simmons continued. Death was a familiar theme in his ministry and he handled it like a doctor.

"She married Cassius Cambridge after the war, and they had eight children, the eldest being a daughter who is much fairer than the rest. That must be your daughter. The daughter and five boys survived. Annabelle, Cassius, and their children worked a forty-acre farm outside Sangster Station all her married life. She died at age forty-five. After Annabelle died, her daughter, Maybelle, and Maybelle's husband Jonas occupied the farm with her father and five brothers. Cassius died a few years after Annabelle in 1895." He turned and looked off into space, remembering happy times with Annabelle's family.

"Yes, I know that family well. I baptized, married, and buried many of them. The five brothers married and moved away. You see, Annabelle had left the farm to her only daughter and eldest child. That is not how things usually go in this part of the country. Maybelle's five sons took the place of her brothers raising crops and animals. Two are still on the farm with their parents."

Pat again expressed his sadness at Annabelle's death, but was pleased to hear all the minister had said about his daughter and her family's good fortune.

Reverend Simmons continued. "If you have room in your riding machine, I'd be happy to ride with you and take you to their farm. I've never ridden in a car before."

"That would make things much easier, Reverend. There is plenty of room. We would appreciate your coming along," said Millicent.

They rode out of town a half mile south over a road that had never seen a "riding machine" and was not kind to the first one. Negroes on forty-acre Reconstruction spreads poured out of their houses or stopped their work to stare at the Pierce Arrow and to comment excitedly about it. The sun broke through shallow white clouds as though witnessing a triumphal Roman procession.

Two miles farther along the dusty road, they came to a modest, whitewashed farmhouse set near the road with several outbuildings of varied sizes and shapes looking as though grown by nature. The farmyard was bordered by apple and peach orchards and a vegetable garden. Behind them yawned fields of corn, soybean, and cotton.

Pat saw his daughter. She walked confidently, gracefully from the front door toward them in her long blue dress and white apron. Her hair, worn in a bun, accentuated her handsome face. She favored her mother, but was lighter, with a narrower nose and a sharper chin. He could see his daughter, Katherine, in her. Her eyes fell on the Pierce Arrow, Reverend Simmons, Millicent, and then on Pat. Puzzlement spread across her face and that of the tall colored man standing with her.

Reverend Simmons greeted Maybelle, her husband, Jonas, and their two teenaged sons. He inquired of their health and then introduced Pat and Millicent. Jonas was a dark, burly farmer, fortyish, with a few strands of grey hair, rough, thick hands, and broad facial features. All stood silent for a few seconds staring at one another. Then Reverend Simmons started to explain the reason for their visit.

Jonas moved closer to his wife and took her gently by the arm, saying, "Please, let's sit down on de porch." He led them a short distance to a white-railed front porch and bade them be seated on white washed wicker chairs. Maybelle remained standing, clinging to a post. Her body moved side to side and she began to cry as Reverend Simmons spoke on. Jonas stood next to her and held her left hand, looking at her, then at Pat, then back at his wife, still puzzled about all he was hearing. A crow cawed defiantly and flew away as though in regret.

Pat looked away uncomfortably. Millicent squeezed his right hand.

The yard was neat, Pat noticed, unlike the small farms in and around Buffalo, which he remembered as strewn with broken plows, stumps, discarded pots, pails, and furniture. Thirty yards away, a cow and calf grazed behind a fence. A westward breeze carried the fresh scent of their waste across the yard. Only the sucking noise of a nearby calf pulling on its mother's teats competed for their attention.

As the reverend relaxed them with a brief story of the old farm under Annabelle and Cassius, the two parties became freer with their questions. They traced the lives of Annabelle and her family and Patrick and his after the war.

Reverend Simmons, pleased at how open the parties had become, decided his presence was no longer necessary. He excused himself, saying he would walk back and visit with families on the way.

Jonas assumed the patriarchal role of the pastor. He stayed close to his wife and held her hands when feelings threatened to overcome her as she talked about her mother and father. Pat's attention fixed at first on the beauty of her face, then on the calloused hands, strong arms, and shoulders. This woman, he knew, spent most of her life in heavy work, gardening, tending animals, and cooking. He guessed she was at least two inches taller than he.

As the conversation slowed, Jonas broke it off and invited the two visitors to remain for dinner and the night, if they wished. Pat and Millicent went to the trunk of the car and brought back food, soft drinks, and the small gifts Millicent had bought in town.

After a dinner accompanied by light conversation, Maybelle sent the boys out to feed the cows, the chickens, and the geese. She waited until she was sure they could not hear her before speaking. "My Mammy was in love with you, Mista Pat, and never lost those feelins. She loved my father, sure 'nough, but she kept you deep down in a secret store. She never held hate in her heart for no man, least of all for you, Mista Pat."

"Maybelle, I felt the same way about your mother. I dreamed of her all my life. I have suffered terribly not being able to make up to her or you for what I didn't do. Now I can die in peace because I've seen you, the flower of your mother." Pat struggled to his feet and pressed his lips onto her forehead. That night, everyone went to bed, but no one slept through.

By the second day, Millicent became the center of attention. Maybelle wanted to know more about this strangely elegant and sophisticated lady. Later on, when they were alone, she and Jonas talked about Patrick and Millicent, but she dismissed any thought of a long relationship with them. For one thing, she could see he was not well; also, seldom did white people befriend colored folks, even when one of them was a daughter.

Jonas agreed with her. He said he doubted they would ever see these whites again, but he liked them and trusted them. They had come a long way to see her because they knew Pat was near the end of his life. He had no fear they would cause them any trouble.

Toward noon, after lunch and a guided tour of the farm, Millicent tried to focus conversation on Maybelle and her family, but Maybelle turned the conversation to her.

Pat and Jonas walked through the orchard until Pat became tired. They sat under a tree and Pat questioned Jonas about the farm. Jonas talked at length about his plans to increase his acreage, as forty acres barely sustained them. "Let me help you do that," Pat pleaded. "It would ease the terrible guilty feelings I've had over the decades and allow me to die a happy death."

Millicent contributed $100 to the gift, Pat $25—all he owned. Jonas and Maybelle talked by themselves about their reluctance to accept such a large amount of money from these two white folks. At length they agreed, however, that the offer was too important to the whole family to refuse. Once their decision was made, elation swept over them and Maybelle and Jonas expressed their deep gratitude to these generous strangers.

For the boys, the two days had been an unusual experience. They had white friends, both boys and girls, but understood that these friendships would end when they all got older. Millicent and Patrick were the first adult whites they had spoken to in anything but short, polite phrases, eyes averted.

Just before Millicent and Pat drove off, Maybelle gave her father a red scarf that first her mother and then she had treasured for thirty years. Pat held it to his cheek and a tear traced a glistening line to his chin as they left.

Pat and Millicent returned home with a world of new feelings and thoughts, wonderful thoughts about Maybelle, Jonas, and their family. They had had no contact with Negroes in the North. They admitted to close friends that it had been hard to understand the family's speech, but that it was easy to see how much they cared for one another and what good parents Maybelle and Jonas were.

Following Pat's annual physical in January 1914, the doctors told him he had but months to live. His kidneys were inflamed. Movement brought pain to both sides of his body. He could not lie down comfortably, let alone walk or sit at table to eat. His pulse had slowed; his heart was beating unevenly.

He was not surprised at the news and decided to make one last trip to Buffalo to visit with John, by train because it was a smoother ride and more comfortable. Milly accompanied him.

On Sunday afternoon, Bob's wife, Mary Alice, cooked a huge dinner. Around the dining room table sat Bob, John and Johanna, their children James, Mary, and Katherine, their widowed daughter-in-law, Amelia, Amelia's children, and Patrick and Milly. Bob's six children crowded the kitchen table and included a toddler, William Joseph Donohue, born in 1912. They talked of happy memories and good times. They cried and laughed and they sang the latest from Broadway well into the night, around an upright player piano pedaled by Mame's eldest daughter, Alice.

On Sunday, April 14, Milly accompanied Pat to Buffalo by train once again. His niece, Mary, was dying of consumption. As they taxied to the Ward, anger overwhelmed him. How could God take his beautiful niece? She was so full of innocence and joy. He idolized her. By the time he got to Mary's side, she was in a coma and the coarse sounds of death were all that remained of her life. An hour later, she died in Johanna's arms. Pat shared cries of pain with Mary's parents.

Certain this was his final visit to Buffalo, Pat asked one more favor of Milly, to accompany him to Holy Cross Cemetery. There, because Pat no longer knew exactly where it was, they inquired at the office and asked that a workman accompany them to Mary's grave, unmarked for nearly twenty-five years.

Garrett had offered to pay for a stone for his daughter's grave, but Pat had refused. "It's my duty alone," he had said. Garrett had left an amount for a large monument in his will two years later, but once again, Pat had not allowed his children to use any of his father-in-law's money for that purpose. "I'll do it," he proclaimed loudly. "It will just take time."

As they stood alongside the grave and prayed a silent prayer, Pat said to himself, "I will use my last dollar to remember you, Mary." He made up his mind he would somehow fulfill his promise.

In late July, Johanna wrote to say the consumption had reappeared and John was gravely ill. Pat insisted on visiting John once again, even though he was not much stronger than his brother. In a most unusual ceremony, both men asked to receive Extreme Unction at the same time from Father Lynch, the pastor at Our Lady of Perpetual Help. It was common practice to administer the last rites at the point of death. For them, Father Lynch made the only exception he would make in thirty years as a priest.

As Pat left the house, leaning on Milly, he knew he was leaving his brother for the last time, but with a smiling face, he promised to celebrate Christmas with him.

On the train returning to Bath, he said his rosary. His mind slid through the ghosts of a lifetime like they were all players on a New York stage: his parents, Patrick and Catherine; Gramma Joy, Theresa Haggerty, and Bishop Timon; the 155th and the 164th fighting side-by-side; Tipping and Mooney and PM; his wife, Mary, and his children, Katherine, Bobby, Minnie, Nellie, and Annie; John and Johanna and their children, Mary, John, James, and Katherine; Annabelle, Maybelle and Jonas; and this marvelous woman holding his hand.

Four women were the great loves and anchors of his life. His brother had kept him in the game, at bat, and flying around the bases for seventy years.

His sudden sobbing startled Milly and the others in the car with them. He knew he had no funds for Mary's grave. It was now up to those he left behind.

Pat died at seventy years of age on Saturday, August 8, 1914, with Millicent easing him into eternity. John lingered on and died peacefully two months and a day later, Johanna stroking his forehead and whispering a prayer. Both men died without fear, and with only a deep sense of the people they would miss, especially their wondrous women.

Both men's burial services had the same recessional, written a year earlier, ironically by an Englishman, Frederick Weatherly, and played perhaps for the first time at funerals in North America at their services. It was their request before dying that only the second verse be sung and that it be dedicated to the women they loved.

> *And when ye come, and all the flowers are dying*
> *And I am dead as dead I well may be*
> *Ye'll come and find the place where I am lying*
> *And kneel and say an Ave there for me*
> *And I shall hear, though soft you tread above me*
> *And all my grave shall warmer, sweeter be*
> *For you shall bend and tell me that you love me*
> *And I shall sleep in peace until you come to me.*

Pat had one other request, one that left everyone but Milly wondering: to be buried with an old red scarf in his hands, woven around his well-worn rosary.

Glossary

Abatis: A line of sharply pointed, chopped tree limbs installed in the ground outside the main defense line, slanted outward toward the enemy.

American Protective Association or APA: Founded in Iowa in 1887, it pushed an anti-Catholic political agenda at local and state levels of government. According to the APA, loyalty to the pope was irreconcilable with loyalty to America. Sought to prevent Catholics from holding public office and from teaching in public schools. Disappeared about 1910 but lived on in the minds and speech of Catholics, especially Irish Catholics, for much longer.

Americans: Term used by nineteenth century sociologists to denote aristocratic, generally wealthy, culturally elite Protestants of English ancestry from New England as distinguished from more recent immigrant groups like Germans and Irish. "Americans" controlled business, government, and community institutions in Buffalo in the first half century from its founding.

Anglo-Irish: English who immigrated to Ireland after Cromwell conquered the island in 1650; controlled its main businesses and estates of thousands of acres until years after Irish independence from England in 1922 and in some cases still today. Became a common term among Irish people and educated Irish immigrants.

Artillery: Cannons or other large caliber firearms; a branch of the army armed with cannons. On occasion, artillery men operated as line infantry.

Banshee: In Irish mythology, a female fairy whose wailing foretold someone's death.

Battery: The basic unit in an artillery regiment. Batteries included six cannons, one hundred fifty-five men, a captain, thirty other officers, two buglers, fifty-two drivers, and seventy cannoneers with the horses, wagons and equipment needed to move and fire the cannons.

Bayonet: A metal blade shaped like a long knife that could be attached to the end of a musket rifle and used as a spear in hand-to-hand combat.

Breach: A large gap in a fortification or line of soldiers exposing the inside of the fortification or line to penetration by an attacking enemy.

Breastworks: Breast-high earth works or barriers, made of logs and soil, to protect soldiers from enemy fire.

Bullet screens: Light defenses, often built from a farmer's fence rails, generally with some earth mounded against them.

Butternut: Term applied to Confederate soldiers by Union soldiers because of the yellowish-brown color of their jackets.

Caliber: The distance around the inside of a gun barrel measured in millimeters or thousands of an inch. Bullets are labeled by the size of gun they fit.

Campaign: A series of military operations that compose a distinct phase of a war, e.g., the Overland Campaign waged by General Grant in Virginia from May 1864 to April 1865.

Cap: A tiny brass shell holding fulminate of mercury. When the trigger is pulled, the hammer slams into the cap, igniting gunpowder which flames into the chamber of the musket gun, igniting a wad of gunpowder, which blasts the bullet out of the barrel.

Cartridge: A roll of thin paper holding a small amount of gunpowder in the bottom and a ball or bullet in the top. A soldier had to tear off the top of the cartridge and ram it down the barrel of his rifle, one of nine steps to firing a muzzle-loading rifle.

Cavalry: Military mounted on horseback, often used to scout enemy positions and movements or to attack enemy cavalry. Cavalry could dismount and serve as infantry.

Cholera epidemics: The First Ward was prone to cholera epidemics because it was built on low-lying land that retained sewage water and bred virulent bacteria. Buffalo was ravaged by cholera epidemics in 1832, 1835, 1849, and 1854. Cholera is caused by the bacterium vibrio cholerae, transmitted by water or food that is contaminated by the feces of an infected person.

Clogs: Originally, wooden-soled shoes used in Irish dancing.

Colors: A flag identifying a regiment or army.

CSA: Confederate States of America, which were South Carolina, Mississippi, Florida, Alabama, Georgia, Louisiana, Texas, Virginia, Arkansas, Tennessee, and North Carolina.

Contraband: Slaves who escaped or were freed by the Union Army, often encamped near a Union Army post and employed by its soldiers. After mid-1863, 200,000 freemen and former slaves joined the U.S. Colored Troops.

Community of the True Inspiration or Ebenezer Society: A breakaway German Anabaptist church founded in the 18th century; between 1842 and 1846, purchased 5,000 acres of land that formerly belonged to the Seneca Nation Buffalo Creek Reservation in West Seneca, New York. Because of the growth of Buffalo, they started a move to Amana, Iowa, in 1855 and completed it over the following decade. The site of their first settlement is still known as Ebenezer.

William 'Fingy' Conners: Born in 1857, he lost a thumb as a child and was thus nicknamed "Fingy." An uneducated tough, he took over his parents' saloons on Ohio Street as a teen and used them and his gang to organize labor crews in the port of Buffalo; organized 7,000 unskilled laborers in Great Lakes ports; controlled Buffalo government construction contracts; influenced state and national elections; purchased the Buffalo Courier and Express newspapers and large Florida real estate holdings.

Demonstration: A military movement used to draw the enemy's attention from the main attacking or withdrawing force.

Dysentery: Intestinal disease brought on by a variety of pathogens (viral, bacterial, and parasitic) causing severe diarrhea; one of the leading causes of death in the Civil War. More soldiers died in the Civil War because of disease than as a consequence of battle.

Earthwork: A field fortification such as a trench or line fortified with earth and logs.

Elevate: To empty a lake freighter of its grain or ore, contained in separated sections or holds.

Enfilade: To fire across the length of an enemy's battle line from one of its flanks.

Episcopus Ordinatus: Latin for the consecrated bishop of a Roman Catholic diocese.

Fatigue duty: Physical, noncombat work, e.g. cleaning up the camp, repairing structures, digging latrines, building roads or fortifications, kitchen duty.

Fenians: Term first used by John O'Mahoney for the American Irish republican society he formed in 1858 to free Ireland from British rule; adapted from "Fianna" or Gaelic warrior bands who lived apart and could be called upon to defend the land. Became an umbrella term for various Irish revolutionary groups.

Flank: The end or wing of a battle line; as a verb, to move around the end of an enemy's battle line.

Furlough: Leave from duty granted by a superior officer. Furlough papers described the appearance, unit, and time of leave and return.

Gabions: Cylindrical wicker baskets filled with rock and earth used to build field fortifications.

Grand Army of the Republic: The GAR formed as a fraternal organization of Union veterans in 1866 to promote housing, pensions, and other veterans' issues in Congress.

Hedge Schools: Schools started in poor rural areas of Ireland from the 18th century on by educated local men. Even though the National School system was established in 1830, due to lack of resource commitment, hedge schools continued until the 1890s. Called "hedge schools" because they were held outdoors alongside the ever-present hedges of the Irish countryside. They were also held in homes, barns, and other buildings, particularly during uncomfortable weather.

Know Nothing or Native American Party: An anti-immigrant, anti-Catholic national political party active between 1845 and 1855 and directed especially against German and Irish immigrants. Died after the election of 1856 when Millard Fillmore ran unsuccessfully on its line, but lived on in the vocabulary of Irish Americans. Membership was limited to white men of English ancestry.

Kyrie Eleison: Greek meaning, "Lord, have mercy." Found in the Roman Catholic mass.

Lake Carriers' Association: A Great Lakes, American flagship, shippers' organization controlling freighters moving commodities like grain, ore, salt, and limestone among Great Lakes ports.

Low Mass/High Mass: A pre-Vatican II Council (1961 to 1965) distinction. Low masses required a smaller donation and had no musical instrumentation and usually no singing. Only two candles were lighted at the altar. Six candles were lighted for a high mass, which was celebrated with music.

Maire: Irish name for Mary, pronounced "Moira."

Marine leg: A long boom suspended from the side of a grain elevator, lowered into the holds of freighters with a conveyor belt of buckets attached to elevate, i.e., empty the bulk grain or ore in a hold.

Military Units: The army was the largest organizational group of soldiers. One company was said to be equal to 50-100 men and up to four platoons; ten companies equal to 300-1,000 men or one regiment; four regiments equal to 2,500-3,000 men or one brigade; two to five brigades equal to 6,000-10,000 men or one division; two to five divisions equal to a corps; one to three corps equal to an army. A company was commanded by a captain, a regiment by a colonel, a brigade by a brigadier general; an army, a corps, or a division by a major general, and the whole Union Army by a lieutenant general who was also commander-in-chief.

Muzzle loading: Rifle muskets loaded from the muzzle end of the gun by jamming a cartridge down the barrel with a ramrod, a metal rod attached beneath the barrel.

Parrott Gun or Rifle: A type of artillery piece designed by Robert Parrott of the West Point Foundry, Cold Spring, New York. Produced ten- and twenty-pound models for field use by both the army and navy and up to 200-pound models for fortresses.

Pickets: Soldiers posted in small units spread several yards apart and 200 to 500 yards in front of the main defense line to provide advance warning of an enemy attack or to filter an assaulting line.

Plug: A baseball fielder could throw a runner out by hitting him with the ball, i.e., "plugging" him, when he was running between bases.

Quartermaster: The officer responsible for armament, clothes, food, and other supplies for the troops.

Redoubt: An enclosed fieldwork or fort used to protect a garrison from multisided attacks. Called a salient or lunette if shaped like a half-moon and attached to a fortified line of defense.

Rifle pit: A shallow hole used by pickets with earth and log mounded in front from which a soldier shot from a prone position.

United States Sanitary Commission: Established by Congress on June 18, 1861, but privately financed and staffed by volunteers to assure and supervise appropriate care of Union sick and wounded.

Seanachaite: Irish storytellers skilled at inventing or retelling ancient Celtic and other legends.

Skirmish: A minor attack to probe the enemy's line for weakness.

Sutler: A private business near or within a military encampment that sold practical and comfort items (canned foods, clothes, pen knives, etc.) to soldiers.

Union: The section of the country that remained loyal to the federal government during the Civil War: Connecticut, Delaware, Illinois, Indiana, Iowa, Kansas, Kentucky, Maine, Massachusetts, Michigan, Minnesota, New Hampshire, New Jersey, New York, Ohio, Pennsylvania, Rhode Island, Vermont, and Wisconsin. West Virginia became a Union state in 1863, seceding from Virginia. Union soldiers were also called Federals.

Vedette: A mounted sentry stationed in advance of a picket line.

Veteran Reserve Corps: Wounded and partially disabled soldiers were allowed to remain in service in the VRC to do noncombat, light duty, e.g., hospital service, brig guard duty.

Vincentians or Congregation of the Mission: Founded by St. Vincent de Paul in Paris in 1624. The order is a loose federation of congregations of Roman Catholic priests and brothers whose principal mission is the instruction of the poor in the faith and the formation of the clergy. It has hundreds of houses in 86 countries and had over 4,000 members at the turn of the 21st century.

WASP: Of White Anglo Saxon Protestant ancestry.

WCTU: Women's Christian Temperance Union, formed in 1874 in Cleveland, Ohio, to educate and agitate against the use of alcohol. It evolved to stand for women's rights in an era when women could not vote, hold property, or retain their children in case of divorce.

Welland Canal: Twenty-six miles long, connecting Lakes Erie and Ontario across the Niagara Peninsula, thus bypassing Niagara Falls. Part of the St. Lawrence Seaway System, it allows lake freighter traffic amounting to 40,000,000 tons to move between the western Great Lakes region and the Atlantic Ocean and beyond. Opened in 1830 and modified for the fifth time in 1972.

Whiteboys: Eighteenth century Irish secret society members who wore white smocks during nighttime raids against landlords and tithe collectors. Became a general name for Irish who carried out violent raids on English interests in Ireland well into the 19th century.

CPSIA information can be obtained
at www.ICGtesting.com
Printed in the USA
LVHW041305260921
698719LV00003B/70